PENGUIN BOOKS

# Last Chance

Gregg Hurwitz is the *Sunday Times* bestselling author of *Orphan X* and *The Nowhere Man,* the first Evan Smoak novels. He is also the author of *You're Next, The Survivor, Tell No Lies* and *Don't Look Back.* A graduate of Harvard and Oxford Universities, he lives with his family in LA, where he also writes for the screen, TV and comics, including Wolverine and Batman.

## BY GREGG HURWITZ

### TOR TEEN BOOKS
*The Rains*
*Last Chance*

### THE ORPHAN X NOVELS
*Orphan X*
*The Nowhere Man*

### OTHER NOVELS
*The Tower*
*Minutes to Burn*
*Do No Harm*
*The Kill Clause*
*The Program*
*Troubleshooter*
*Last Shot*
*The Crime Writer*
*Trust No One*
*They're Watching*
*You're Next*
*The Survivor*
*Tell No Lies*
*Don't Look Back*

# Last Chance

### GREGG HURWITZ

PENGUIN BOOKS

PENGUIN BOOKS

UK | USA | Canada | Ireland | Australia
India | New Zealand | South Africa

Penguin Books is part of the Penguin Random House group of companies
whose addresses can be found at global.penguinrandomhouse.com.

First published in the United States by Tom Doherty Associates 2017
First published in Great Britain by Michael Joseph 2018
001

Set in 12.5/14.75 pt Garamond MT Std
Typeset by Jouve (UK), Milton Keynes
Printed and bound in Great Britain by Clays Ltd, Elcograf S.p.A.

A CIP catalogue record for this book is available from the British Library

ISBN: 978–1–405–93830–3

www.greenpenguin.co.uk

TO THE NAYAKS

Chetan and Shelly
Eka, Asha, and Kanu

Because sometimes you *can* choose your family

It ended in sacrifice. I suppose we always knew it would. That we couldn't possibly make it through unscathed. But I never dreamed it would turn out the way it did. The way the world went upside down and our lives with it. Now that it's over, I hope you take something away from what happened to us. Two brothers and a girl from Creek's Cause – who would've ever thought we'd make a difference?

The world changed.

We changed it back.

*The day after the day after tomorrow,*
*in a state nestled among others . . .*

**ENTRY 1**     *I wake up in the perfect darkness of Uncle Jim and Aunt Sue-Anne's ranch house, and there's a split second where everything is fine. I'm six years old, and life is good. And then I remember.*

*My parents are dead.*

*The reality crushes in on me. My throat closes, and for a few minutes I struggle to breathe in the inky black of the guest room. It's not that I'm about to cry – I've done plenty of that already. It's that I can't seem to find any air.*

*It was their anniversary last week, and they'd gone to Stark Peak to celebrate. They'd been drinking, probably too much. Depending on which version you heard, Dad ran either a yellow or a red, and a muni bus nearly broke their Chrysler in half.*

*It had to be a closed-casket funeral.*

*I finally figure out how to breathe again, and I roll over on the couch and look down at my big brother sleeping on the floor beside me.*

*People talk about sibling rivalry, but you should know right away that Patrick is awesome. And not in the dumb slang way, like when people talk about new pop songs and high scores on* Call of Duty. *I mean, like what the word actually means. He's big for his age, but it's not just that. Patrick is the kind of tough they don't make in real life. He's never lost a fight. I've never seen him cry, not even at the funeral. He can herd cattle already and ride a horse like the horse is part of him. He wears a black cowboy hat, and it doesn't look like he's playing dress-up; it looks like he's a friggin' eight-year-old cowboy.*

I

He's asleep, but barely. He's really lying there to watch over me because he knows that while I'm tough like kids around here have to be, I'm a long ways from awesome like him, and when you're awesome like him, you protect your kid brother.

I think of a brown box on the kitchen table downstairs.

The one with the STARK PEAK POLICE DEPARTMENT stamp on it.

I slide off the couch as quietly as I can and step over Patrick's body. He stirs but doesn't wake up. Uncle Jim and Aunt Sue-Anne have ordered twin beds for us, due to arrive any day now. They're gonna turn their guest room into our bedroom. I know I should be grateful, but instead it just makes me feel all gray and bleary inside.

Once those beds show up, that means it's final.

I sneak out of the room and creep down the hall. It's an old ranch house, and the floorboards creak, so it's slow going. I take the stairs even slower.

The brown box waits, centered on the table like a pot roast.

The cop who dropped it off today said it holds Mom and Dad's 'personals,' whatever that means. We'd agreed to leave it be until morning. I'm not supposed to be here.

But I need to see.

My heartbeat thrums in my ears. I lift the lid, half expecting something to jump out at me. A smell rises. Lilac perfume – the smell of Mom. And something worse, an iron tang that reminds me of the way the air hangs heavy around the Braaten slaughterhouse. I take a moment to think about that one and try to keep my heart from clawing out of my chest.

The box is mostly empty. Just a few items are nestled in the bottom. Dad's Timex.

I pick it up. The face is cracked, the time frozen at 10:47.

The minute my life changed forever.

2

My lips are quivering, and I think about how Patrick's lips would never quiver, not in a million years.

I set the watch down. Thanks, Dad, for drinking that extra Martini. I hope it was worth it.

Something black in the corner of the box catches my eye.

It's soft to the touch. I lift it to the dim light.

It's Mom's fancy clutch purse.

The outside is stiff and stained, reeking of lilac from when her perfume bottle cracked open. I think about the force of a muni bus hitting a perfume bottle. And then I think about it hitting other stuff.

I gather my courage and unsnap the purse. I tilt it to look inside.

A trickle pours out, like tiny diamonds. No — glass. At first I think they're shards from the perfume bottle, but there are too many of them. As they brush my fingers, I feel that they're not sharp, not sharp at all, and I realize that they're pebbled glass from the shattered windshield.

They tumble on to a spot of moonlight at my feet, and I see that they're tinted crimson.

Somehow this brings it all home. I am a six-year-old kid without a mom or a dad. This is who I am now.

I am alone here in the kitchen, holding the last relics of my parents. I am alone in the world. Even inside myself I am alone, a tiny spotlit figure in a giant dark warehouse.

My face twists. My cheeks are wet. My shoulders shudder.

I don't realize I'm crying until I hear Patrick's feet thumping the stairs behind me, and then I'm turning around, and he's hugging me, and I hear his voice in my ear. 'I got it from here, little brother.' My face presses into his arm, and I cry and cry and think I'll never stop, and he knows not to say anything else.

I feel like I'm coming apart, my insides gone jagged, shattered

3

*into as many pieces as there are bits of glass at my feet. It's not just the worst I've ever felt.*

*It's the worst anyone has ever felt.*

*Until nine years later, when it would feel like a Sunday stroll through town square.*

Light seeped in around the edges of darkness, like morning peeking around curtains. But there were no curtains.

Rings of fire ignited my wrists. My ankles screamed. Were they tied? A crunching sound scraped my eardrums at intervals.

The woods came into focus.

Only problem was, they were upside down.

Blinking, I sourced the crunching sounds. Sleek black boots walking in concert, packing down dead leaves.

Drones.

Alien life-forms wrapped head to toe in flexible black armor. Their suits were human-shaped, as seamless as if they'd been poured on. You couldn't see anything beneath them. Each one was as airtight as an astronaut suit, right down to the polished helmet. Which made sense, since the things that inhabited the suits – the Harvesters – seemed to exist in gas form.

Fighting through my fear, I tried to find my bearings.

I was suspended from a sturdy branch, carried through the woods like a field-dressed deer dangling from a sapling. My shoulders throbbed like you wouldn't believe. I craned my aching neck and peered up at the nearest Drone. All I saw was my own pale face reflected back from the dark-tinted face mask.

I was big for my age, decently strong from years of

baling hay and chopping wood and all manner of ranch chores. But I didn't feel big now.

The tips of pine trees swayed against a clear blue sky. As we headed upslope, I noted the position of the sun. Slowly, it dawned on me just how screwed I was. The Drones were taking me back to the Hatch site.

The Hatch site at the old cannery, where all the kids and teenagers from Creek's Cause and the neighboring towns had been taken. Everyone under the age of eighteen had been rounded up. Caged. Strapped to a conveyor belt. Their bellies used as pods to incubate some new lifeform. They floated now on slabs of sheet metal, their eyes rolled back to white, their bodies stretched beyond recognition as something alien grew inside them. That's where I was headed.

What I would have given to be back in that kitchen crying over my dead parents.

**ENTRY 2**     It's hard to say what was worse, the pain or the terror.

Let's hope you never find yourself debating that question.

My circulation was cut off, my arms and legs gone all pincushiony. My head bounced around, jarred with every goose step that the Drones took. It ached like it had never ached before. My hands and feet, bound to that branch, felt like they might just snap off.

Despite all that pain, the answer to the question finally came clear.

The terror was worse.

I needed some way to distract myself from the jagged ball of dread gathering in my stomach. To distance myself from . . . *myself*.

Okay, then. Pretend you'll get yourself out of this mess.

Pretend you're gonna live.

That you'll find another notebook.

Start a fresh journal.

Write down what happened to you. What *is* happening to you right now.

What would you say about *that* guy?


My name is Chance Rain. I'm fifteen years old. I would say nice to meet you, but I'm a little busy right now, you know, dangling from a branch being carried to my death and all that. To say that things suck would be an understatement.

And I don't just mean that they suck right here, right now. I mean, things *globally* suck.

It's hard to believe that it's only been a month since fragments from a broken-up asteroid hit Hank McCafferty's fallow field and buried themselves deep in the earth. But these weren't just meteorites. They were *seeds*.

Stalks shot up quickly and then burst, releasing spores into the air. McCafferty inhaled those spores, and they took him over, spreading through the white matter of his brain, controlling him as sure as a bulldozer operator controls the blade from inside the cockpit. McCafferty's belly bloated up, and his legs carried him to the water tower by Charles Franklin's farm. He climbed to the top of the tower, and then his stomach exploded, releasing a new kind of spore.

A second generation of spore that rode the winds right into town.

Every single adult in our town was transformed. Us kids and young teenagers, we were fine. The cutoff age, it turned out, was eighteen. As in *precisely* eighteen. If you were seventeen, then on your next birthday at the exact instant of your birth you'd turn, too. You'd take a single breath and then – *boom*.

Your eyes would shrivel to ash and blow away so you'd have tunnels straight through your skull. Your eyeholes would grow transparent membranes, virtual screens that fed information back to the Harvesters.

So we all have *that* to look forward to.

7

Except for Patrick, who had already turned eighteen and stayed exactly the same. As far as we knew, he was the only person in the world with immunity. Which made sense because, you know, he's Patrick.

So that's how they attacked us, the Harvesters. From within.

And in case you thought we were special in our little farm-and-ranch town of Creek's Cause, we found out soon enough that they'd sent thousands of other asteroids into thousands of other towns and cities all around the planet.

The Harvesters were clever, you see.

They made the human adults do their dirty work for them, made them lay the foundation for the invasion. Once you turned, you were nothing more than a remote-operated Host with a hijacked brain. Our very own aunts and uncles and shopkeepers and teachers ran us down, captured us, and delivered us to the Hatch sites.

Unless we killed them first.

And we'd killed plenty. Me and Patrick and Alex and the others who'd holed up at Creek's Cause High School, hiding from the living terrors that roamed our town.

Alex Blanton was Patrick's girlfriend, between us in age. The three of us had been best friends since forever, and then she and Patrick had turned into *she and Patrick*, and she and I had stayed best friends. She had long dirty-blond hair and a wide smile that I tried not to think about too much, because . . . you know, we were friends. Like I said.

A couple of weeks ago, she'd been taken by the Harvesters. I'd rescued her from the Hatch site, and afterward she'd kissed me.

I tried not to think about that too much either.

Especially after I brought her back to Patrick.

Yesterday the three of us had snuck to the Hatch site again to kill the Queen Harvester, who was impregnating all the kids.

We'd known it was a suicide mission.

While Patrick and Alex created a diversion, I'd shot the Queen from four hundred yards out with a bolt-action Ruger M77 Hawkeye.

As you can imagine, her Drones freaked the hell out.

When I tried to escape, I hid inside a hollow tree where someone else was also hiding. He said he was a Rebel. He looked like a Drone, except his armor was battle-worn, scuffed-up charcoal instead of polished black. He was badly injured. He told me that the Rebels had been mostly killed off by the Harvesters. He'd been looking for me.

As in *me*, Chance Rain.

He told me that Patrick and I had to carry out some sort of mission. That we were the key to the survival of the human species. That the Harvesters knew who we were and were looking for us everywhere. That if we were killed, everyone on earth would die.

No pressure there.

And then he died before he could give me any specifics.

I fled to a cabin on Ponderosa Pass. It was supposed to be our meeting place. Except Patrick and Alex never showed up.

But the Drones did.

Like I said, a suicide mission. When we'd said our good-byes, Patrick had taken his shotgun, Alex a revolver. We'd made a vow not to be captured alive. It was either the cabin or the business end of a gun, and I'd been the only one to make it to the cabin.

And so now here we are. Patrick and Alex are dead. I'm hanging from a branch like a gutted deer, about to be delivered to the Harvesters. When I die, the last hope for humanity dies with me, though I have no idea why.

Basically, everything is as bad as it could possibly be.

And this little exercise of trying to find distance from my predicament isn't working very well. In fact, I think it's safe to say it's failed abysmally.

The Drones quickened their pace. I jounced along, a sack of firing nerves. Sprigs poked my cheeks. Underbrush scraped my ribs. I thought I might pass out.

The Drones hiked the slope of Ponderosa Pass with ease. Each jolting footstep brought a fresh agony. We moved up, up, up.

At last we reached the brink.

The Lawrenceville Cannery was in a valley that topped the pass like the gravy dimple you smush into a mound of mashed potatoes. It had been in the middle of a massive expansion before the Dusting. Among the dense trees were pieces of construction gear, mounds of rubble, slumbering backhoes.

We passed fallen trees that the Drones had razed in their pursuit of me, that first furious chase. Stumps poked up out of the earth like shaving stubble. As we made uneven progress, it lurched into sight through the trunks, an upside-down blur way below that finally came into horrific focus.

The Hatch site.

The huge cannery doors rolled back to expose the inside of the factory. The cages and crates stacked against the back wall, many of which still held kids. The reconfigured conveyor belt, designed to carry strapped-down boys and girls to their end. It snaked across the factory floor before continuing through a hole cut in the wall. The Hosts stood around like windup toys whose batteries had run out, eyeholes bored through their skulls. There was Mr Tomasi, my former English teacher, his shaggy hair looking even shaggier, his corduroy blazer worn through in patches. I could see right through his eyeholes, right through his head. Like the other Hosts, he seemed to be waiting for the operation to resume.

The operation that had been shut down when I'd shot the Queen.

The Drones carried me forward through the trees, past a storage warehouse, into a copse of pines. My breath quickened, jerking my chest.

The trees thinned a bit, and I corkscrewed my head, seeing inverted flashes of the Hatch site flickering through the branches, growing closer. I caught a glimpse of where the conveyor belt emerged from the wall of the cannery. The belt ended at the edge of a massive foundation that had been poured for a construction expansion – a job that, like every other job, had been interrupted by Asteroid 9918 Darwinia. Dozens of Drones stood shoulder to shoulder. The Queen's sprawled armor lay at their boots. Even from this distance, I could see the hole I'd put through her helmet.

The foundation itself was covered with a thousand slabs of sheet metal that floated above the concrete plain by some magnetic force. The slabs were arranged in rows – a sea of dominoes. Each slab supported the body of a kid who had been implanted with offspring by the Queen. All those boys and girls laid on their backs. Giant humps rose from what used to be their stomachs and chests. Their bodies had literally been turned into cocoons. *Husks*, the Rebel had called them. The bulging growths inside had split the kids' clothes. Their skin, stretched to the breaking point, was translucent. Through it I could see the hard edges of broken bones . . . and something much, much worse.

Another life squirming inside each dead-to-the-world kid. Feathering the skin with stretch marks. Pulsing.

Almost ready to hatch.

More Drones patrolled the aisles between the slabs, tending their depraved crop. That's what it all resembled – some kind of gruesome farm.

And then the Drones carrying me turned, my view disappearing. For a moment I could see only tree trunks. I was carried over a rise in the forest floor, my shoulders jolting. My hip brushed against bark. A muscle cramped at the base of my neck. Pine needles streaked overhead.

At last we broke through the tree line, stepping out into the open.

Countless Drone helmets rose in unison to note my arrival. They swiveled toward me, every last one of them, moving as a single piece.

I hadn't thought it would be possible for dark-tinted face masks to convey rage.

I swung there on the branch, blinking against the sudden light, completely exposed before the waiting phalanx of Drones.

A terrible insectoid screeching filled the air. Though none of the Drones moved, mist shot out of valves around the necks of their armor, dissipating in the air. The cries echoed off the walls of the valley, stirring birds from the treetops.

Panic overwhelmed me, a wet blackness that filled my lungs. I struggled against my restraints, shouting and trying to kick myself free.

We started the final descent.

**ENTRY 3**    For a moment there was only blind panic. Pain brought me out of it. I realized that all my bucking and squirming just made the restraints dig deeper into my wrists and ankles. Sunbursts dotted my vision; I was light-headed from hanging upside down for so long. Freaking out certainly wasn't helping things.

I tried to calm myself. What would Patrick do? I pictured him with his half squint, staring out from beneath the brim of his black Stetson. He'd take whatever was coming. Spit in the mask of the nearest Drone. Go down like a man.

I closed my eyes. Drew in a shaky breath. Released a shakier one.

*Good-bye, big brother. You taught me well. I'll try not to embarrass you now.*

I thought about Alex wearing her fiercest scowl, the one she used to reserve for the ice-hockey rink. I'd seen her shoot her own father after he'd transformed. I'd seen her almost take the head off a Host with her hockey stick. I couldn't imagine her bowing down to anyone.

I took another breath, this one steadier.

*Good-bye, Alex. You were part of what kept me going. If I couldn't be with you, at least I could be near you. Because of you I always wanted to be more than I am. I'll try to be that now.*

My exhale, smooth as a saddle horn.

*I hope you guys were together at the end.*

I opened my eyes.

*See you soon.*

For the first time, I let my muscles relax. I lolled from the branch, swaying hypnotically. We crossed the parking lot, heading for the cannery and the foundation beyond. The Drones that were gathered around their dead Queen grew closer with every step. Several paces beyond at the corner of the foundation, a cracked-open meteor the size of a Volkswagen rested on a nest of shattered concrete.

As I was carried across the front of the factory, some of the kids cried out from their cages. A girl sobbed hoarsely. Tiny fists pounded bars. I heard my name called – a survivor from Creek's Cause? – but couldn't turn my head far enough to see who it was.

We passed the cannery, nearing the foundation. A stench wafted over on the breeze. The putrid smell, I realized, came from the floating Husks – more precisely, from the Hatchlings growing inside them.

My captors paraded me before the other Drones, showing off their prize. I hung there, observed by all those face masks, and braced myself for whatever was coming.

I pictured the dying Rebel hiding with me in the dark core of the massive tree. The guttering glow of his mask. His hand resting on mine. *No matter what, they must* never *find out who you are. Do* not *let them take you. We will contact you when we can and tell you of your mission. Until then you have one job: Stay alive.*

One job. And I'd failed.

The dead Queen's armor lay beneath me. The jagged hole in the helmet looked like a mouth. There was only

15

blackness beneath, an empty suit. The armor still held her form, taller and more slender than that of the Drones. One of her arms tapered into a stinger that she'd plunged into the bellies of countless kids and teenagers. I shuddered off the memory. Then I stared up at the rows of face masks.

'Well,' I said. 'Let's get this over with.'

They gazed back blankly. A faint breeze carried the stink of the Hatchlings. I could hear them inside the Husks, straining the flesh, the wet sucking noises making my stomach roil.

My peripheral vision caught a movement. Mr Tomasi, lumbering over. His work slacks were missing one leg from the knee down, and bone glittered through a wound in his thigh. He wielded a box cutter.

Extending the slender blade, he crouched, a black silhouette except for the two holes where the light shone through. His shadow darkened my face.

I confess, I might have closed my eyes.

I heard a slicing sound, and then the foundation rushed up and hit me.

He'd cut my restraints.

Already he was shuffling away.

I went to stand up, but then a boot came down on my neck, pinning me to the concrete. The tread ground into the hinge of my jaw so heavily that I thought the bone might snap.

A Drone reached down, grabbed my arms, and ripped me to my feet. His gloves weren't really gloves, just an extension of the seamless suit. They felt as cold and hard as metal, but somehow they were still flexible. They dug into my biceps now and I thought they might break right through the skin.

I glared into the impenetrable mask. Glared at the life-form beneath, which – from what little I'd gleaned – was composed of gas swirling inside the airtight suit.

The Drone spun me around so I faced the sea of floating Husks. The smell hit me hard, and I gagged. Crushing me in his grip, the Drone marched me across to where the cracked-open meteor had landed. I say 'landed' instead of 'crashed' because the inside was a perfect globe of a cockpit. The walls were rimmed with transparent screens that seemed made of the same organic matter that formed the eye membranes of the Hosts.

Bluish lights flickered across the screens, data scrolling quicker than I could register. Thousands of subscreens tiled the display, speeding through what looked like live footage. Each one flipped every few seconds, showing new scene after new scene. A few lodged in my mind: Towering high-rises on some desolate, trash-blown city street. A Third World slum, sheets flapping from ropes. A freeway on-ramp crowded with empty cars, some of them smashed into a center divide.

Were these the feeds from the Hosts mapping out the standing infrastructure of our planet?

A similar bank of subscreens mirrored the first, digesting all that footage. Every line, every angle, the composition of every object – each was delineated by some sort of digital outline, charted like Google Maps.

The computing data was awesome. Everything connected to everyone watching everything. How could we possibly stand a chance against it? That's how we'd die, all of us. Tumbling into the void of omniscience. I felt like a speck of dust free-falling inside the brain of God.

Sweat ran down from my hairline, stinging my eyes. I reminded myself to breathe.

Shouts rang out behind me, and I looked over my shoulder. Through the rolled-back factory doors, I had a partial view of the kids in the crates. Which meant they had a view of me. The insides of the crates were lost to shadow; all I could make out were skinny arms thrust through the bars, waving, grasping, reaching for me. The whole wall looked like a multilimbed monster.

The Drone clenched my neck and turned my head back to the split-open meteor. I faced the curved interior straight on. Something in the cockpit must have registered me there, because all at once the screens went dark.

Wind froze the perspiration across my shoulders. My stomach leapt. I peered into the halved globe and waited and then waited some more.

A light lasered from the center screen so suddenly that I cried out. It shot a few feet above my head. Heat radiated down on me. I looked up to see where the light had expanded to form a bluish sheet. Flat and contained, it hovered there, projected into thin air. It was a perfect square, just wider than my shoulders. A single ray of light tethered it to the cockpit, a string holding a kite in place.

The sheet began to lower.

The heat grew more intense, making my scalp prickle.

I went to run, but two Drones held me in place.

My chest heaved with panic breaths; I couldn't stop it any more than I could stop the downward creep of that blue sheet.

Just before it reached me, I lowered my gaze to protect my eyes. A burning spread across my crown, and then my hair felt singed, and then –

*atcgggaatccctaacgtccccaatttaaggggggaactctacggactaccta*

My brain emerged, gasping for air almost literally. The light scanned through my insides like a heated metal plate. I felt it moving down my neck, inside my throat. My chest caught fire, and then my stomach burned. The worst was next. Sweat popped out across my forehead, rolled down my cheeks, pooled in the hollow of my neck. Thighs. Knees. Shins.

At last it was over.

The sheet zapped back inside the cockpit.

The screens seemed to power off.

The Drones released me. Jerking in a breath, I stumbled forward. The heel of my hand struck the bottom of one of the screens, and it rippled like water. As the Drones yanked me back to stand, my palm came away gooey. I wiped it on my jeans and waited to see what would happen next.

The screens ignited, showing hundreds of readings. Cells. Hair strands. Twisting ladders.

On one of the side screens, a rendering appeared, every last contour of a face and body, rotating on display. There I was – Chance Rain, in wireframe.

My insides had been mapped as thoroughly as all those street and city views.

My DNA, broken down and analyzed.

The Rebel's voice echoed again inside my head: *No matter what, they must* never *find out who you are.*

Good luck with that.

The screens zoomed in on one of the DNA ladders. And then it pushed further into one of the chromosome rungs.

I remembered reading about genetics in Mrs Wolfgram's science class. She'd been a good teacher, Mrs Wolfgram.

The last time I'd seen her, Patrick had obliterated her head with a Winchester shotgun.

On the meteor screen, my chromosome rung magnified even more, the map of me growing larger until a section of base pairs was visible.

All of the base pairs, like everything else, were depicted in blue.

Except for one.

That one was rendered in red.

And it was blinking.

I blinked right back at it.

Its edge looked jagged, like one set of teeth on a zipper.

'What the –'

My next word was drowned out by a roar overhead. I barely had time to pull my gaze north when a meteor streaked down and embedded itself in the parking lot across from the other one. The earth shook, flipping the few remaining cars on to their sides. The meteor plowed up a wake of asphalt.

It rested there, smoldering, the air around it gone wavy with heat.

Then it cracked open with a popping noise.

The jagged exterior hid the smooth orb of a cockpit inside. As the meteor hinged wide, I saw her inside, a sleek black form, slender legs drawn up to her chest.

The Queen uncoiled from the cockpit.

My guts turned to ice.

We'd risked everything to kill the last Queen, and here was another one, plopped down from the heavens to take her place. How many more were there? What had we even been thinking? The fight suddenly felt pointless. Not that I'd be around much longer to worry about it.

The Queen's lustrous black suit held the faintest curves of a woman's shape. She walked so gracefully that she practically glided across the ground. The closer she got, the taller she seemed.

At last she loomed over me.

'You are Chance Rain.' Her voice was digitized, feminine and yet seemingly without life. Amplitude bars flickered across her tinted face mask with each syllable. The helmet itself seemed to be translating. 'You are one of the two.' She wasn't asking; she was telling me.

I swallowed hard, managed to move my head up and down.

'Where is Patrick Rain?'

I felt my mouth start to wobble, so I bit down on my cheek. Warmth spilled through my mouth. 'He's dead.'

'That is acceptable,' she said, the amplitude bars dancing like blue fire. 'You must be voided, too.'

I channeled my inner Patrick and spit in her face.

Behind me the kids cheered from their cages. Blood-laced saliva dripped down the Queen's face mask.

She had no emotional reaction. Her head cocked, as if gauging how to respond to this display. What did getting spit on even mean to her?

Mist burst from her neck valves – a show of aggression.

At this proximity the shriek was earsplitting. She reared up. Her stinger arm twisted behind her, a tentacle drawing back to strike. Small sensory bumps squirmed along its entire length, but I wasn't watching them.

I was watching the tip, tapered to a vicious point.

It flicked once. The stinger firmed, swelling with what looked like muscle.

The Drones held me in place. My feet were numb. My body had turned to soup. I could feel my face, contorted into a mask of my own.

I took my last breath.

That's when we heard it.

A distant rumble, followed by a crashing sound and the roar of machinery. The Queen wheeled around to look. Way up at the brink of the valley, the cab of a semitrailer truck burst into view, blazing straight through a patch of young pine trees. On either side of the semi, protruding like tusks, were undercutters. The giant chain saws, usually attached to a backhoe, were designed for cutting rock – or clearing forest. Which they were doing right now, carving a path straight through the pine trees. The Drones had used the detached undercutters yesterday to knock down some of the trees in their search for me. It took a moment for my brain to process that they'd been rigged on to the semi.

The massive truck barreled down the slope toward us, crushing everything in its path, snapping trunks like beanstalks, bouncing over the timber, its ten mighty wheels roaring for traction.

The sun glinted off the windshield, turning it into a rectangle of fire. As the truck pulverized the last row of trees and smashed on to level ground, it skidded sideways. The glare lifted from the windshield.

Through the dusty pane, I made out a shadow behind the wheel. A male form.

Wearing a cowboy hat.

**ENTRY 4**     'Holy *crap*,' I said.

But no one was listening to me.

I took advantage by wrenching free of the Drones and throwing myself aside.

Facing the truck, the Queen puffed up to her full height. The Drones spread wide across the foundation. A cluster of them broke loose and charged.

The semi truck bounced violently over the curb, hurtled on to the parking lot, and demolished the Queen's meteor. Rock fragments and blue-tinged goo exploded across the hood.

The tires screeched as the truck rocketed into a too-sharp turn. Those vicious undercutter tusks swung toward the advancing Drones. The driver's window was rolled down, and I caught a perfect glimpse through.

It was Patrick all right.

My throat clutched. My mouth guppied, looking for air. For a moment I thought maybe the Queen *had* skewered me with her stinger and this was some weird afterlife dream.

The vanguard of Drones flew toward the semi. The semi raced to meet them.

At the last minute, Patrick raked the wheel to the side. One of the giant chain-saw blades swept right through the Drones' legs. Amputated armor spun, suddenly airborne.

Black mist exploded out of the leg holes with enough force to propel the suits off the ground. Some shot a few feet off the asphalt; some skipped across the parking lot; others spun in dying circles on the ground. In each suit the pressure of the expelled smoke lessened until nothing was left but the deflated armor. The Drones had been bled from their suits, their life matter disintegrating into the air.

The second undercutter whisked around to meet the next line of Drones. A few ducked and were severed at the midsection. Others tried to leap over the undercutter and had their boots cleanly removed. One Drone almost got away, catching only a nick in his heel. Any penetration, no matter how small, was enough. Black gas geysered from the wound with a teakettle scream of expelled air.

The semi 180'ed, lifted up on to its side wheels, threatening to tip over. When the driver's side swept past, I swore I saw Patrick's black Stetson dip as he gave me a little nod. The weighty back end spun toward me, pushing a wall of air before it, blowing my hair flat.

In front of me, the Queen reared up, stinger curled menacingly behind her. Gas shot through not just her neck valves but through a line of valves along her sides, too, framing her in fearsome spouts of black smoke.

The truck swept by, hammering into her, wiping her from view. Empty pieces of her armor rained down on the foundation. I stared with disbelief at the rear of the truck.

Through the dissipating smoke, a figure slowly came clear standing on the metal plate above the drive wheels. She was fastened loosely on to the back of the cab, cargo straps crisscrossing her chest like bandoliers. Her arms appeared first, glistening with sweat. Her hands gripped a shotgun. Not just any shotgun.

Patrick's Winchester.

The hands jacked the pump – *shuck-shuck* – and aimed to the side, firing into a lunging Drone's chest. He shot backward, propelled by the buckshot and the bursting spouts of his own dying self.

The black mist cleared.

I tried to swallow, but my throat was too dry.

She lifted the shotgun to rest against the ball of her shoulder and stretched out a hand.

'Well,' Alex said, 'what are you waiting for?'

**ENTRY 5**     I finally unlocked my legs and jumped forward. Alex and I clasped hands.

Feeling the warmth of her palm pressed to mine, I finally allowed that, yes, this was real. They were alive. I could've choked on my relief.

Alex started to haul me aboard, but I pulled back.

'Wait,' I said. 'The others.'

She looked past me. Exhaled.

'Okay,' she said, then swung the shotgun up past my cheek, rested it on the ledge of my shoulder, and fired behind me. It felt as though someone had banged a pair of cymbals inside my head. Over the ringing in my ears, I made out the screech of air exiting punctured armor. Alex barely paused. Unhooking the cargo straps, she stepped free. 'But we'd better move it.'

She hopped off the semi and landed beside me, firing off two more shots at charging Drones.

Turning to the truck, I jumped on the runner and stared through the passenger window at my brother.

'Patrick!'

But he was way too focused to celebrate a returned-from-the-dead reunion. 'Focus,' he said. 'We got work to do.' His hand rooted in the backpack resting on the bench beside him. 'Use this.'

I saw my preferred weapons glinting inside. 'My baling hooks!'

'Better.'

He came up instead with what looked like a power drill and slid it across the seat to me. I reached through the window and caught it by the handle.

A nail gun.

Behind me I heard Alex fire and fire again. Through the windshield I could see more Drones sprinting toward us.

'I removed the muzzle guard so it actually fires nails like in the movies.' Patrick revved the engine. 'Now, get going.'

I hopped down. Patrick dropped the truck into gear again and shot forward, chewing through the wave of Drones just before they reached us.

With Patrick covering our backs, Alex and I went shoulder to shoulder and faced the foundation.

Drones left their positions among the floating slabs, streaking toward us. The Husks were distended to their breaking point. The Hatchlings squirmed more vigorously inside their humps. It seemed like they could sense the commotion.

Alex wrinkled her nose against the stench as she fumbled to reload. 'Is that . . . ?'

'The Hatchlings,' I said. 'They reek.'

The Drones were closing in, and Alex was still struggling with the shells. I raised the nail gun, gripping it with both hands. The strip of nails swung beneath my fists like an ammo belt.

I pinged off a shot with a pneumatic *pffft*, but it fell short. It took another try for me to figure out the range, but then I sank a sixteen-penny nail into the face shield of a Drone. For a second, nothing happened.

Then black mist piped out from around the nail, a tiny leak. The pressure grew stronger until it shoved out the nail, which clinked on to the concrete. The Drone lifted his hands, trying to cover the hole. Air blasted through his fingers. His hands flew away as the pinhole expanded, blowing out more chunks of face shield until the entire mask disintegrated in an oil-well burst. Newton's third law kicked in and shot him back on to his butt. The suit sat there, an empty shell.

Alex and I looked at each other. A smile tugged at her mouth, but I could see that her lips were trembling. Her fingers shook, too, as she slotted the next shells into the magazine tube beneath the barrel. Fighting off panic, we turned and mowed down the advancing Drones.

Between them we caught glimpses of the foundation. One of the Husks started to give way. For an instant I could make out a suggestion of the child's body it used to be, and then it was just stretched skin, a shape distorted beyond recognition. A fissure opened in its side with a moist yielding. I swear I saw a long finger poke out through the gap. The other Husks wriggled and bulged.

If we waited any longer, we were going to find ourselves in the middle of a massive Hatch. I couldn't imagine what the things inside would look like.

Or what they'd do to us.

We unleashed another volley at the Drones, clearing enough space for us to turn and run to the factory. Over on the parking lot, Patrick was wheeling the semi truck into tight doughnuts, crushing his attackers. None of the Drones could get close to the cab.

Not yet anyway.

Alex and I wheeled around the corner of the cannery and through the rolled-back doors.

The Hosts were waiting.

They stood around the assembly line, blocking the wall of crated kids. Some were strangers. But a few weren't. Mr Tomasi. The Durant brothers – Gene and Billy Joe. Afa Sibanda, a dreadlocked Tongan ranch hand who used to work McCafferty's harvests. It was always worse when you knew them before. Their eyeless faces showed no humanity, no sign of who they had been. And yet you could still recognize them.

Mr Tomasi was nearest. He'd been one of my favorite teachers. He'd taught me *Lord of the Flies*. He'd once told me I was a good writer, that I should think about college. He liked to listen to baseball on the radio.

Lifting the nail gun, I fired a shot at his head. It missed the mark, puncturing his throat. Fluid oozed around the nail, draining down his chest. It had no effect; he kept on coming toward me and Alex just like the others.

So I put another nail through his forehead.

He fell.

I looked at him there, lying still on the floor. Emotion rose up in me, but I beat it down. Not here, not now. What was alarming wasn't what I'd done to Mr Tomasi. What was alarming was that I could force myself to get over it.

The kids erupted, banging their locked crates.

'Get me out!'

'Over here! Kid – over here!'

Alex blasted away, the scattered buckshot taking out two Hosts at a time. I shot the Hosts on either side of Mr Tomasi, clearing a path to the kids. While the remaining Hosts descended on Alex, I hurdled the bodies, ran to the cages, and started unlatching them as fast as I could. It took everything I had not to look over my shoulder every two seconds.

The first few kids spilled out and ran away.

I shouted at them, doing my best to keep the fear from my voice, 'Help me open these! Open the other cages!'

First one girl stayed to help and then another. The more we freed, the more helped free other kids. They poured forth, tumbling over the conveyor belt.

Alex cried out, and I turned and looked over the current of fleeing kids to see Afa swat her to the ground. He was the last Host standing. He drew back a powerful arm. A single punch would knock her unconscious – or worse.

Pure dread chilled my veins, freezing me to the spot. A half second passed, an eternity of wasted time, before I shattered free.

I ran to Alex, sliding over the conveyor belt, and slammed into Afa from the side just as he threw his punch. My weight barely budged him, but the impact was enough to make him swing wide. His fist smashed into a metal control box, knocking it off the wall. I bounced off him and landed next to Alex, the nail gun sliding away.

We stared up as Afa turned.

His hand was badly damaged from the blow. His pinkie was missing, the stub sending out a jet of fluid. His middle and ring fingers dangled from threads. The flesh at his remaining knuckles had been peeled back to the bone.

With his good hand, he reached for the steel lever that operated the conveyor belt and wrenched it free. Wielding it, he came at us.

I could hear the semi truck revving outside and the smack and hiss of the undercutter blades tearing through Drones – Patrick was too busy to save us.

Alex didn't have time to clear the shell from the shotgun, so she swatted at Afa with the stock. He knocked the shotgun aside. Alex and I backed to the wall – nowhere to go. Afa raised the steel lever.

Then something hit him from behind, shuddering his massive frame. He staggered forward. Another blow came, then another.

The others were coming to our rescue, hammering into him like a wave.

He wheeled around. A few of the smaller kids flew free, but more and more tackled him until he was brought down to his knees. He fell on to his hands, kids tumbling over his frame. The steel lever clanged on the floor, spinning slowly until one end kissed my feet.

I grabbed it. Stood up.

'Everyone get back!' I shouted.

The kids peeled off Afa in all directions, his giant frame exposed like that of a breaching whale. I wound up with the lever, waiting until I had a clear shot.

Afa's head swung up to face me. I looked straight through his eyeholes.

You wouldn't have thought a single swing could do so much damage.

Afa shuddered on the floor, his skull caved in, his hijacked brain done for good.

I heard my voice as if from a distance, the words coming out soft and husky. 'Sorry,' it said to what was left of Afa. 'I'm sorry.'

I hoisted Alex to her feet. She grabbed the shotgun as she rose.

The other kids and teenagers had poured outside, dodging Drones, scattering in all directions – literally running for the hills. Since the battle raged on in the parking lot between Patrick's *Mad Max* truck and the Drones, most of the kids made for the foundation, sprinting between the floating slabs.

Alex grabbed my arm and pointed.

With dread I looked across to where the kids streamed between the Husks. At first I was confused by what I was seeing over there. The entire foundation seemed to be alive, a pulsing, organic mess. The movement wasn't just from the fleeing kids wending their way through the slabs. It was *on* the slabs, too. The Husks no longer resembled children at all. The humps stretched up so high they looked like giant eggs set on end. The walls of flesh were pulled taffy-thin. Beneath the translucent sheets of skin, bipedal creatures stirred, finding their feet. They reared up, shoving their arms wide, clawing at the Husks to get free.

The panic I'd done my best to tamp down inside erupted, pinpricking my skin, putting a sheen of sweat across the back of my neck.

'Oh, my God, Chance,' Alex said. 'It's happening.'

**ENTRY 6**     We ran for Patrick in the truck, waving our arms. He'd made short work of most of the Drones who'd gone after him. The parking lot was littered with pieces of armor. A Drone torso skittered across the asphalt like a dying rocket, trailing black smoke.

Patrick spotted us and slowed the semi. A Drone hopped on to the runner, reaching through the driver's window for the wheel. Patrick hit him with one of my baling hooks, cracking his face shield. Then he kicked the door open and flung the Drone away.

The truck was still slowing. Patrick finished the skid, waiting for us to reach him.

Alex and I dodged Drones in various stages of injury. One rested on his knees and elbow. He had a sleek black glove clamped over a hole in his neck. As we ran by, Alex kicked his arm. His hand flew off the hole, and his life mist blasted out of him.

We jumped into the truck, the three of us lining the bench seat. We stared through the windshield with disbelief.

It was like being at the most horrific drive-in movie ever.

Covered with birth sludge, a wave of Hatchlings tore loose from their Husks. It was hard to get a good look at them. Fluids dribbled down their bodies. It was unclear what parts were them and what parts were shrapnel from the burst Husks. Bits of bone and viscera coated their bodies. Clumps of skin clung to their faces. They had nostril holes but no noses. Their eyes, shiny and beetle-black, looked like giant pupils.

The Hatchlings were shaped mostly like humans, that much was clear. Two legs, two arms, a head atop a torso. Their flesh looked soft and mucusy – sluglike. They were tinted salamander orange.

My eyes were drawn to one Hatchling who stood wobbling at the edge of his floating slab. He jumped like a raptor on to a kid's shoulders. Clawed hands and feet dug into the boy's back, a spray of crimson puffed in the air, and then they sank out of view beneath the fray.

My gorge rose up and pressed at the back of my throat.

The kids reversed, bucking and screaming, colliding with one another. It was like watching a herd of spooked horses driven into a labyrinth.

The Husks continued to crack open. Most of the Hatchlings looked to have wiry, masculine builds. Their muscles were so defined that they were like living anatomy sketches. But one in about every twenty was a rotund feminine form.

The male Hatchlings dove for the boys and girls, bounding after them in low hops, bent forward at their torsos like apes. They weren't trying to capture the kids as the Hosts did.

They were ripping them apart.

Not all were successful. Some of the Hatchlings toppled off their slabs and landed with a wet splat. Others stumbled in lurching circles as if trying to learn how to use their legs.

Over the noise of the idling engine, I heard Patrick's teeth grind. He dropped the gearshift into drive and stomped the gas, throwing Alex and me back in our seats.

We rocketed for the foundation, cutting down Drones left and right. Patrick screeched to a halt at the edge of the foundation, and we piled out.

Alex tossed Patrick the Winchester Defender and drew the revolver from the rear waistband of her jeans. I raised the nail gun.

For an instant we stood there frozen at the fringes, watching the massacre. One of the male Hatchlings hopped over to a female and held something out to her.

She took the offering in her three-digit hands and bent her face to it.

She was partially turned, so I couldn't see what it was, but I did see the thick liquid streaming down her arms, dripping from her elbows.

When she lifted her head, her chin was stained red.

That was all it took.

Rage overpowered our terror.

We charged in.

Given the stench, it was like wading into a sewer.

Alex grouped three rounds in the chest of the female. The Hatchling staggered back, dropping her shank of meat. But then something insane happened. The wounds closed right up, the gloppy flesh filling in the holes.

Patrick fired the shotgun at her, but the pellets seemed to move straight through her skin with no effect. She bared her teeth and hissed.

The sound made my flesh tighten.

It wasn't until my finger cramped that I realized I'd

been firing and firing the nail gun. Her skin absorbed the nails as readily as it had the bullets.

Patrick put a hand on my wrists and lowered my arms. 'It's not working.'

'What will?'

Instead of answering, he sprinted forward at the female Hatchling. As he neared, her hiss turned to an airy shriek.

Just before he reached her, Patrick slammed into one of the floating slabs, shooting it toward her like an air-hockey puck. The metal edge caught her just beneath the chin and took her head clean off.

Alex made an incredulous noise. It sounded like a laugh, but darker.

It broke us from our momentary paralysis. She and I joined Patrick, banging the slabs into Hatchlings even as others continued to claw their way free of their Husks. In between it all, kids and teenagers fought and screamed and died. It was mayhem.

I sent one slab rocketing into the lower back of a male about to shred a little girl. Alex kicked the slab of a Hatchling that hadn't yet freed himself from his Husk, spilling the living sac on to the ground. It was trampled into orange slop. The remaining Drones leapt into the fray, using their bodies to protect the Hatchlings. The slabs knocked into one another, starting a chain reaction, clipping Drones and cracking their suits.

The Hatchlings and Drones held the advantage, though. There were just too many of them. As I leaned my weight into another floating slab, a Husk split open right next to me, releasing a burst of rotten-egg funk. Acid clawed up my throat; could I puke and fight at the same time? The

Hatchling pulled himself erect on the floating metal pane, facing away from me. That gave me my first up-close look at the slender humanoid form, the tight muscles wrapped in newt skin. The three wide digits of each hand tapered into pointy nails, a gradual hardening with no clear delineation where the flesh ended and the claw began. I was close enough to touch the bulge of his calf. If he turned, he could dive right into me, leading with the points of those nails.

Instead he jumped in the other direction, on to the back of a teenage girl, and rode her down on to the ground. Her scream cut off with a gurgle. I realized I was holding my breath. I realized, too, that I was on the verge of screaming.

The Husk he'd left behind lay on the slab before me like the sloughed skin of a snake. Staring down at the cracked-open chrysalis of the young human form, I couldn't believe it had once been a kid like me. The flesh had turned translucent, as if all the nutrients had been sucked out of it. I suppose they had.

The Hatchling raised his head from his feast. I grabbed the slab and slammed it into the back of his skull. He wobbled a bit, trying to stand up. I rammed the metal edge into his head again, smashing it into the neighboring slab. I kept smashing and smashing until I felt something grasp my shoulder.

Yelling, I spun away, swinging wildly. Patrick side-stepped me, pointing.

I lifted my head. As far as I could see, Hatchlings continued to break free of their Husks. They came spilling toward us from the full sweep of the foundation, tumbling over themselves like an army of rats.

Patrick's voice rose over the commotion. 'Back to the truck!'

As we sprinted toward the semi, kids were picked off on either side of us, taken out as if hit by cannonballs. I found myself running next to a heavy kid a few years older than me. He was running out of steam.

'Keep going!' I shouted. 'Just keep –'

A moist smack and he was gone.

Something warm dripped down the side of my neck. The noises behind me were indescribable. I kept running. Patrick was in front of me, but I didn't see Alex.

I yelled her name. Behind me metallic thunderclaps grew closer and closer. It took a moment for me to register what they were. The Hatchlings were bounding across the slabs, hammering down on to the floating metal rectangles.

'Alex!' I shouted.

The thunderclaps quickened. Orange-tinted blurs darted into my peripheral vision. Patrick wheeled around in a full turn, getting off a shotgun blast without breaking stride.

And then it was the two of us running shoulder to shoulder, weaving through the wobbling slabs, hurdling fallen bodies. The semi truck waited ahead, tantalizingly close.

'Where is she?' Patrick yelled.

I didn't know.

I wouldn't have thought I could have felt more terrified, but losing Alex in this sea of horrors proved that I still had a ways to free-fall before I hit bottom.

As I reached the edge of the foundation, a Hatchling reared up right in front of me. There'd be no time to veer. He leapt for me. I slid on to my back beneath a slab. The concrete was slick – I didn't want to know with what.

I flew beneath the floating sheet metal, feeling a weird pull at my joints and bones. Above me the Hatchling clanged on to the slab, making it bounce low enough to touch my nose.

As he tumbled overhead, I shot out the other side, popped up on to my feet, and kept running. Thank God for Little League slide practice.

I felt heat at my back – the breath of the Hatchlings? Was that even possible?

Patrick and I broke free of the last line of slabs and withered Husks. The passenger door of the semi was open. Patrick dove in first. I crowded his back, grabbing the door to yank it shut behind me. Patrick's momentum carried him across to the driver's seat. Before he could get there, the driver's door flew open and a form shot in from the other side, beating him to the space behind the wheel.

The smile Alex managed was nervous, wobbling on her face. Even so, it brought a wave of relief and affection that I felt in my spine. 'I'll drive,' she said.

Hatchlings pelted the door behind me with enough force to dent the panel. They hammered the cab from all sides. I banged down the door lock.

Alex redlined the engine, throwing us into a screeching turn. The tires smoked and shot gravel. A fat female Hatchling flew at us, plopping on to the windshield and cracking it. Two males followed in her wake, smearing the glass, blotting out our field of vision. The crack spiderwebbed.

We weren't moving.

'Go, Alex!' Patrick shouted.

Alex's hands whitened around the wheel. Concern twisted her forehead. 'I *can't*.'

The banging intensified, Hatchlings smashing into the truck from all sides. Something struck the roof hard, denting it in low enough to tap Patrick's black cowboy hat askew. My heart knocked my ribs. I peered out the window and saw the front tire spinning uselessly in a puddle of orange slime. The tread caught another Hatchling by the foot and sucked him under. They were turning to mush beneath us, giving the tires no traction. It was worse than snow.

We were stuck.

The smell crowded the cab like something physical, pressing through our nostrils, down our throats.

A male Hatchling slapped against my window, inches from my face, scaring the crap out of me. His mouth spread on the pane, thick tongue dragging across the glass. His incisors gleamed. Others piled into him, layers deep. His claw clicked against the door handle.

Alex hit the steering wheel with the heels of her hands, screaming, though I could barely hear her over the sound of bodies striking the truck. Her hair flicked across her face, caught in the corner of her mouth.

Now we could see nothing but orange on all sides, as if we'd been dropped into a bowl of Jell-O. The wipers squeaked back and forth ineffectually, still trying to perform their duty, laughable and heroic. Another female smashed on to the windshield. The glass groaned all around us.

At any second it would give way.

**ENTRY 7**     'Scoot over!' Patrick yelled.

Grabbing his shotgun, he tumbled over Alex and into the driver's seat.

He unlocked the door.

'Patrick!' Alex shouted. She grabbed his arm, but he twisted free.

I looked past him through the driver's window. Amid the churning sea of orange, I made out a flash of polished black – one of the Drones pressing himself into the mix.

Patrick reared back, his shoulders knocking Alex into me and me into the passenger window. He raised one of his cowboy boots and pistoned it into the driver's door.

It flew open into the mass of bodies. Leaning against us, Patrick raised the shotgun, aimed it down the length of his body between his boots, and fired.

The blast tore a hole through the orange wall. The pellets wouldn't hurt the Hatchlings – we'd learned that already. So what the hell was he doing?

Patrick shucked the shotgun, the shell flying over his shoulder and pinging off my cheek. He fired again through the temporary hole.

And hit the Drone.

The Drone exploded, blast mist firing out of the armor gashes, blowing back our hair. But it also blew back the Hatchlings, clearing a small circle by the driver's door.

A makeshift grenade.

Patrick rolled forward, lunging out of the truck and on to his feet in the short-lived clearing. He swept his boot across the ground, kicking the deflated armor before the front tire.

Then he jumped back an instant before the Hatchlings regrouped. They hammered the door into the frame behind him hard enough to knock him across the bench seat. Alex ducked, so I caught my brother's full force, both of us piled against the passenger window. My face was mashed to the glass. On the other side, I could see nothing but bulging black eyes and fangs snapping for purchase.

Alex jackknifed sideways beneath Patrick's legs and stomped on the gas pedal.

The tires spun in place and kept spinning.

And then the front tire grabbed the armor, yanking the truck into a partial turn. Hatchlings flew away from one side and slid from the cracked windshield as cleanly as if we'd wipered them off. Only one female held her place, clinging to the lip of the hood.

The tire pulled itself farther on to the armor, and then we shot free.

Patrick and I seesawed toward the driver's side, but Alex shouldered up into place, ramming us off with her elbow so she could hold the wheel.

On the hood the female Hatchling drew back a plump fist, aiming for the center of the spiderweb.

The shotgun rolled across Patrick's knees.

Without looking over, Alex grabbed it, digging her finger through the trigger guard, and swung it in front of her.

She fired through the windshield, turning the Hatchling's face into an orange smear. The Hatchling rose up, and then the wind caught her and lifted her off the truck like she'd been tied to a passing plane.

Through the shattered windshield, air blasted our faces. Our eyes watered. Alex didn't let up, though, not for a second. We careened across the parking lot and bounced violently on to the slope of the hillside.

A shuddering exhalation left Alex, making a sound like a moan.

In the rearview mirror, we could see them bounding after us in that terrible apelike gait. They were falling farther and farther behind.

I had forgotten to breathe. I told my lungs that now would be an okay time to start again.

We veered upslope, jolting in our seats, dodging felled trees and stumps left behind when the Drones had cleared a swath of the mountain in their pursuit of me. A half-depleted gravel pile flew by on the right, and then a familiar knoll lurched into sight ahead.

The rise from which I'd shot the Queen.

I squinted into the wind. My eyes locked on a massive tree stump a few strides from the knoll. I couldn't see inside, but I could tell that it was hollow.

'Stop!' I yelled. 'Stop here!'

Alex hit the brakes. I tumbled out of the cab, falling on to a soft patch of moss. The Hatchlings surged up the hillside at us, a tide of orange. I tried to rise, my sneaker skidding out on the moss. It felt like I was moving in slow motion.

'Whatever you're doing,' Patrick said, 'do it faster.'

I ran to the giant hollow stump and peered inside.

Sure enough, there lay the Rebel's empty suit like a cast-off shell, left behind when he'd died. And his helmet. I'd dropped it there after twisting it off to peer down the neckhole. I'd found only wisps of smoke.

I snatched up the helmet and turned.

Alex and Patrick were staring at me, their eyes flaring.

'Chance,' Patrick said. His voice was dead calm, like the time he told me to hold still before he shot a rattlesnake coiled two feet behind my heel.

I knew he was trying not to panic me, but it had the opposite effect.

I didn't know what was wrong, but his and Alex's eyes were locked on a spot a few inches to my side.

And then the smell hit.

Rancid. Like rotten eggs.

I knew I had to turn my head. But I really didn't want to.

Something detached from the bark of the tree beside me – it seemed to be made of the tree itself. A shadow flickered toward me.

A long, three-digit hand.

Even as it reached for me, I could see the color of the skin changing from a barklike pattern to a familiar orange.

A single word spun at me through the panic whirl of my thoughts: *chameleon*.

The hand clamped over my forearm, singeing my skin. I yelled. I couldn't help it.

You would've, too.

**ENTRY 8**    As the hand tightened on my forearm, the burn intensified. It felt like acid eating through my skin. I tried to wrench free. The Hatchling peeled away from the tree, his camouflage changing from cracked brown to shades of olive and black that matched the surrounding forest.

His other claw resolved from the trunk, rising in the air.

A memory flash hit me from moments before – those pointy nails mangling a boy's body with the efficiency of a blender.

I twisted and swung the Rebel's helmet with all my might. It cracked against the Hatchling's head, denting it in.

He reeled back, his grip loosening just barely.

But it was enough.

I dropped my weight to the ground and ripped my arm free. It lit up with the pain of a thousand hornet stings, but this was no time for pain. Already the crater at his temple was filling itself back in.

I ran for the truck.

The Hatchling scrambled after me.

The other Hatchlings were surging up the slope toward us, now only twenty yards away. They crashed through the underbrush, leapt over branches. I heaved myself into the cab across Patrick's lap, and Alex floored the gas pedal. The Hatchling lunged for me. I pulled my legs inside an instant before a tree trunk took the swinging passenger door clean off.

It smacked brutally into the Hatchling, wiping him from view.

I stared down at myself in disbelief. My legs remained intact. My feet were still attached to my legs.

When I lifted my gaze through the open doorframe, I saw the other Hatchlings hurtling after us. Their camouflage cycled rapidly to keep up with the terrain. Colors flickered across them as if their skin were TV screens.

It looked as though the valley itself had come to life, as though the ground and trees were pursuing us.

I bit my lip and hunched over my scalded arm, waiting for the sting to let up. We rumbled toward the rim, the truck slowing as the terrain steepened. The Hatchlings were gaining on us. Given the camouflage, it was hard to pin them down. They seemed to sprout from the mud and drip from the branches.

I looked away. It was almost too much to stand, thinking about what would happen when they caught up.

Alex's voice cut through the air. 'We've got a problem.'

'As in a *bigger* problem than problems we already have?' I asked.

She pointed at the gas needle.

A quarter tank and dropping rapidly.

Now an eighth.

'The fuel line must've busted,' Patrick said.

'How?' Alex asked.

'I don't think there's anything behind us that you *didn't* run over,' I said.

The truck lumbered upslope toward the rim. I glanced

back. The living forest was closing in, bits and pieces surging into clarity. Here a claw. There a gaping mouth.

'Well,' Alex said, 'at least it can't get any worse.'

A low whooshing sound filled the cab, and then flames licked up from beneath the hood.

The truck was on fire.

**ENTRY 9**    A yellow blaze in front of us.

An army of Hatchlings behind.

The semi – on fire, running out of gas, underbrush wadding against the grille as we labored up a steepening slope.

Heat blew back across our faces. Branches crackled beneath the charge of hundreds of tridactyl feet.

Alex was literally standing on the gas pedal, her butt up off the seat, her elbows locked. *'Go, go, go, go, go!'*

We slowed, slowed, nearly stopping at the rim. The truck coasted for a weightless moment. Then toppled over the edge.

The forested downhill slope, spotted here and there with freshly cut tree trunks, seemed to stretch forever. Gravity seized the truck. We started to pick up pace again.

I shot a look back through the rear window. For the moment the Hatchlings were out of sight behind the brink.

I grabbed the backpack and Patrick's sleeve. 'We got one shot,' I said, fumbling for the door handle. 'Let's take it.'

Alex looked across at me, her ice-green eyes holding on mine. She nodded.

I pulled the door handle and fell back, bringing my brother with me. He grabbed his shotgun before we tumbled out of the cab. We hit a patch of soft dirt – our first luck all day. Even so, his weight crushed into me, bruising my shoulder.

I kicked-pushed him up off me, and we ran a few strides, jumped over an outcropping of shale, and skidded down a long rocky slope into a ravine filled with dead leaves.

A moment later dust kicked back into our faces and Alex rattled down on her stomach, slotting neatly between me and Patrick. Her face held a worn-out frustration that I didn't recognize. I knew how she felt; it seemed the onslaught would never end.

We lay there, panting against the forty-five-degree slope.

A few precious seconds of rest.

Soon enough the ground started to vibrate against our cheeks. The pitch rose bit by bit until the earth shook with footfalls. Were the Hatchlings going to sniff out our hiding space? The noise grew even louder. Pebbles shook free, raining down across our heads. We had to turn our faces.

The sound grew thunderous. It felt like they were on top of us already. It seemed impossible that they wouldn't spot us. We braced ourselves, chests heaving.

To our left, way downslope, the semi truck bucked into view, fire erupting from the hood. A stream of Hatchlings followed it. The truck crested a bulge in the mountainside and vanished, hurtling down Ponderosa Pass.

Following its wake, the stream of Hatchlings passed overhead for one full minute. And then another. They seemed to ripple across the earth, their skin changing against the rocky backdrop.

Sometime after minute three, the shimmering movement stopped.

We were still panting.

'My God, Chance,' Alex said. 'We'd better take care of that.'

I followed her gaze to where my arm rested on the shale between us. The flesh of my forearm was swollen and red, a massive hive.

A hive in the shape of a three-fingered hand.

We hiked through the dense woods. Patrick took the lead, shotgun slung back over one shoulder. He bent aside a branch for Alex, and she in turn handed it off to me. We were making decent headway down Ponderosa Pass, though we had to take a meandering route to avoid the one that our burning truck and the Hatchlings had blazed through the woods. On our way we were looking for a cabin, a ranger station, a trailer – anything that might have a first-aid kit.

'We're not supposed to be alive right now,' Alex said. 'We were supposed to take out the Queen, shut down the Hatch site.' A bitter laugh. 'Sacrifice ourselves nobly to win the battle.'

'And you're mad that we survived?' Patrick asked.

'Yeah, I'm mad.'

'Why?'

'Because after what we just saw, winning a battle isn't enough,' Alex said. 'We have to win the *war*.'

The Rebel helmet swung at my side. How bizarre that neither Patrick nor Alex had asked me about it. I hadn't had a chance to fill them in on any of it. Not that the fate of the world depended on me and Patrick. Not that we had to stay alive for some mission. Not that I'd met a friggin' Rebel from outer space who'd told me about the Harvesters.

I said, 'About that –'

But Alex wasn't done talking. 'That's the problem with not dying when you set out to. I mean, you make all your plans. And other stuff, *complicated* stuff . . .' She placed another bent-back branch in my hand, and our fingers brushed. '. . . you think you're not gonna have to deal with. Because you won't be around to figure it out. But then – *surprise*.' She shot me a quick look over her shoulder, which I swear was loaded. 'You're alive. And things are more complicated than ever. And you have to figure it out, no matter who gets hurt.'

My mouth had gone dry.

'We'll figure it out,' Patrick said. 'How to kill those things. But first we gotta get back to town, warn everyone, and regroup. I want Chatterjee's take on the Hatchlings, too.'

I also wanted to hear what our former biology teacher would have to say about all this.

As Patrick kept on about war strategy, I found myself wondering if I'd mistaken what Alex was saying. Maybe she *was* just talking about the war. Had I misread her look? Had I misread it because I'd wanted to?

'. . . has to be a way to inflict bigger damage,' Patrick was saying.

I stared down at the Rebel helmet. Then I cleared my throat. 'Look, you guys aren't gonna believe this. . . .'

'You ran into a Rebel alien who told you that you and I are the key to the survival of the human race before he evaporated in a puff of smoke?'

My mouth opened. I closed it.

Patrick bulled forward through some dense shrubs. Alex followed him, smirking. She has this smirk that pulls her mouth a little bit to one side.

In case you were wondering.

'Wait,' I said. 'How . . .? When . . .?'

Patrick reached into his backpack, dug out my well-worn notebook, and slapped it against my chest. 'We found your journal in the cabin,' he said.

'But I hid it.'

'I know,' Patrick said. 'Under the pillow. Not exactly a mastermind hiding place.'

'Well, I didn't figure . . .' What were they doing on the bed?

A memory hit me: *My fingers brushing Alex's neck as I fumble with the clasp of her necklace. Alex leaning into me. Her plush, plush lips.*

I shook off the thought. 'So you know everything.'

'Everything you wrote down,' Patrick said. 'And you were pretty thorough.'

I could've sworn that *that* was loaded, too.

'They chased us half the night,' Alex said. 'We had to hide in a gully. We must've gotten to the cabin right after they caught you. At first, when you weren't there . . .' When she spoke again, she sounded as tough as ever. 'But then, like Patrick said. We found it. We knew the early entries, obviously, but we read the end. How you killed the Queen and she was made of mist or whatever. What the Rebel said about you and Patrick needing to carry out some *über*-mission. How the Drones were closing in on you at the cabin.'

'I thought you were crazy with all that stuff,' Patrick said.

'I, on the other hand, thought you were only half crazy,' Alex said.

'So we decided to go in hard.'

I thought of them blazing down the hillside in that semi. 'That you did.'

'Patrick followed their tracks,' Alex said. 'After a bit it was pretty clear they were taking you to the Hatch site.'

'I thought we might get there too late,' Patrick said. He hooked my neck and pulled me close so our foreheads bumped. Then he stared at me, emotion flickering beneath the surface of his dark eyes. I must've grown some, because I didn't have to tilt my head all the way back to look at his face. I wondered when that had happened.

'If you'd died before we got there,' Patrick said, 'I would've killed you.'

I smiled, but he didn't. Patrick doesn't smile much.

He let go of my neck and started walking again. 'Now let's break into that house and get your arm cleaned up.'

At the same time, Alex and I said, 'What house?'

Patrick pointed down below, but I saw nothing except branches and leaves. Alex looked at me with one eyebrow cocked. I gave a shrug. Was he hallucinating?

We cut through a copse of pines, and finally I saw it.

An A-frame built of dark wood nestled into the hillside. Giant windows reflected back the surrounding trees, blending it seamlessly into the forest.

'That's the problem with you two,' Patrick said. 'Too busy yammering to pay attention.'

**ENTRY 10**    The house must've belonged to rich folks before it all went down. Polished floorboards, plush bearskin rugs thrown down before a massive hearth, sparkling granite countertops.

I sat on one of those sparkling countertops in the kitchen, biting my lip and trying not to make a noise as Alex wiped my forearm with a baby wipe from the first-aid kit. A *baby wipe* – as if the pain weren't bad enough.

'Quit whining, Little Rain,' she said.

'I'm not saying anything.'

'Your *posture* is whining.'

'My posture is stoic.'

She feigned a poke at the hive, and I flinched. She smiled, pleased with herself, then tossed the baby wipe into the trash. 'I'll be right back.'

She headed up the stairs to the second floor.

In the china hutch, a softball glove had been shoved in among the nice dishes. I tried not to think about the owner of that glove. Who she used to play catch with. Where she was now. *If* she still was.

That was part of it now. Stopping your brain before it ran off and led you where you didn't want to go.

To distract myself I dug around inside the first-aid kit. I came up with a few packets of Benadryl. I remembered Aunt Sue-Anne giving me Benadryl one time after Ben

Braaten pushed me into a patch of stinging nettle by Hogan's Creek. I tore a packet open with my teeth and dry-swallowed two pills. Then, figuring now was no time to be slowed down by hives, I took two more.

Patrick came in through the back door. 'I got the generator turned on,' he said. He stopped and looked at me. 'Quit whining.'

'I'm *not* whining. Why does everyone say I'm whining?'

'Your face looks whiny.'

'Your face looks stupid, but you don't see me pointing it out.'

*That* almost earned a smile.

Patrick took off his hat, armed sweat from his forehead, and seated the Stetson back in place. His pendant had popped out from the collar of his shirt. The silver jigsaw-puzzle piece, strung on ball chain like a dog tag, fit the one around Alex's neck. As you could probably guess, Patrick wasn't really a jewelry guy, but he wore it for her. He shoved the pendant back inside the collar now. His eyes scanned the kitchen. He pulled a butcher knife from the block by the sink, appraised it approvingly, and slid it into his backpack.

Alex's feet tapped back down the stairs. She spun around the newel post, a box in hand.

'What's that?' I asked.

'Oatmeal bubble bath.'

'Now's not really the time.'

'Ha-ha.' She busied herself at the sink, stirring a couple of teaspoons into a bowl of warm water. Then she tore a dish towel into strips and soaked them. Her forehead furrowed a bit when she worked, and her lips were pressed together.

I noticed Patrick noticing me noticing her, and I cleared my throat and looked away. 'When they got me at the Hatch site,' I said, 'they put me in front of one of those meteor ship things, and it scanned me.'

'*Scanned* you?' Patrick said.

'Like my cells and DNA and stuff. It all showed up on the screens – a magnification of my chromosomes. One of my base pairs was . . . screwy.'

Alex kept tapping the strips into the glop with a fork like she was following some kind of recipe. '*Screwy?* Is that the scientific term?'

'It was all red and blinking. Definitely what they were looking for. And it had a missing part. Like it was . . . I don't know, *altered* in some way. Whatever's wrong with me, it got the second Queen there in a hurry.' I paused. 'Or what's *right* with me.'

At that, Patrick's head snapped up. 'The immunity.' He was usually so inscrutable, but now he was practically beaming with hope. 'Maybe that's the same thing I have.'

You see, when it turned out that Patrick was immune to the spores that made folks transform at the age of eighteen, we'd hoped that it was hereditary – and that maybe, as his brother, I had it, too. But then we'd found out that our mom had had fertility issues and that she'd used embryo transfers to get pregnant. No one knew whether my dad and she had chosen different egg donors. So maybe I'd inherited the same immunity Patrick had. Maybe I hadn't.

I have to admit that seeing my blinking base pair on that gooey meteor screen, along with all this talk of me and Patrick being the saviors of the human race, had already gotten me hoping that I had whatever weird genetic immunity Patrick had. Optimism seemed like a dangerous indulgence these days, but what else could be so important about my chromosomes?

'The Harvesters are hunting us down for a reason,' I said.

'Because their spores can't mess with us.' Now Patrick was smiling. A real smile. 'Man, that's a relief. I've been counting the time, you know . . . you have left. Twenty-eight months, seventeen d –' Patrick caught himself.

Alex had stopped stirring. She was over at the sink, her back turned.

'Alexandra,' he said. 'I'm sorry. I didn't mean –'

She turned, wearing a smile. It was an honest smile, but there was something else in it, too, something less happy. 'Oh, come on, Patrick. You think I'm not thrilled that Chance could have immunity like you? It's the only bit of good news in this whole crappy situation. At least let's enjoy it.' She cleared her throat. 'Stop looking at me like that, you guys.'

'Fifty-eight days,' I said.

'I know when my birthday is,' Alex said.

'Maybe there's –'

'Let's not "maybe", okay? Let's just not. We know what this is. We know the cards we've all been dealt. We'll play them the best we can until we can't anymore.'

Patrick stepped forward and put his hands on her shoulders, the brim of his hat shadowing his eyes. 'No matter what, we're gonna take down these bastards before your birthday. You're gonna be safe. I don't know how yet, but I'm gonna make sure of it.'

'You can't promise that, Big Rain,' she said.

'I just did,' he said.

She looked up at him. She didn't move, but I sensed her muscles unclench. She softened. I'd known that feeling, the comfort of Patrick stepping in, saying he was gonna take care of something. He always had. He always did.

I wondered what it would be like to have that power.

Patrick cocked his hat back. 'I'm gonna go look for clean clothes. We can each grab a shower, and then we'll head back to town.'

He walked down the rear hall. I heard a door swing open and creak closed behind him.

Alex came over to where I sat on the counter, the bowl in her hand. She lifted one of the strips and let the extra muck drip into the bowl. Then she took my hand in hers, gently, and turned my arm over.

She wrapped my forearm. She was standing close, her stomach brushing against my knees. I could feel her breath against the hollow of my neck.

I told myself not to look at her lips.

Or the edge of her eyebrow where it met her temple.

Or the strokes of her collarbone, barely visible above the stretched-out hem of her dirty T-shirt.

'Eve Jenkins'll be happy to see you when we get back, that's for sure,' Alex said.

Eve. Dark hair, straight bangs, a round face with a dimple in one side when she smiled at me, which was often. She was sweet and she was cool.

She wasn't Alex.

Alex's head was still dipped, but she looked up at me through her eyelashes. It was unfair, that look.

For some reason I couldn't grasp, I felt a surge of anger. 'What are you doing, Alex?'

She looked at me directly now. I'd never talked to her that way. 'What do you mean?'

'Patrick's my brother.'

She took a step back. 'I've known you pretty much since *birth*, Little Rain. I'm aware of the relation.'

'When we were hiking on our way here. I know what you were saying. It's not all in my head.'

Her pissed-off expression stayed the same, an unreadable mask. For an awful moment, I thought that maybe I had it wrong. The heat in my chest and face started to mutate from anger into earth-shattering embarrassment.

I was about to break the silence when she said, 'You're right.'

I was glad I hadn't blurted out anything else.

'This is stupid. *I'm* being stupid. This isn't right.' She set down the bowl next to me. 'Look, Chance. I thought you were dead, okay? We both thought you were dead. And . . .'

'And *what*?'

'You know how I feel about your brother. I've felt that way about him for practically as long as I can remember.'

I looked through the big picture windows at the dark landscape dissolving into dusk.

'But the thought of you being gone made me feel so . . . I don't know. *Alone*.' She started to chew her thumbnail. Thought better of it. 'Does that make sense?'

*Yes.*

'No,' I said.

I couldn't look at her. Not right now.

'There's not a handbook for this, Chance. We're teenagers.

60

We're not supposed to be trying to survive every minute. Counting days. Thinking about dying. Thinking about the people we . . . the people we're closest to just being *killed* in some awful way. Everything feels raw. And jumbled up. How are we supposed to know what we need to get through it?'

*I don't know. I'm not sure of anything. And the things I* am *sure of are fighting each other in my head.*

'You're supposed to know. You're supposed to be with Patrick.'

'I *do* know.' She was playing with the side of her necklace, twirling the silver links. The jigsaw pendant surfed into view above her collar and then vanished. 'But it's more complicated than just that.' She shook off the thought, annoyed. 'You don't get it. Maybe you're too young.'

*I'm not too young. It's so damn complicated that I'm drowning in it.*

'Right,' I said, staying fixed on the windows. 'I'm too young.'

She took in a deep breath, held it, exhaled slowly. 'I'm sorry, okay? I didn't mean it like that.' She lifted her hand and rested it on the side of my face. Her palm was cool, soft. For the first time, I let myself look directly at her, into those green eyes.

For a moment we just stared at each other.

Then she leaned forward to kiss me on the cheek. Her mouth caught the edge of my lips.

I might have turned my head a little.

I'm not sure.

She pulled back a few inches, and then we were close, breathing, just us in our grimy clothes with her hair swept forward like a curtain framing our faces.

A noise from behind us.

Patrick clearing his throat.

Alex stiffened. I felt my shoulders knot. We turned.

Patrick was staring at us, his eyes unreadable. He had a stack of folded clothes across his arms.

Guilt hit me like a dropped anvil.

My big brother. My protector. My best friend.

All at once I felt tired. Bone-deep tired.

Patrick said, 'How's the patient?'

'Fine,' Alex said, scooping her hair behind her ear with her fingers. 'We were just . . . I just finished wrapping his arm with oatmeal. That should help the swelling, and it won't make him drowsy and useless like Benadryl would.'

Given what had just happened, it took a moment for the words to register.

'Um.' I swept the torn packet behind my back. Blinked heavily. 'Benadryl makes you drowsy?'

'Uh, *yeah*,' Alex said. 'Everyone knows that.' Her eyes picked over me.

I scooted aside a little, in front of the crumpled packets.

'Oh, no, Chance.' She reached behind me, came up with the wrappers. 'You didn't.'

I blinked again. My eyelids suddenly felt like they were made of concrete.

'It's no big deal,' Patrick said. 'He can nap it off. It's not like we have to go right this second.'

A deep rumbling carried down the mountain, vibrating the bones of the house. Far away. But growing louder.

Alex spun slowly to face the big glass windows and the gathering dusk beyond. 'What the hell is that?'

**ENTRY 11**     Patrick shoved us up the stairs in front of him. In the top hall, an attic hatch marred the perfect ceiling. Patrick yanked on the dangling cord, the ladder unfolding with a thump. He lunged up, shouting at us to follow.

The Benadryl had kicked in big time, leaving me groggy. I paused on the rungs halfway up and shook my head.

The rumbling sound grew louder yet.

I forced myself to climb.

The attic wasn't really an attic. It was a dormer room with thick, shaggy carpet. The walls were lined with file cabinets and storage boxes. Coming off the ladder, I kicked a box, and it spilled its contents – yellowed photo albums and an old varsity-football jacket.

Pieces of someone's life.

Alex and Patrick were crowded over by an oval window, one of those specialty ones with a starburst grid. It looked like the wheel of a big boat. Patrick's whole body was tensed, his shoulders flexed up like the hackles of a dog.

'Whaa?' I slurred.

'Shh.' Alex waved me over.

My first step was wobbly. I evened out my balance the best I could, stumbled to the window, and took a knee behind them, trying to peer over their shoulders. The window, three stories up, poked above the nearby treetops, giving a view of the northeast side of Ponderosa Pass. Stifling a yawn, I shifted to peer between Alex's head and Patrick's hat. Way across the flats, I could make out a collection of buildings in the distance. Stark Peak – the closest thing to a big city we'd had growing up, an hour and a half by car before the alien invasion. The giant spire atop City Hall lorded over the cityscape. I remembered going there for a field trip in third grade, our class tittering in the grand marble lobby lined with saltwater aquariums. Growing up here, we were about as far as you could get from an ocean, so you can imagine us kids gawking at the coral and the clown fish, moray eels and puffers. It was like encountering creatures from another planet, but – as I've learned since – a lot more pleasant.

I'd always thought I'd get to see the ocean someday. Breathe in the salty breeze. Swim in the waves. Bury myself up to the neck in sand.

So much stuff I wouldn't get to do.

I could hear the rush of the tide, a low rumble washing around me, and –

Alex jabbed me with an elbow, and I fought my eyes open.

She used to play ice hockey, so getting elbowed by her is a different kind of elbowed.

Somehow I was sitting on the plush carpet. I rubbed my arm. 'Ow.'

'We can't have you falling asleep right now, Chance,' she hissed.

'I waasun susleep.'

She snapped her fingers in front of my face. 'Look at what we're dealing with.'

'I already looked.'

'No. You didn't. You gave a glance and then fell back on your –

'Chance,' Patrick said in his no-fooling-around voice. 'Get up here.'

I got.

They scooted aside to make room for me, and I finally had my first good look at the mountain.

At first I didn't believe what I was seeing. I squeezed my eyes shut, hard, and then forced them open again.

A column of Harvesters poured over the brink of the pass from the Hatch site. The procession was made up mostly of Hatchlings, but there were plenty of Drones and a few Hosts. The Hatchlings' camo flesh morphed to match the terrain, creating a weird optical illusion. The ribbon of movement spilled down the folds of the mountain, headed, it seemed, directly for us. It disappeared from sight just beyond the bulge of trees fronting the house.

In spite of the Benadryl, I felt suddenly quite awake.

I stared at the swell of forest before us, waiting for the vanguard to emerge. But Alex smacked me again with an elbow and pointed to the north.

It seemed the Harvesters had changed course in that dip of land before the A-frame. We couldn't see this, only where the war parade emerged a half mile to our left on the side of the mountain. Down in the foothills, it was joined by two other streams of Harvesters, one presumably coming from the tractor plant at Culverside and another from the hay-pressing factory in Pinedale.

Their ranks swelled, but they held the marching

formation. They cut north, moving toward Stark Peak. Incredulous, I let my eyes rise to the cluster of buildings at the horizon. Every few miles another tributary poured in from another town, the living yield of another Hatch site. Drones. Hatchlings, mostly male, some female. The occasional Queen bobbing into view higher than the rest, like a lord riding one of those fancy chairs slaves used to carry them around in.

In the flats by Lakewood and Springfield, cattle trucks joined the parade. Were Hatchlings driving them? Hosts? The Harvesters were moving everyone and everything to Stark Peak, a long column stretched out across the highway like a war supply line.

Closer to us, right at the base of the foothills, a commotion broke out. A cluster of Hatchlings bulged from the heavy traffic of the march and spread through a trailer park. From here they looked like angry insects, monsters in a video game. They swarmed the dirty little compound, kicking through doors and windows and emerging from the double-wides dragging kids in their wake.

The kids bucked and kicked, their mouths spread wide in terror. Over the thousands of marching feet, we couldn't hear their cries. Their heels gouged trails through the dirt.

The Hatchlings hauled the kids toward the cattle trucks. Through the slats I could see movement. My stomach burned, all acid and stress.

A gate swung open, and we saw inside.

Bodies mashed together into a block of life. Squirming, sobbing, screaming. One girl's thin arm rose above the fray.

Alex had pressed her knuckles to her mouth. She wasn't making a sound, but I could feel the energy pouring off her like heat.

The Hatchlings herded the new kids up the ramp, packing them in with the others. Except the last kid. They tossed him back to two female Hatchlings instead.

I had to look away.

When I looked again, the kid was gone, the truck gate was closed, and the procession continued.

'We gotta clear out of here and get back to the school,' Patrick said. He wasn't whispering, but his voice was low, as if the Harvesters could hear us huddled here in the dormer. 'Or that's gonna be us.'

It would have been impossible for them to spot us, but Alex and I had drawn away from the window.

Another wave of grogginess swept through me, and I yawned, my eyes watering. I wanted to curl up and sleep for a hundred years. I wanted to scream and run. I wanted to give up. I wanted to fight.

A violet light spilled through the feathered clouds, illuminating Stark Peak from the west – the pale buildings shimmering with the sunset's last gasp. I lifted my hand, blocking out the Harvesters and their war march, leaving only the cityscape and the wide-open sky. Alex glanced over at me and then did the same, peering over the tops of her fingers.

She said, 'This would've been beautiful once.'

Patrick was up and ready, crouching, a dark silhouette in the darkness of the room. 'Let's go. We got work to do.'

He wasn't big on sunset gazing.

Alex stood. I told my limbs to move, but they didn't listen. I stared at them blearily. Yawned again.

Patrick slapped me across the face hard enough to force my head to the side. 'C'mon, Chance,' he said. 'We need you to snap to.'

I found my feet.

**ENTRY 12**    We tiptoed down the stairs, my cheek still stinging from Patrick's hand. The sound of the army outside seemed even louder, antlike skittering on a massive scale. The cacophony swelled, footsteps jarring the ground, rolling through the earth in waves. I watched a coaster slide across the kitchen counter a millimeter at a time.

Though the swell of trees shielded the house from view, we shied away from the big windows. Patrick led us to the rear door. He wore the backpack, Alex carried the Rebel helmet, and they'd split up the weapons. They didn't trust me to carry anything. I didn't trust myself either. I was swaying on my feet like a drunk hobo.

Alex turned the deadbolt quietly. There was no point taking any chances, and besides, fear makes you do dumb things.

We crept out the back, and the smell hit, a gust on the chill breeze that made me want to retch. The earth vibrated, tickling my feet through the soles of my boots. Pine needles trembled all around us.

Patrick knifed his hand and pointed straight downhill. Alex nodded. I tried to nod through my Benadryl haze, but the sludge in my head seemed to be growing thicker. I'd never been terrified and exhausted at the same time.

We picked our way through the trees, sliding downslope, sometimes on our feet, sometimes on our butts. The rumbling of the Harvester army grew fainter until it was barely audible, the hum of an insect. Night came on faster than seemed possible.

I leaned against a tree, nodding off.

I sensed a shift in the air and jolted awake, holding up my hands. Sure enough, Patrick was there, his arm drawn back for another slap.

'I'mbawake,' I slurred.

'Stay that way.'

We cut back and found the main road winding down the pass. We let it guide us but kept to the side in the foliage. We hadn't gone far before we spotted a pair of Hosts on the asphalt – a female and a male, Chaser and Mapper. We hunched behind a boulder and spied on them.

The woman wore a yellow housecoat split down the back, no trousers, and one slipper. Tatters of the man's suit trousers swung above his bloody ankles, but his jacket, shirt, and tie were perfectly in place. He had his head bent, his eyeholes aimed at the ground, and he walked in an expanding spiral pattern of right-angle turns. Like all male Hosts, he was a Mapper, vacuuming up the terrain and beaming it back to the Harvesters.

The Hosts, I noticed, were getting more ragged every day, their bodies starting to give out. Their muscles couldn't handle the abuse their hijacked brains were putting them through. Hosts didn't eat, didn't drink, didn't rest. The Mappers mapped and the Chasers chased. I couldn't imagine that they'd be around much longer.

While one threat diminished, a greater one grew.

As if to remind us, the shifting wind brought a faint murmur of the distant Harvester force.

We waited until the Hosts' backs were turned, and then we slipped away. For a time we walked through the darkness in silence, our footsteps soothing and rhythmic.

Soon enough the motion lulled me to sleep. My heel jarred against the hard dirt, snapping me awake. I fought my head up, my eyes open.

'We're gonna be walking all night,' Alex said.

She was right. It was a long way down to the barricade of fallen pines and our car parked off the highway beyond. Reaching up with my thumbs and forefingers, I pinned my eyelids open. Patrick looked back at me and shook his head. I brushed a spiderweb from my neck and kept stumbling along.

The rumble of the Hatchlings had faded away entirely at some point, but I didn't know when. The relative silence felt so reassuring. I could taste the pine at the back of my throat, a fresh, earthy tang.

A whinny carried out of the darkness, freezing us where we stood. A moment later a distinctive clopping echoed between the tree trunks.

Alex spun around to face me, that wide smile springing up on her face. I was grinning, too. Patrick was looking at us.

He wasn't grinning.

The clopping grew louder, and then it burst through the trees and reared up before us. An Andalusian stallion, seventeen hands high, with a white star gleaming on the side of his chest.

*The horse galloping beneath us, a churning machine. Reins threaded through my fist. Alex behind me, one arm looped around my waist, her body sealed to mine, the heat of her cheek pressed between my shoulder blades.*

71

Patrick's head was slightly cocked, the Stetson tilted just enough to trickle dew from the brim.

Alex cleared her throat. 'We . . . um, rode him down the pass after Chance got me.'

Patrick said, 'You guys rode a horse together?'

Alex nodded. 'Yeah. We found him in a stall. It was like . . .' She clamped her lips, as if wishing to take back the sentence. 'Magic.'

*Magic.* Heat crept up my neck, flooded my face.

Between my exhaustion, the stallion's materializing out of the gloom, and the suffocating guilt filling my chest, I felt like I'd tumbled into some weird dreamscape.

I fought off a yawn.

Patrick took a half step back into a roadside culvert, one boot toeing the lip. He rested an arm across his raised knee and studied us. 'Okay,' he said. 'Get your horse.'

Alex hesitated a moment. Then she walked over to the stallion. He reared up again, his silky black coat shimmering in the moonlight. She lifted a hand to his nose.

The horse turned and cantered off down the road.

Alex and I stood there paralyzed, feeling ridiculous. I debated running after him, but that would've been even more ridiculous. His horseshoes sounded like clanging pots against the asphalt. His majestic tail swished back and forth, and then he was gone around a bend. The yellow wash of the moon reflected up from puddles in the street.

Patrick said, 'Guess we can scratch "magical horse rescue" off the list of options.' He turned and faced something behind him in the culvert, a shadowy mass covered with branches. 'But I have a better idea.'

*

72

Patrick straddled the off-road motorcycle, Alex sitting on the seat behind him.

I was in the sidecar, my knees up around my chin.

They'd pulled the bike up out of the culvert and on to the main road while I'd sat on the edge of the asphalt and fought to keep my head upright.

Patrick glanced down at me. I felt like an elephant on a tricycle. I wasn't certain, but I thought I could detect a smirk on his face.

'Ready?' he asked.

The Rebel helmet was wedged in my lap. I adjusted my weight awkwardly in the cramped sidecar. A far cry from galloping down the pass on a black stallion with Alex at my back.

I nodded miserably.

At least I had my weapons of choice again. The wooden handles of the baling hooks felt reassuring inside my fists. But not as reassuring as the metal curves protruding about a foot from between the knuckles of either hand.

If we were gonna blaze down the pass on a motorcycle (and sidecar), I had to be armed.

Patrick rose up even higher, kick-starting the dirt bike. As we veered out into the middle of the road, I felt the Benadryl surge into high gear. I suppose 'low gear' might've been a better term.

It was like a blackout, punctuated with gunshot flashes.

– the black sky scanning overhead until the stars went dark and –

– Alex smacked my head. I came to just in time to register a Host fly out of the woods at us. My hand whipped a baling hook at his head, slashing through the throat when –

– I bucked in the seat, cracking my nose on my knee, and then –

– another smack knocked my head, also courtesy of Alex. I started violently out of my drugged slumber, flailing instinctively with the hooks, one tip sinking into meat inches from my face. Empty jack-o'-lantern eyes peered at me. I'd impaled the head through both cheeks. The body scraped along next to the sidecar, sandpapered by the road, and Alex was screaming and –

– the wind riffled my hair. I tilted my head back drowsily. The moon, a bulb shining through the heavens. It blurred, and –

– the motorcycle's beam illuminated a decaying Chaser ahead, muscle and bone showing through her pale skin like an X-ray. Patrick didn't slow. A smack of tire meeting rotting flesh, and I saw her arms fly up over her head, and –

– my head was bumping along the metal edge of the sidecar, painful and yet somehow peaceful, and then –

– Patrick prodded me out of the seat. My hand slipped on the curved metal side, which was coated with spilled guts. As I toppled over, I caught sight of the motorcycle's red-spattered fender. The hard ground rolled beneath me, bringing into view –

– the stupid stallion chewing a bush at the side of the barricade. As we passed, Alex gave him a smack on the hindquarters and sneered, 'Thanks a *lot*.' The horse tossed his mane, and I blinked and saw –

– my boots slipping on the mossy logs of the barricade. A fallen pine banged into my chest, and I realized I was sprawled flat, a dollop of sap poking my cheek. I thought about how nice it would be to just close my eyes and –

– float above the highway past the barricade. For some reason Patrick's butt was below my head, upside down. I felt his words rumble through his body and into mine: 'I got it from here, little brother.' His voice was as steady and comforting as ever, but a rush of heat hit my face as I realized that – humiliation of humiliations – he was carrying me. I caught a sideways glimpse of Alex looking at me –

– jouncing up and down, the ball of Patrick's shoulder jolting into my gut. Still upside down. Marshy reeds sucked at my brother's boots. I managed to lift my wet-sand head to look behind us and immediately wished I hadn't. A mass of Hosts closed in, arms raised, eyeholes like bullets through their skulls showing –

– Alex breathing hard, her chest heaving. At her feet were the sprawled remains of a half dozen Hosts. Patrick shucked his shotgun, a shell spinning free in the night air, glinting until it fell with a plink on to the moist earth. A hard surface dug into my back, and I rolled my head to see that I was lying on the roof of the Mustang where Patrick probably hurled me so he could turn and fight –

– clear of the reeds, tires spinning before catching the rocks we'd laid down as tracks to get us out of the marsh and on to –

– the highway unspooling before us. I tilted forward in the backseat and leaned heavily against the front headrests.

Patrick stared forward, one hand on the wheel, his Stetson low over his eyes.

Alex gave a half turn, the glow from the high beams casting her smooth cheek in a pale yellow light.

She said, 'Welcome back, Little Rain.'

**ENTRY 13**     We made it across the valley without major incident. Minor incidents were of course unavoidable. Once we reached the outskirts of town, we snaked off the highway up a bumpy dirt road into the forest. We left the Mustang with the hood steaming and its grille dripping remains. Then we threaded back through the trees toward town and the school – our base camp – beyond.

Darkness folded around us, the treetops blotting out the stars. Beneath the oatmeal bandage, my forearm pulsed with heat. I tightened my grip on the baling hooks. And then I remembered.

I dropped my hooks, letting them dangle from my wrists on their nylon loops. Putting my fingers in my mouth, I gave a piercing whistle.

I faced the dark woods. Patrick and Alex stopped behind me. Alex had a gun in one hand, the Rebel helmet in the other. We waited and waited some more.

And then we heard them coming, darting through the underbrush, paws scrabbling across the hard ground. The Rhodesian ridgebacks I'd raised burst into the clearing, panting and wagging and bumping us with their noses like playful dolphins.

My giant puppy, Cassius, jumped up on me, resting his muddy paws on my shoulders and slurping my face. Smiling, I pushed him off. He rammed his side into my knees until I scratched his back. He was a black-mask ridgie – the band of dark fur covering his nose and eyes contrasting with the rest of his honey-tan coat. Like the others, he had a narrow band of reversed fur running down his spine, a wicked-looking racing stripe. He'd put on another ten or so pounds since I'd seen him last, his powerful chest widening with muscle. He was the second-biggest now, behind Tanner – and that was plenty big. These guys were bred to hunt lions, so imagine what they did to Hosts.

Deja, Princess, Thor, and Grace bumped Cassius aside, competing for my attention. I took a knee and greeted them all. Atticus sat aloofly until they were done and then trotted over. I noticed he was limping. When he drew near, I lifted his front paw. The pad beneath was badly torn. Dread hit me like a dropped stone, rippling through my insides. How long would he make it out here injured? He nuzzled my palm and then backed away.

They were feral now.

I called Cassius and Tanner back over and said, 'You look out for your brother, you hear?'

They cocked their heads, furrowed their brows, wagged their tails. Silly human making silly human noises.

The others were sitting in a semicircle around me. 'Release,' I said, and started walking.

They surrounded us as we moved through the woods, keeping us inside the pack. This forest was their home now; here they ruled over all things living and not.

As we reached the edge of town, they started to fall away. Patrick, Alex, and I halted and looked across the unfenced backyards. It took a moment for our eyes to focus through the darkness. Something had knocked over the Woodrows' barbecue grill. But there was no movement.

Cassius whimpered at my heel, and I turned back to the pack, scratching him behind the ears. I snapped my fingers, and Atticus hobbled forward.

I gestured toward town, but he backed up, whining.

'C'mere,' I said. 'Don't be stubborn.'

I tried to examine his paw again, but he darted away, slinking among the trees, his eyes glinting out at me. I thought of Zeus, my biggest boy, who'd died protecting me. Something cracked in my chest, threatened to break.

I looked back at the pack. 'You guys better protect him,' I said. 'That's your most important job. He's your big brother, and he took care of you all these years. Now's your turn.'

Patrick rested a hand on my shoulder. 'Sun's gonna rise soon,' he said gently – or at least as gently as Patrick said anything. 'We gotta move.'

Atticus kept his distance. He didn't want to go with us. It's not like we had that much to offer anymore. If I were him, I'd have preferred the woods, too. I went to him slowly, holding out my hand. He licked it. I kissed his head – musk, dirt, and cinnamon.

'Release,' I told the dogs, and they trotted off, Atticus limping behind them.

We stepped out from the tree line and hustled along the side of the Woodrows' house, stepping over the fallen barbecue. Then we peeked up the street. The neighborhood here was little more than a cluster of single-story houses hugging the high school.

Most of the action (and I use the term loosely) in Creek's

78

Cause used to take place in town square, a mile or so south. Not that there was much to the square – a few blocks rimmed with restaurants and shops, a supermarket, two traffic lights, a big church perched at the edge of a grassy sprawl. It had been reduced mostly to blood smears and shattered windows, a ghost town haunted by the grown-ups who hadn't left to help at the Hatch site.

Now Patrick, Alex, and I picked our way up the residential street, hiding behind hedges and abandoned cars. We made slow but steady progress toward the tall chain-link fence guarding the school's perimeter. As the first light of morning filtered over Ponderosa Pass in the distance, we snuck across the school parking lot and flattened ourselves to the ground in front of a gate.

Patrick reached up, his hands working the combination lock securing the chain. He spun the dial back and forth and then tugged. Nothing happened.

I sensed movement on the streets behind us. Grandpa Donovan emerged from the Swishers' old house and plodded on to the sidewalk, his head canted forward. Across the street from him, a worker I recognized from the Piggly Wiggly supermarket stepped out on to the porch of the Rose residence.

They were mapping the *interiors* of buildings now?

Grandpa Donovan shuffled toward the next house in the row. One of his coverall straps had come unhooked, and it swayed in front of his stooped form. If he lifted his head three inches, those eyeholes would register us here. That would bring Hosts scurrying from all directions. And that would likely reveal the high school as a hideout – the last bastion of safety for the kids and teenagers of Creek's Cause.

'Move it,' Alex said to Patrick.

Patrick's hands stayed steady. He rolled the dial through its combination once more and tugged. Again there was no give.

The sun inched higher above the horizon, exposing us even more on the strip of lawn lining the fence. I'd been holding my breath. I tried not to move anything but my eyes, which tracked the Hosts on the sidewalk.

Grandpa Donovan finally disappeared into the neighboring house, but the supermarket stocker continued heading down the street directly toward us.

I grabbed Patrick's arm. 'We have to split,' I said. 'We gotta find somewhere to hide.'

We'd just started to rise when we heard a rattle overhead.

Eve Jenkins's slender hands reached through the chainlink, working the lock. It released with a dry click, and she swung the gate open.

We scrambled inside on all fours and then ran for cover, diving into the shadows in front of the school. The supermarket worker kept on toward us. For a moment I thought he'd spotted us, but then he turned crisply on his heel and padded up the steps to another house. We exhaled together, a chorus of relief.

'Ben changed the locks after you left,' Eve whispered.

Patrick nodded, his mouth a grim line. 'Of course he did.'

'He said it was for safety.' She shook her head. 'But I've been keeping an eye out for you.' She reached over and squeezed my forearm. 'I'm happy to see you.'

To my side I sensed Alex's face swivel to face me. I could practically feel her told-ya-so smirk.

Eve's eyes moved to the Rebel helmet. Only then did I realize how futuristic it looked.

Patrick grabbed the helmet and shoved it into the backpack. 'Nothing Ben needs to see,' he said.

We kept close to the side of the school until we reached the broad stone steps. Sure enough, Ben Braaten, the self-appointed head of security, waited behind the front doors. His hand rested on the bolt gun tucked into the front of his jeans.

When fired, the compressed-air gun shot a steel rod several inches forward. It was designed to whack the thick skulls of cattle. It worked even better on Hosts.

Ben's face, scarred from the car crash that had killed his brothers, stared at us blankly. He was as tall as Patrick but beefier, the only kid I'd known to go head-to-head with my brother in a fight. I waited for Ben to remove his hand from the stun gun. It took a moment longer than I would've thought.

His eyes picked over us, catching on the conspicuous bulge in the backpack. 'You're alive,' he said.

'Sorry to disappoint you,' Alex said.

A scar gnarled Ben's upper lip, so it was hard to tell whether he was sneering. Sweat glistened in his crew cut. A fingerprint of shiny crimped flesh marred his forehead at the hairline.

'Alex,' he said, 'you know I'm happy *you* made it.'

Patrick walked past him, brushing his shoulder. Alex and I followed my brother down the hall to the gym.

Rows of beds lined the basketball court, and on one side the bleachers had been pulled out from the wall. The morning sun shone brightly through high-set windows. Pennants for Creek's Cause High's various sport championships hung from metal beams way up in the ceiling, a reminder of how much that stuff used to mean – school records and rivalries and who was going to state. How dumb it all seemed now.

The surviving kids and teenagers – about a hundred in all – were just stirring.

JoJo spotted us first. Her eight-year-old face lit up with happiness, and then – instantly – her eyes filled with tears. She ran over, her yellow stuffed animal flapping under her arm. She jumped up, arms and legs koala-clamping around me, her stuffed animal mashed against my cheek. One of Bunny's ears was wet from chewing.

JoJo's tears were hot against the side of my neck. She squeezed me harder, and I patted her back. I could feel the ridge of her spine through her skin – it never ceased to surprise me how little she was. And how fragile.

Her brother, Rocky, came in her wake, flicking his head to clear the black curls from his eyes. We bumped fists. He was two years older than JoJo and playing it cool, but I could see how relieved he was that we'd returned.

We were the closest thing to family they had anymore.

'Everything okay?' I asked.

Rocky averted his eyes and gave a single-shoulder shrug.

JoJo whispered into my neck, 'It was *awful* without you.'

I rubbed her back some more. 'It's okay now, Junebug.'

She pulled away and looked at me through uneven brown bangs. She'd cut her hair herself, and you could tell. 'You don't understand,' she said. 'Ben tries to take over when you guys are gone, and he's sucky and totally unfair.'

I set her down. A murmur rolled around the gym as the others noticed us and started hopping off the beds.

'Doesn't Dr Chatterjee keep him under control?' Alex asked.

'He *tries*,' she said. 'But you know Ben.'

As if on cue, Dr Chatterjee entered the gym, moving jerkily on his leg braces.

Our biology teacher – and former family doctor – was the one adult we knew who'd made it through the Dusting. He'd helped us close in on a working theory of what had happened to the adults in our town. We believed that the spores attacked the white brain matter of people over the age of eighteen, spreading through the myelin wrapping the nerve cells of their frontal lobe. Once the frontal lobe was under control, so was the rest of the Host organism. That's why kids and most teenagers were protected – our white matter was still coming in. Since Dr Chatterjee had multiple sclerosis, his white matter already had missing patches. The spores couldn't gain a foothold, not in his brain. So he was still him.

We'd voted him the leader of the survivors, not that Ben had been too pleased about that one.

Chatterjee gave us a smile that rivaled JoJo's and started for us. Before he could get across the basketball court, the other kids crowded in on us, thumping our backs and asking us a million questions. The returning heroes.

I had to confess, after everything we'd been through, it felt pretty good.

Only Ben and his lackeys, Dezi Siegler and Mikey Durango, didn't join in. They stayed in a tight huddle over by the bleachers, whispering to one another out of the sides of their mouths, their eyes pinned on us.

Eve took our weapons back to the storage room so we

weren't standing there in the mob with guns and steel hooks. As the kids quietened down and started their morning routines, Chatterjee finally shouldered through. He gave me and Alex a hug, an unusual show of affection. And then he shook Patrick's hand. Patrick inspired a kind of formality.

Dr Chatterjee said, 'I'd imagine there's quite a bit you need to fill me in on.'

Alex said, 'You have no friggin' idea.'

**ENTRY 14**     Being in Dr Chatterjee's biology classroom made me sad now. Maybe because of how much I'd loved it back when things were normal. Once his MS progressed, forcing him to hang up the stethoscope and take up a whiteboard marker, he'd needed a helper in his classroom. Someone to input grades, erase the board, sharpen pencils – all the fine-motor-coordination stuff that was increasingly tricky for him. He usually chose me.

I never took to math or history – but biology? It was one of my favorite classes, right there with English. Darwinism, meiosis and mitosis, parasites and hosts – I ate all that up. Maybe that made me a nerd, but I didn't really care. Patrick had once told me that I seemed more at home inside books than outside of them. Until recently I hadn't understood that he'd meant it as a compliment. It was useful now, what I'd learned. But for some reason that made it less beautiful to me.

When I was contemplating spores eating their way through my aunt's and uncle's brains or how my chromosomal base pairs had been altered or the fact that a whole race of aliens wanted to kill me . . . well, it took the fun out of all that old-fashioned learning.

Dr Chatterjee sat behind his desk now. A thin film of dust covered the blotter, the rubber DNA model, the out-box still filled with the last round of graded papers. Janie Woodrow, who used to sit next to me, had gotten an A-minus on her report about Cartesian divers. Janie's overbearing single mother, who didn't countenance imperfection, would have had a stern talk with her about that minus.

I used to give Janie a hard time about her Japanese pens and her impeccable flash-card system. Even the rubber bands around the index cards had been color-coded. The last time I'd seen her had been the night of the Dusting. Don Braaten had pinned her to the middle of the road in town square. His knee in her back, his hands winding duct tape around her wrists. He'd been wearing overalls still stained with blood from the slaughterhouse, and I could see straight through his eyeholes. Her cheek had been mashed into the yellow dotted line. I was too far away to see if she'd been crying, but I'd known Janie Woodrow to cry at a lot less.

It's probably not such a mystery why I didn't like being in Dr Chatterjee's classroom anymore.

'How 'bout you, Chance?' Chatterjee said.

I'd zoned out.

'Huh?' I said.

Chatterjee glanced at me through his round wire-frame glasses. He'd been sitting cocked back with the Rebel's helmet in his hand, contemplating it like Hamlet with the skull. Or had that been the other guy, the gravedigger?

Patrick, Alex, Eve, and I sat in the front row.

Back in the auditorium, we'd filled in the others on the big-picture stuff, from the Hatchlings to the march to Stark Peak. The news had drawn the usual reactions. Disbelief, tears, a few nervous breakdowns. But when it came to all that business about me and Patrick saving the world, we'd decided to heed the Rebel's advice and keep it to ourselves. This discussion was only for behind a closed and locked door.

'I said, what do you think the Drones *are* beneath the armor?' Chatterjee was a few days unshaven, his beard coming in salt and pepper. 'Just swirling DNA?'

'Yeah,' I said. 'In a gas state.'

He hefted the helmet and stared in the face mask. 'So the suit must replicate gravity conditions on their home planet. If, say, they evolved to live in metallic hydrogen as on Jupiter or Saturn, then in the massively lower gravity field of Earth, they'd be unable to maintain a solid state.' His faint singsong accent gave his voice a pleasing ring. 'It's a very clever system, isn't it?'

'That's one word for it,' Alex said.

But Chatterjee was undeterred. 'First they send spores that make the indigenous life-forms do the heavy lifting and pave the way for their arrival. They design their suits to mimic the dominant life-form here. Us. Then they use the nourishing, healthy tissue and hormones of our young to grow their own next generation. Their offspring come out adapted to the host atmosphere.' He removed his spectacles and polished them on the lapel of his shirt. 'Which means they don't need us anymore.'

'Except for food,' I added.

Eve blanched.

'These Hatchlings,' Chatterjee said. 'They're tridactyl humanoids?'

'What they are,' Alex said, 'is horrifying.'

'We have to understand them to beat them,' Chatterjee said.

'We saw these things, Dr Chatterjee,' Patrick said. 'And with all due respect, we're not gonna beat them with *understanding*.'

'How, then? All you have to go on are a Rebel's dying words. He said his compatriots will contact you about this . . . mission you're required for. But they have no way to do so.'

'That's why we have to contact *them*,' I said.

Patrick and Alex looked over at me. Only then did I realize that I hadn't discussed this plan with them. I'd thought it was self-evident. That was the problem when you were as close as we three were; I sometimes forgot that Patrick and Alex weren't inside my stream of consciousness.

'Chance,' Chatterjee said, in a gentle, let's-not-rile-up-the-mental-patient tone. 'You have no way to contact them either.'

'Why do you think I risked my life to go back for this?' I reached across the desk and plucked the helmet from his hands.

'Wait,' Patrick said. 'Sit down a second. This isn't safe.'

'As opposed to *what*, Patrick?' I said.

For that he had no answer. I knew I was being cocky, but I liked the way it made Alex look at me.

'You heard Dr Chatterjee,' Alex said. 'The suit is designed to replicate their home planet's gravitational conditions. Heavy gravity means massive pressure. That thing could pop your skull like a grape.'

'That's just a theory,' I said, waving her off. 'Besides, I saw a bunch of their screens back at the Hatch site. There are controls and stuff.'

'Labeled in English?'

'The mask *translates* to English, Alex. That means it probably understands it, too.'

'This is crazy, Chance,' Eve said.

'Like I said, compared to what? Marching into Stark Peak and confronting ten thousand Hatchlings? Give me

88

an option that's safe and sane and I'll shut up.' I stared at them, daring anyone to speak. I shook the helmet. 'Whatever answers we're gonna get are in *here*.'

Before anyone could stop me, I tugged the helmet over my head. The rubbery insulation gave with a faint pop and sealed around my neck. It felt airtight in here, an underwater quiet. At first nothing happened. I stood there like an idiot with a giant Rebel helmet on my head.

I pictured what I looked like to the others. To Alex.

Major fail.

I cleared my throat. 'Okay, then. I was wrong.'

At the sound of my voice, the helmet lit up. No – not the helmet. The entire world.

A vivid metallic blue that was impossible to describe because it was a shade I'd never encountered before. Everything I looked at was outlined with hundreds of lines that mapped every shape and contour – the writing on the whiteboard, Patrick's mouth shouting at me, a rotting apple core in the trash can. The lines sparked and fizzled, and I remembered that the software or whatever it was had been damaged in the Rebel's crash.

I staggered around, knocking into Eve's chair. Between the lines, the static, and the actual environment, it was hard to keep my bearings. Chatterjee's face swept by. I felt Patrick grabbing my shoulders.

Then there was a *foomp* sound like a vacuum cleaner trying to suck up a baseball. The insulation around my neck tightened. The air cramped around my temples. I felt my sinuses caving in. All the bravery and confidence I'd felt moments ago evaporated.

'Controls,' I croaked.

89

A thousand symbols I couldn't understand blinked to life, scrolling across my visual field. Confused, I batted at them. The clamp grew stronger. My head was going to cave in because I'd decided to show off. My vision dotted. I pictured what I would look like when they unscrewed the helmet. I'd have one of those tiny shrunken heads, the kind that witch doctors made in cartoons.

Patrick grabbed me around the waist, and Alex pulled at the helmet, her foot buried in my gut.

We fell over. Patrick took out two desks and Eve. I rolled to my knees. A roar – my surging blood – filled my head. My hands scrabbled across the face mask. My vision swam. I fought for focus.

I could hardly get my vocal cords to work, and when they did, I forced out one croaky word: 'Pressure.'

All the symbols flew away except for a circular icon blinking a few feet off the middle of the face mask like the tip of a rhino horn. Sucking for breath, I smacked the virtual icon with the heel of my hand. It must've looked like I was giving a high five to an invisible friend.

Air hissed out vents in the sides of the helmet, thin jets of steam slicing my peripheral vision. The pressure relented. I yanked on the helmet with both hands, but still it wouldn't give. The hissing kept on, and a moment later I could finally snatch in my first breath.

I fought the helmet off and barfed on the tile.

Eve rubbed her head. Alex untangled herself from a chair. Sprawled on the floor, Dr Chatterjee readjusted his leg braces.

Patrick sat up. 'Okay,' he said. 'That went well.'

**ENTRY 15**     That night I slept like I'd never slept. No dreams, no nightmares, just a twelve-hour block of dense darkness. When I came to on my bed, the gym was lit up with full daylight and the others were busy with their tasks. I couldn't believe that all that light and noise hadn't woken me.

Patrick's and Alex's beds were empty. Alex's sheets were strewn and rumpled, but Patrick's bed was made as tight as a marine's.

I stretched, inventorying my aches and pains. The good thing about getting up late was that there wouldn't be a line for the bathroom. I stumbled to the boys' locker room and peeled off the oatmeal bandage. It had done the trick – the swelling was pretty much gone. Only the faintest outline of the Hatchling's hand remained. I tossed the sticky strips of fabric into the trash and took a two-minute ice-cold shower. The water pipes still worked fine for now, but we often kept the generator off, saving the power for emergencies. Which meant no hot water.

I dried off, dressed, and headed to the cafeteria, passing a few lookouts in various classroom windows. Others on cleaning duty mopped the floors. It was comforting to see the kids working in shifts, minding a schedule. The Hatchlings might be beserking through Stark Peak right now, but at least we still had our little survival routines here at Creek's Cause High. Despite the perimeter fence, we kept lookouts posted 24/7. So far the Hosts had made no effort to penetrate the school, but after seeing a few of them map the interiors of houses yesterday, I was nervous that they'd change whatever passed for their minds.

The cafeteria offered slim pickings. I had a brown apple, an energy bar, a scoop of crunchy spaghetti, and a glass of water. While I chewed a mushy bite of apple, Leonora Rose smiled at me sympathetically from the next table.

Even though she was closer to Patrick in age, she and I had always been better friends. One of my first memories was of her at four years old pushing me in a stroller, wearing her mom's shoes, the high heels clopping up the sidewalk. How eager we'd been to grow up. Now the kids counted every new morning with dread; each day brought them twenty-four hours closer to their eighteenth birthday. In the meantime we did our best to ignore the trickling hourglass and get by.

Leonora said, 'We're running low on food. Ben says we're gonna have to do a supply run to the Piggly Wiggly soon.'

'What does Chatterjee say?' I asked.

She shrugged. One side of her straw-colored hair had been braided into a neat pigtail, but the other was loose and wild. I wondered if she'd been unable to find another hair tie or if she'd just given up. One of her front teeth was now inexplicably gray.

'I don't know,' she said. 'I didn't ask him.'

The implications of that were troubling.

She picked mold from a piece of bread. 'Not that it matters anyway,' she said. 'At least to me.'

And I remembered: Her eighteenth birthday was the next one up. A familiar sinking feeling took hold inside me, the sensation of falling and falling.

'When?'

She gave a wan smile. 'Tonight. At 10:03.'

I felt my cheeks get hot, emotion rushing into my face. No matter how often we confronted it, it was impossible to get used to.

'It's okay, Chance,' she said, getting up abruptly to clear her tray. 'Really. It's just how it is now.'

Though I'd lost my appetite, I forced myself to chew the rest of the apple. Then I went back to the gym. Alex was there now, her hair taken up in the back. She was practicing swings with her hockey stick. She didn't use a puck – that would make too much noise. She wound up and sliced the blade of her stick an inch above the polished floorboards again and again. Her jaw was set in a firm line, her eyes focused – the don't-bother-me-I'm-practicing face.

Except now she wasn't practicing for hockey.

Patrick was on the bleachers. I walked over and sat down next to him.

He knocked my knee with his.

I knocked his with mine.

We watched Alex swing and swing.

'I'd hate to make her mad,' I said.

'Yeah,' he said. 'I don't recommend it.'

I smiled.

'Leonora's up next.' I nodded toward the whiteboard that Dr Chatterjee had positioned at the edge of the basketball court. It had all of our birthdays and times of birth listed in order.

'I'd noticed that,' Patrick said.

My eyes found Alex's birthday there, a couple up from the bottom. Less than two months away. She'd been a New Year's baby. That had once been something cool about her, something to celebrate. It was as if fate had reserved the start of the New Year for her to make her even more special.

Now it was something to dread.

I glanced over at Patrick and saw him looking at the board also, and I knew he was focused on Alex's name up there, too. His eyes were shadowed beneath the brim of his cowboy hat, his mouth a firm line. He was someone who liked solving problems, but right now there was nothing that could be solved.

I changed the subject. 'You got my notebook?'

'I slid it under your mattress this morning,' he said. 'You were out cold. So I drew a flower on your cheek with Magic Marker.'

My hand flew to my face. 'Really?'

He tapped my spread hand so my palm smacked into my cheek. 'No.'

I punched his arm. It was like punching a steel pipe. I didn't shake my throbbing knuckles, though, no matter how badly I wanted to.

'Dr Chatterjee and I hid the Rebel helmet in my backpack and locked it in his classroom,' Patrick said, all business again. 'The last thing we need is anyone else finding that thing.'

'I think I can figure out the controls. I'll try it again tonight after everyone goes to sleep.'

'We'll see,' Patrick said.

'I'm not asking permission,' I said.

He looked out at me from beneath the Stetson. The brim gave the faintest dip. I took it as a nod.

Down below, Alex had finally set aside her hockey stick and headed for the TV she kept on the lowest bleacher. Ben was in his usual spot on a folding chair over by the double doors. He was watching Alex, too, with this flat, expressionless stare that made me think of what he'd look like with twin tunnels through his head instead of eyes.

Alex noticed him as well. 'Did you check the TV when we were gone?' she asked.

'No one checks the TV,' Ben said. 'Except you.'

If his grin could talk, it would've said, *Silly girl*.

Early on, Alex had scrounged up the crappy little TV with rabbit ears from the teachers' lounge and plugged it into a twelve-volt battery with an outlet. Even after all the channels had gone dark, she still checked them religiously.

She turned it on now and flipped the dials. Her usual ritual.

She did it often enough that everyone pretty much ignored it.

The screen buzzed with nothingness.

'It breaks my heart when she does that,' Patrick said quietly. 'But then I think it would break my heart if she *stopped* doing it.'

I hopped down the bleachers to my bed and pulled out the notebook. Leaning back on to the balled-up sweat-shirt I used for a pillow, I contemplated where to start. I like to go in order, to write the stuff that I've seen first-hand, but sometimes I get information after the fact and circle back and write it in the margins. It's a pretty messy notebook, but it's all we have.

As far as I know, it's the only active historical record left on Earth.

If you think about it, that's pretty cool. But if you think about it longer, it's terrifying.

I read to where I left off. Closed my eyes. Put myself back there.

And then I wrote.

*I wake up in the perfect darkness of Uncle Jim and Aunt Sue-Anne's ranch house, and there's a split second where everything is fine. I'm six years old, and life is good. And then I remember.*

*My parents are dead.*

**ENTRY 16**     After a lookout shift and something resembling dinner, I found JoJo and Rocky on the bleachers, and we played twenty questions.

'Is it bigger than a hippo?' JoJo asked.

'Yes,' I said.

'Is it bigger than a lizard?' she asked.

Rocky groaned. 'If it's bigger than a hippo, it's bigger than a lizard.'

'Not if it's Godzilla,' she said.

'Godzilla is a *fictional* lizard.'

'Who said we weren't including fictional animals?'

'Because you just don't.' Rocky shook his head, his dark, curly bangs swaying. 'Right, Chance?'

'Is that one of your questions?' I asked.

'No,' he said at the same time JoJo said, 'Yes.'

'No,' I said.

Rocky said, ' "No" you *don't* include fictional animals or "No" you *do* include them?'

'Is that another of your questions?'

Rocky smacked his forehead in mock despair. JoJo giggled.

'No!' Rocky said just as JoJo said, 'Yes!'

'I *do* include fictional animals,' I said. 'And you're down to your last question.'

'But that's stupid,' Rocky said. 'If fictional animals count, then you could include anything. It could be a flying elephant.'

'Dumbo!' JoJo said.

'That's correct,' I said. 'I was thinking of Dumbo.'

'No way,' Rocky said.

'Yes way. I swear.'

JoJo said to Rocky, 'I told you I know what I'm doing. There's a technique.'

'It's not *technique*.' Rocky glared at his younger sister. 'It's the luckiest guess in the history of the known universe.'

'You're just mad that I'm indrewitive.'

'You are indrewitive, Junebug,' I said, mussing her already mussed hair. My palm came away sticky. 'When's the last time you showered?'

Before she could answer, I heard a throat clear behind me. When I turned, Leonora was standing there. I stood up quickly.

Everyone was watching her.

That's what happens when you get close to your time.

She plucked at her fingers with her other hand. 'Look, Chance. I only have a couple of hours.' A nervous laugh escaped her, a high-pitched twitter that held no humor. 'And I . . . I want it to be you.'

We had the attention of everyone in the gym. Patrick's bed creaked as he stood up. Ben sidled over from the doors.

'Um, why do you want . . .? Are you sure you . . .?' I realized I was stammering, so I closed my mouth.

Ben rested his hand on the butt of the stun gun he'd used many a time at his dad's slaughterhouse and many a

98

time since then. 'I can handle it,' he said. 'I know what I'm doing. It'll be the easiest. The most humane.'

'No,' Leonora said. 'I want it to be Chance.' She took a step forward. That one crazy pigtail still stuck out at the side. 'You were like a little cousin to me growing up. You know me better than anyone . . . left.' A tear clung to her bottom eyelid. 'So I guess that makes me closest to you.'

I couldn't talk, so I just nodded. She gave me a businesslike nod in return and walked away.

Dread gathered in my gut, building itself up over the next few hours. I paced around the gym with my head lowered, counting the floorboards. Eve asked me if I wanted to talk, but I just shook my head. As the time drew near, I walked over to Patrick on his bed.

'You know where Leonora is?' I asked.

'She wanted it to happen in the art studio. Alex is with her.'

'Okay.' I nodded several times too many. 'Okay.'

Patrick stood up. 'Want me to go with you?'

'Yes,' I said quickly.

We walked over to Ben, who was sitting in his chair by the gym doors.

'Can I borrow your stun gun?' I asked.

For once Ben didn't make a crack. 'Of course,' he said, handing it over. He touched my arm as I walked past. 'Good luck.'

Patrick and I headed through the dark halls toward the art studio. I was breathing too fast, my chest jerking. My hand was sweating on the stun gun.

Patrick glanced over at me. 'You got this?'

'What if I can't do it?' I said.

'You can,' Patrick said.

'I don't want to mess this up for her,' I said. 'I don't want her to feel not taken care of in her last minutes.'

'She won't,' Patrick said. 'I promise you that.'

We turned the corner into the art room. Leonora was sitting in a chair, and Alex was behind her with a brush, working out the tangles in her hair.

Leonora managed to produce a smile. 'Hi, guys. Thanks for coming.'

Like it was a birthday party.

I guess in one sense it was.

My eyes jerked to the clock, which showed 9:59. Four more minutes.

A sloppily made cupcake impaled by a too-big pillar candle sat on the floor at Leonora's feet. I'd heard that Eve had scraped together some ingredients for it and given it to her at dinner. The cupcake had only a single bite missing. Couldn't blame her for not having much of an appetite just now.

Alex popped out the hair tie and brushed through the pigtail. Leonora's hair looked really pretty now, falling about her shoulders. Alex had done a great job. It must have taken forever.

'You look beautiful,' Alex told her.

Leonora crossed to the mirror over the paint sink, and her hand flew up to cover her mouth. 'I can't remember the last time I looked this normal.'

'Not just normal,' Alex said. 'Beautiful.'

'But beautiful is normal for you,' Patrick said.

Even here, now, under these circumstances, Leonora blushed a bit. She dabbed at her eyes, took a deep breath, held it. Then she said, 'I think I want to lie down.'

Her legs got weak, so Alex and I helped her on to a canvas tarp that Ms Dumone used to use as a drop cloth beneath her easel. The color had left Leonora's face except for circles of red on her cheeks. She looked much younger than her seventeen years and 364 days.

'Let's wait and make sure, yeah?' she said. 'In case I have some miracle immunity like Patrick.'

We all knew that wouldn't be the case.

'Of course,' I said.

The stun gun was wobbling in my grip. Leonora reached out and placed a cool hand on my wrist. 'Okay, Chance. Maybe get it in position?' She tapped her left temple. 'Let's do it here.' Another nervous laugh, like an escaping bird. 'Don't want to mess up my good side.'

I lifted the stun gun, but now it was shaking even worse, my whole arm trembling. I could feel a lump rising in my throat, and I thought, *Don't you dare cry. Don't you dare make this about you.*

'C'mon now, Chance,' she said. 'It's almost time.'

I stared at the smooth, pale skin of her temple.

*— four-year-old Leonora shoving me in the stroller up the uneven sidewalk —*

Sweat stung my eyes.

*— and I'm giggling as I bounce over the tree-root bumps in the pavement —*

Behind me the second hand ticked on the art room's wall.

*— I hear her clip-clopping behind me in her mom's high heels —*

Leonora's shiny hair pooled around her head. Blinking through tears, she looked up at me. 'It's okay, Chance. Really it is.'

*— and she's singing to me: "'He went to bed and bumped his head and he couldn't get up in the morning.'"*

I felt like I was stuck inside my own body, peering out through a concrete mask. I couldn't stop my arm from shaking, but I couldn't move the stun gun either. I thought I might throw up or run out of the room or start crying. It was an awful, awesome responsibility. And I wasn't up to it.

'I have a suggestion,' Patrick said, crouching next to me and sliding the gun from my grip. 'Why don't I do this part and Chance can hold your hand. I mean, that's the part that matters, right?'

Leonora nodded, her head rustling on the tarp.

The relief was so intense that my vision spotted for a second. I blinked it clear and focused on Leonora.

Tears slid sideways off her face. She reached for me with her hand, and I took it.

Patrick moved himself to the side, holding the stun gun to Leonora's temple. Alex rested a hand on her leg. They kept their bodies cleared out of the way so it felt like it was just me and Leonora. I fought off my shame at needing my big brother to cover for me and concentrated on her. I petted the back of her hand.

The clock ticked and ticked, practically echoing off the walls and the tile floor. It sounded like a bomb counting down.

'I'm glad I got to know you,' I told her.

She squeezed my hand hard enough to crush my fingers, and I let her.

Then she shuddered. Darkness crept across her eyes until they looked like giant pupils – like the eyes of Hatchlings. Then came a quiet crackling sound, like termites chewing. Her eyeballs turned to dried bits of ash and fell away, leaving two tunnels through her head.

I looked away.

Patrick's arm firmed, and then there came a hiss of compressed air and the wet smack of the steel rod firing.

Patrick rolled her gently in the tarp. Still I kept turned away.

He stood up, and Alex did, too. I found my feet but kept my gaze lowered to the floor. Inside me, emotion surged like hot lava – grief and guilt and bone-deep horror.

'Chance,' Alex said. 'It's okay.'

Patrick stepped in front of me. I still didn't look up, but I saw his shadow. Then he held out his arms a little. The hot lava boiled, ready to explode right out of my chest.

I stepped forward, hugged my brother tight, and wept like a damn baby.

**ENTRY 17**    I woke up in the middle of the night and checked the clock – it was almost 2 a.m. We'd agreed to meet in Chatterjee's classroom after the others fell asleep so I could give the Rebel helmet another try.

It'd be good if it worked.

Or at least if I didn't puke my guts out all over the floor again.

I eased off my bed so the springs wouldn't squeak and went to wake Alex. Her bed was empty.

That was weird. We'd planned to walk over together.

Patrick wasn't in bed either, but that made sense since he was on lookout duty, keeping an eye peeled from Mr Tomasi's room. I snuck out of the gym and made my way to my old English classroom.

Patrick was sitting cross-legged on Tomasi's desk, facing the bank of windows.

'All quiet on the western front?' I asked.

Without turning, he said, 'Northeastern. And yeah.'

Patrick didn't always get my references.

'I thought Alex might be here with you,' I said.

'Nope. Check Chatterjee's – maybe she's there already.' He turned his head to check the clock, and I caught a sliver of his silhouette. 'I got ten more minutes till Dezi relieves me. I'll meet you guys there.' His head swiveled away to face the windows again. I stared at his broad shoulders.

All business. That's Patrick.

I withdrew.

As I walked back out of the humanities wing to head for Chatterjee's, I noticed movement outside through one of the windows. Instinct kicked in, and I dropped to the floor. For a minute I breathed into the cold tile. When I finally peered over the sill, I saw a figure on the swing set in the sheltered picnic area.

Oh.

I let myself out through a side door and sat down in the swing next to her. We swayed back and forth on our toes. Even though the building shielded us from the street, the last thing we could risk was creaking chains. For some reason I knew not to say anything. I sensed she just wanted me there.

'I couldn't sleep,' Alex finally said. 'I try to push down all the memories of before, but sometimes they slip to the surface. Imagine that. With everything going on out in the real world, I'm most scared of what's inside my skull.'

'You had a nightmare?'

She tilted her head, as if the question confused her. 'A wisp of a memory. My dad pushing me in a swing at Hammond Park. This was before Mom left. I couldn't have been eight years old yet. The summer sky, his hands on my back, the wind against my cheeks – I felt it like I was there. One of those timeless moments, you know?'

I did know. I'd never considered it directly, but I realized that I'd always thought of swings as timeless also. I'd figured that someday my kids would sit on swings, too, and be pushed by me, and then my kids' kids would be pushed by them. But when this set rusted and crumbled to the ground, who would build the next one? There were no more adults, and there'd be no more kids. Not in this world.

Alex said, 'I know that you and Patrick never got along with my dad — or him with you guys — but I remember how safe he made me feel.'

Sheriff Blanton had always thought Patrick and I were trouble, two broke ranch kids going nowhere. He couldn't stand his daughter's dating Patrick. He used to warn her, *Rain only goes one direction. Down.*

'He was a good dad,' I said.

'I shot him in the head,' she said. 'I know it wasn't *him*, but it was what was left of him, and every time I think of my daddy, even pushing me as a little girl in a swing, that's where my mind goes. From a swing set to the bullet I put through his forehead. I can handle one memory or the other, but when you put them together, well . . .' She blew out a breath. 'That's what I can't stand. That life contrasted with this one.'

'But we can't forget who we were before either,' I said. 'Or all we'll have is what's out there.'

She kicked her legs straight. The chains groaned, and she moved her shoes quickly back to the ground. 'What's the point of remembering if it only makes it hurt more?'

'I guess that's our job now,' I said. 'To take who we were before and try to bring it to this. Try to protect those seeds and grow them.'

'Even here?'

'Even here.'

The breeze shifted, bringing the smell of grass and rotting flesh from the neighborhood across from the school.

We drifted forward and back, forward and back, not going anywhere.

'Patrick and I had a fight,' she said.

I thought about my brother on Mr Tomasi's desk, staring out those windows, and I realized he wasn't just focused. He was mad.

'When I first woke up from the dream,' she said, 'I went to talk to him. But I can't talk to Patrick about stuff like this.' Alex turned in her swing to face me, the chains twisting overhead. Her ice-green eyes fixed on me. 'Not like I can talk to you.'

I felt a guilty rush, more pleasant than not. It was like eating a piece of stolen candy, delicious and unhealthy. I wanted to say a hundred different things, but I didn't know if any of them were the right thing to say, and so, with effort, I turned away from her vulnerable gaze.

'Patrick only thinks about *now*. About what has to be done. About the next step. And that's safe and reassuring, and we need that more than ever.' She blinked and held her eyes closed for a moment, her long lashes arcing out. 'But there's also something . . . missing in that.'

The moonlight caught half of her face. It was hard not to look at her lips, not to remember what they felt like.

'It's my fault,' I said. 'When my parents died, he had to step up. He couldn't be a normal eight-year-old. I wasn't strong enough. So he had to be. I never would've made it without him.'

'I'll let you in on a secret.' She leaned closer to me, and I could smell the lavender skin lotion she wore that she'd foraged somewhere. 'He wouldn't have made it without you either.'

There was only maybe a foot between us. I wanted so badly to lean forward into her.

Instead I said, 'We should get to Chatterjee's.'

She tilted off the swing, and I followed suit. We slipped back inside and walked quietly down the dark corridor. We'd just rounded the corner when I came chest to chest with two of Ben Braaten's lackeys, Dezi and Mikey. They must've been heading to relieve Patrick on his lookout duty.

'Look who's sneaking around behind his big brother's back,' Dezi said.

'I'm not sneaking anywhere,' I said. 'We were just talking.'

'Sure you were.'

'Don't live down to your reputation, Mikey,' Alex said, breezing by him.

Mikey grabbed her by the biceps and spun her around. He was a husky kid, the starting center on our football team. His hand encompassed Alex's arm; it looked like if he squeezed, it would snap.

'Watch your mouth, little girl,' he said.

Alex tried to twist away, and he yanked her into him, wrapping her in a bear hug from behind and lifting her off the floor so she couldn't get traction with her feet.

My temper flared, and I charged at him.

Dezi blindsided me.

At least that was what I thought happened. I felt knuckles crush my cheek, and then I was lying on the floor and Dezi and Mikey were chuckling down at me. I started to get up, and Dezi kicked me in the stomach. My mouth was bleeding, the breath knocked out of me. I could hear Alex yelling and twisting in Mikey's grasp.

Dezi set his hands on his knees, leaning over me. 'C'mon, Little Rain. Why don't you get up?'

I tried to suck in air but couldn't find any. Drops of blood fell from my bottom lip, tapping the tile. I tried to rise but was having trouble moving.

A voice issued from the darkness in the hall behind us. 'I got it from here, little brother.'

Dezi whipped around just as Patrick melted into view, barely more than a dark form with a cowboy hat. I didn't see what happened, but there was the sound of flesh hitting flesh, a grunt, a crack, and then Dezi spilled on to the floor next to me. Unconscious.

'Don't you *ever* put your hands on my brother again,' Patrick said. 'Or on Alex.'

Mikey released Alex, shoving her away. He swung at Patrick, but Patrick ducked, the punch sailing over his Stetson. As he rose, Patrick kicked out one of Mikey's legs and hit him with a cross on his way down.

Mikey struck the floor next to Dezi.

The three of us, in a neat little row.

Patrick wasn't winded. He hadn't rushed, hadn't even moved that fast. He'd just ambled in and taken care of business like he always did.

I didn't think I could feel any worse about the guilty pleasure I'd felt from my talk with Alex, but there it was.

Patrick looked over at Alex. 'You okay?'

She rubbed her biceps. 'Yeah. I'm fine.'

He looked at me. 'Good?'

'I am now.'

'Let's go, then,' he said. 'We got work to do.'

He offered me his hand, and I took it and stood up. Wiping my mouth, I followed my brother down the hall.

Eve and Chatterjee were waiting in the classroom, the Rebel helmet out and ready on his desk.

'What took you so long?' Chatterjee asked.

'I overslept,' I said.

Eve glanced at my split lip but didn't say anything. I'm glad she didn't, or I would've probably snapped at her. I felt guilty for betraying Patrick, even though I hadn't really betrayed him. I felt embarrassed for getting my butt kicked by Dezi friggin' Siegler. And I was envious of Patrick for how he'd coasted in and delivered an ass-whuppin' like the High Plains Drifter.

The last one bugged me most of all, because I was never envious of my brother. That's not how we worked. We looked out for each other, and we were happy for each other.

Five minutes on a swing with Alex had turned me into a jerk.

'Well,' Dr Chatterjee said, 'perhaps we should discuss procedures for –'

I grabbed the helmet and shoved it on to my head, partly to move things along, partly to hide my face. Before anything could happen, I said, 'Pressure.'

The blue lights flared to life, that circular icon blinking in the middle of the face mask. Because the helmet wasn't crushing my skull yet, I took a moment to study it. It had notches along the perimeter. A dial that seemed to be floating in the air about two feet from the helmet.

I reached out and twisted the virtual knob.

The insulation tightened around my neck, starting to cut off my circulation.

I twisted the dial the other way, and the pressure lessened.

I said, 'Done,' and the dial vanished.

Progress.

I took a moment to be proud of myself. Okay. Now what? I hadn't thought much past this. I suppose I'd figured that the helmet would give me some direction, but no. Just the blank face mask staring back at me.

'Message,' I said.

Nothing happened.

'Transmission,' I said.

More nothing.

'Phone home.'

Still nothing.

'Customer service.'

Through the face mask, I could see Alex shaking her head, her forehead lowered into her palm.

I chewed my lip, thinking, until the taste of blood reminded me that it was split.

'I am Chance Rain,' I said.

The helmet ignited with blue lights everywhere. And then a series of symbols appeared in a row, turning over like slot-machine reels. Fascinated, I watched them whir until they landed on English letters.

It was a note spelled out for me.

THIS CONDUIT NOW OPEN. A TRANSMISSION HAS BEEN SENT. CHECK BACK DAILY FOR RESPONSE.

The blue lights vanished.

I took off the helmet, looked at the expectant faces surrounding me. And I grinned.

For the first time in a long time, I'd done something right.

**ENTRY 18**   In the dead of night, every night, I checked the helmet, but no message waited for me. By day we did our tasks, took our shifts, and tried to stay safe.

A week passed, and then another.

Our food rations got lower, our meals staler.

We grew sick of waiting, sick of hiding. Patrick and I might have been the key to the survival of the human species, but right now we had nothing to do except wash clothes, clean toilets, and check the perimeter fence.

One night, walking back from a late-night stretch watching the southwest quadrant from the second floor, I spotted Patrick and Alex on the swing set outside. The very same one that Alex and I had sat on. She was wearing his cowboy hat, they were twisted on their swings so they faced each other, and they were making out.

So much for their big fight. So much for Alex saying she could talk to me differently. Who was I kidding anyway? If *I* had to choose between me and Patrick, it would be no contest.

I felt creepy spying on them, and so I pulled back from the window, closed my eyes, and took a moment to get my head right.

These were my two favorite people on the planet. They belonged together. I was happy for them. These feelings were all genuine, and I kept my eyes closed until I felt them in my heart, strong and true.

Then I headed back to the gym.

Eve stirred as I moved toward my bed, poking her head up from the jacket she used as a blanket. 'You drew the graveyard shift, huh?'

Her bangs formed a razor-straight line right above her eyes. Hair was always a problem for the girls these days, but for some reason Eve was able to keep hers looking perfect. It was a rich shade of brown that matched her eyes, though her irises had yellow flecks that lit them up.

I don't know what came over me, but I leaned down and kissed her. At first she stiffened, caught off guard. And then she melted a little, her hand rising to my cheek. It felt good.

As in really good.

We pulled away. She took in a sip of air.

'Good night,' I said.

She smiled just barely, but it was enough to bring out that dimple in her right cheek. 'Night.'

The next morning was back to business as usual. Eve worked the supply station, and when I walked by, we awkwardly said hi and went on with what we were doing. We didn't make eye contact the rest of the day.

That's me, Casanova-Pants.

Later I saw Alex checking the TV set on the bleachers, spinning through endless screens of static. She was leaning over, one foot up on the bottom bench, her forehead scrunched with focus.

I really wanted to not find her attractive.

I really wanted to not like her more than Eve.

I really wanted to choose which emotions to pluck out of my heart and flush down the toilet.

She looked up, caught me gawking and contemplating toilets. 'Whatcha need, Little Rain?'

I mumbled out an excuse and took off.

Like I said, Casanova-Pants.

At dinner there was a confrontation in the cafeteria. Patrick and I heard the ruckus behind the serving counter and ran over.

Ben, Dezi, and Mikey surrounded Dr Chatterjee in a half circle. His back was to the wall, but he didn't look intimidated. He looked angry.

'I absolutely will not,' he was saying.

'We're hungry,' Ben said. 'We can eat more and then just go get more.'

'No,' Dr Chatterjee said. 'We will ration what we have as planned. I've specified a calorie amount for everyone based on his or her weight and that's what we will stick to. There's a schedule we will maintain to minimize risk. When the food stores hit a certain level, we will run a foraging mission. We're not going to throw out our entire plan because you and your compatriots want an extra sandwich, Mr Braaten.'

'What if I don't like that plan?'

'Then you'll shut your mouth and go along with it regardless. We voted on it. And this is a democracy.'

'A democracy with *you* as the leader.'

'Yes, Mr Braaten. That's how democracies function. With leaders.'

'Give us the keys to the pantries,' Dezi said. His face sported a bruise from when Patrick had taken him down.

'I will not,' Chatterjee said. 'And you will not speak to me that way, Mr Siegler.'

'The key,' Dezi said again.

Mikey said, 'We're not asking.' He stepped forward, pressed a finger into Dr Chatterjee's chest, and gave a gentle push. Chatterjee stumbled back on his leg braces and bumped into the wall but kept his balance.

A ripple of excitement and discomfort moved across the tables. The others were on their feet, straining to see what was going on.

It struck me that there was much more at stake in this moment than food rations.

Patrick stepped behind Ben, his boots scuffing the cheap linoleum. Ben turned.

They faced each other. Years of tension simmered between them. You could practically feel the heat in the air.

Ben Braaten was the only person I'd ever seen fight Patrick to a draw. Patrick had called him out in their freshman year after Ben emptied out my backpack in the creek. Twenty minutes of punches and grappling behind Jack Kaner's barn had ended with them bloody and exhausted, their clothes covered with dirt and bits of hay. Too worn out to keep at it, they'd finally limped off in opposite directions.

'Get your guys under control,' Patrick said to Ben. 'Or I will.'

Ben studied him, his expression changing, making his scars shift and realign like living things. The round mark of damaged skin at his hairline looked like a bottle cap, right down to the crimped edges.

The air back here was so thick with the smell of lettuce and ketchup I felt like I was breathing in the food itself.

'This is a democracy, remember?' Ben said. 'I don't have "guys."'

Mikey and Dezi moved away from Chatterjee, who pushed himself back on to his wobbly legs and straightened out his clothes. Ben walked by us, banging Patrick's shoulder, his lackeys following him out.

'I'll keep an eye on them,' Patrick told Dr Chatterjee.

'I'm not scared of them,' Chatterjee said. 'Not one bit.'

Patrick said, 'You should be.'

**ENTRY 19**    I dragged myself out of bed yet again in the dead of night. Dezi was standing guard at the doors. I wondered why he was at the post instead of Ben.

'Where you going?' Dezi asked.

'To take a leak.'

He didn't move.

'I assume you don't want me to hose on your leg,' I said. 'So maybe step aside?'

Reluctantly, he did. But when I went to pass, he put his arm across the doorway, right at my face level.

'One of these days, your mouth's gonna get you into trouble,' he said.

'You mean like you'll sucker-punch me?'

'That wasn't a sucker punch.'

'Try hitting me sometime when I'm actually looking at you,' I said. 'And see what happens.'

'Good idea.' He moved his arm away. 'You're lucky your brother is your brother,' he said.

'Yeah. I am. But for different reasons than you think.'

As I walked the dark halls, I dug the key to Dr Chatterjee's classroom from my pocket. There were only two keys, and he'd trusted me with the second one. I'd earned it, I supposed, by sticking my head into the Vacuum Helmet of Doom.

As I turned the corner into the science wing, I noticed

that something was wrong. Chatterjee's door was open, and a splinter of wood stuck out from the jamb. I heard clanking inside.

Bracing myself, I crept forward.

The classroom looked empty, but I heard movement behind the desk. Ben rose up into view.

He was holding the Rebel helmet.

He noticed me standing there.

'What the hell is this?' he asked.

I rushed forward and snatched the helmet from him. He was too surprised to react. At least not right away.

'I took it off one of them,' I said. 'When I shot the Queen.'

Shadows covered his face. 'Why's it locked in here?'

'Why are *you* in here?'

'I'm looking for the keys to the pantry.'

'Dr Chatterjee said —'

He leered at me, mocking: ' "*Dr Chatterjee said, Dr Chatterjee said.*" God, you are such a wuss. Wake up, Chance. It's a new world. We don't have the luxury of a democracy any more than the cavemen did. Me and my boys — and even you and your brother — we're the ones who keep this place safe. So yeah, I think we should eat more. Keep up our strength. Because when the Hosts come crashing through that door, it ain't gonna be little JoJo and some crippled teacher who holds 'em off. You and I both know that. Sooner or later you gotta admit it to yourself.'

He stepped forward. I let the helmet swing loose at my side. A weapon. He took note and halted his advance.

'Chance, I'm only gonna say this once. Hand over that helmet or I'm gonna shove it up your —'

'Hey, Ben.'

At Patrick's voice we both spun around.

Ben looked at him. 'Your brother was gonna hand over the helmet so I could take a look at it.'

'No,' I said. 'I wasn't.'

Patrick stepped into the classroom. 'I don't think he was, Ben.'

Ben's jaw shifted to one side and then back. But he kept his mouth closed.

'The keys to the pantry are hidden somewhere else,' Patrick said. 'So I can save you some time there.' He looked at me. 'C'mon, let's get going.'

Helmet in hand, I started out.

'Where you going?' Ben asked.

'Away from you,' I said.

Patrick and I stood in the quiet of Mrs Olsen's history class. The walls were bedecked with posters of various wars. Allied forces storming Omaha Beach. The fall of Saigon. Paratroopers jumping into Iraq.

And then there was me with a goofy helmet.

I put it on, fired it up, and adjusted the settings. I'd gotten good at this part – plenty of practice.

This time I felt a jolt of excitement after I announced my name. Instead of the blank screen I'd grown accustomed to, virtual symbols scrolled across my visual field.

My body language must've changed, because Patrick said, 'What? What is it?'

'Hang on. I'm not sure.'

At last the letters rolled into place. MEETING TIME: 24 NOVEMBER AT 2400.

'Okay,' I said. 'Where?'

The slots rotated again. This time instead of letters, two long numbers came up, one on top of the other. Each one had thirteen decimal places.

I thought for a minute.

'Is this latitude and longitude?' I asked.

More whirring and then: YES.

'Show me on a map, please,' I said.

My view changed with dizzying speed. All of a sudden, I was flying through space. The stars didn't get long and streak by *Star Wars* style; they blipped past me so fast they were like strobe lights.

I wobbled on my feet. Patrick's hand grabbed my elbow, steadying me.

I flew through space.

There was the Milky Way.

Now I was in it.

Pluto whipped by in a blur.

Neptune scorched past. Then Uranus.

I rocketed through the rings of Saturn.

Jupiter.

Mars.

And finally the familiar blue-and-green globe.

A breath and I was plummeting toward North America.

About to smack down somewhere in the middle.

My view slowed, slowed, like at the end of a bungee-cord jump.

Our state.

A valley, edged by a familiar mountain range.

Creek's Cause.

Slower, closer, a fifty-square-acre view zooming to twenty and then ten.

A rooftop I knew as well as the back of my hand.

The image froze for an instant, and then the lights went out.

I unscrewed my head from the helmet and sucked in a lungful of fresh air. A wave of vertigo came on, and I almost fell over, but Patrick caught me and set me back on my feet.

I grabbed his shoulders.

'Day after tomorrow at midnight,' I gasped. 'We're going home.'

**ENTRY 20**    The hardest part before we left always was saying good-bye to JoJo. After nightfall most of the kids were gathered in small groups playing cards or chess with pieces carved out of soap like in prison movies.

JoJo was sitting in my lap hugging Bunny, and Rocky leaned into my side.

'I don't get why you always have to leave,' JoJo said. 'And you take Alex and Patrick with you, and they're our next-favorites.'

'Every time we've left, we've brought back information,' I said. 'And information is power.'

'You sound like a teacher,' Rocky said.

I made a face. 'Okay, scratch that. I mean, the more we learn about the Harvesters, the more we'll know about how to beat them.'

'You think you can beat them?'

I thought about being one of two people in the whole world chosen to save humanity and felt a charge of pride. 'Yeah, I think we have a shot.'

On his bed across from me, Patrick slotted shells into the magazine tube of his shotgun, one after another. Alex prepped her fingers like she used to before hockey games, wrapping protective bands of medical tape on her fingers in the spaces between her knuckles. She stripped each piece from the roll and bit it off. Her hockey stick rested against the inside of her thigh. She looked tough as hell.

Every time we left the school, we were stepping into a war zone. I had to ready myself, too, but right now there was an eight-year-old who needed me, and suddenly that felt more important to me than anything else.

'Today's Thanksgiving,' JoJo said. 'I bet you forgot that.'

'I did.'

'Do you *hafta* leave on Thanksgiving?'

'I do.'

She crossed her arms. 'I don't feel like I have so much to be thankful for.'

I almost told her right there about my role, how I was the savior of the planet, destined to carry out a secret mission, but the words sounded ridiculous in my head before I could say them. Like hearing about the wonder that is me would make JoJo feel any better. I didn't make *me* feel any better.

I put my hand on her head. Her hair – still tacky. 'Is that dried Sprite?'

'No,' she lied, indignant.

'I'll try to bring you back some good news, Junebug,' I said.

'Who's gonna look out for me when you're gone?'

'Your big brother,' I said, and Rocky puffed up a bit. 'And Eve.'

Eve glanced up from the same magazine she'd been leafing through for a month and gave a wave. She and I hadn't really spoken since that kiss. I don't know what I'd thought would happen, but it had only made things awkward between us.

124

'And Eve's gonna make sure you shower, too,' I said, loud enough for Eve to hear.

Keeping her face in the magazine, Eve held out a thumbs-up.

Rocky and I laughed. But when I looked back at JoJo, she was crying. I gave her a hug. 'What's wrong?'

She sniffled a few times, wiped snot on her sleeve. 'We're all stories. That's all we are, really. There was a story of a brother and sister whose parents died. And they wound up here in this awful place but found someone to look after them. Right?'

My throat felt dry, so I had to swallow before I could talk. 'Right.'

'So now you're part of our story and we're part of yours. But when you leave . . .' She clutched Bunny tighter. 'I don't get to be part of your story.'

I turned her around so she was facing me. 'You'll always be part of my story, Junebug.'

But her tears kept rolling into her worn stuffed animal.

'I'll tell you what,' I said, taking out my notebook from beneath the thin mattress. 'When I see you again, you'll tell me everything that happened to you guys. And I'll tell you everything that happened to us. And we'll write it down together in here, okay?'

She nodded.

Patrick walked over to the supply station, shotgun over his shoulder, and retrieved my baling hooks. He came back, stood over me, and let them dangle in front of my face.

He started to say something, but I cut him off. 'I know, I know,' I said. 'We got work to do.'

I kissed JoJo's sticky head, slid her out of my lap, and picked up my hooks.

It was a long haul to our house. If we cut through town square instead of circling, we'd knock off at least an hour of slow going through the surrounding streets. But darting out into the open carried obvious risks.

Alex, Patrick, and I huddled behind a parked truck by the hospital, peering across the big lawn. An ambulance had smashed into the central fountain, turning it to rubble. At the edge of the grass, the church rose up, seemingly abandoned. Power cables draped the streets, which had been jackhammered in spots when the lines were cut. A few cars and trucks remained where they'd been the instant the Dusting had moved through town. All the windows of the One Cup Cafe had been shattered. The only movement I could make out was in Bob n' Bit Hardware, which was lit with a guttering orange light from the old-timey blacksmith forge in the back.

'What do you think?' Alex whispered.

'Looks clear,' Patrick said. 'And we haven't seen any Hosts yet.'

It had been eerily quiet on the way here. We'd taken all the usual precautions, but we hadn't spotted a single Host. That had never happened before.

'If we keep going at this pace,' Alex said, 'we won't make the house by midnight. And missing that meeting –'

'Is not an option,' Patrick finished for her. He looked at me. 'What do you think?'

' "Fortune favors the bold," ' I said.

'So that's a yes,' he said, slightly annoyed.

I nodded. 'We've been here watching for . . . what? Ten minutes? And we haven't seen a thing. If we shoot the diagonal across the lawn and cut up the slope into the hills behind the general store, we're home free.'

'Big if,' Alex said.

'All ifs are big these days,' Patrick said.

'Aren't you two extra cocky ever since you were promoted to the Most Important People in the World?'

'You gotta admit,' Patrick said. 'It is an impressive title.'

He held up a fist, and I bumped it with mine.

'You Rains are intolerable sometimes,' Alex said. 'You should remember: Rain only goes one direction –'

*'Down,'* we all whispered together, and stifled our laughter.

'So are we gonna do this or are you guys gonna just sit around and feel important?' Alex said.

I looked at my brother. 'I say we just sit around and feel important.'

Alex smacked me. I pretended it didn't hurt.

'Okay,' I said. 'Seriously? I say we go for it.'

We all looked at one another and came to an unspoken agreement through that telepathy thing that sometimes happened when it was just the three of us.

Patrick crept out from behind the truck, and we followed him in a V formation. We walked across the sidewalk. Stepped on to Main Street for the first time since it all began.

It felt liberating and terrifying at the same time.

We slipped past a long-dead pickup with a broken driver's-side window and stepped on to the lawn.

I'd thought I'd never stand in town square again.

Keeping alert, facing different directions, we walked along, moving past a knocked-over bench. Squirrels darted up trees. I almost tripped over something and looked down. It was a man's loafer.

With a rotting foot still in it.

We kept on, moving right across town square.

Despite the cold I was sweating through my undershirt. Our eyes picked across windows, doorways, vehicles. Now and then I shot a glance at the general store and the woods beyond. The finish line.

We neared the center of the square.

Most of the water had spilled out of the fountain, but what remained was thick with scum. It reeked like death.

We shuffled past it.

We made it two-thirds across the square.

Then on to the sidewalk. The deserted shops and restaurants lined the street before us like a row of teeth. We stared at the general store, which was nestled back into the hillside and the woods beyond.

Patrick halted.

'Patrick,' Alex said. 'What's up?'

'*Shh.*'

I heard it, too. A buzzing sound.

It stopped.

'Maybe the wind?' Alex whispered.

We took another step, and then it came again, a little clearer. We froze.

This time it didn't stop. The breeze shifted, carrying it to us again, and now it didn't sound like one noise.

It sounded like a lot of noises.

A cloud of tiny black dots appeared over the roof of the general store. Billowing.

No – *swarming*.

Flies.

A figure cut through the swarm, shuffling forward into view on the roof. His head came into sight first.

With holes in place of eyes.

And flies spurting through those holes.

They hummed all around him, more than used to fill the air around the Braaten slaughterhouse, more than I'd ever seen in one place at the same time.

As the figure moved forward, his torso came into view. He was backlit by the moon, his silhouette perfectly black but breath misted in front of where his mouth would be.

He took another step and made a rasping sound – his feet scuffing the tar-and-gravel roof.

But it came at us in stereo.

I blinked sweat from my eyes, trying to make out the movement behind him through the teeming air.

Six more eyeless forms resolved in the swarm behind him, trudging forward, seeming to bleed up from the roof itself. Their heads oriented toward us as we stood there in the open.

I swept a gaze up the slope of the hill behind the general store.

The entire rise was in motion, like a landslide.

A horde of Hosts pouring through the trees beneath a river of flies, heading on to the roof.

Heading toward us.

**ENTRY 21**    There were no Drones or Hatchlings among them, searching for us. That was good. And though the Hosts were coming for us, it seemed they were falling apart, their decomposing flesh drawing flies. Their eye membranes had rotted out, which meant they likely couldn't transmit. But still, we couldn't let them get close just in case one of them scanned our image and sent it back to the Harvesters.

Alex, Patrick, and I were still there, rooted to the ground, stunned by the sight before us. The Hosts kept on, their flesh moldering away, their limbs held together by the rags of their clothes. The hand of the man in front was little more than a spade of bone, his forearm dangling from ligaments, twisting in the breeze. But some of the others still looked sturdy, firm-muscled Hosts running on to the roof. The humming pepper cloud of flies swayed in the air, heaving back and forth like a single living thing.

The man in front tumbled over the roof and fell to the sidewalk. His legs splintered wetly, his torso smacking concrete. His head rotated up, his arms clawing him forward.

Until a hefty second Host smashed down on top of him.

They poured over the brink like lemmings, slopping on to the ground. For a moment it seemed they'd all disintegrate by their own doing. But something awful was happening. That muck of body parts was building itself up.

Like a ramp.

At last Alex and Patrick unfroze themselves.

They turned to run, but I yelled at them. 'Wait! We'll never make it! The Chasers'll get us.'

The Chasers – the women – looked fast and fierce.

Patrick and Alex stared at me like I was crazy. The flies swirled around me now, pelting the nape of my neck. It was impossible to separate the flies from the panic I felt churning the air around us and inside me.

The Chasers would catch up to us. And it would be awful.

'There's no cover in the square!' I shouted.

One of the Hosts leapt off the roof, hit the ramp half-way down, and tumbled. Even from this distance, I could hear the snap of breaking bones. Part of me wanted to fall to the ground, cover my eyes, and give up. But another part of me rose up, stitching together the final threads of an idea that might just save us.

'What do you propose?' Patrick asked.

Ahead, two Chasers ran smoothly right off the edge of the roof on to the mound of bodies. They kept their feet down the ramp.

There was no time to explain.

'Follow me!' I screamed. 'I have a plan!'

I sprinted into the current of flies, right for the oncoming Hosts. I prayed that Patrick and Alex would trust me. I could hardly see through all the flies.

The first Chaser neared, and a blast took off her head from the nose up.

Patrick, running beside me, shucked the shotgun.

As if I'd needed to worry.

I squinted into the onslaught of flies, saw Alex sprint up on my other side. A Chaser came at her, and I impaled her temple with the tip of my baling hook, then wrenched the metal free.

Alex caught the next one beneath the chin with her hockey stick, the head flopping back and nearly off. Through the hatched-open neck, I caught a glint of dull white building blocks – the vertebrae topping the spinal cord.

I thought Alex was yelling in horror and revulsion but realized it was me.

Flies beat at my eyes, my lips.

Ten more Hosts swept down the ramp. Too many.

'Chance,' Alex said, shielding her mouth with an arm. 'Might be a good time to tell us *what the hell you're thinking*!'

I swallowed a mouthful of panic bile, cut left hard, and bolted for Bob n' Bit Hardware. Behind me the shotgun roared and roared, Patrick cutting a wake.

I shoulder-smashed through the front door, spilling into the dark aisles. Alex flew through next, knocking into me. We dominoed over into Shower and Sink Fixtures, knocking items from the shelves. Patrick turned in the doorway, facing outside – shuck-shuck *boom*, shuck-shuck *boom*.

'I can't hold 'em off!' he shouted.

'Let them in!' I yelled, scrambling to my feet.

The forge in the back workshop threw off a dangerous orange glow, casting licks of light around the walls and on to the waist-high mounds of bullets. Over by the anvil, a few rifles lay twisted and useless. Beside them a crate held shackles that the gunmetal had been turned into. A few old-fashioned weather vanes leaned against the wall, linked by a glistening spiderweb.

Bob Bitley was still kneeling on the floor where I'd left him, his head bowed, a pair of tongs protruding from his eyeholes. Fluid puddled the floor beneath his knees. His skin oozed around him, his face sitting off-kilter like a too-big mask. Flies circled his head, a buzzing cloud. They'd gotten in through the rolled-open rear door.

I gave him a wide berth, scrambling over the heaps of rounds that glittered and jingled like treasure. As I bee-lined for the forge, a series of loud crashes shook the store. I shot a glance back. Patrick had tilted over a tall display of gardening tools, trying to block the Hosts. They climbed over the wreckage, blank-faced and eyeless, their hands straining in the air.

I positioned myself behind the forge and kicked it as hard as I could. It didn't yield a bit. It was fastened to the floor. I kicked again, jabbing my heel into the metal side, releasing a fairy dust of sparks. It gave slightly.

Alex finally got what I was doing and sprinted over to help. Her knee brushed Bob Bitley, and he crumbled, keeling over and collapsing, the tongs ringing against the concrete.

We synchronized our blows so we hit the forge at the same time. It tilted up a bit this time, the giant bolts rattling in their holes.

The Hosts kept pouring into the hardware store, driving Patrick back to the doorway of the workshop. The Winchester spoke and then spoke again.

'Guys!' Patrick shouted over his shoulder. 'We're running out of room here!'

Alex's cheeks were flushed, her eyes lit with the flame. 'On three,' she said. 'One, two, *three*.'

We hammered our heels into the forge as hard as we could. It groaned upward. When the bolts snapped, they sounded like gunshots. The whole thing toppled, spilling the glowing contents across the mounds of ammunition.

'Run!' I screamed at Patrick.

He fired one last time. As he stepped back into the workshop, Hosts poured across the threshold after him.

We sprinted out the rear door into the back alley. Alex was already outside, rolling it shut. As Patrick flew through, the edge of the door clipped his shoulder and sent him tumbling. A Host arm shot through the gap. Smashing shut, the door took it clean off. Bodies thudded against the other side, fingernails scraping.

As Alex leaned her weight into the handle to keep the door closed, Patrick jammed a shovel beneath the gap, kicking it until it was wedged into place.

The door shuddered, more and more Hosts packing into the workshop. The wood splintered. A leg smashed through, exposed bone and muscle dripping crimson. A hand burst out next, knocking Alex's hair so it fluffed up beside her head. She reeled back. The whole panel started to give way.

I pictured the orange spill of the forge melting into those bullets and wheeled around.

The general store loomed next to us at the alley's end, its back tucked into the hillside. We couldn't see up on the roof, but the moonlight threw stretched-out shadows down on to the alley. Judging from those shadows, the Hosts had thinned out. There were only a few dark silhouettes now, the last stragglers spilling from the woods on to the tar-and-gravel roof above.

We wouldn't have time to wait for them to clear out.

We took off down the alley toward the general store just as the explosions started.

At first there were a few bangs, followed by moist smacks. They intensified, popcorn getting up a head of steam on the stovetop. Patrick and Alex followed me through the rear exit of the general store. As we hurdled the back counter and barreled up the aisles, the explosions quickened. A few rounds penetrated the wall, zinging overhead.

We careened outside as the detonations reached a drumroll pitch, the ammo snowballing until it sounded like one continuous roar. Most of the Hosts had followed our trail into the Bob n' Bit, but those that remained outside lunged for us.

We didn't slow down. We couldn't. My baling hooks were a blur before my face. Alex's hockey stick whirred by. We cleared a path to the ramp of squirming bodies.

Then we waded up it.

Our legs sank in to the ankles. We had to fight our way through the last of the Hosts even as we bulled our way up the putrefying flesh. Flies typhooned around us.

Patrick's shotgun choke was set wide, so we let him lead. He cleared two Hosts with a spray of pellets. I felt a cheek cave beneath my boot, a guppying mouth locking around my heel.

As we charged up the last hard-fought yards of squirming ramp, fireworks erupted behind us, sending shrapnel flying. At last we pulled free of the wriggling slope on to the solid roof.

There were only a few Hosts left when the explosions behind us surged into a massive ka-*boom* that knocked us off our feet. I flew sprawling over one shoulder, my cheek scraping gravel. As I fell, I caught a crazy sideways glimpse of the general store's walls and roof flying apart.

A wave of heat ripped across us, the flies dropping dead, hammering the roof all around us like hail. My ears rang. I rolled over to face the threat, but the Hosts who'd stood between us and the woods had collapsed into heaps. The explosion had disintegrated their failing bodies.

Patrick stood over me, his black cowboy hat blotting out the moon. He offered me a hand. We grasped around the wrists, and he yanked me to my feet. I staggered a little, and Alex caught me.

'Nice shortcut, boys,' she said.

Together we limped off the roof and up the slope, at last losing ourselves among the trees.

**ENTRY 22**     Our old house looked haunted.

Not haunted-house haunted, but haunted like when you see a news story about a car accident and there's an empty shoe sitting on the stained asphalt. Haunted like the kill floor of the Braaten slaughterhouse after hours. Haunted like my mom's purse filled with colored glass, nestled there in the bottom of a cardboard box from the Stark Peak PD.

Patrick and I stood shoulder to shoulder before the porch of Uncle Jim and Aunt Sue-Anne's ranch house, staring up. Ever since that muni bus had turned Mom and Dad's Chrysler into a crumpled tin can, this had been our home.

They'd died here in front of this house, Jim and Sue-Anne, at my hand and Patrick's. There was no sign of blood in the dirt, not anymore. We'd brought their bodies upstairs, and nature had cleaned up the rest.

Alex lingered behind, giving us space. The moon had lost itself behind invisible clouds, the sky as thick as ink. We were an hour and fifteen minutes early for our meet with the Rebel. Which, given the dreary mood settling over me and my brother, felt like an hour and fifteen minutes too long.

Patrick said, 'Why don't we rinse off our boots.'

Not a question.

The hose coiled next to the porch still worked. We sprayed off the gunk. After our adventures at the general store, there was plenty.

We finished, walked up to the screen door, and paused.

'Okay,' I said.

'Okay,' Patrick said, and palmed the screen open.

A layer of dust had blown through the mesh, powdering the entryway. We walked in, our wet boots leaving perfect prints. I rested my hand on the newel post and looked up the stairs.

'Should we?' I asked.

'Prob'ly.' Patrick turned to Alex. 'We're gonna pay our respects.'

'I'll wait down here,' she said. 'Take whatever time you need.'

We made our way upstairs and then down the hall. The last time we'd been inside was the night we'd found Hank McCafferty on top of the water tower, spores drifting out of his split-open body and riding a wind current into town. We'd rescued Rocky and JoJo that night. We'd killed Jim and Sue-Anne, too, after they'd transformed. And found Alex locked in a vintage steamer trunk.

It had been a long night.

We paused outside Jim and Sue-Anne's door. We could smell them from out here, but it wasn't as bad as it might have been. If it were summer, it would've been a whole other story.

Patrick turned the knob.

Two lumps beneath the covers where we'd left them, side by side. Uncle Jim's hat tilted on top of the pillowcase draped over his head. They looked peaceful.

We stood at the footboard.

Patrick took his Stetson off, held it against his chest. An oddly contrived gesture, especially for him, but we were flying blind here. He cleared his throat. 'Glad you guys have each other,' he told them.

'They're starting to stink,' I said.

'Respect, Chance.'

'Seriously, Patrick. This isn't respect. This is stupid.' Our run-in with the horde of Hosts at the general store had left me raw and callous. Angry even, in ways I didn't understand. 'We're talking to rotting corpses.' I gestured at what remained of our aunt and uncle. 'How would *you* like to be like this?'

'Probably not much,' he said. 'For a variety of reasons.'

'We should do something. Like bury them.'

'We have more pressing concerns right now. Plus, it's not like they know the difference.'

'Fine.' I looked back over at their covered bodies. It was clear to me that those decomposing forms on the bed had nothing to do with my aunt and uncle anymore. Like all those Host bodies ambling around, they'd had the essential parts of who they used to be plucked out of them. I had to say something, though, because Patrick was looking at me expectantly, and I was the one who usually found words for stuff like this. I cleared my throat. 'Sorry, Uncle Jim. Sorry, Aunt Sue-Anne. I wish we could've done better for you.'

Patrick gave a nod at that. 'Anything else?'

'Let's get out of here.'

We closed the door behind us.

Downstairs, Alex had prepared a meal at our old kitchen

table. She'd even set out silverware on Sue-Anne's lace tablecloth and lit a few candles. She must've found a can of pumpkin-pie filling and two cans of green beans in the pantry, because there they were, open and placed before Sue-Anne's hideous holiday china.

'Check me out, getting all domestic,' Alex said. 'Now, sit.'

We did.

The smell of human bodies lingered in the air. The green beans were slimy and cold, and even a few twists of Sue-Anne's big wooden salt mill couldn't help. The pumpkin-pie filling was gloopy. The flickering candlelight reminded me of those times during power outages after tornadoes blew through, turning the power lines into spaghetti. It was the saddest Thanksgiving dinner ever.

But also sort of wonderful.

'Okay.' Alex wiped her mouth with a fancy cloth napkin and tossed it on to her empty plate. 'We all need to say what we're thankful for.'

'You go first,' I said.

'Fine. If I had to say what I'm grateful for . . .' Her eyes lowered to her plate, an uncharacteristically shy gesture. 'It's you two. My boys.' She looked at us. *'What?'*

Patrick's lips pursed in that not-quite-a-smile thing he did when he was amused. 'We didn't say anything.'

She threw her napkin at him. 'I'm serious. It's always been us, and it'll always *be* us. And that's what I'm grateful for on this screwed-up Thanksgiving.' She adjusted her silverware, though it needed no adjusting. 'You next.'

'My little brother,' Patrick said. 'And . . .' He pretended to think awhile until Alex glared at him. Then he half grinned and said, 'And the love of my life.'

Alex had her jigsaw pendant out, and she was rubbing it with her thumb. She realized and dropped it back beneath her collar. They both looked at me.

'Same thing,' I said. 'It's you two bozos. Duh.'

'And *Eve*,' Alex said, ribbing me, but I could tell her heart wasn't in it.

I kicked her shin gently under the table, and she said, 'You'd better eat more, Little Rain, if that's the strongest kick you can manage.'

We laughed, but then all at once Patrick stood up so fast his chair toppled over.

Standing past the threshold of the kitchen a few steps into the living room, a form stood in darkness.

**ENTRY 23**     We stared across the kitchen table at the shadowy figure in the living room.

Charcoal space suit, tinted face mask.

Patrick grabbed for his shotgun, but I said, 'No, it's okay. It's him.'

Alex twirled her hockey stick. 'Looks just like a Drone.'

'That's what I told you guys.'

'Patrick Rain. Chance Rain. And . . . Girl.' Amplitude bars wobbled on the face mask with each word as it translated, a blue glow that widened and closed like a mouth.

'Really?' Alex said. 'That's all I get? *Unnamed Girl?*'

I moved toward him. 'It's us.'

Patrick and Alex came reluctantly, keeping their weapons. I brought my baling hooks, too, because – why not?

We stood in a loose ring on the carpet.

It was all so surreal. Standing in our living room, talking to a Rebel from another planet, a planet that had been overtaken by the Harvesters just like they were trying to overtake Earth now. The few surviving Rebels had tried to fight back, had come here to warn us before the Harvesters wiped out another people and notched another planet in their win column.

I cleared my throat uncomfortably. I didn't exactly have a lot of experience dealing with saviors from other worlds, but I imagined there was some kind of etiquette for it. 'Would you like to . . . um, sit down?'

'Why?' The digitized masculine voice sounded not so much robotic as perfect, all the flaws and irregularities smoothed out.

'I don't know,' I said. 'To relax.'

'Why would I want to relax?'

'It's just what people do here,' I said. 'When we talk.'

The Rebel sat abruptly on the carpet. Alex stifled a laugh.

'I meant on the couch or an armchair or whatever,' I said.

He repositioned himself, and then we all sat around the low glass table like we were having tea. Moonlight seeped through the closed metal slats of the venetian blinds in the big front window, laying patterns across the carpet and our faces.

I could sense Patrick and Alex studying him. They hadn't seen a Rebel up close like I had. His suit was airtight and seamless like those of the Drones, but in contrast to their sleek, polished armor his was chipped and scuffed up. The color was different, too, a matte charcoal compared to the shiny black of the Drones'.

Patrick leaned forward, elbows on knees, folding his hands. 'This mission I keep hearing about. You came here looking for us.'

'Yes,' the Rebel said.

'Why did you know who we were already?' I asked.

'Because,' he said, 'we put you here.'

I tried to swallow. 'Uh, *what*?'

Patrick pulled back, his spine straightening one vertebra at a time. Alex's mouth was hanging open.

The amplitude waves flared back to life. 'We managed to smuggle a group of genetically modified human ova into the fertility banks here.'

A blue light shot out from his chest plate, projecting a hologram above the glass table between us. We watched, captivated.

It showed a guy in an old-fashioned-looking biohazard suit, like something from one of those atomic-bomb documentaries. We couldn't see his face behind the tinted eye shield. He lumbered down a cold tile corridor in a building that had been shut down for the night. In his puffy glove, he held a medical canister made of surgical steel. He pressed a code into a keypad, and two doors to a freezer unit opened with a hiss. He disappeared into the wisps of cool air.

Just as quickly as it had materialized, the moving image vanished.

'It was a dangerous endeavor with very low odds of success,' the Rebel said. 'We tried this at myriad fertility banks around the planet. Only two ova made it through the entire birthing process and took.'

I was breathless. 'Only two,' I repeated. 'Me and my brother.' My throat was so dry that the words barely came out.

'Yes. Both at the Stark Peak Fertility Bank. It seems conditions were more favorable there.'

'So you've been following us ever since?'

'We were only able to track you through your birth. The risks were too great to continue monitoring you from there. But we are pleased you are both healthy and viable.'

My spinning mind caught on an image of Patrick breathing in the spore-infected air. His genetic immunity hadn't been luck or chance. It had been carefully engi-neered. *We* had been carefully engineered. There was too much to process. Part of us had been *designed*?

'Wait a sec. We're one of you? From *there*?' I jabbed a finger at the roof.

'We do not have much time,' the Rebel began.

'No,' Patrick said. 'Wait a minute. We just found out we're friggin' *aliens*, so we get a question or two, okay?'

The blue light glowed in the mask: 'You are not one of us. But you are not entirely human either.'

I had no idea what to do with that information. Not right now. There was too much to consider. So many ramifications.

'This means you knew *years* ago,' I said. 'You knew that there would be an invasion *before we were born* —'

'Yes. And the Harvesters already suspect where you were born. That is why the first asteroid hit near your town.' The soothing voice seemed so at odds with the information being conveyed.

'So we should go on the run,' Patrick said. 'Get as far away from here as we can.'

'No. Being out in the open is more dangerous. It is imperative that you remain hidden.'

'We need to hide so the Harvesters can't capture us?' I asked.

'Now that the Hatchlings have successfully been birthed, they no longer need to,' the Rebel said.

'Why's that?' Alex asked.

The Rebel said, 'Because if the Hatchlings find you, they will devour you. As they will all other humans they come into contact with.'

I tried to swallow, but my throat was like sandpaper.

'The Hatchlings,' Alex said. 'They'll take over from the Drones?'

'Yes. Since the Hatchlings are adapted to live here, the Drones and Queens will eventually leave this planet in their hands. And they'll go search out new galaxies to Harvest. They are not well equipped for this world.'

Alex held up a hand. 'Because they're made of gas, right? The Harvester Drones and Queens? Like you?'

The Rebel's head dipped in something resembling a nod. He pressed his palm to his chest, and his charcoal armor ignited with a network of thin blue tendrils, like the circuitry of a computer chip. The glowing filaments flickered in and out, and then suddenly the suit turned clear and we could see what was inside.

I felt the blood rush to my face. Alex gasped.

Clouds of gas swirled inside the airtight suit, floating around organs. But the organs were as translucent as the mist, and I could see through them like holograms. My anatomy knowledge wasn't great, but I could make out a heart and a lung. What looked like two livers. A spinning brain that drifted down a leg and bounced back up, levitating through the stomach, the chest.

'Our bodies evolved under a different atmospheric and gravitational system,' the Rebel said.

'You evolved to live in metallic hydrogen,' I said.

'Not precisely metallic hydrogen, but similar.'

'Like on Jupiter or Saturn.'

'Jupiter, yes,' he told me. 'Saturn, no.'

'Oh,' I said.

I was learning things people hadn't known since the beginning of time. Scratch that. Since *ever*.

'Chance,' Patrick said. 'Let's just –'

'So the Harvesters,' I said, 'their whole invasion, it's all designed for them to birth a generation suited to Earth's environment?'

'Yes. The first phase of a Harvesting comes in the form of plants seeded by asteroids.'

'The Dusting,' Alex said.

'Yes, the . . .' The mask darkened, and I realized that he – or the mask's translation feature – was searching for a word.

'Spores?' I said.

'Pollen. The pollen enters certain members of the indigenous population.'

'Like McCafferty,' Patrick said.

The Rebel continued, 'It penetrates their very cells, scours the twisting ladders of DNA to pluck out specific letters it requires. Then it mutates and releases a different version of the pollen with keys fitted precisely for stretches of the host species' genetic code.'

'And that's the second phase,' Alex said. 'The one that turned all the grown-ups into Hosts. Chasers and Mappers.'

'It makes use of the adults of the indigenous population to pave the way for the Harvesters' occupation.'

'By stealing kids and turning them into egg sacs,' Alex said.

'By turning the young into Husks, yes. During the pupal stage, Harvester offspring absorb bits and pieces of the indigenous DNA from their Husks, stealing traits more suitable to the new environment and integrating them into their genetic makeup.'

'The Harvesters . . .' Alex coughed into her fist. 'They've done this before?'

The tinted face mask swiveled to address her. 'Yes.'

'How many?' she whispered. 'How many worlds?'

The Rebel's chest plate created a new hologram. I recognized our solar system immediately because of Saturn and Jupiter. Except Jupiter was blinking red, and so was Earth. Then the solar system dwindled to a point, one blinking red dot in the swirling Milky Way. And shot through the galaxy were rivers of blinking red stars, veins of infection.

The hologram zoomed out again. Now the Milky Way itself was a single red dot in an ocean of other galaxies. A *universe* of blinking red dots.

The hologram vanished.

No one said anything for a minute.

Then I rallied.

'And that's where we come in, right?' I said, pride swelling in my chest. 'Me and Patrick. It's why you gave us immunity. For our super-important mission. Because we're the saviors of the planet.'

Now the blank screen rotated to me. For a moment it was as black as midnight. If it had a face, it might've looked puzzled. Then the amplitude waves spoke again.

'We did not put you here as saviors,' the Rebel said. 'We put you here to sacrifice.'

**ENTRY 24**     I sat there stinging in the aftermath of what we'd just been told. My head throbbed; my ears rang. It felt like I was waking up from being coldcocked.

Patrick was on his feet, the Winchester dangling at his side. The moonglow through the closed blinds scrolled across the contours of his body. 'Come again?'

'Every organism has a purpose,' the Rebel said. 'There are workers, fertilizers, spreaders, soldiers. Your and your brother's purpose is to die.'

'Like now?'

'Not yet. But soon.'

I reached out a wobbly hand like I was trying to shape the air, but I was really trying to shape my own thoughts. 'Explain . . . can you explain what the hell you're talking about please? Like *now*?'

The Rebel sat perfectly still. If it weren't for the amplitude waves on his mask, he might've been a statue. 'We injected a viral vector into selected human ova stored in fertility banks for women who were infertile.'

'Like Mom,' I said, my voice hoarse.

'What's a viral vector?' Alex asked.

'Our scientists take a virus designed through natural selection to penetrate human cells –'

'Like smallpox,' I said.

'Not *like* smallpox,' the Rebel said. 'Smallpox.'

'You injected us – the eggs that made us . . . whatever – with friggin' *smallpox*?' I said.

'Yes.'

He tapped his chest, and another hologram floated into existence. This one showed a bunch of oval cells with what looked like dumbbells inside them. A high-magnification image of smallpox? In the hologram a needle pierced one of the cells and withdrew the interior matter. Through the pounding in my head, I wondered how anyone could operate a needle that small.

'First we excised the DNA sequences that made it virulent,' the Rebel said. 'We rendered the smallpox inert.'

'So why use it?' I asked.

'Because it's a suitably spacious virus.'

'Spacious? Who cares if it's spacious?'

'Chance,' Alex said gently. 'Let him talk.'

She reached out, took Patrick's hand, and tugged him down to sit next to her again on the couch. She put a hand on his knee.

My own knee was bouncing up and down. I was jittery with nerves and fear. I put my palms on my thighs, tried to still them.

'Because what remains after we remove the virulent sequences is a biological vehicle with lots of . . . cargo room,' the Rebel said. 'This allows us to fill this storage space with new genetic material.'

A new needle appeared now in the hologram, filling the punctured cell with fresh matter.

The Rebel said, 'The virus acts as before, but rather than infecting the organism –'

'Us,' Patrick said. 'We're the *organisms*.'

The Rebel continued unwaveringly, dispassionate and clear, 'Rather than infecting you, it transports this new genetic material into your cells. More precisely, it transports it to the target DNA sequence on the chosen chromosome, where it inserts itself.'

Now we watched a blue-light rendering of the viral vector channeling through the cells of an organism, burrowing into the DNA ladders, and then injecting its new genetic contents.

'A Trojan horse,' I said.

'I do not understand.'

'Never mind,' I said. 'So what is this new genetic material you put inside me and Patrick?' My tone was bitter, laced with anger.

'Immunity to the pollen, as you suggested earlier. That is what protects you from transformation on your eighteenth year.'

'And?' Patrick said through clenched teeth. He went to stand again, but Alex kept her hand firm on his thigh, holding him down.

'And a dispersal mechanism buried inside your cells. Designed to weaponize you.'

'Weaponize . . .' I couldn't finish the thought.

The hologram vanished. The Rebel was silent for a moment. Maybe this was his version of struggling for an explanation. 'We discussed the pollen of the Harvesters. How it affected select members of your adult population?'

'Yes.'

'Your genetically modified DNA contains a stretch of coding designed to do the same to Hatchlings.'

'The dispersal mechanism,' I said. 'We blow up like McCafferty and release a spray that kills the Hatchlings?'

'That is a crude manner of understanding it, but yes.'

'I'd love to hear the *un*-crude manner,' Alex muttered.

'So that's what I am?' I said, my voice shaking. 'A weapon of mass destruction?'

'Patrick is the weapon,' the Rebel said calmly. 'You are merely the fail-safe.'

I sat there, shaking. 'I'm not even the damn weapon?'

'You are the backup weapon. We need you to activate as well in case the primary dispersal mechanism fails.'

A horrifying image scratched its way into my brain: McCafferty's swollen body, blown open atop the water tower. That was gonna happen to Patrick. That was gonna happen to me. What would it feel like? Would part of me know?

I shoved away the fear, grabbed for my anger. It felt safer.

'Well, that's terrific.' I stood up, banged my hands against my sides. 'Not only is my immunity *useless*, since I'm designed to die, but I don't even get to sacrifice myself in some dramatic, meaningful way, since I'm just Mr Secondary. So much for our awesome secret mission. So much for us being humanity's salvation. The most important people on the planet. Our one job: Stay alive at any cost. For what? So we can *die*?'

'Chance,' Alex said. 'You gotta keep your voice down.'

I leaned forward and jabbed a finger in the Rebel's mask. 'This *sucks*.'

I sat. Caught my breath. Temper tantrum over.

The Rebel remained motionless.

After a minute or two, Patrick got up and sat next to me on the couch. He put his arm around my shoulders, gave a squeeze, and then let go. He looked at the Rebel.

'Okay,' he said. 'So if I do it – detonate or whatever – successfully, then Chance can live, right?'

'That risk cannot be taken. The slightest error in your dispersal mechanism will lead to failure. The odds of activation success of the primary mechanism solely are 57.4563 percent. The odds of success for both primary and secondary mechanisms are 89.5332 per cent. Every life on your planet is at stake –'

'I don't care about everyone on my planet,' Patrick said. 'I care about my brother.'

'Patrick,' I said. 'If you go, I go. That's how it's gonna be.'

He was staring at me, his face as stubborn as ever.

The Rebel said, 'A secondary benefit of your . . . spray, as you put it, is that it will additionally wipe the Harvester pollen from the air.'

Slowly, I shifted my gaze back to the Rebel. 'You mean it gets rid of the spores that transform us?'

'It disintegrates them on contact. We engineered it to do so, of course. There would be no point in preserving your planet if we could not save the remaining host organisms *on* the planet.'

I looked past Patrick to Alex. Her face was red like she was going to cry, but she didn't cry. Not Alex.

Patrick turned his head and looked at her, too.

She pressed a hand over her mouth. She knew she was the reason.

We wouldn't die to save all of humanity.

But we'd die to save her.

'Okay,' I said. 'So let's go do this, then.'

The Rebel said, 'It is not that simple.' Same infuriatingly rational tone.

I almost laughed. 'Of course it's not.'

'We understand how the Harvesters affect the host species,' he said. 'But the Hatchlings are different on every planet.'

'Because they have to steal DNA from the host organisms that suit each environment,' I said, in my best let's-move-this-along voice.

After all the crap that just got dropped on us, I figured I was allowed some attitude.

'That is correct. Decades ago we were able to prepare you and your brother as dispersal mechanisms.'

Patrick said, 'Call me a mechanism one more time and I'll punch you in your floaty brain.'

The Rebel looked at him. Then continued, 'When given the destructive pollen, your bodies are designed to replicate it on a massive scale and release it, spreading it to the Hatchlings. It will replicate inside the Hatchlings using their DNA code and trigger them to pass it from Hatchling to Hatchling, cleaning the air in the process. It is engineered to spread at a massively accelerated rate.'

'What about the Drones and Queens?' I asked.

'They've been accounted for as well,' the Rebel said. 'The dispersal will make your planet uninhabitable by Harvesters for approximately twenty-four thousand years.'

'Sounds good to me,' Patrick said.

'But because we did not then know what genetic form the Hatchlings would take on your planet, we could not engineer the destructive serum.'

'So we're dispersal mechanisms with nothing to disperse,' I said.

'You are primed. But not yet armed. It was not possible until the Hatchlings were born. Until we could capture one. We had to examine their unique physiology before we could design a serum precisely fitted to their DNA. Precisely engineered to destroy them.'

'Have you done that?'

'At great cost.'

'What does that mean?' Alex asked.

'The Harvesters raided our last remaining outpost in an attempt to locate the destructive serum we were engineering. They killed us.'

'Except you?'

'And one other. He escaped with the serum. I have received broken transmissions from him, and I believe him to be coherent. I will meet with him. When I do, I will send you another set of coordinates for a meeting. We will bring the serum and inject you.'

'And then it just . . . works?'

'You are exquisitely designed. Once the serum goes into your bodies, your bodies will know what to do with it.'

'What do we do until then?'

'Check the helmet. Every day. And stay out of sight. We cannot risk your being devoured by a Hatchling.'

The last word was barely out of the Rebel's mouth when the big front window exploded, the venetian blinds billowing inward. Shards flew at us, scattering across the couch, the armchairs, the carpet. The metal blinds ripped free of their mounting, wrapping around the bulging form on the carpet behind the couch.

It rose. Shook free of the blinds.

The stench hit us.

The hardened fingertips of either hand clicked against one another like jaws.

Nostril holes quivered.

The Hatchling drew himself up to his full height.

**ENTRY 25**    The Rebel stood between us and the Hatchling. He raised an armor-sheathed arm, pointing. 'Flee.'

The Hatchling swatted him aside like he weighed nothing. The Rebel flew sideways across the room and hit an empty armchair. It toppled over, flinging him into the bookcase. Hardcovers rained down over him.

I shot a quick glance at Alex and saw that she was as scared as I was. If a Hatchling could overpower a Rebel that quickly, what the hell were *we* supposed to do?

The Hatchling dipped low on his haunches and then leapt right over the couch, arms spread, claws glistening. Patrick fired the shotgun right through his chest.

The mucusy skin absorbed the pellets, but still the blast was enough to halt his momentum. He twisted in midair and crashed through the glass table.

I swung the baling hook at his head. He turned, mouth open, and the tip sailed through his spread lips and embedded inside his cheek. The hook slowed down as if it had hit mud, my arm continuing the swing in slow motion. My biceps strained. The metal burrowed through the moist orange flesh even as the wound healed up along its wake. At last the baling hook popped out the other side. The cheek sutured itself closed as the Hatchling pulled himself from the glass table.

'Crap,' I said.

The Hatchling rose, his camouflage skin flickering, different patches changing to match the carpet, the couch, the wall behind him. Glass stuck out of him everywhere – a dagger in his side, a triangle in his cheek beside his nostril holes, a series of shards rising like quills from his thigh.

And then his skin healed, pushing out the glass. The shards fell to the floor, clinking against the wreckage.

Hopelessness descended on me, a blanket of despair.

He jumped at me, and I closed my eyes, remembering the burn I'd felt when the Hatchling had grabbed my forearm in the woods near the cannery. What would it feel like to have the thing land on top of my entire body?

I felt it clamp down on the nape of my neck, and I yelled. When I opened my eyes, I was flying backward.

Patrick had seized me and hurled me out of the way. In his other arm, the shotgun swung up. He shoved the muzzle into the Hatchling's neck and fired.

Most of the neck flew away, spattering the back wall. The head hinged to one side. I prayed it would topple off.

But no. It stopped.

Then, slowly, tendrils of skin constricted and pulled the head into place again, seating it again on the stump of the neck. As the flesh knit itself together, Patrick backed up, bumping into me.

'We can't kill it,' he said. 'Let's go.'

We bolted for the kitchen. Alex was in the lead.

Behind us the Hatchling heaved himself forward. The Rebel, on his feet once more, tackled him. The acid flesh seemed to have no effect on the armor. But the Hatchling overpowered him quickly, backhanding him. The Rebel spun around and fell into the heap of glass. I prayed his suit wouldn't crack.

Alex hip-checked the kitchen counter on her way to the side door that let out on to the cattle enclosure. Patrick slid over the counter, and I followed him. At the kitchen door, we piled into one another like dominoes.

We heard a series of thumps as the Hatchling bounded across the living room toward the kitchen. He leapt so high he struck the ceiling. Chunks of drywall crumbled down behind him. His claws pounded the floor when he landed.

Alex yanked the knob, but the dead bolt was thrown. She reached for it, but there wouldn't be time.

I turned. At first I couldn't see the Hatchling, but I smelled that he was close, felt the air from his movement brushing against my face. I sensed a ripple of motion fly up off the counter and realized that he was up there above us, camouflaged against the ceiling. He ghosted overhead, hurtling toward us. His hunched shoulders smashed the light fixtures, the contact making his flesh resume its natural orange hue. Sparks cascaded down. He led his descent with his claws, a bird of prey swooping in for the kill.

Patrick grabbed Alex around the waist at the last second and yanked her away from the door, hurling her across the floor tile like a bowling ball. Then he shoved me away, diving on top of me. We skidded painfully into the refrigerator.

The Hatchling hit the side door like a wrecking ball, blowing it out of the wall, frame and all.

Sliding beneath the table, Alex racked up two chairs,

her hockey stick spinning off toward the living room. The plates and silverware jumped. The big wooden salt mill fell over and rolled off the edge of the table. One of the candles toppled, igniting the lace tablecloth.

Patrick and I stood up, our backs to the hard metal of the fridge. The overhead lights fizzled. The Hatchling turned, framed by the jagged mouth he'd knocked into the side of the kitchen wall.

We had nowhere to go.

He dipped down and hopped once, landing right before us. The claws of his feet tapped the tile. He leaned toward us slowly. His stink wafted into our faces. A foot away. Now two inches.

I clutched for Patrick's hand, found it.

A salamander-orange lip wrinkled back from a set of fangs. Pearly-white incisors gleamed. The smaller teeth were just as sharp.

This was it.

Then there was a clunk.

The Hatchling stiffened.

Then he shrieked.

He twisted on to his heels. His face lit with agony. The screams continued, loud enough to hurt my ears. He was clutching at his back, his spine twisting. He dropped on to his knees, and as he fell away, we saw Alex standing behind him.

She held the wooden salt mill in one hand. It had snapped in half from the force of the blow.

A trickle of salt spilled out of the splintered core, dribbling down on to the Hatchling.

He writhed and screeched.

The salt ate into his skin, shriveling him up like a slug. His body was pocked with holes, his damaged guts and organs exposed. His limbs stopped rasping against the floor.

And then there was only the stench, hanging heavier than a cloud of car exhaust.

Behind Alex on the table, the lace crackled, a neatly contained garden of flame. The fire fluttered across her features, and I thought it might be the most romantic lighting I'd ever seen.

She poured a mound of white crystals from the broken shaker into her palm. Then she lifted it up and smiled that smile.

'Kryptonite,' she said.

She walked over to the sink, plugged the drain with the stopper, and dumped the rest of the salt in. Then she turned on the hot water.

Patrick and I remained frozen against the refrigerator.

Alex shot us a look. 'You can move now,' she said. 'Go check on the Rebel. Tell him Unnamed Girl just kicked some Hatchling ass.'

For once Patrick was speechless. He straightened his black cowboy hat. Nodded at the sink.

'What are you doing?' Patrick asked.

Alex walked a quick circuit of the kitchen, retrieving her hockey stick, picking up my baling hooks where they'd fallen. Then she stuck them in the salt water in the sink, dunking the blade of her stick and the ends of my hooks beneath the surface.

'Preparing,' she said.

Shaken, I walked over to the living room.

The Rebel rose unevenly. His armor now sported a few more scratches, but the suit had held. He looked at where the Hatchling lay puddled on the kitchen floor. 'Amazing,' he said.

'The salt?' I asked.

'Yes,' he said. 'And Girl.'

'I agree. On both counts.'

'We need to evacuate immediately,' he said. 'The noise will draw more.'

I nodded. 'Okay.'

When I turned around, Patrick was coming back up the hall from Uncle Jim's old study, cradling a dozen boxes of shotgun shells in his arms. 'Rock salt,' he said.

Uncle Jim had used them to scare wolves away from our livestock.

The Rebel said, 'I must leave now to track down my compatriot and the serum.' He stepped across the melted mess of the Hatchling without bothering to look down. 'You, too, should leave as quickly as possible.'

'We will,' I said.

The Rebel slipped through the gash in the kitchen wall and vanished into the night.

Alex pulled my dripping baling hooks from their saltwater bath and tossed them to me. Then she whipped her hockey stick clear of the sink. The blade gleamed wetly.

'Ready?' she said.

'Not yet.'

I looked at my brother, and I could tell he could read my mind, like always. He gave me a nod.

I walked over to the hedge of flame rising from the dining-room table. I stabbed the edge of the lace tablecloth with the tip of my baling hook and yanked it, flame and all, off the table and on to the carpet of the living room.

Orange and yellow spread, a billowing second carpet on top of the first one. It caught the wallpaper and climbed to the ceiling, tendrils wrapping around the doorway into the hall. The curtains went up all at once with a sound like a rush of wind.

We kept our eyes on the flame, watching the fire devour our old house as we moved backward out through the hole in the kitchen wall and into the cool night.

We gave it some distance. When we got to the barn, we paused.

The big barn door was still rolled back from when we'd left in a hurry that awful night two months and a lifetime ago when it had all begun. I'd been out here baling hay, and Patrick had come to fetch me.

I could see the metal catch inside where the baling hooks were supposed to hang.

Back when they were still used for hay.

I turned my attention again to Jim and Sue-Anne's ranch house. I thought about my aunt and uncle up there on the second floor, resting on the bed where they'd slept for so many decades. I didn't want to leave them to the flies and maggots. Flame licked at the downstairs windows. Black smoke poured from the chimney and then started leaking through the shingles.

The last piece of our old life, up in flames.

Maybe it would burn itself out. Maybe it would catch and take down the whole house.

I found myself hoping for the latter.

**ENTRY 26**    JoJo sat with her back to the base of the slumbering band saw in shop class. She let Bunny hop down one of her legs and then up the other. A dirty stuffed animal with one half-chewed ear making her way along JoJo's filthy jeans.

This is what passed for fun now.

Rocky stood over by the window. Stained with grease and powdered with sawdust, it was dirtier than any of the other windows at the school. He'd scrubbed a scuba-mask viewing circle in the pane with his sleeve, and he peered through it now.

JoJo thought back to when she first got Bunny. Mom had given Bunny to her when she'd visited Mom in the hospital. Mom had needles in her arms and all kinds of crazy tubes going everywhere, and JoJo had been scared to go into the room to see her. Rocky had held her hand really firm and said, 'You'll make Mom feel bad.' And so in JoJo went.

Mom hadn't looked much like Mom. Her hair was pasted to her face. Her curls dark with dried sweat. Her skin looked like paper. Her lips were chapped, and they had sores on them.

And Rocky had hugged Mom, and JoJo remembered thinking how brave he was to just march right up there and do that. The last thing she wanted to do was cuddle

164

with Mom right now, which made no sense, because she loved her mother more than anything. When Dad took Rocky to get ice-cream cups from the cafeteria, JoJo had been left alone with Mom.

Mom said, 'I have something for you, my sweet, sweet girl.' And she'd reached an arm trailing tubes over to the nightstand and pulled open a drawer. JoJo remembered thinking how much it must have hurt to move that arm with all the needles stuck in it, pulling beneath the tape. Mom must've really wanted to give her whatever she was reaching for.

And out from the drawer she came.

Bunny.

The best stuffed animal JoJo had ever seen.

She was yellow, Bunny, since it was around Easter and that's when stuffed-animal bunnies were different colors.

JoJo remembered feeling something beneath her face, warm and bright. Something like joy. But sad, too. And she could see it in Mom's face as well. And Mom said, 'Sweet girl, I know how much you love me.'

And JoJo thought, *How? How do you know? Ever since you got sick, I haven't figured out how to say it, not once, not ever.*

Maybe because it felt too scary to say it.

So she nodded.

And Mom said, 'I'm hard to hug right now with all these pokes in me and cords everywhere. So I thought I could give you this little bunny. And you could hug her instead, since I'm so hard to reach.'

She handed Bunny to JoJo.

And JoJo squeezed that rabbit as tight as she'd ever squeezed anything in her life. She put all of her love and fear and guilt into Bunny, and Bunny took it all and turned it yellow, the color of the sun, the color of sunflowers, the color of forgiveness.

When JoJo opened her eyes, Mom smiled at her and her eyes crinkled at the edges, and Mom said, 'I felt that. I felt every last drop of it.'

And JoJo had never let go of Bunny since.

Bunny hopped down her left leg now, leaping over the hole in the knee of her jeans. Hopped back up her right leg.

It was getting boring.

Rocky had barely moved from that window.

It was his third time on lookout duty, and he wasn't gonna screw it up. JoJo stood next to him and let her eyes scan the front of the school. No movement on the lawn.

No Mappers, no Chasers, none of those crazy creepy Hatchling things Chance had told them about.

'Do you ever wish you were older?' JoJo asked.

It was the biggest classroom at Creek's Cause High, crammed with machines and workbenches. Her voice echoed off the hardware.

Rocky spun around and shushed her. 'You gotta stay quiet, JoJo. I'm working. You're not even supposed to be here.'

She walked away and sat down by the belt sander.

'And no,' he said. 'I don't wish I was older. If we were older, we'd be closer to eighteen, and you know what happens when you turn eighteen.'

'But imagine if you were fifteen instead of ten,' she said. 'Like Chance. Or if I was seventeen and tough like Alex. Or eighteen like Patrick.'

'Nobody's like Patrick.'

'Fine. But I still hate being eight. It's useless being eight. Especially right now. Eight's just the age of the kid who gets *eaten*.'

Rocky whirled away from the window to glare at her. 'Don't say that.'

'It's true, though.' She didn't look at him as she spoke. She looked at Bunny instead. You could talk about this stuff to Bunny. She didn't get mad like the others. 'The only thing that's useful anymore is being big. And no matter what I do, I'm not gonna grow fast enough to go up against any of those things. And you aren't either.'

'I'm on lookout, aren't I?'

He turned back to the window for a while. Then he looked back over his shoulder. JoJo was hugging her knees to her chest. She wasn't mad. She was upset.

She was chewing on Bunny's ear, the one that looked less like an ear and more like a nub every day.

He said, 'Quit chewing on Bunny.'

'Bunny likes it when I chew on her.'

'Just . . .' He swung back to his scuba-mask spot in the window for a peek. 'Another half hour and we're done. Then we can play cards.'

'I'm sick of cards.

'Or hide-and-seek.'

She was great at hide-and-seek. She'd found nooks and crannies all over the school, the best ones to squeeze into and disappear.

Since Rocky was too busy being a big-shot lookout to play with her, she made Bunny jump across the sawdusty floor and up the side of the machine and –

With a blare the belt sander fired up. The old machine

rattled, the gritty paper whirring by. It scared her so badly that she fell back, Bunny skittering away out of her grip.

'Shut it off,' Rocky hissed. 'Shut it off!'

But she was too terrified to move.

He bounded away from the window and clicked off the belt sander. He was breathing so hard she could see his chest heaving beneath his T-shirt.

Already she heard footsteps pounding up the corridor. Ben swung through the doorway, Dezi and Mikey at his heels.

'The hell was that?' Ben said.

'I'm really sorry,' Rocky said. 'I accidentally –'

'I did it.' JoJo stood up, smacking sawdust off her legs. 'I was playing with Bunny, and she hopped over the power button. I thought the power was off.'

'We were testing the generator,' Dezi said.

'Bad luck,' Rocky said.

'For you,' Mikey said.

Ben pointed at JoJo. 'She's not supposed to be in here.'

'I was just letting her keep me company,' Rocky said. 'She gets scared when she's alone.'

'We don't got room for "scared,"' Ben said. 'Not anymore.'

'It didn't distract me,' Rocky said. 'I swear. I've been on lookout every second.'

Dezi was over at the scrubbed circle on the window. He pulled away from the pane quickly. 'Then I suppose you spotted the Host standing on the sidewalk staring right at the school.'

Rocky's chin dipped. 'No. I had to run over to shut off the machine.'

'Then you were distracted,' Ben said.

'I guess so. Yeah.' Rocky was studying his shoes. 'I'm sorry.'

Ben walked over and picked up Bunny where she'd slid.

JoJo felt her lips start to wobble, and she willed her tears not to fall. She managed a single word, and it sounded squeaky and strangled: 'Don't.'

Ben tore off Bunny's head.

Her insides, the cottony stuffing, stuck up out of her neck.

JoJo's face got hot, and then she felt the wet on her cheeks splotching the floor and said, 'Don't', again, even though he already had.

Ben looked at her, his head canted. The burned skin at his hairline was shiny and stretched tight. The shadows were severe here in the room, darkening his other scars from the car crash. His face looked like a jigsaw puzzle.

He tossed her Bunny's head.

It skidded across the floor and bumped into her leg.

She picked it up and squeezed it to her chest. Even if it was just Bunny's head, it was still Bunny.

Ripping Bunny's body into pieces, Ben crossed the room, dropping bits of stuffing and patches of fabric on the floor. When he reached the window, he stayed a few feet back and peered through the rubbed-clear circle. Everyone was quiet. JoJo tried not to sniffle too loud.

Then Ben's shoulders relaxed. 'It's gone,' he said.

'Okay, good,' Rocky said. 'It won't happen again.'

'Take off your shirt,' Ben said.

Rocky blinked at him a few times. He rolled one of his sneakers over on to its side, then back again. 'What?'

Ben reached on to one of the workstations and picked up a bundle of rubber clamping bands for holding stuff together when you glued it. He flopped them into the palm of his other hand a few times like a cat-o'-nine-tails from a pirate movie.

'Take. Off. Your. Shirt.'

Dezi and Mikey sidled up on Rocky, one on each side. Trembling, he pulled his shirt off over his head. His arms looked so thin. He balled up the shirt and held it in front of him like a shield. Even so, he looked pretty scrawny.

'Turn around,' Ben said.

JoJo stifled a cry in her chest.

Rocky hesitated, so Dezi spun him around and shoved him over the workbench. Rocky made a noise that wasn't quite a cry.

Ben walked over and stood behind him. 'You put the group at risk.'

'No.' JoJo heard herself talking as if from afar. '*I* did.'

Ben looked over at her. 'Then this is your fault.'

He whipped Rocky, the bands slapping his bare flesh. Rocky grunted through gritted teeth.

Ben whipped him again. Already welts were rising on Rocky's back.

JoJo squeezed Bunny's head. She thought about what she'd just said, about how the only useful thing anymore was being big and how she wasn't gonna grow up fast enough to be any use. She'd never felt more useless than now.

There was nothing she could do but watch her big brother get whipped.

Ben hit him another time. Then he drew back his arm again, the bands flicking overhead.

'Stop!'

Dr Chatterjee entered the room, his leg braces clinking across the tiles.

'Put those down immediately, Mr Braaten.'

'Or what? You're gonna stop me?'

'No,' Dr Chatterjee said. 'But *they* are.'

Kids came pouring through the doorway behind him. Eve and the Mendez twins, and then a trio of guys from the football team, and then pretty much everyone else. They filled the shop class, crowding around Ben, Dezi, and Mikey.

Dr Chatterjee held out his hand. It had a slight tremor from his disease. 'Give me those bands.'

Ben stared at him, his jaw shifting. Then he looked across the other faces. 'None of you understand what it'll take to keep you safe,' he said. 'Rocky abandoned his post. We could've had Chasers through our front doors without any warning.'

'The bands, Mr Braaten,' Chatterjee said again.

Ben whipped them into Chatterjee's palm harder than was necessary. It sounded like it hurt, but Chatterjee didn't make a noise. He tore them out of Ben's grip.

'Eve, please check on Rocky,' Dr Chatterjee said.

Rocky kept his back turned to everyone. He pulled on his shirt, wiped his cheeks. 'I'm *fine*,' he said.

Eve glared at Ben. 'Patrick would never do this.'

'Patrick's got two things going against him,' Ben said. 'He's not here. And he's not in charge.'

'Right,' Chatterjee said. 'But I am.'

'According to who?'

Eve raised her hand. Chatterjee turned to the others. One by one, all the hands rose.

Dr Chatterjee said, 'One more episode like this and you will be dismissed from your position as head of security. You won't be allowed to carry a weapon, patrol, or take shifts as a lookout.'

'You need me,' Ben said. 'When trouble comes – and it will – I'll be your best bet. You won't *dare* to sideline me.'

Chatterjee wobbled forward another step. Firmed his balance. Stared Ben dead in the eye. 'Don't doubt it for a second,' he said.

Ben stared back at him, but he must not have liked what he saw, because he brushed by Dr Chatterjee. Dezi and Mikey followed him, the others parting to make way. Then everyone filtered out the door.

Dr Chatterjee walked over to Rocky. 'You're all right?'

Rocky nodded.

Dr Chatterjee rested a hand on Rocky's shoulder, and Rocky stiffened. He didn't want to be touched. JoJo knew how he felt.

Chatterjee said, 'I promise I won't let that happen to you again.'

His leg braces clanked on his way out, and then it was just JoJo and Rocky again. Rocky stayed turned away. His head was bent, and his shoulders were shaking.

But he wasn't making a noise.

Sitting on the floor, clutching the Head of Bunny, she stared at her brother, feeling even more helpless than before. What could she do?

Rocky made little noises, still trying to hold it in.

JoJo remembered how Mom had given her Bunny to squeeze at the hospital so JoJo could feel what she needed to, but in a way that didn't make it too scary. She thought for a moment.

'Rocky?' she said. 'I'm scared. Will you hold my hand?'

At first Rocky didn't respond. Then he straightened up a little. One hand lifted and wiped his cheeks. When he turned around, his face was red, but the tears were gone.

She stood as he approached and took his hand on their way out.

**ENTRY 27**     We walked through the woods, our boots packing down dead leaves. Though Patrick and Alex were close, I could barely see them through the mist. It floated between the trunks like a slow-moving river, eddying around the branches. The leaves turned the moonlight into a mosaic on the forest floor. It smelled of mulch and pine.

We walked in silence. There wasn't much to say after what the Rebel had told us.

Patrick and I, we'd get to save humanity. We'd get to save Alex.

But we'd have to die to do it.

A wall of vertical bars emerged from the mist ahead. Wrought iron.

Patrick and Alex slowed, but I walked forward, set my hands on the bars, and peered through at the rows of gravestones. I'd nearly lost my life in here a month back. I'd wandered inside through the thick mist, not noticing that the place was filled with Hosts. Thankfully, I'd tucked in behind a Mapper, and Mappers don't look up unless something catches their sight. I'd walked slowly and silently behind him, matching his footsteps as he charted his course through all the other Hosts. If any of them had raised their heads a few inches, it would've been the end of me. But none had.

It had taken me hours to get out.

Patrick came up on one side of me and Alex on the other. We looked like three jailbirds there gripping the bars.

'We don't even get to wind up in there,' I said to Patrick. 'We'll be exploded all over the place like Mr McCafferty.'

'Beats turning into a Host,' Alex said. 'Or getting eaten by a Hatchling.'

'Look at Unnamed Girl, all upbeat,' I said.

She bumped me with her hip. 'I'm not Unnamed Girl,' she said with a Clint Eastwood squint. 'I'm the Girl with No Name.'

We stared at the ghostly headstones, morphing in and out of the fog. Patrick put his arm around Alex.

I looked at my brother. 'We're not human. We're not Rebels. There's no one like us. Except us.'

'And me,' Alex said. She pushed off from Patrick and walked up the fence line, trailing her hand along the bars, her fingertips making the faintest dings against the metal. 'I consider myself an honorary whatever-you-are.'

She moved a ways off, giving us space. I guess she figured we needed some brother-to-brother time. Especially right now. Alex was good like that.

Patrick squinted out from beneath his black cowboy hat. 'So what exactly are we?'

'We're time bombs,' I said. 'That's all.'

'We could save the entire planet,' Patrick said. 'That's pretty cool.'

'Great,' I said. 'So they'll build a statue of us in town square.'

Patrick made his half grin. ''Member how boring you used to say it was living here? Ranching and farming? Two restaurants in town? The same faces day in, day out? That would've been us till we died. We would've worked and married and maybe had kids and wound up in there' – he aimed a finger through the bars – 'like everyone before us.'

'Yeah,' I said. 'We would've.'

'I could've been happy having that life,' he said.

'I know.'

'But not you.'

I didn't answer. I knew he was trying to make me feel better about being a hero. But I wasn't a hero. He was. He saw the big picture, how everything added up. I just didn't want to die. Not like that, not ever.

Patrick said, 'You used to talk about how there was a whole big world out there.'

I finally nodded.

'Well, maybe this is the price of playing in that big world,' he said. 'We get to now, whether we want to or not. We get to do this for Rocky and JoJo and Chatterjee and Eve.'

'And Alex.'

He looked at me. 'And Alex.'

'Thirty-seven days,' I said.

'I know when Alex's birthday is, Chance.'

A flash of a memory hit me: *Patrick sprawled on top of a carport, his oxygen mask knocked off his face. He'd just inhaled air. Infected air. We'd both thought he was gonna die. 'I know how you feel about her,' he'd told me. 'Take care of her. And make sure she takes care of you.'*

'We never talked about it,' I said. 'What you told me on top of that carport.'

'What's to talk about?'

I stared at him.

He stared at me.

'We're both gonna be dead soon, Chance,' he said. 'Does it really matter anymore?'

Before I could reply, I noticed that Alex was backing up toward us, her knuckles dinging the bars in reverse. She didn't stop until her shoulder blades bumped into Patrick.

'There's something out there,' she said.

We heard the crunch of a footfall. Twigs snapping. Underbrush giving way. The mist mushroomed around us. We couldn't see farther than a few feet.

We went back-to-back-to-back, our weapons raised.

Then a sound issued out of the fog.

A rumble.

I relaxed. 'Don't worry. It's the dogs.' I lowered my baling hooks and gave a whistle.

The noises that answered me didn't sound like my Rhodesian ridgebacks at all. Had the pack gone rabid?

'Chance?' Alex said. 'Wanna tell your doggies to chill the hell out?'

A face emerged from the swirling mist.

It barely registered as human. The missing eyes were the least of it.

The lower jaw had fallen off. Rot holes in the flesh showed the larynx pulsing with every breath, making a terrible ragged noise that called to mind a snarl.

More upright forms appeared behind it.

Wheezes and wet rumbles issued from damaged faces.

They weren't ridgebacks.

They were Hosts.

**ENTRY 28**     The Hosts blended into the dense fog so we couldn't get a handle on how many there were.

Patrick raised his shotgun, but I grabbed the barrel. 'Hang on,' I said. 'We need the rock-salt shells for the Hatchlings.'

The front Host lunged forward, and Patrick cracked him with the butt of the shotgun.

He said, 'It's not a waste if it keeps us alive.'

A few more Hosts melted from the mist. Five now.

No – six.

Male and female. Mappers and Chasers.

When the first one went to lunge again, Alex swung at him with her hockey stick. She made good contact. The blade sank into the Host's neck and stuck. Alex yanked it free, and the body collapsed.

We retreated.

The Hosts followed us through the mist. I could hear more feet shuffling on the hard earth, just out of sight.

Even though it was freezing, my shirt was matted to me with sweat. 'How many are there?'

No one bothered to answer.

'Keep the fence at our backs,' Patrick said, 'so they can't surround us.'

And that's what we did, making clumsy, awkward head-way. The Hosts stalked us through the mist, stumbling

178

between tree trunks, disappearing and then easing back into sight. All the while that ragged breathing filled the air, seemingly everywhere around us.

'I'm shooting the next one that gets close,' Patrick said.

'You'll get off one shot,' Alex said. 'That leaves a bunch more.'

'You've got a hockey stick. Chance has his hooks.'

'That leaves a bunch more minus two,' she said.

'It's a fight, not a math class,' Patrick said. 'The equations don't always add up.'

'All I'm saying is, if this breaks down into a free-for-all, we're gonna come out on the losing end.'

'It's not just that,' I said. 'A gunshot could draw any Hatchlings in the area. Then we'd *wish* we were just dealing with Hosts.'

The wrought iron ticked across my shoulder. We were moving along the north wall of the cemetery. Which was all well and good.

Except it ended in about ten feet.

The Hosts seemed to sense this. They drew nearer, saliva drooling from the holes in their throats, matting their shirts. Alex swung at one, knocking him back.

We reached the corner. The intersecting fence line ran back toward the heart of the woods. But town lay ahead, through the open forest.

'We gotta keep moving toward town,' Patrick said. 'Tree to tree. Don't get caught in the open.'

With his shotgun leveled, he led the way off the fence to the nearest tree. Sure enough, a bunch of Hosts materialized from the fog to circle us. We swung our weapons, carving out a bubble of space as we advanced. Our steps moved in concert as we held a tight formation. In situations like this, Patrick, Alex, and I didn't have to talk to stay on the same page.

We reached the trunk and put our shoulder blades to it so we faced outward. The Hosts thrust in at us. I whacked one on the head with the side of a baling hook, and he stumbled to the side, his ankle snapping. He hopped back up on one foot, the other leg twisting loosely beneath his knee.

The weak link.

They faded back again. We couldn't see them in the fog. We could *hear* them.

That was even worse.

'When we move,' I said, 'we push past the injured one.'

A breeze whipped through, clearing the mist momentarily, the Hosts appearing at the edge of visibility. We charged for the Host with the broken ankle, knocking him aside, swinging our weapons and sprinting for the next tree. We repositioned ourselves with the trunk to our backs.

More horrible ragged breathing. More ropes of saliva.

It was gonna be slow going.

And yet we didn't have a choice.

We progressed that way, moving from tree to tree. The mist turned to snowfall, so light you could barely feel it. The flakes spun around us, frosting our hair, like something from a fairy tale.

A scary-ass fairy tale.

The Hosts grew impatient. As we bolted for the next tree, one of the females dove, got a hold of the cuff of my jeans, and nearly pulled me off my feet. Patrick dealt her a jab with the shotgun, and she released me just as my other boot slipped on a patch of ice. Alex caught me under the arm, hauled me to my feet, and we scrambled to the next pine.

Two others took advantage of the opening and charged Alex. She raised the hockey stick just in time, their gnashing mouths slamming into it, pinning her to the tree. Pulling her head back, she thrust the stick handle into their open maws, gagging them. The wood shoved through the hinges of their jaws with a crackling noise. Still the voice boxes lurched visibly in their throats, making gargling noises.

They kept driving into her, their legs scraping up snow.

I jabbed at them with my baling hooks, ripping them off Alex. They drifted back into the mist, quick as cats. When they reappeared, I noticed a new one now. And then another.

How many were out there, hiding in the mist?

'We're not gonna make it the whole way to town,' Alex said. 'One slip. That's all it'll take.'

'Not a good way to go,' I said.

'Nope.'

'Plus, then we couldn't save humanity.'

She managed a weak smile.

Patrick wasn't amused. 'We didn't come this far to get taken by a few rotting Hosts.'

'Tell *them* that,' I said.

We made a break over the next crest. At the peak a gnarled whitebark pine thrust up like a giant bonsai tree. As we made for it, the Hosts slanted in at us. We regrouped at the whitebark, flailing at them, driving them back. Our shoulders scraped the trunk, bark powdering down over us.

We were panting now. It took effort for me not to double over to catch my breath.

Above the rush of the wind, we could hear the babbling of Hogan's Creek. I squinted into the flurry of snow. There it was way below, frigid gray water snaking through sheets of ice. The ground on either side was sloped and free of brush – free of cover of any kind.

We'd never make it across.

There was no point in saying it. It was clear as day.

I tilted my head back to the trunk, my breath still firing in my lungs. 'Okay,' I said. 'Do we start shooting now?'

'And draw the Hatchlings?' Alex said.

'I think we're out of options.'

'No.' Patrick pointed. 'There.'

At first I couldn't see what he was pointing at. But then I noticed the faint glow through the pines.

A farmhouse.

The Widow Latrell's.

Those lights had been burning for weeks and weeks.

'We make it to the house,' Patrick said. 'Regroup there.'

We steeled ourselves, gathered our strength. Then we fought and kicked our way to the next tree. And the next. And the next.

The farmhouse came clearer through the thickening snow. A mile away. Now a half. At last it was only about a hundred yards off.

But we were tired. Too tired.

One of us was bound to make a mistake.

I'm sorry to say it was me.

As we ran for the last trees before the cleared space that passed for a front yard, my boot hit a slick of ice.

A moment of weightlessness.

I hit the ground on my stomach.

Right away I felt a powerful grip clamp down on my boot.

A Chaser.

The bones of her hand wore tattered flesh and stringy tendons like a lacy glove.

She ripped me backward into the pack.

**ENTRY 29**    The pressure on my boot was relentless. I slid back into the heart of the cluster of Hosts, my chest and stomach skating over ice. My chin bumped along the ground.

I looked back at Patrick. His gun was aimed, but if he fired, the pellets would tear into me, too. I rolled over and hammered my heel into the Chaser. She recoiled, readjusting her grip, and I yanked my foot free.

The others dove in at me from both sides.

Alex thrust her hockey stick toward me, and I grabbed at the slanted blade with numb fingers. She ripped me forward just before the Hosts piled on to me.

By some miracle I held on.

Fingers brushed the back of my shirt as I jetted out of the embrace of the mob. One of them tore at my sleeve and came away with a swatch of fabric.

Alex shot me like a puck on to the slick patch of open ground before the widow's porch. I spun in a half circle, the snow-filled night sky rotating crazily overhead. Patrick and Alex were running backward toward me, holding off the seething tide of Hosts. Barely.

I shot to my feet.

The porch was about fifty yards away now.

Not a speck of cover.

The Hosts' gurgles rose in a terrible chorus as they bunched in the snow, a wave ready to break.

It broke.

They bounded at us.

We turned and ran.

Their ragged breath chased us. The tapping of footfall quickened. Snow streaked my vision. Patrick jacked the shotgun.

'Now!' he yelled.

We spun around. The Hosts, blurs against the whiteness. Feet away.

Patrick leveled the Winchester.

Another noise rose above the din.

Howling.

*Dog* howling.

The Hosts spun, disoriented by the noise.

Ridgebacks barreled out of the trees on either side of the front yard, arrowing in at the Hosts. A perfectly executed attack.

After all, they were bred to hunt lions.

Tanner hit first, bulldozing the biggest Mapper, knocking him right off his legs. Deja and Princess lasered in on the Chaser who had grabbed me. Grace had one of the others by the scruff of the neck, whipping her head back and forth. Cassius held the rest at bay. He straightened his front legs and sank down behind them, ready to pounce, his square head lowered. He was issuing a rumble of a growl that would've frozen a grizzly.

Cassius drew himself back up to his full height, the rumble growing even louder, an animal sound that drowned out the animal sounds of the Hosts.

Then he lunged.

Tanner streaked into the mob after him.

We watched the ridgebacks dismember the Hosts. It felt like watching a massacre. At last the dogs paused, staring at the streamers of mist, but no more Hosts emerged from the snow.

It was over.

The ridgies circled us, wagging their tails, nuzzling our palms. A victory dance. We petted them in long strokes along their sides – their reward.

The celebration was cut short.

'Wait a minute,' I said. 'Where's Atticus?'

I looked around, growing frantic.

I pictured the last time I'd seen him. He'd been limping. I thought about how much losing a step could cost you in the wild.

My gaze moved from dog to dog, and then I searched among the trees. Cassius sat in front of me and cocked his head, his forehead wrinkled in that distinctive ridgeback way.

'Why didn't you protect your brother?' My voice rose with emotion. 'You had *one job* – one job more important than any other. And that was to protect your brother.'

The dogs were cowering, and I realized I was yelling.

A sting of guilt now, to add to the grief.

'Brothers always protect each other,' I said. 'No matter what.'

Patrick rested a hand on my shoulder. 'Chance,' he said. 'It's not their fault.'

Alex scratched Cassius's head and then Deja's.

But the dogs were still shifting from paw to paw, their

tails tucked, looking at me. Uncomfortable, upset. After all, I was the one who'd raised them.

I lowered to my knees and held out my arms. The dogs crowded in, leaning against me, and I hugged them, buried my face in their fur.

'I'm sorry,' I said. 'Good dogs. Good, good dogs.'

'Why don't we bring them inside?' Patrick said. 'Give them some food.'

I rose, and we walked to the house. The dogs loped along beside us. When we stepped up on to the porch, they halted.

Alex opened the door, and we turned back.

The dogs stared at us, waiting. They were panting, wearing big dog smiles. Their breath misted the air.

A familiar sadness tugged at my chest. No matter how many times it happened, I couldn't get used to this part. But I had to.

'Release,' I told them.

They bounded off into the forest again, playing and nipping at one another. A blast of snow sheeted the air, and when it cleared, they were gone.

Alex and Patrick were already inside, the door left ajar for me. I took a moment to gather myself and then stepped in after them.

They were standing frozen in the foyer. I almost bumped into Patrick.

I said, 'What are you –'

Patrick raised a finger to his lips.

A scraping sound carried up the stairs from the basement, as unsettling as the tines of a fork across a plate.

It wasn't the Widow Latrell. She'd headed into town at

the beginning, along with most of the other Hosts. In a fight for our lives, Patrick had kicked her into the forge. We'd watched her burn, watched the flesh of her neck bubble as sparks flew up all around her. She was long gone.

Which prompted the question:

What was down in the basement?

**ENTRY 30**    Patrick edged across the foyer and nudged open the door to the basement.

Pitch-black.

The scraping grew louder.

Patrick inched slowly across the threshold, leading with the muzzle of the shotgun. Alex and I crowded behind him, braced for a fight. He used the Winchester to ease the door further ajar. The hinges complained. Light fell across the top step, but the rest stayed bathed in darkness.

He firmed the shotgun to his shoulder. Reached for the light switch with his other hand. Clicked it on. A bare bulb dangled about halfway down the staircase.

No one – and nothing – on the stairs.

The stairs ended at a wall – you had to turn at the bottom to enter the basement. There was something on the wall.

A smudge.

Dark.

As if someone had flicked a paintbrush across the drywall.

Our eyes adjusted.

Picked up the crimson tint of the smudge.

The scraping kept on, rising up the stairs at us, lifting the hair on my neck.

Patrick put his boot on the second step. It groaned. The third.

I followed.

Because brothers always protect each other. No matter what.

Alex pressed up against me, guarding our rear. The tips of her long blond hair brushed across the side of my neck, my cheek. We descended. It felt like an eternity. At last we neared the bottom.

The basement gaped to our right, but aside from the smell of dank concrete and the feel of open space we could sense nothing.

The scraping didn't get louder. It didn't get quieter either.

Alex cleared her throat, the noise making me start.

Patrick stepped off the bottom stair and faced the darkness, the shotgun pointed into the mouth of the basement.

'Oh,' he said.

'What?' I hissed. 'What's "Oh" mean?'

He stepped forward. My night vision was kicking in, enough for me to make out a shape squirming a few feet into the basement. Like a sack of grain. But alive.

It wasn't moving toward us. It wasn't moving away from us. It was just squirming. And scraping.

Patrick reached across, put his hand over the light switch.

'You might not want to see this,' he said.

'Too late for that,' Alex said. 'Turn on the light.'

The light went on.

At first I didn't recognize her. Lips rotting away, exposing a toothy grimace in her otherwise expressionless face. Clumps of hair fallen out around the holes through her head. Her face was moving. Maggots in her eyes.

It was Gladys Jenkins.

Eve's grandma.

She'd been friends with the Widow Latrell. They used to knit or play bridge or do whatever old ladies did.

She clawed at the concrete. The scraping sound wasn't her fingernails.

It was her finger *bones*.

Her nails had torn out already. They lay yellow and cracked on the floor, like cheese curds. She was wearing one of those long flower-print dresses with a high collar and poofy sleeves. The hem was hiked up over one knee, and we could see where her compression socks ended. A white stick of bone poked out of the side of her thigh. From the looks of it, she'd shattered her hip, too. That whole side of her dress was sopped with blood.

She was trying to pull herself forward still, like a wind-up car spinning its wheels against a wall.

I realized with horror that she'd been doing this since the Dusting. Day after day down here, broken and sprawled on her stomach, literally scraping her fingers to the bone.

I remembered her baking fresh cookies for Halloween and thinking about how much effort that took when she could've just bought bags of candy at the Piggly Wiggly like everyone else.

'Her eyes,' Alex said. That was all she could manage. Her voice sounded strangled.

Patrick reached out his hand toward me, palm up. He flicked his fingers: *Give it to me.*

'It's okay,' I said. 'I got it.'

But I didn't move.

His hand stayed there, steady as can be.

I gave him one of my baling hooks.

He put it straight through the top of her head.

The scraping finally stopped.

Patrick wiped the hook back and forth across his thigh, then handed it back to me.

'Come on,' he said, his voice husky. 'Let's find something to eat and then get back to school.'

His boots creaked the stairs on the way up. Alex and I stood there a while longer, shoulder to shoulder, staring at what used to be Grandma Jenkins. I could hear Alex breathing hard.

I felt something brush the backs of my fingers. Alex's hand.

I took it.

**ENTRY 31**    'There are Hatchlings here in our town,' Patrick said. 'Not just Hosts.'

Alex and I stood next to him on the bleachers, facing out at the crowd of kids and teenagers gathered on the basketball court below. Weak morning light filtered through the high windows. Dust danced in the yellow shafts. We'd made our way here without incident, slipping into the school before dawn broke.

Dezi piped up first. 'You said they all went to Stark Peak.'

'We saw them headed there initially,' Alex said. 'But looks like they're spreading out.'

Ben lifted the stun gun from the waist of his trousers. 'We can handle a few stragglers.'

'No,' I said. 'You can't.'

'We've handled the Hosts, haven't we?' Ben said.

'The Hatchlings are much, much worse.'

'Why's that?'

'Because,' I said, 'they're hungry.'

A silence descended over the gym. One of the Mendez twins started sobbing. Mikey hushed her.

'They won't get us in here,' Ben said. 'The Hosts didn't even manage to map this place. At least not the inside. So as far as the Harvesters know, the school doesn't even exist.'

I thought about Grandpa Donovan going from house to house in the neighborhood across the street, vacuuming up all the floor plans with his blank eyes.

'The Mappers aren't done,' I said. 'Not yet. For all we know they still have this place on their list.'

'The Mappers – like the rest of the Hosts – are falling apart,' Ben said. 'When I was on lookout yesterday, I saw Mr Alessandri out there. He was decomposing. His shins literally fell apart. Just gave way. He was lying in the middle of the street, useless, until a coupla coyotes dragged him off.'

'It's true,' Alex said. 'The Hosts are in bad shape. But trust me. You don't want to take any chances. With them *or* with the Hatchlings.'

'Because of that,' Patrick said, 'we gotta buckle down security even more. We should limit all missions off school grounds.'

'We still need to make the occasional food run.' Ben looked across at Dr Chatterjee. 'At the discretion of our beloved leader, of course.'

'Besides,' Dezi said, 'you guys are the ones who keep going off school grounds.'

'That's because they're risking their necks to tell us what's going on out there,' Eve said. 'We'd be in the dark if it wasn't for them.'

'We're working on a plan,' I said.

I regretted it the minute it came out of my mouth.

'Oh?' Ben's glare sharpened. 'What plan is that?'

'We're not sure yet,' Patrick said, covering for me. He put one foot up on the bench in front of him and leaned his elbow across his knee. 'That's why we've been scouting.'

'So you're out there making some secret plan with that alien helmet you got,' Ben said. He turned to the others. 'That's right. They've got info they're keeping from us, and we're supposed to sit around here, not ask questions, and starve.' He swiveled back to us. 'Is that about the score?'

There were a few more grumbles of support than usual. This caught me, Patrick, and Alex off guard.

I said, 'We're still figuring out what the helmet does.'

I was drowned out by shouts. Just a handful of voices, but they were loud. I looked across the crowd at Dr Chatterjee and noticed him looking nervous, too.

He took a few steps toward the front.

'The food is the real issue at hand,' he said. 'As of now our food stores are still above the designated thresholds.' He removed his eyeglasses and polished them on the hem of his filthy shirt. 'By my calculations we don't need to go on the next foraging run for another three weeks.'

'My calculation's simpler,' Ben said. 'We get more food. We eat more food.'

'There are more variables than that,' Chatterjee said.

'Right,' Ben said. 'Like, it's to all your advantage to keep me and my boys well fed. We're the ones who're gonna have to fight when the Hosts come. It's not like JoJo's gonna save you.'

A few teenagers laughed.

'The supermarket's *right there*,' Dezi said.

'Every time one of you steps out of this building,' Chatterjee said, 'you are risking not just your own life but the lives of everyone in here.'

'That's only if they follow us back here,' Ben said.

Several more voices rose in defense of Ben. I was

surprised to see Jenny White and Kris Keuser nodding along.

Chatterjee held up his arms. His hands shuddered slightly from the tremor. 'Okay,' he said. 'We can certainly discuss whether we'd like to approve an early food run.'

'We don't need to *discuss* it,' Ben said. 'I want a vote. This is a democracy, right? That's what you keep telling me.' He turned to the others. 'Don't you want a vote? Don't you guys want more food? *Better* food?'

Several scattered cries of agreement came.

Chatterjee's Adam's apple lurched as he swallowed down whatever he was about to say. He held silent for a moment. When he spoke, his voice was calm. 'Very well,' he said. 'All those in favor of an earlier food run, raise your hands.'

About ten hands shot up immediately – Those of Ben and his lackeys. But slowly more and more hands went into the air. From high on the bleachers, Patrick, Alex, and I watched, stunned, as they continued to rise.

At last Chatterjee tallied the votes.

Thirty-eight for.

Fifty-seven against.

Ben and his crew had lost by a decent margin. But still – it was the closest he'd ever come to collecting a majority. From his expression I could see he understood the significance of that. He looked over at us, and something in his smile reminded me of a wolf.

Hungry. Biding his time.

As the crowd dispersed to get on with the day, JoJo ran over to me. I picked her up and carried her over to my bed. That's when I noticed Bunny.

Or, to be precise, Bunny's head.

'What happened?' I asked her.

I sat down on my bed, the cheap springs creaking beneath our weight. Across the gym I noticed Chatterjee pull Patrick aside and start talking to him. Chatterjee's expression was very serious. I didn't like it one bit.

'Ben tore her head off,' JoJo said.

I felt a ticking in my stomach, like a bomb. '*What?* When?'

'Right before he whipped Rocky.'

At first I didn't register the words. I gazed at JoJo's knitted brows. Her big brown eyes. There was a white-noise rush in my ears. I looked over at Chatterjee and Patrick across the gym.

I realized now what Chatterjee was telling Patrick. And I realized I wouldn't be able to get there in time.

It seemed to happen in slow motion.

I started to dump JoJo off my lap.

Patrick's spine went ramrod straight.

Chatterjee grabbed for his sleeve.

Patrick's arm pulled free as if Chatterjee weren't holding it at all.

JoJo slid on to the mattress.

I stood up.

Hurdled Alex's bed.

Patrick sliced through the beds.

Ben stood clustered with Mikey and Dezi.

Ben turned around as Patrick approached.

Ben started to smile.

And Patrick decked him.

He knocked Ben into a 180, sending him crashing through two beds, racking them up like bowling pins. For an instant Mikey and Dezi were shocked, frozen in place. Ben got up and charged Patrick, hitting his gut in a football tackle, knocking him through a few bystanders and over the top of another bed.

The frame spun up on one leg. The pillow went flying.

'Enough of this. Quiet! You're making too much noise.' Dr Chatterjee tried to get at them, but his unsteady balance wouldn't allow him to push through the crowd.

Ben and Patrick grappled and punched. It was brutal. I got there but couldn't break through the ring of spectators either. The others were cheering, most of them for Patrick but a good number for Ben, too.

It was like that night behind Jack Kaner's barn, the two of them going at it and going at it, two rabid dogs who wouldn't quit. Ben landed an elbow to Patrick's jaw, Patrick's Stetson flying off. Patrick beat at Ben's face. Ben drooled blood, but Patrick kept on.

I could hear my brother's voice, a growl through clenched teeth: '– ever touch a smaller kid again –'

And then Ben snapped his head into Patrick's chin, knocking him off his chest. Patrick landed propped up on the corner of an upended mattress. Ben rolled on to his side and tried to get up, but his hand slid out from under him and he just lay there on the slick floorboards.

They were five feet apart, both of them laid out, glaring at each other, panting.

At last I shouldered through the onlookers and headed for Patrick. Dezi and Mikey came into the cleared space, too, pulling Ben away, checking on his cuts and bruises.

'I'm fine.' Ben swung his arms roughly, pushing them away. 'Don't touch me.'

I picked up Patrick's cowboy hat. Crouched over him. Held it out. 'You seem to have misplaced this,' I said.

When my brother grinned, blood filled the gaps between his teeth. 'Would you mind putting it on me? I'm a little worn out.'

Alex was next to me now, too, kneeling beside him, worried. 'Patrick, what the hell were you think –'

Patrick cupped her face, pulled her down, and kissed her. Her long hair vined around his forearm. When he let go, he left a bloody lipstick stain on her cheek.

Alex pulled away and sat back on her heels. Truth be told, she looked a little breathless.

He regarded her. Then he said, 'Are you gonna help me up or just keep gawking at me?'

Alex crossed her arms. 'I haven't decided yet.'

**ENTRY 32**   Late night. I couldn't sleep. No one else could either.

With all the tension in the gym after Ben and Patrick's fight, it felt like if you struck a match, the place would combust.

I leaned back in my bed, pen in hand, notebook open across my knees. I was way behind on entries and scribbling as fast as I could. There was a ton to catch up on, and as the Unofficial Historian of the Human Record, I had a responsibility to keep going. I stretched my neck, shook out the cramp in my hand.

The half-moon was caught perfectly in one of the casement windows above the bleachers, as if snared in a spiderweb. It was a rich shade of yellow, almost gold.

I thought about how peaceful it must be up there on the moon right about now. All that rock and hardened lava orbiting around us like always. In the stars it didn't matter that every adult in the world was dead. Didn't matter that Hatchlings were coming to devour us alive. Or that I'd had to hold Leonora Rose's hand while Patrick fired a steel rod through her skull.

Alex was sitting up across from me on her bed with a needle and thread, stitching Bunny's neck closed. She was biting her lip, furrowing her brow with concentration the way she did. Her shirt was torn and ragged, her hair tangled, her face streaked with dirt, but I have to say in that spill of golden moonlight she didn't look bad at all.

She glanced up, caught me watching. I didn't avert my eyes. She smiled at me.

It was a different kind of smile. Not flirtatious. But like she was happy to see me looking at her and didn't care if I knew it. I felt it spread all through me, that smile, like a sip of something warm on a freezing night.

Her smile faded. We held our eye contact. I was vaguely aware of Patrick on the bed behind hers, lying back, pressing an ice pack to his swollen eye.

Finally Alex returned her attention to Bunny's severed head. Someone had to.

I'd just started writing again when I became aware of whimpering a few rows over. I was used to this – ever since the Dusting, kids had all kinds of night terrors. At any given moment, you'd hear two or three kids in the darkness, chattering in terror, pleading in sleepy murmurs, or lurching awake, gasping for air.

This time, though, it was JoJo.

I got up and hurried over to her. She was thrashing around her bed in slow motion, almost gently, fending something off. One bed over, Rocky was out cold, his mouth popped slightly open, his curls falling across his milk-pale cheek. He was her big brother, sure, but he was only ten years old himself. Right now he looked even younger. I wanted him to sleep.

I rested a hand on JoJo's stomach and jiggled her a little. Her eyes opened.

She started crying silently right when she saw me, her arms shooting out around my neck. I picked her up and shushed her.

'Nightmare about the Hosts?' I whispered.

She buried her face in the side of my neck like she did, and I felt her head shake. 'No,' she said. 'Ben.'

That's all she said.

'Why don't you come hang out with me for a while,' I said quietly.

'Yes, please.'

We walked back over to my bed, and she sat down in my lap. 'Tell me the story about the cemetery again,' she said.

'It's scary,' I said.

'Yeah,' she said, 'but it's got a happy ending.'

Her hair was still a mess. It smelled like lollipops – I swear there was part of one stuck in there somewhere. I brushed a snarled tuft aside and let her lean back against me.

Keeping my voice low, I told her the story about how I'd found myself alone in the fog-drenched cemetery at night. How I'd made my way to my parents' grave. How, when the fog cleared, I'd seen that I was surrounded by Hosts. A big group of them had all but filled the cemetery, and every direction I looked there'd been an eyeless form rising from the mist. The only way I'd survived was by sneaking out behind a Mapper who hadn't raised his head once.

'And you stepped where he stepped,' JoJo said. 'Your feet in his footprints.'

She always relished that detail.

'Yes.'

JoJo said, 'And you passed within *inches* of other Mappers, but they never looked up either.'

'That's right,' I said.

'And even though it took hours, you made your way out.'

'You can tell this story better than I can by now.'

JoJo reached for my notebook and pulled it into her lap. 'You're writing about your last expedition?' she whispered.

'Yes. I'm catching up on everything Patrick, Alex, and I saw. What we learned.'

'Let's catch up on what me and Rocky saw, too,' she said.

'That sounds like a good idea.'

'That way we'll be part of each other's story, like you said. Forever and always.' She looked over her shoulder at me, her dark eyes shining in the moonlight.

I felt something catch in my throat. I thought of the mechanism hidden in my DNA, waiting to destroy me. 'Forever and always, Junebug.'

'How do we do it?'

'You know how to tell a story,' I said. 'You just did. Tell me what happened to you when we were gone, and I'll figure out how to write it.'

'I was sitting in shop class against the big saw-machine thingy, letting Bunny jump up and down my leg,' JoJo said.

So I wrote:

*JoJo sat with her back to the base of the slumbering band saw in shop class. She let Bunny hop down one of her legs and then up the other. A dirty stuffed animal with one half-chewed ear making her way along JoJo's filthy jeans.*

*This is what passed for fun now.*

I showed it to her. 'How's this?'

She read it solemnly and then looked up at me again.

'My jeans aren't that filthy,' she said.

I gave her the same look that Patrick used on me, the one our father had used on both of us. 'Those jeans,' I said, 'are the filthiest jeans in the history of filth.'

She almost smiled.

Together we wrote out the rest, from Ben tearing Bunny's head off and whipping Rocky to Chatterjee marching in and putting Ben in his place. I swear she seemed to calm as we got it down on paper. Maybe that's one of the points of stories – purging stuff out of our heads on to the page.

She was nodding off just as we finished, and I carried her over to her bed and tucked her in. She stared up at me. Her eyes looked huge – Disney orphan eyes.

'What if you leave again and don't come back?' she asked.

I answered instinctively. 'I won't.'

'You can't promise that,' she said. 'You can't.'

I was about to offer her some fake assurance, but then I thought again about how I was nothing more than a dispersal bomb. I closed my mouth. The truth of it fully hit home in that moment: Fifteen years old and I was going to die. I was *designed* to die. I suppose in a way all of us are, but there seemed to be a special horror in knowing the how and when.

'You're right,' I said. 'I can't.'

'I don't need you,' she said. 'I *don't*.'

She rolled away angrily.

I stared at her back. 'Okay.'

I moved to leave, but she reached behind her and grabbed my thumb with her little fist. At first I thought she was pouting, but after a few moments I realized that she'd fallen asleep still gripping my thumb.

I had to slide my hand free without waking her. I guess she felt about me how I felt about Patrick. As long as he was around, I knew I was safe. I wondered if I was up to my responsibility to her in the days I had left.

Who would take over for JoJo when I was gone?

On the way back to my bed, I spotted Eve sitting on the bleachers. I hadn't had a chance to talk to her alone in a while, so I detoured over to her. She grinned when she saw me coming. I sat next to her, and she took my hand, lacing her fingers through mine.

It felt awkward, since we weren't really boyfriend and girlfriend. I guess we weren't really *not* either. I wasn't sure what to do, so I held her hand.

'I have to tell you something,' I said.

She looked nervous. She let go of my hand. 'What?'

'We saw your grandma,' I said.

Eve shook her head a little, as if that wasn't what she was expecting. I wondered what she *had* been bracing herself for.

'Okay,' she said. 'So you saw her. She's like my mom and dad and everyone else, right?'

'We took care of her,' I said.

I realized that I meant it in both senses.

'She's at peace now,' I added, though the words felt formal and clunky in my mouth.

Eve nodded a few times. 'I feel like there's less of me left every day,' she said.

Her eyes darted away, and her lips pursed, bringing out that dimple in her cheek. She looked so sad that I kissed her. I know that's a dumb reason to kiss someone, but I wanted to do anything to make her feel better.

She was pretty, and her lips were soft, and her face was warm.

But I didn't feel anything. Aside from guilt, I mean.

All I could think about was the way Alex's hand had brushed against mine in the Widow Latrell's basement. How that little gesture had brought something good to that awful moment – a tiny light in the darkness.

When I pulled back, Eve was still leaning toward me, her eyes closed. She opened them. 'I wish I wasn't older than you,' she said.

'Why?'

She blinked back tears. 'Nothing. Forget it.'

I could tell from her expression that I'd done something wrong, but I wasn't sure what.

She ducked her head a bit and hooked a strand of hair over her ear. 'Good night, Chance.'

When I got back near my bed, Patrick was sleeping, his breaths long and even. I pulled the ice pack off his face. Even in the dark, his eye looked red and swollen.

I turned to say something to Alex, but her bed was empty.

I scanned the dark gym but didn't see her, so I headed out toward the double doors. Of course Ben was sitting watch on his metal folding chair, his arms crossed, his stun gun tucked into his jeans.

'Sneaking out after your brother's girlfriend?' he said, not bothering to lower his voice at all.

'Where is she?'

'Girls' locker room. Maybe you two can swap lipstick.'

I walked past him.

Dezi and Mikey were working the front-door shift, and they turned and stared at me as I passed, their eyes glinting.

I reached the girls' locker room and cracked the swinging door slightly. 'Alex?'

Only the drip of water and a faint rumbling of pipes answered me.

I eased the door open and stepped inside. The lights were off, the generator shut down for the night.

It started up then, the grinding sensation in my stomach that signaled panic. I used to feel it maybe twice a year. Now it was more like twice a day.

As I passed the open stall of the showers, the dripping grew louder. The smell of mold and tile cleaner laced the air.

When I came upon the first bank of lockers, I heard a faint sound. The brush of metal against metal.

*Snip-snip.*

I crept forward, on high alert.

*Snip-snip.*

I rounded the lockers.

There Alex sat on the worn wooden bench that ran between the banks of lockers. She was covered by shadow. Her head was tilted forward, her hair dangling over her face.

She almost looked like a Host.

I heard a strange noise then. Not the snipping but a fainter breathy sound.

Alex was crying. I'd never seen her cry. Not like this at least.

I took a heavier step to announce my presence, not wanting to startle her. Her head turned slightly to take me in, though I couldn't see her eyes through the drape of hair over her face. Her arms were limp, her hands resting loosely in her lap.

I remembered that snipping sound – scissors? – and wondered what the hell she was doing here alone in the darkness.

'What's wrong?' I asked.

'The water's shut off for the night. I hate to sound like a princess, but I just want my friggin' hair clean. Just once. I just want . . .'

She shook her bangs out of her face and wiped a tear off her cheek with her shoulder like a little kid. I still couldn't make out her hands in her lap. I didn't say anything, because I had no idea what to say.

After a time she said, 'New Year's baby. That's me.'

I knew this, of course, but I kept my mouth shut because I figured she needed to tell me anyway.

'A month and a few days,' she said. 'That's all we have left.'

I eased closer to her. I straddled the bench facing her but left some distance between us, giving her space.

'You're scared the plan won't work?' I asked. 'That you'll transform?'

She made a sound like a laugh, but it was the most humorless laugh I'd ever heard. 'If I transform, I won't know anything. So no, I'm not scared of that. I'm sad I won't be with you guys. And if the plan *does* work, you guys are gone. Then I don't want to be here anyways. I don't want to be left behind.' She gave another non-laugh. 'God, this is so screwed up. Who would've ever thought we'd have to weigh all this?'

She shifted a little, and her hands came clear now. One of them clutched a pair of scissors. The other a hank of her long hair.

She raised the scissors, and – *snip-snip* – another lock fell away.

I stared at the blond curl resting across her palm, so long that the ends dangled a good six inches on either side. How many months – years – had it taken her to grow it that long?

She stared at it, then let it fall to the floor. 'Maybe this is part of it. We give up what we like. What makes us *us*. Our parents. Our friends. Our clothes. Our hair. If we give up enough, then there's nothing to lose. And if we're gonna make it, we have to act like we've got nothing to lose.'

She swiped grime off her cheek. Then she peeled off her shirt. Beneath, a thin cotton tank top.

The collar dipped low across her chest. Her arms were lean and muscular. Her skin was streaked with dirt. Her chest rose and fell with her breaths. Her collarbone was shiny with sweat.

Emotions tumbled through me one after another. I couldn't keep them straight.

She handed me the scissors. 'Do it,' she said.

'I don't want to.'

'Why not?'

'Alex,' I said. 'Alex, your hair is . . .'

But there was no way to tell her anything about her hair that made sense in words.

She took my hands, folded them around the metal handles. 'Please, Chance.'

So I took the scissors.

I stood behind her.

And I cut off that beautiful long hair.

She stayed perfectly still, her head bowed as if in prayer. When I looked at the mound of wavy blond hair puddling around my boots, I felt a sense of loss that made it hard to breathe.

When I was done, she took the scissors from me and cut the few stray wisps that fell over her face.

Her hair sat choppy and uneven across her forehead, over her ears, along the back. Only on her could this have looked good.

Not good. *Great.*

She looked like some badass comic-book heroine. Postapocalyptic Girl.

She stood up, ran her fingers through her hair, shook free the loose strands. She looked at me. I couldn't keep my eyes off her lips, so I glanced away at the empty shower stalls.

'Have you talked to Patrick about any of this?' I asked.

'Patrick doesn't get this stuff,' she said. 'Patrick is just Patrick. The same as he was before.'

'That's because he's strong,' I said.

She regarded me evenly. 'Yes, strong. Strong and brave. The bravest guy I've ever known. But what does it say about him if none of this changes him?'

My mouth opened, but I had no answer.

Alex walked by me, and all at once we were close in the aisle between the lockers. She leaned over. Kissed me on the cheek.

I felt it everywhere in my body.

'Thank you,' she said.

I managed a nod.

She moved past me toward the door.

I stood there for a moment with my thoughts and the slow drip of the shower nozzles. Then I followed her out.

She was a few steps ahead of me in the dark hall. I hurried to catch her, my footsteps echoing hers.

She turned the corner into the next corridor and was suddenly jerked out of sight.

I sprinted after her. As I rounded the corner, I saw a shadow lurch at my face and I ducked. The fist skimmed across my cheek, mashing my upper lip into my teeth, hard enough to topple me. I cracked my head on the tile. Warmth spread through my mouth where my molars had cut into the inside of my cheek. Dark spots blotted my vision.

Dezi laughed down at me. 'Man, you just don't learn, do you?'

Mikey was holding Alex from behind, pressing his huge body into her. 'Nice haircut, Alex. You look like a d –'

She stomped on his instep with her heel, and he yelped and shoved her away, hard enough to make her head snap back on her neck. She hit the floor, jolting on her knees, and spilled over next to me, her breath leaving her in a whoosh. She was gasping for air, the wind knocked out of her.

'You're so pathetic,' Dezi said to me. 'You think everyone doesn't know that you're crushing on Alex? You think everyone doesn't laugh at you behind your back?'

He stepped forward and kicked me in the gut.

I curled up, coughing.

'We're so sick of you three,' Mikey said. 'Acting like you run the place. But times are changing.'

Behind them in the hall came a ticktock of approaching boots.

My brother's broad form emerged from the shadows, his hat pulled low. Nothing but a band of shadow where his eyes should be.

Dezi and Mikey bladed their bodies, facing him and keeping an eye on me and Alex at the same time.

'I got it from here, little brother,' Patrick said.

He stepped toward them.

'No,' I said, getting my feet under me. 'I got this.'

I punched Dezi in the knee and felt it buckle. As I rose, I elbowed him in the side of the head, and he fell away. Mikey was looking at me with shock. Before he could react, I hit him as hard as I could in the solar plexus. He grunted and doubled over, and I decked him, driving my fist into his chin with everything I had. It knocked a string of spit loose from his mouth as he went down, pile-driving into the tile.

Alex was up now, leaning against the wall, still catching her breath. 'Nice . . . cross . . . Little Rain.'

Patrick looked above Dezi's and Mikey's squirming bodies at me. I could only see the bottom half of his face beneath the hat. His lips and chin seemed carved from stone. His mouth tensed with a touch of amusement. There was approval in there, too, maybe even pride.

I sensed a shift in the darkness beneath the brim of Patrick's hat – his eyes moving past me to Alex. 'I like the hair,' he said.

The heat of his invisible gaze found me again. He gave me a little nod.

I nodded back.

A trickle of red was streaming down my temple from where it had struck the tile. I wiped it off, spit blood, and headed back to my bed.

**ENTRY 33**      Over the next few days, Dezi and Mikey stalked me. Dezi had to wrap his knee in an Ace bandage, and his limp was pretty pronounced. But he deserved it. I tried to make sure I stayed within eyeshot of Patrick, and he tried to make sure he stayed in eyeshot of me.

Twice a day like clockwork, Alex checked the crappy little TV. She'd kneel at the base of the bleachers, plug it into that twelve-volt battery, and spin her way through a sea of static. She'd click to every last channel, giving the old-fashioned dial a full turn, and then she'd wiggle the rabbit ears and do it again.

Night after night Patrick, Alex, and Eve would gather with Dr Chatterjee in his classroom and watch me put on the Rebel helmet to see if the coordinates for our next meet had been beamed to me. Night after night the helmet held no new information.

I wasn't sure what I was hoping for.

No message meant we couldn't save the world. Or Alex.

A message meant the serum was ready and Patrick and I would go to our highly unpleasant deaths.

We trusted Eve and told her we were waiting to meet with the Rebels again. But we left out the specifics of the serum and how Patrick and I were due to, you know, explode. It was my choice, and I'm not sure why I made it. I just felt like that was something private for me, Patrick, and Alex. It had been the three of us for as long as I could remember, and even if Eve was my not-really-girlfriend, something felt wrong about including her. We didn't tell Chatterjee either, mostly not to worry him. We would tell them in due time, once we had the serum in hand. Maybe it was selfish, but dealing with their concern on top of my own mounting dread felt like too much. Plus, the more people who knew, the bigger the risk of Ben finding out. And Ben finding out would change everything.

We went through our routines numbly, the three of us locked inside our secret. JoJo took to carrying Bunny around by the ears, the stuffed-animal head swinging at her side like a kettlebell. The food supplies got lower, the necessity of a grocery-store run growing more urgent. We were down to wilted iceberg lettuce, browning apples, and open-faced lunch-meat sandwiches made on bread with holes where we'd picked out the mold.

Given all the lookout shifts and stress, exhaustion settled into me, bone-deep. I found myself nodding off one day while I was supposed to be mopping the hallways. When I finally got back to the gym, Alex was busy with her futile TV ritual, on her knees before the tiny screen.

The desperation of it struck me differently, maybe because I was so tired. I walked over and rested a hand on her shoulder.

'Alex,' I said. 'Maybe it's time to stop.'

She kept on twisting the dial through fields of static. 'It's my form of praying,' she said.

What could I say to that?

I left her alone. Patrick was on perimeter duty, and Eve was handling the supply station, so I took the opportunity to catch up with my notebook entries. As soon as the sun was down, I dozed off hard into a comatose serenity.

Until I felt a cramping in my throat.

Pain spread like fire through my body, my trapped breath swelling, swelling, until my chest and stomach bulged out. This was it, my genetic programming taking over, transforming me into a dispersal mechanism. I had no choice. It was terrible. And yet a small piece of me wanted to yield. Once I gave in, would it actually feel *good*?

My eyes flew open.

It took a moment for me to identify the dark figure leaning over me as Mikey. But there he was, his hands fastened around my neck. I struggled against him, but he was much stronger than me. He hunched over my bed, his shoulder muscles popping with exertion, his forearms as thick around as tree branches. As my vision wobbled in and out, I recognized Dezi's silhouette to his side. Dezi was standing with his arms folded, enjoying the show. My pent-up breath burned even worse, igniting my chest. I flailed and flailed but couldn't manage to squeeze a sound out through my compressed throat.

Sweat dripped from Mikey's forehead on to my face. His features were twisted, snarling. There was nothing in them that I recognized. Fury had overtaken him. He was as far gone as a Host.

Realization dawned. He wasn't trying to hurt me.

He was trying to kill me.

My eyesight fuzzed over completely, spots bleeding into spots.

A crack echoed off the high ceiling of the gym.

The pressure released.

I drew in a screeching breath and then another. As my vision restored, I saw Mikey drop away, his body collapsing like a sheet of rock crumbling from a cliff face.

Alex stood behind him, hockey stick in hand.

She turned to Dezi, and Dezi flinched.

Alex said, 'You'd better drag him out of here, or you'll get the same.'

Dezi bent down out of sight with a grunt, and then I heard the rustle of clothes and deadweight dragged across the polished gym floor. It was so dark that no one else had even seen what had gone down.

I managed to sit up, my cough turning into a hacking fit. My Adam's apple felt as though it had been crushed.

Alex sat next to me, her arm around my shoulders. Slowly, I got my breathing under control.

'You okay?' she asked.

I tried to talk, but only a rush of air came out. I had no voice. So I nodded.

Alex said, 'We're falling apart.'

I nodded again.

'Those Rebels better get in touch with us soon,' she whispered. 'I don't know how much longer Chatterjee's gonna be able to hold it together here.'

'Not . . . long,' I whispered hoarsely.

'You need some water or something?'

I shook my head.

'Get some rest, okay?'

I nodded.

She settled back on to her bed. I looked across the gym

to the far corner. Mikey had regained consciousness. He was sitting on the edge of his mattress, doubled over, rubbing the back of his head. Then he threw up on his feet.

The sight warmed my heart.

I lay down on my bed, but I couldn't sleep. Alex was right. The fabric of the new order we'd established here was tearing. Ben and his crew were growing bolder by the day. If they hurt me and Patrick bad enough, there'd be no meeting with the Rebels, which meant no serum, which meant that everyone on the planet was done. Another moral obligation for us to endure.

I found myself on my feet, walking through the dark halls to Dr Chatterjee's classroom. I fished the spare key out of my pocket and let myself in quietly through the repaired door.

As I had so many times before, I pulled on the Rebel helmet.

No glow. No response. Same blank screen of the face mask.

I tried to speak through my bruised voice box but still couldn't. I swallowed and then managed a faint rasp: '*I am Chance Rain.*'

The helmet lit up with a blue glow. This part never got old – having my head stuck into an advanced alien technology. But the screen stayed as empty as ever.

I reached to take the helmet off when suddenly the face mask came to life, virtual symbols rotating through variations.

I realized I was holding my breath.

Once again the message rolled into place. MEETING TIME: 15 DECEMBER AT 1700.

The date and time at which I would be given the means to kill myself.

I finally understood what people meant when they said that they felt their heart thumping in their chest. I could feel every pulse, sense the blood shoving itself through my veins.

'*Where?*' I said in that same hoarse whisper.

The slots scrolled again through endless unfamiliar symbols, finally settling on two numbers, each taken out to thirteen decimal points. A latitude and a longitude. Like I was communicating with a machine and not a human.

'*Show me on a map.*'

The helmet slammed me into outer space. I was moving almost too fast to process. I stumbled a little and then righted myself. Stars winked by.

Milky Way.

Pluto.

Saturn.

Mars.

I decelerated into North America, the view finally slowing.

Our state. The valley.

Creek's Cause flew by.

The flat plain to the west of the high school, miles out.

Closer, closer.

Flatland. It all looked the same.

I traced the vein of the highway.

An exit sign blipped past: STONE SPREAD, 137 MILES.

I skimmed across a single-lane road, forging north.

Another sign: STONE SPREAD (POP. 53).

A scattering of ragged homes and barns, long abandoned.

A dusty stretch of earth a half mile past a row of dilapidated stables.

A spot no different from any other spot.

The image froze for an instant, and then the blue glow extinguished.

Breathing hard, I pulled off the helmet. The room flipped around me, my sense of balance out of whack. I pressed my hands to my head and waited for the spinning to stop. I took a step, waited out the vertigo, and then walked evenly to the rear classroom door that let out on to the back fields.

As much as I wanted to rush to Patrick to give him the news, something stopped me there at the rear of the classroom.

I turned and looked behind me. School desks in neat rows. The lingering smell of whiteboard markers. Colorful diagrams of amoebas and protozoa.

My gaze settled on my old seat. Fourth row, second from the front. How many notes had I taken in that chair? How many lectures had I listened to? Daydreaming at that desk, I'd imagined dozens of futures for myself. None of them involved what was waiting for me on December 15.

A few weeks' time. That's all I had left. I had a sudden awareness of the seconds ticking away, the bomb planted inside me waiting to blossom into . . . into *what*?

I turned heavily back to the rear door. The knob felt ice cold against my palm. I eased the door open and stepped outside.

The night chill seeped through my clothes. The clouds

were as dark as gravy against the midnight sky, the moon blotted from sight.

I scanned the perimeter for Patrick, but the gloom was too thick for me to make out much of anything. The entire school was fenced in, a concession to worried parents a while back when school shootings seemed to sweep across the country. I started out across the field toward the base-ball diamond. The chain-link running along the first-base side looked out past a row of Dumpsters and on to the rear of the grocery store. I kept my attention pegged there as I approached. Unmowed grass flicked across the toes of my boots, giving off whispers. The earthy smell, clean and fresh, rose to my nostrils.

Patrick always worked his way clockwise around the perimeter, so I figured I'd go the other way to ensure that our paths crossed. I couldn't wait to share the Rebel update with him and start laying plans.

I stepped from the dew-wet grass on to the dirt of the infield, making sure to tag first base out of habit. Keeping a sharp eye out for any movement among the Dumpsters behind the Piggly Wiggly, I hugged the chain-link, head-ing for home plate. I got halfway down the line when my foot kicked something in the dirt. It skittered away.

I looked down and froze.

A severed zip tie.

My eyes traced a bunch of smudges in the dirt back to a gap in the chain-link fence. An L-shaped cut, big enough for someone – or *something* – to shove down the flap and step through.

The slit in the fence had been there forever – we'd snuck through it ourselves on our first approach to the school after the Dusting. But Patrick and I had repaired it shortly after, suturing up the gap with zip ties under cover of night.

The rest of the cut zip-tie loops lay clumped at the base of the fence like maggots.

I walked over to them and stared down, trying to quiet the sense of unease building in my ears.

I had to run to warn the others, but I was having a hard time getting my legs to listen. I took a step back and then another.

A crunching sound finally broke through my shock.

Footsteps.

Too late I realized that I'd been so focused on what might be on the far side of the fence that I'd lost track of what might already be in here with me.

Fear clawed its way up my throat.

I turned.

Two large shadows were right on top of me, attended by a drone of circling flies. Clicking bones held together by rotting flesh and tattered grocery-store uniforms.

Black coasters for eyes.

**ENTRY 34** . I tried to scream, but no sound came out.

My throat, still wrecked from Mikey's near strangulation.

The Hosts were five feet away and closing in – no time to turn and run. One of them still clutched the pair of bolt cutters he'd used to cut the zip ties; it dangled at his side. The breeze wafted the reek of rotting flesh into my face. One of the flies pinged off the side of my head.

My hands were raised, spread. I tried to turn them into fists.

I stared at the eyeholes and realized – they were angled slightly down.

Mappers.

My mouth was still open in a silent scream. My brain raced, a thousand thoughts compressed into microseconds.

They hadn't picked up on me yet. They were charting the school grounds. Thank God I hadn't screamed. If they recorded me here, it would alert the Harvesters to the school. More would come. Everyone would die.

Out the other end of this flurry of thoughts spit a single command: *Don't be seen.*

Four feet away.

From my throat issued a tiny creaking sound, a

snuffed-out moan. It was the only noise my throat could manage. The Hosts didn't key to it.

Three feet.

They were side by side, their shoulders aligned but an arm's length apart.

Two feet.

I rotated on the balls of my feet, blading my body. I put my arms flat at my sides, willing myself to occupy the thinnest profile imaginable.

One foot away.

I closed my eyes. Sucked in my stomach. Blew out a breath to compress my chest.

I was inanimate. A rock. Carved from wood.

The buzz of flies intensified. The Hosts were close enough that I could sense the heat of their bodies, could feel the air move.

I tensed so hard that my muscles cramped. My calf knotted. The arch of my right foot locked up. A nerve shot down my neck into my shoulder.

Sandwiching me. Fabric whispered against my chest. *Don't breathe.*

The crunching sounds continued, the footsteps advancing uninterrupted.

I kept my eyes squeezed shut even as I heard them move away. The noise changed as the Hosts forged on to the grass, the long blades brushing across their feet. Only then did I allow myself to open my eyes.

I watched them continue on, vacuuming up the lay of the field with their eye membranes. I released the breath I'd been holding.

There was no sign of Patrick anywhere. He'd probably

already circled and was working his way across the fence line in the front.

I was on my own.

Finally unlocking my legs, I stepped lightly back on to the grass behind second base, willing my boots not to scrape against the ground. Then I sprinted for the school, giving the Mappers a wide berth.

I hit the math-and-science wing at a full sprint.

Mrs Wolfgram's classroom door was ajar.

The black rectangle of the doorway stared back at me.

I swallowed down bile, crept closer, put my face to the dirty window.

Not just one Mapper inside the room but two.

If I ran inside to face off with them, I'd be spotted. If I killed one of them, another would map my body contours and convey my position to the Harvesters. Even if I killed them all, they'd blip offline abruptly at the same time, which would no doubt raise suspicion. Either way the Harvesters would know that there were kids on the premises. The high school would be blown. They'd send more Hosts or worse – Hatchlings.

There was no way to stop the Mappers and remain invisible at the same time. My insides twisted with frustration, wrung like a wet towel.

I reversed course, jogged an arc around to Chatterjee's room. My panic flared a notch higher when I saw another Mapper in there, covering the floor I'd occupied minutes before. He was really tall, six and a half feet, with narrow hands and elongated fingers. He'd been a stocker at the Piggly Wiggly. I didn't remember his name, but the mean kids called him Boo Radley.

He finished spiraling his way through Chatterjee's classroom and stepped into the corridor, turning to head for the heart of the school.

Toward the gym.

Where a hundred or so kids were sleeping.

I bolted along the side of the building, hurdling bushes and sprinklers.

As the classrooms whipped by, I spotted another Host inside, veering off into the chemistry lab.

I peered through window after window, searching for someone to warn. I passed the labs and then the physics rooms with no luck.

Through the open classroom doors, I caught flicker-glimpses into the halls – Boo Radley shadowing my movement as he progressed through the school. Flecks spun around his head, flies in perpetual motion. I ran ahead of him, hoping to spot one of the kids. But I was running out of room – and time.

At last I came around the corner to the final hall that ended at the gym. Desperately, I peered through the nearest window and spotted movement up ahead.

JoJo.

She trudged through dim blocks of light falling through the panes. She wore one of my T-shirts, which drooped down over her knees. Bunny's head swung at her side. Her cheeks looked plump, her eyes puffy with sleep. She turned for the bathroom.

I tapped on the window with my fingertips. It took everything I had not to hammer the glass with the heel of my hand.

At first she started, scared. Her head swiveled over.

A few blinks as she registered it was me. And then she walked over to the window.

'Chance?'

I tried to talk, but only a strangled croak came out of my injured throat.

She leaned closer. 'You okay?'

I pointed violently down the hall behind her. My mouth moved, but it could barely force out the word: *'Mappers.'*

'What? What's wrong?'

I waved my hand again down the hall but then realized that my crazy gesticulations weren't helping. I waved for her to come even closer. She leaned in, her temple kissing the window. I put my face to the glass and choked the words through my vocal cords.

*'Bunch of Mappers . . . inside . . . heading for the gym. . . . warn others.'*

Her eyes widened. She pulled back from the window, shot a glance up the corridor. And then she sprinted for the gym.

Only now did I see that Rocky was farther down the hall on front-door lookout. She grabbed his sleeve and yanked him up off his chair. He ran at her side, the two of them barreling along.

I pressed my cheek to the window, peering in the other direction up the hall. A swirl of flies came into sight around the corner. A distorted shadow fell across the floor, stretched over the tiles and up the opposite wall, holes of light showing where the eyes would be.

Any second and Boo Radley would step into sight.

Frantic, I whipped my head back toward JoJo and Rocky.

She reached the door to the gym, yanked it wide, and they vanished through. The pneumatic closer stalled the door as it swung shut. It moved in infuriating slow motion, the seam at last vanishing.

I turned back just in time to see the tall Mapper step into view.

He moved with his spine erect, almost regally, floating down the hall. A living halo of flies pulsed above his head.

He walked right past me.

Helpless, I watched him go. His heels were cracked. The skin of one ankle was rubbed through, the Achilles tendon straining, vibrating like a plucked cello string.

Behind him more Hosts appeared and entered the other classrooms off the hall. They were finally mapping the school interior. Every square inch of it.

Boo Radley trudged toward the double doors to the gym. Soon enough those talonlike fingers would curl around the door handle.

Too late I remembered that we'd barricaded the gym's other exits to protect against a Host invasion.

The door Boo Radley headed for was the only way in or out.

The kids were trapped inside the gym.

**ENTRY 35**     After JoJo burst through the doors with her breathless announcement, the gym erupted in panic. Kids and teenagers hopped up from their beds and cowered at the base of the bleachers.

Ben yanked his stun gun from the waist of his jeans. 'I'm gonna kill any of them that come inside,' he said, keeping his voice as low as he could manage.

Dezi and Mikey stormed past Eve into the supply station, grabbing for Patrick's Winchester. Eve protested, but Mikey shoved her aside.

'What are you doing?' Eve said. 'If that shotgun goes off in here, every Host within a mile'll hear it.'

Chatterjee rolled off his mattress and fumbled with his leg braces. 'Everyone stay calm. *Quiet*. If you're this loud, they'll all come stampeding in here.'

That got everyone to hush.

'We need to plan our counterattack,' Rocky said.

'There's no time for a plan,' Ben said. 'Not anymore. We take him down fast and hard.'

'JoJo said there are a *bunch* of Mappers inside already,' Eve said. 'If we kill one, our cover'll be blown. They'll know we're here. They'll hunt us down.'

Sweat dripped from Ben's hairline, tracing the pathways of his scars. 'We're out of options,' he hissed.

JoJo hopped up on the bleachers. 'Hey. Hey.' She was

raising her hand. 'There is *one* other option. It'll even let us keep the high school.'

'Shut up,' Dezi said. 'We're handling it.'

'You guys gotta listen to me,' JoJo said.

No one did.

Alex stepped up on to the bleacher beside her. 'Let her talk,' Alex said.

Something in her tone made everyone stop. They looked at JoJo.

'Fine,' Ben sneered. 'What's our other option, JoJo?'

'We let him in,' JoJo said.

A sound echoed through the gym – the click of finger-nails against the door handle.

JoJo whispered, 'Everyone take your shoes off. *Now*. And get behind me. Stay as quiet as possible.'

She hopped down and ran across the basketball court to the side of the doors. The others moved behind her, a wave sweeping across the floorboards. Ben headed over last. But he kept his stun gun at the ready.

'If he spots us,' Ben said, 'I'm killing him.'

The door eased open.

The Host was so tall he had to duck to get through the doorway. He entered and stood there a moment, his head tilted down, eyeholes aimed at the floor.

Boo Radley.

Right to his side, the big group of kids and Chatterjee quivered in a mass against the wall. JoJo stood at the fore-front, Bunny's head clutched defiantly in hand.

If Boo Radley'd turned his focus even slightly, he'd have seen them all cowering there.

But he didn't.

Instead he walked to the center of the gym. Then he started his spiral pattern, turning at ninety-degree angles, picking his way through beds as he moved outward.

He kept walking and turning, expanding slowly.

The kids remained silent. Not a cough. Not a sneeze. Not a whimper.

As Boo Radley got to the outer edge of the beds, JoJo directed the others with hand gestures, like a traffic cop. The group padded lightly, their socks quiet against the floorboards, a few teenagers skittering out ahead, others scurrying to catch up. They spread through the beds behind Boo Radley as he made a turn. It was like musical chairs without the chairs, a dance in tight quarters. Every kid had to place every step carefully. Dezi limped to keep up.

Boo Radley reached the far wall and rotated, the kids swinging again to his blind spot, moving of a piece like a school of fish. They let him map, stepping where he stepped, keeping behind him.

Boo Radley walked along the wall, and JoJo gestured for everyone to head to the center of the room now. They swept behind her again, trying not trip over one another's heels. Rocky barely got out of Boo's way, the long fingers of the swinging arm skimming across the back of his shirt.

Boo traced his path along the bleachers, scanning through the benches to take in the space beneath. Then he mapped the far wall and pivoted on a heel.

The kids flattened against the west wall, two bodies deep.

Boo walked past them, his footfall and the buzz of flies

231

the only sounds in the gym. He reached the double doors and plucked at a handle with his long fingers. The door swung open silently on greased hinges. He started to duck through.

Way down at the end of the row, Maria Mendez stepped out of line so she could watch him leave.

And kicked an empty Dr Pepper can.

It clattered on the floorboards.

It might as well have been an A-bomb going off.

Everyone froze.

Alex dove and caught the can. The silence sounded even louder than the rattling.

Boo Radley stopped. He reversed back through the door. Started to turn.

JoJo stepped out in front of everyone like a conductor. She stuck her arm to the side and swung it downward as she sank below the line of beds. Everyone flattened to the floor a second before Boo Radley rotated around.

His eye membranes fixed on the wall across from him.

Even at his height, he'd be unable to see over the final rows of the beds.

Only the blank wall beyond was visible.

He swiveled back to the doorway and passed through.

When the door sucked closed behind him, it was as though the walls themselves exhaled.


I was half crazy with anticipation by the time I saw Boo Radley exit the gym and step back out into the hall.

He was leaving them alone?

It made no sense.

Before I could react, the rear classroom doors banged

open around me all at once. I grabbed my chest and flew back against the wall, knocking my head. I stayed frozen flat against the building as the Hosts exited the school through the row of rear doors. They drifted out toward the baseball field and the waiting slit in the fence.

Staring at their receding backs, I kept telling myself to breathe. I took it a gulp at a time. Once the Mappers were a little ways off, I spun off the wall and ran through the nearest door. I collided with Patrick in the corridor, who was flying in from the front doors. I banged off him like the losing bumper car and gave a yelp.

His jigsaw pendant had spilled out of the collar of his shirt. For Patrick this signaled full dishevelment. 'What the hell went down in here?' he asked.

My voice still didn't work, so I shook my head.

He hauled me to my feet, and we sprinted to the gym.

He yanked the door open to reveal everyone inside.

Safe.

They were gathered around JoJo, who along with Bunny's head was holding court: '– figured if we let 'em map the school, then they'll think we aren't here. And I remembered what Chance did in the cemetery, how they couldn't see him because he tucked in perfectly behind a Mapper.'

She grinned proudly and hugged Bunny's head to her chest.

I cleared my throat, glared right at Ben. 'Good thinking, JoJo,' I said. 'You saved us all.'

My voice was still strained, but at least I'd found it again. It was worth it to see Ben's face.

'Where'd the Mappers go?' JoJo asked.

'Back fields.'

'Can I see?'

Patrick nodded. 'I think you've earned it.'

JoJo led a small group of us out into the hall. We lined up against the windows, our breath fogging the glass at intervals.

The Mappers were more than halfway to the baseball diamond by now.

As we watched, they stopped walking one by one. Then they tilted their heads up to the heavens.

Their eye membranes glowed to life, dozens of spots of blue.

Familiar clicking sounds carried back to us. Throaty and irregular.

The Mappers were uploading all the data they'd just gathered. Data that showed the school to be empty.

A sense of wonder settled over us as we watched them across the dark fields. The blue spots floated like fireflies.

The Mappers finished, their heads nodding forward, and then they plodded toward the fence.

Boo Radley went down first. That worn ankle simply gave out, the tibia shoving its way through the ankle hole. His other leg kept churning even though it was tilted off the ground, and then he collapsed into a pile, his rotting body disintegrating before our eyes.

Another Host dropped, and then they went down in twos and threes, putrefying puddles on the outfield grass. Only a few made it to the fence and stepped through, trudging off into the darkness beyond.

We stayed there lined along the hall, watching breathlessly. It was impossible to look away.

For a while parts squirmed on the ground. A foot waving in the air. A head quivering on the fragile stalk of a neck. Fingers clutching soil, clawing their arm forward right out of its shoulder socket.

As dawn cast its pale light across the fields, the remains were still. A murder of crows swept in, picking over the offerings.

Dr Chatterjee backed away from the windows first, removing his glasses and rubbing his eyes. 'Well,' he said. 'That should buy us some more time.'

Ben came off the wall next. 'Not if we starve to death,' he said.

No one had the heart to argue. It was the most battle-worn I'd ever felt without a battle.

We streamed back toward the gym. I couldn't help but pause and gaze once more across the fields.

A raven dipped its beak into one of the puddles and came up with a glistening morsel. It flew off, banking against the dappled orange clouds.

It was odd what passed for beautiful these days.

**ENTRY 36**    Foraging runs are governed by two rules:

Stick with your crew.

And never leave a man behind.

For the grocery-store run, we took out two crews, ours and Ben's.

Ben had his group of five, stocked with the usual suspects. And we had ours, led by Patrick. In addition to me and Alex, we had Eve, Rocky, Jenny White, and Kris Keuser.

There hadn't been many volunteers.

Though we hadn't spotted any Hatchlings close to the high school yet, Patrick's Winchester was loaded with rock-salt shells and Alex had taken her hockey stick and my baling hooks to the cafeteria kitchen and baptized them again with salt water.

It was past midnight on December 14, and the waxing moon lent a pale gleam to the wild grass of the baseball outfield. Each crew pushed two empty wheelbarrows – Rocky and Kris steered ours. We reached the zone where the Hosts had disintegrated on the outfield grass. Over the past days, the puddles had bled together, leaving a soupy film across a patch of center field. The smell made my eyes water. For a moment I thought the organic matter was moving again. A trick of the moonlight? But no, it was throbbing with life. I went on alert, leaning closer.

Maggots.

My first thought was, *How boring*.

Jenny White gagged a bit.

I put my hand on her back, but she shook me off and threw up, contributing to the sludge.

'Shut her up,' Ben hissed from over by the fence.

'She's *ten*,' I whispered. 'Cut her a break.'

Jenny wiped her mouth, and we continued on. The two packs moved separately, Ben's crew angling up the first-base line while we took a circuitous route through left field, skimming along the third-base dugout.

Ben reached the slit in the fence first. He'd repaired it himself after the Host invasion, cinching up the chain-link with a series of combination padlocks from old gym lockers. He had every last combination memorized. He went to work now unlocking them. Our crew waited over by the dugout. The purring of the first dial carried over to us, followed by a metallic click as the lock opened. The process went on for a very long time.

At last we watched their dark forms vanish through the fence line. Dezi stumbled a bit on his way through, given his bad knee, sending a rattle of metal through the night air. Ben grabbed Dezi's shoulders and held him balanced on one leg, perfectly still, halfway through the fence. Then he and Mikey guided Dezi through.

After they filtered between the Dumpsters and faded into the darkness, Patrick held up his hand, holding us in place. We waited another five minutes, and then my brother lowered his hand. We crept across the infield dirt.

Ben had laid the gap open perfectly like an unzipped jacket. He'd let the loose padlocks dangle from one side of the slit so their weight tugged the flap wide. Despite all the ways he was awful, I had to admit he was really useful when it came to stuff like this.

Rocky and Kris parked our empty wheelbarrows beside the two left by Ben's crew. We breezed through the fence, lifting our feet carefully so as not to jangle the chain-link. Then we huddled up behind the rows of Dumpsters.

Ben's guys had already forged into the grocery store through the rolled-up door of the loading bay. We crossed the asphalt, climbed on to the dock, and slipped inside. Ben had left the door open for us. We found him and his crew in the back room, which was rimmed with freezers.

The doorway to the main floor was covered with dangling plastic strips. Terror bubbled up in me as I saw them bulge inward at us. They fell away, revealing Mikey steering a flatbed cart into the room.

I exhaled shakily. Ben's dark eyes found me. 'Feeling jumpy, Little Rain?'

'You'd be an idiot not to,' Alex said.

Ben rested his hand against the door of the nearest freezer unit. 'Still cool,' he said. 'This bad boy's never been popped.'

Mikey moved the cart close, and Ben opened the door. The freezer was packed with cuts of meat. Ben rubbed his hands together to warm them; it made him look like a cartoon robber about to plunder a bank.

His guys started stacking vacuum-sealed cutlets, chops, and fillets on to the flatbed. Ben looked up at my brother and jerked his head toward the plastic curtain. 'Roll out.'

Our job was to secure the main floor and load up on nonperishables.

We pressed through. The plastic dragged across my face, falling away to reveal the main floor. It was chilly — the front doors had been breached by Hosts way back at the beginning.

Patrick signaled for us to break up between the aisles as we'd discussed. We split off in twos to complete our various tasks. Mine and Patrick's was to deal with the shattered sliding front doors.

Rocky and Eve started grabbing armloads of Cheerios, crackers, and energy bars. Jenny and Kris peeled down the aisle toward canned goods. Alex stayed alone in the back. We'd said that her job was to provide overwatch, but it was really to keep an eye on Ben and his crew.

Patrick and I eased our way to the front of the store. The night wind whipped back my hair. Despite the cold, I armed sweat from my forehead.

We reached the sliding doors. One of them had been smashed in by the Hosts, but the other was intact. The doors were made of heavy-duty Lexan. Jack Kaner had installed them last July after an F2 tornado ripped through and turned all his windows to slivers of glass.

As I stared across the parking lot, I felt my heartbeat revving up, a *thump-thump-thump* at my wrists and the sides of my neck. Town square was barely visible beyond the lot, a lake of black framed by the blocky shadows of the hospital, the church, the One Cup Cafe.

A body lay at the edge of visibility, either a rotting teenage kid or a dead Host. It was twisted grotesquely, as if it had landed there from some great height, the torso jackknifed back over the hips, arms splayed. I wondered how it had happened.

When Patrick tapped my shoulder, I jumped.

He pointed at the emergency metal gates tucked into the wall at either side of the doorway. We gave a last scan of the parking lot and then leaned our weapons against the wall and set to work. I dug my hand into the crevice on the left side and hooked the handle at the end of the gate.

It expanded outward with a screech.

I froze. Bit my lip. My eyes were scrunched shut against the noise. I pictured it rolling across the parking lot, town square, the whole stupid valley, and echoing back from Ponderosa Pass fifty miles away.

I looked behind me at Patrick. His eyes were wide, his Stetson cocked back on his head. He eased a breath out through his teeth and made a calming gesture with his hands: *Slower.*

He grabbed the gate handle on his side of the doorway and extracted it one painstaking inch at a time. Rather than screeching, it made a grinding noise. Patrick eased off the pressure even more, and the grinding slowed to a series of metallic ticks as the rusty hinges accordioned open.

I followed his lead, guiding the other side of the gate out to meet his in the middle.

I felt exposed there in the open mouth of the store, my whole right side laid bare to wind and darkness. But I forced myself to move as slowly as I could.

As the gate stretched open, my side of it would give a tick, and a few seconds later Patrick's would. It sounded like a clock winding down.

We backed up toward each other. At last I felt my brother's shoulder blades bump into mine. An industrial-size padlock dangled from the metal loop, and Patrick freed it. I fastened the thick hasp, and he hooked the padlock through, clicked it, and extracted the key.

When he exhaled, his shoulders lowered a solid inch. He stepped away from the doorway, picked up his shotgun, and turned to face me.

He whispered, 'Now let's –'

He read my face and stopped.

My mouth had gone bone-dry. A sheen of panic sweat covered my body – it had sprung up instantly. My throat clutched. I couldn't force out a single word.

I didn't have to.

Slowly, Patrick turned his head toward the window just behind him.

On the far side of the pane, no more than six inches away, nostril holes quivered and blew twinning plumes of mist against the glass.

Eyelids flickered over bulging black pupils. Even in the darkness, the orange hue of the flesh was clear. The mouth parted as I dreaded it would.

And kept parting.

Jagged teeth stretched wide, each one tapering to a gleaming, pearly point.

The Hatchling reared back and launched himself into the window.

**ENTRY 37**     The Hatchling hit the pane with the violence of a head-on train wreck. The collision threw off a warbling noise with resonance I felt in my bones, so loud I cringed and ducked at the same time, as if either would help. The Hatchling reeled back a step, his feet scraping against the pavement. He squared to us again, gathered himself up, and then beat against the Lexan, leaving streaks of orange mucus laced with blood. He kept going. Claws. Elbows. That horrid face, smeared against the pane.

It was so terrifying it took a moment for me to register what was happening. The tornado-resistant Lexan glass had held. Unlike the sliding front doors, which could come unhoused from their tracks, the windows were secured solidly in their frames.

For now it was like watching him from the safety of an aquarium.

Not that that helped calm me down any.

The breeze shifted, blowing the fetid smell through the bars of the gate. My gorge rose and soured the back of my mouth.

Patrick and I stepped away from the window.

'Oh, my God,' Jenny White said from somewhere behind us. 'That's not real. That *can't* be real.'

We tore our eyes from the flailing spectacle, looking

behind us. Rocky, Eve, Kris, Jenny, and Alex had stepped into view from various aisles, staring in disbelief.

Alex said, 'Will the gate hold?'

'Solid steel,' Patrick said. 'It's as strong as the Lexan.'

The Hatchling seemed to be hammering the glass in fast-forward. Ropes of blood painted the window. Claws scoured the Lexan. His head struck the pane again and again. It was like he couldn't believe he couldn't break through. For a moment I wondered if he might beat himself to death against it.

But then he pulled back from the window. He staggered a few steps and straightened himself up. He turned to the parking lot.

He released a high-pitched whistle. Steam vented from hidden glands ringing his neck, misting in the air around his head so it looked like a lion's mane. He was pushing the noise out of himself with such force that he doubled over from the exertion.

Inside the Piggly Wiggly, we clamped our hands over our ears.

Ben and Dezi spilled through the back door.

'What the hell is going –' Ben froze.

I'd never seen fear on his face before. I'd never seen him even approximate the expression he was wearing now. His face seemed to flatten out, the skin pulled wide, broadening the scars. It made him look so young – I could recognize the kid he used to be before the car crash.

Mikey stuck his head through the plastic curtain. He blinked twice at the sight and then withdrew. I can't say I blamed him.

Dezi hobbled forward. 'Kill him,' he said, raising his

voice to be heard over the Hatchling. 'Patrick – *shoot that thing!*'

But Patrick knew as well as I that there was no point. The rock salt wouldn't penetrate the Lexan any more than the Hatchling could. And Patrick couldn't fire through the locked gates covering the front entrance; half the pellets would ricochet off the steel bars and wind up embedded in his own face.

At last the Hatchling finished his cry. He drew himself back upright.

An instant of silence. And then the faintest rumbling.

'What's that noise?' Kris said, his voice slowed with shock.

At the outer edges of the parking lot, bounding through the mist, came the answer.

Four of them.

Six.

No – ten.

A pack of Hatchlings, called in for the kill as sure as coyotes answering their leader's howl.

And it hit me. We were in an aquarium, all right. On the wrong side of the glass.

The Hatchlings bounded toward us, dipping low like apes as they neared. And then they leapt.

They hammered the Lexan like a volley of cannonballs, the force great enough to shudder the walls of the grocery store.

They bounced back and rose again, shaking themselves off.

They came once more, a second wave of attack. This time they leapt *above* the Lexan panes. We heard the crunch of claws sinking into stucco. For a peaceful instant, they were gone from sight. The front of the grocery store and the parking lot looked as desolate and quiet as ever.

Then we heard the sets of claws pulling free. Punching back in.

Moving upward.

'What are they doing?' Rocky asked.

'Maybe . . .' Ben coughed to clear his throat. 'Maybe they're going away.'

Now came a moaning of the ceiling beams. Plaster fell from above, fine as silt. We stared up with dread. A few bits trickled down on to Rocky's shoulder.

There came a terrible scrabbling sound. Claws grinding. *Digging.*

Ben walked backward down the aisle, retreating toward the freezer room a single slow-motion step at a time. Dezi limped after him. All I saw was their necks, the underbelly of their chins. My gaze shot north again. We couldn't take our eyes off the ceiling. We stayed still and quiet, as if that could make us disappear.

Kris whispered, 'Are they really gonna –'

A Hatchling crashed through the roof, shooting down in a shower of wood and plaster. He plummeted, positioned like a swooping hawk, claws leading the way. He landed directly on top of Kris, shredding him to pieces before his body even struck the floor. The Hatchling didn't land on a body. He landed in a pool of what the body used to be.

We all watched, stunned. The floor where Kris had been was a Cuisinart mess.

The Hatchling lifted his head, his mouth stained Joker red. The rest of his skin morphed into different shades matching the colorful labels on the shelves around him.

Then he leapt six yards, landing on top of Jenny White. It was like some awful checkers move. The Hatchling's sewage reek permeated the store. And the smell of torn-open flesh.

Another crash rent the ceiling behind Alex. Then a spot of roof gave way over in the dairy section. Another by the fruit bins. Rotten apples rolled across the tile every which way.

The Hatchlings rocketed down through the roof like bungee jumpers with the cords cut.

Ben screamed. It was too high-pitched to be called a yell – it was an out-and-out scream, shot through with the purest terror I'd ever heard. The sound sent a wash of pins and needles over my skin.

And got me moving.

I ran at the Hatchling feasting on Jenny and sank my baling hook into the top of his head. The hole smoked around the steel tip, the salt water doing its trick.

The Hatchling craned his head around toward me, his lips spread in a piercing cry. The force of his neck muscles was almost enough to wrench the hook from my hand. He tried to swipe at me, but I tugged the hook free and jumped back.

He fell on the floor, seizing.

Jenny had died as fast as Kris, her body unrecognizable except for the clotted mass of long brown hair.

I sprinted for Rocky and Eve in the next aisle.

As I rounded the endcap, Patrick hip-checked me out

of the way, sending me flying. I caught an upside-down view of him standing in the precise spot where I'd been an instant before, unloading the shotgun directly up into the ceiling.

The rock salt tore the plummeting Hatchling to pieces. Chunks of flesh and spatter rained down all around us. A glob hit my bare forearm, stinging my flesh before I shook it free.

I rolled on to my feet, came up behind Patrick.

'Thanks,' I said.

'Yup.'

We bolted around the corner and up the last aisle, where Rocky and Eve stood stunned and speechless. Past them at the end, Alex maintained a wide stance, her hockey stick raised.

A rotund female Hatchling had landed between her and the door to the freezer room. Alex stared past the Hatchling at Ben and Dezi on the far side.

The rest of the Hatchlings filled the store behind us, cutting off all other routes. But if we could get through this female, we could escape out the back.

'Distract her, and I'll hit her with the stick!' Alex shouted to Ben and Dezi.

Ben's chest heaved. He tried to step back but tripped over his shoes and fell. He got up, one hand held out, shaking. He gripped the stun gun.

'That won't work,' Alex said. 'Not on them.'

Ben's wild eyes found her. 'I'm sorry, Alex,' he said, his voice cracking.

He turned and ran for the freezer room.

'*Wait!*' Alex shouted. 'We need numbers! Get back here!'

Dezi followed Ben, slowed by his bad knee. As he hustled toward the freezer room, he favored one side so heavily that it looked like he was skipping.

The female ran after him. Her claws made a terrible grinding sound against the tile. Dezi tried to run faster. His bad knee folded beneath him. He staggered.

The female reached him.

We didn't see it so much as hear it.

Wet thrashing. Screams. Ripping skin.

Ben reached the plastic curtain. He paused, turned back to look at us. The strips cascaded down across his shoulders, rustling against his clothes. He looked directly at me and Patrick. His cheeks glistened with tears. His face shifted, something showing through the fear.

Something like remorse.

He vanished through the plastic curtain. The metal door behind it banged closed. A dead bolt slammed home.

He'd locked the Hatchlings in here. With us.

We could hear the others bulling through the store, closing in.

Alex came up behind the female and hammered her with the hockey stick. The female grunted and rolled off what was left of Dezi. Alex pressed the blade to her throat and leaned all her weight on to it.

A sizzle as the salt coating scorched through the Hatchling's flesh. The salamander-orange head nodded to one side, nearly severed. Alex followed up with a slap shot that sent the head tumbling through the air, denting the metal door on impact.

Patrick and I corralled Rocky and Eve, rushing them toward Alex and the freezer room beyond. Alex kicked the female's body aside, clearing the aisle for us, and started for the plastic curtain.

We got only a few steps when two Hatchlings skidded into sight around the aisle's end. They lost their footing, smashing into the shelves of rotten milk. As they popped back on to their feet, their skin transformed from milk white to its native orange. They were quickly joined by a third.

We spun around to run to the front of the store. It was clear. I coughed out a single note of relief.

As we started racing toward freedom, Patrick pulled up first, spreading an arm to hold us back.

'*Wait,*' he said.

He was staring intently at the displays before the cash registers.

Sure enough, they blurred and came to life, bipedal forms peeling away from their backdrops.

As the camouflage faded, four Hatchlings resolved into 3-D. We'd nearly sprinted right into them.

Shoulder to shoulder, they started toward us.

The three Hatchlings behind us advanced as well.

The noose, tightening fast.

**ENTRY 38**      Patrick fired at the group of four Hatchlings. Rock salt glanced off their flesh, leaving smoking spots of black. The Hatchlings hissed at us but didn't drop.

'Why isn't it working?' Rocky said.

'We're not close enough to break skin,' Patrick said.

'What do we do?'

Patrick shrugged and *shuck-shucked* the shotgun. 'Let them get closer.'

'I'm not wild about that idea,' Alex said.

We backed into one another, an outward-facing huddle. The aisle sign swayed overhead: MILK & DAIRY.

An idea swirled around the panic typhoon in my head, and finally I managed to grab hold of it.

I broke apart from the others, setting my shoulder blades against the glass-fronted refrigerator units. 'Hold them off,' I said. 'I have a plan.'

'What are you doing, Chance?' Eve shouted. 'Get back here!'

I launched off the glass doors and hurled myself into the rise of shelves opposite. Loaves of bread spilled down, pummeling my head. But I felt the base of the unit give a bit.

I drew back and hurtled at the bakery shelves again. They tilted up. I shoved into them like a football player driving into a workout sled.

The shelves toppled.

Not the whole aisle of course, just that section.

It crashed into Condiments & Sauces.

'Follow me!' I yelled, vaulting a raft of tumbling baguettes, scaling the rise even as it fell.

Patrick got off a blast in either direction, driving back the Hatchlings a few steps. My brother and the other kids clambered after me.

I was hoping the units would topple like dominoes across the store, but I wasn't that lucky. The bread unit landed at an angle a few feet above the floor, propped against a rack of Tabasco sauce. I threw myself into the shelves of Tabasco, leading with my shoulder. The rack was already wobbly from the impact, and I sent it over the tipping point.

It hammered through into Drinks & Snacks. I landed painfully on top of the metal shelves. Two-liters of Coke battered my shoulders.

Behind me I heard screaming and shotgun blasts. As I shoved myself up on to all fours, Rocky fell on me, knocking me over.

'Sorry!'

We fought to stand amid rolling cans of Sprite and Fanta. Together we leaned into the next unit. Alex was swearing loudly and prolifically.

The unit tipped up and back, up and back, a little more each time. Finally Rocky and I shoved it through into Dry Packaged Goods. The soda shelves smacked into a wall of Campbell's soup cans, the weight of which uprooted their housing unit immediately, sending us spilling into – at last – Baking Supplies.

I skidded out atop a wash of soup cans, somehow staying upright as I freestyle roller-skated my way to the edge of the mess. I leapt clear from the fallen items on to a patch of exposed tile and bolted up the aisle, my eyes scanning the shelves.

'– *please be here please be here please* –'

From behind me: *Boom*. Screech. *Boom-boom*. Screech.

'Chance!' Alex screamed. 'I hope you know what the hell you're doing!'

Finally I spotted it near the end of the aisle. I grabbed the sturdy bag off the shelf, hugging it to my chest.

I sensed a presence at my side.

A Hatchling towered over me.

He'd circled, coming up the row from the rear of the store.

I struggled to open the bag, but it was fastened tight. Cheery red letters jumped out at me: CHILDPROOF SEAL!

I swore.

The Hatchling reared back. His claws flashed.

It was survival instinct. A flinch. Holding up my arms to protect my face from the death blow. Only my hands weren't empty.

They were holding the bag of table salt.

It exploded on impact, covering the Hatchling in a cloud of white crystals. His front half melted, a landslide of orange flesh. His head corkscrewed back on his neck, and he howled.

I dug my boot deep into the mound of spilled salt and kicked as hard as I could. The steel-reinforced toe of my boot, crusted with salt, hammered him right between the legs.

Whatever noise he was making ratcheted up another level.

His body liquefied in patches. He fell on to the tiles, which were coated with more salt. He squirmed, his flesh sticking to the floor and pulling away from his bones like taffy.

I grabbed an armload of bags and ran past Rocky toward the others. 'Grab more!' I shouted, and he scrambled off to do so.

Eve lost her footing on the soup cans and fell hard on to her back. A Hatchling pounced, landing right on top of her on all fours. His head cocked, teeth bared.

I dropped the salt bags except for one, which I swung like a baseball bat into the side of the Hatchling's head. The bag broke open, the flesh dissolving off his skull instantaneously beneath the onslaught of salt. Eve screamed, her hands flailing. Droplets of mucus fell on her, acid eating through her clothes.

I grabbed her wrist and yanked her out from beneath the Hatchling just before he collapsed.

Patrick and Alex backed into me, Patrick firing into the breach again. The five remaining Hatchlings darted over the cascade of fallen shelves, spreading out, readying for an attack. Their skin changed constantly in swirling patterns, picking up the bright colors of the cans and bottles all around them.

'I gotta reload,' Patrick said.

'Fall back here.' I grabbed his sleeve and shoved him into Alex, sending both of them tumbling off the cans into the clear part of the aisle.

Rocky was running back and forth with salt bags,

holding them over his head and flinging them down into the floor. He'd built up a nice line of salt on one side. Eve had already caught on, and she was knocking more bags off the shelf on the other side and stomping on them, splitting them open.

We huddled within the ring of salt. Patrick dropped to a knee, reloading the shotgun as the Hatchlings advanced. The first two hit the salt perimeter at the same time. Their legs buckled, their knees striking the thicker spill, and then they were belly down in the granules, thrashing and screeching.

Another tried the same from the other side of the aisle, liquefying into the floor. Rocky kicked up a spray of white, catching the one behind him as he readied for a leap. As the Hatchling staggered, Eve grabbed up a fistful of salt and hurled it into his eyes. He fell back, his claws tearing at his brow and cheeks, shredding through his own flesh until all that remained was a concave face. He fell back against a rack of Doritos and stayed there, propped up and lifeless.

Alex whipped her head around. 'There were ten. Where's the last —'

A clang overhead jerked us upright. A Hatchling leapt clear over the aisle, banging into the BAKING SUPPLIES sign overhead.

We dove in opposite directions. We must have looked like a human grenade exploding all over the place. But we cleared the way.

Everyone except Patrick.

He wasn't looking up. He was still on one knee, loading the shotgun.

'Patrick!' I yelled as the Hatchling pounded down on the tile right before him.

The Hatchling bent over Patrick, mucus dripping off his torso, tapping the tips of Patrick's front boot.

Patrick remained calmly on his knee, the shotgun propped before him, its butt resting on the tile. His head still lowered, his face invisible beneath the brim of his cowboy hat. He didn't have a chance.

I braced myself to watch my brother die.

The Hatchling flicked its claws and dove in.

*Boom!*

The Hatchling went airborne, flying backward, a hole torn clear through his chest. He whapped the floor a good six feet away.

Patrick hadn't moved. He hadn't even looked up.

He'd simply hooked his thumb inside the trigger guard and applied five pounds of trigger pressure.

Patrick stood up, adjusted his hat. 'Like I said. Just have to let them get closer.' He turned to face us. 'What are you waiting for? We got work to do.'

He cycled the shotgun one-handed and started for the front gate, already digging the key from his pocket.

**ENTRY 39**     The survivors gathered in a solemn semicircle at the base of the bleachers. Never had I heard it so quiet.

Ben sat midway up on one side, me, Patrick, and Alex on the other.

Dr Chatterjee perched on the top bench, staring down imperiously like a judge. Which was appropriate, given what we were dealing with.

When we'd first strolled in, Ben had blanched. But he'd swallowed his astonishment quickly, regaining his usual bluster. After the initial happy surprise of our return, everyone had looked past us at the empty doorway, the mood turning.

Ten of us had left the school. Only seven had walked back in.

No one wanted a replay of the Patrick-and-Ben brawl, so at least fifteen kids had gotten between us and Ben, steering us to opposite ends of the gym until tempers cooled.

Once everyone had settled, Dr Chatterjee had called for a meeting. I had to say, even though we had no procedures in place for a court hearing-type thing, he was doing a pretty good job.

'You lied in your recounting of what happened at the grocery store,' Chatterjee said.

'I didn't lie.' Ben crossed his arms, the sleeves pulling tight across his biceps. 'I said they were stuck in the grocery store.'

'You didn't say you were the one who got us stuck in there,' Alex said.

'How 'bout Dezi?' Ben said. 'He's dead because of the sprained knee Chance gave him –'

'That's irrelevant and off topic,' Chatterjee said. He looked at me. 'And no, it's not Chance's fault that he defended himself when attacked.' When his spectacles swiveled to Ben, the moonlight turned them into glinting circles. 'But the deaths of Kris Keuser and Jenny White . . .' Here he paused. He rasped a hand across his stubble, regaining his composure. 'Those children died because of your actions.'

'No,' Ben said. 'They died because Hatchlings ate them. Let's not lose sight of who the enemy is here.'

'You ran away.'

'Okay, okay.' Ben spread his arms wide. 'You say you represent the law. Is it a legal obligation to rescue someone? In the world how it used to be, I mean. Would you punish someone for *not* running into a burning building?'

'No,' Alex said. 'You'd just think he was a –'

'You didn't just *not help*,' I said. 'You locked us in.'

'You guys were surrounded,' Ben said. 'I thought you were dead. I was protecting myself and my crew. Like in a submarine when you have to close a hatch, cut your losses when a cabin floods.'

'You didn't help because it was *us*,' I said. 'If it was one of your guys, you never would have locked us in.'

'Again, irrelevant. A mom can choose to risk her life for her own baby. That doesn't mean she has to for any

257

random person who might be in danger. No judge would sentence her for that.'

Chatterjee nodded morosely. 'Ben is right,' he said.

Patrick stood up. Everyone in the gym stiffened in anticipation. It didn't take much from Patrick to draw a reaction.

Chatterjee gestured for him to sit down. Patrick held a few beats and then lowered himself back on to the bench.

'A person *wouldn't* be punished for not aiding someone.' Chatterjee glared at Ben. 'But your cowardly actions are not befitting a head of security. You are relieved of your position. You are no longer entitled to stand guard or go on lookout duty.'

An expression flickered across Ben's face so fast you'd miss it if you blinked. It held a kind of anger that's hard to put into words. But then he smoothed out his features into a mask of acceptance.

Patrick said, 'It's not enough.'

Dr Chatterjee said, 'Patrick –'

'We should put him out,' Patrick said. 'He got Kris and Jenny killed. He's not safe to have as a part of us anymore.'

'My ruling is final.'

'Can we take a vote?' Alex said.

Chatterjee pondered this for a moment. Then gave a sad nod. 'All in favor of casting Ben Braaten out of the community?'

A bunch of hands shot up. Chatterjee tallied them mentally. It was too close to count, and from our vantage on the bleachers we couldn't see everyone anyway.

Chatterjee said, 'All those in favor of Mr Braaten's remaining?'

Another set of arms rose. Chatterjee scanned the room, his lips moving as he counted. Then he said, 'It's a tie.'

Ben cleared his throat. 'I haven't voted yet,' he said, and put up his hand.

Patrick stood up, and this time no one told him to sit down.

'Very well,' Chatterjee said to Ben. 'You'll have to turn over your stun gun now.'

That same expression moved across Ben's face, as fast as the flick of a snake's tongue. But he managed a contrite nod. Still, he made no move to give up his gun.

'Do you want to obey, or do you want to leave the community?' Chatterjee said.

Ben smiled, the scars of his face moving into alignment. 'No way I'm risking it out there.'

'Your gun, Mr Braaten.'

Ben pulled the stun gun out from his waistband. Gazed down at it almost lovingly.

Chatterjee said, 'Eve?'

Eve rose from her chair by the supply station, climbed up the bleachers toward Ben, and held out her hand.

For a moment Ben ignored her. He kept staring at his stun gun. Then he lowered his head and offered it up. It was like he couldn't stand to see her take it from him.

Eve brought it down to the storage room and put it away. The congregation broke up.

Ben looked across at Patrick and gave a smart-ass little smirk. Patrick started for him furiously, but I grabbed his arm.

'Don't get distracted,' I whispered. 'Remember what we gotta do tomorrow.' Patrick started to pull away from me, but I tightened my grip. 'We've got bigger concerns.'

His gaze caught on Alex over on her bed, taping her fingers in preparation for the mission. He pulled his arm free, took a step away from Ben, and headed down the bleachers.

I knew what had stopped him. He was thinking about Alex's birthday, same as I was.

Seventeen days away.

**ENTRY 40**    Patrick, Alex, and I left around noon, giving ourselves plenty of time to get to Stone Spread. We'd have to travel with extreme caution in the daylight. After retrieving the Mustang from the woods, we'd circumvented town, taking back roads until we hit the highway. Then we blazed west across the plains, veering around the occasional abandoned car. We didn't see a soul. Or anything without a soul.

I sat in the back, the hot breeze blowing across my face. I couldn't remember the last time I'd ridden in a car during the day.

We hadn't spoken for the past half hour. The implications of what we were heading to do were so vast and complicated that none of us knew what to say. My thoughts returned to my parents.

Scents came to me first: Lilac perfume. English Leather. That lemon soap Mom used to wash dishes. Dad's baby-back ribs.

I thought of my first memory, a view from a bucket swing, sunbeams breaking through tree branches and my chubby hand reaching to catch them. Then others cascaded through my mind. Patrick behind me, teaching me how to swing a Wiffle-ball bat. My first school picture, the mustached photographer adjusting my shirt collar. Swaying on a hammock with Alex, naming the constellations, her bare arm pressed against mine. Uncle Jim helping me deliver my first litter of ridgebacks. Aunt Sue-Anne lying next to me in bed, reading me *The Adventures of Tom Sawyer.* Patrick teaching me how to drive. Alex: the Kiss.

It occurred to me that my life was flashing before my eyes. Considering where we were going, that made sense, but the realization only packed mass on to the lead ball weighing down my chest. I looked at Patrick's profile. He gripped the steering wheel tight with one hand, and his jaw was shifting like it did when he was thinking. I knew he was stewing in his thoughts just like I was.

The signs documented Stone Spread's approach: 127 MILES.

113 MILES.

97 MILES.

Patrick screeched over to the side of the road. Dust clouded across the windshield and then drifted away. He squeezed the wheel with both hands now. Alex and I were looking at him. He was never like this. I didn't know what was wrong.

He said calmly, 'I need to talk to my brother.'

And then he climbed out and walked several paces into the brush at the side of the road.

Alex and I looked at each other. She said, 'Go on, then.'

I got out and walked over to where Patrick was standing, his hands on his hips, staring at the horizon. His hair was matted down with sweat beneath his black cowboy hat. I stood next to him for a while, looking where he looked, trying to see what he saw, but there was nothing out there.

When he finally turned to me, his eyes were moist. I thought maybe he might cry, but then I remembered that Patrick didn't cry. Did he?

He said, 'We will get out there and we will do what needs to be done and save Alex and everyone else, but . . .'

I tried to swallow, but my mouth was too dry. It was hard to look at him, yet I couldn't look away. Inside, I felt like I was free-falling.

Patrick said, 'Remember when you told the dogs that their most important job was to protect their brother?'

I found my voice. 'It is. That's what we've always said.'

'I'm sorry I couldn't protect you from this,' he said. 'And . . . for me . . . it's more than just that. You're more than a little brother to me.'

'What do you mean?'

'I mean – I raised you.' His voice cracked, and I thought that if he started crying, I might die. 'I raised you.'

He shot me a quick look. In his eyes I saw the kind of unconditional love that you hear moms talk about on the morning talk shows.

Before I could respond, he turned and walked back to the Mustang.

Weapons in hand, we stood on the specified coordinates on the battered-flat plain past the beat-down stables. It looked like what it was – a spot in the middle of nowhere.

Wide-open sight lines all around made for easy surveillance. We'd spot anyone coming.

The Mustang was parked behind us. But not too far behind us.

The black helmet swung by my side. I'd brought it in case the Rebels didn't show and tried to contact us again.

Dusk was still a ways off, the sun a rich shade of orange behind a heap of fluffy clouds. We weren't really sure what we were waiting for. But we waited just the same. The Rebels were late. Late enough so I was starting to worry that something was wrong. They didn't strike me as imprecise.

Alex spoke, pulling me from my concerns.

'So you boys are gonna get your serum shots,' she said. 'And then what? You just explode right here?'

'I'm guessing they'll tell us to get to a more populated area,' I said. 'If we disperse the serum out here, the only things it'll affect are the groundhogs.'

'Not if it's carried through the air,' Alex said. 'Look at the Dusting. That wrapped around the entire globe in no time.'

'I hadn't thought of that. I figured we'd at least have more time to, you know . . .' My sentence trailed off. Even the air felt heavy.

Alex swallowed hard, seemed to set aside her sadness. She cocked her head at me. 'Play foosball?' she said.

I grinned. 'Work out a synchronized-swimming routine.'

'Learn how to bake soufflés.'

We were cracking up now, but Patrick wasn't. He was steadily scanning the horizon, squinting against the setting sun.

'Throw ceramic teapots,' I said.

Alex: 'Riverdance.'

Me: 'Become a YouTube star.'

She laughed, smacking my shoulder. 'Overcome my fear of clowns.'

Me: 'Play Mozart on water glasses.'

Alex: 'Cure sleep apnea.'

Me: 'Take up competitive dog grooming.'

Patrick lifted his shotgun. 'Say good-bye.'

We both turned to him, the smiles freezing on our faces.

'What?' I said.

He pointed up in the sky.

A tiny flame, no bigger than a thumbnail. It grew to a silver dollar. Now we heard it, the rush of air. And then the boom of the sound barrier breaking, only carrying to us now.

A meteor.

Of course.

It rocketed closer. We took a few nervous steps back. It didn't slow. It was the size of a refrigerator. A VW Bug.

It zoomed in, pushing a wave of heat before it.

It was gonna pancake us right here on these to-the-thirteenth-decimal-place coordinates.

The helmet slipped from my fingers and hit the dirt with a thud.

'Um,' I said. 'We might want to —'

And then it was on us, the roar drowning out anything I might have said. We bolted to the side, Patrick jostling us in front of him. At the last minute, we dove and felt the heft of the massive object hurtling behind us.

The earth shook. We landed in the dust, the ground vibrating beneath us so hard it jogged my vision. Turning, we saw the giant meteor plow through the barren plain, cleaving the unforgiving ground, shoving up furrows on either side. It missed the Mustang, but the swell of its wake pushed the car up into a thirty-degree tilt.

The meteor traveled a good half mile, sinking to its midway point, throwing off black smoke.

We were on our feet sprinting for it, waving our hands in front of us to clear the air.

Patrick reached it first.

A familiar popping sound drifted through the smoke and then the rumble of the meteor as it slowly hinged open, shoving earth aside.

At last the dark fumes cleared enough for us to see.

A hole the size of a trash-can lid was lasered straight through the meteor. A torpedo blast? Sunlight shone through it. The cockpit was as scorched as the inside of a chimney. A monitor showing our coordinates gave a dying fizzle and went blank. Charred screens, charred seatlike pods, charred control panels.

And two corpses, as black as midnight, still belted in place. Their suits were heat-split, the helmets crushed inward.

The last two Rebels.

Shot down.

It was impossible to tell which was the one we'd met at our house a few weeks back.

The Rebel on the left had a vial the size of a tennis can clamped in his armored glove. Smoke poured out the top.

Patrick skidded down the embankment toward the meteor, careful not to touch the sizzling exterior. He poked at the vial with the tip of his shotgun, and it crumbled into ash. Inside were two blackened test tubes, the glass cracked and singed. The contents had mostly evaporated. Whatever was left was reduced to useless black puddles.

The serum shots for me and Patrick.

The burned residue of the last hope of mankind.

**ENTRY 41**          JoJo stirred in her bed at the commotion across the basketball floor. It was still early in the night, not much past eight, but necessity had put most of the kids on an early schedule that mimicked the sun's rise and fall.

She sat up and cast a look at her brother on the neighboring bed. Rocky was in deep sleep, each raspy breath just short of a snore. Chance, Patrick, and Alex were still gone on their super-secret mission. Groggily, she sourced the noise. Across the gym Ben was talking to Dr Chatterjee intently.

JoJo slid off her bed and snuck across the floor toward them.

'– got a problem outside,' Ben was saying.

She crept closer, crawling beneath Marina Mendez's bed.

'I could not have been more explicit that you were not to be on lookout duty, Mr Braaten.'

'I was going to take a leak. I just happened to glance out the window and notice it.'

'What?'

'It's something new.' Ben lowered his voice even more. 'I don't want to talk in front of the kids. It'll freak them the hell out.'

'Very well,' Dr Chatterjee said, adjusting his leg braces and standing up. 'Then let's go.'

As they padded across the court to the double doors,

JoJo squirmed out from beneath Marina's bed and snuck after them.

Ben and Chatterjee walked quietly across the school's front lawn, heading for the teachers' parking lot. They reached the gate, and Ben withdrew a giant key ring from his pocket, picking out the right key for the padlock.

Dr Chatterjee whispered, 'You're not supposed to have that anymore. You'll turn it over as soon as –'

Ben whispered, '*Sshhh.*'

He released the lock and held the gate open. Chatterjee stared into the inky darkness for a moment and then walked forward in his unsteady gait.

Ben kept at his side, moving along the lawn that framed the side parking lot. There was an odd taste on the breeze. Something foul.

Ben crouched. 'Here.'

Chatterjee whispered, 'What?'

Ben pointed. The lawn was marked with brown dead spots.

Chatterjee blinked down at them.

Footsteps.

It took some doing given his condition, but Chatterjee squatted and touched a trembling finger to the dead grass. Then he shook his hand as if something had stung his skin. He wiped his finger on his trousers.

As he moved to rise, Ben stepped into him, brushing him with the edge of his leg. Unable to react quickly with his orthotics, Chatterjee toppled over off the curb. He landed on the asphalt at the edge of the parking lot, skinning his hands. His glasses flew off.

Flat on his stomach, Chatterjee groped for them.

'Oops,' Ben whispered. 'Sorry. Let me help you.'

His wide boot crunched down on Chatterjee's spectacles, smashing them.

Ben leaned over the fallen teacher. 'It's dangerous out here,' he whispered. 'We'd better get back.'

He started walking away.

Chatterjee managed to shove himself up on to his legs. 'Mr Braaten, you get back here.'

'You might want to be quiet,' Ben said, breezing toward the gate.

'I can't keep up,' Chatterjee said, waving his hands blindly in front of him. 'Please . . . Ben . . .'

He tripped over the curb and spilled on to the grass. Grabbing his shoulder, he struggled back up to his knees. He blinked rapidly at the fuzzy night.

There was no sound save the faint whistle of the wind and a stillness claiming the air. The slightest crunch of earth compressing drew his attention to the wall of the school by the shrubs. A foot setting down?

The brick rise was motionless, and then it wasn't.

It seemed to wobble for a moment, squirming like something living. And then a shape manifested right out of the bricks.

It stood over him, an orange smear against the darkness.

A rancid odor filled the air.

Over toward the school, the gate clinked open and then shut.

The blurry form swiveled to note the sound and then seemed to orient back toward Chatterjee.

Chatterjee's shirt hung about his thin frame, now little more than a sweaty rag. His shoulders bowed with defeat.

And then they straightened.

Biting his lower lip, he forced himself up on to one leg and then the other.

He glared at whatever was before him. 'This way, then,' he said to it. 'Follow me.'

He turned.

And ran *away* from the school.

He banged off the bumper of a Volvo, the force of the impact knocking him into another parked car.

*Whump!*

The Hatchling leapt on to the Volvo's roof, which crumpled under the weight.

Chatterjee ran for the street, putting as much distance as possible between the Hatchling and the children hidden inside the gym. The Hatchling bounded after him.

*Whump!*

Another car roof divoted beyond recognition.

Chatterjee made it through the last row of parked cars.

*Whump!*

The last car in the row.

There was nowhere else for Chatterjee to hide. And no time to run for cover.

He turned to face the blurry form. Drew himself erect. 'All right, then,' he said again.

It jumped.


From her hiding place inside the hedge against the wall of the school, JoJo pressed her hands over her mouth to keep from whimpering. Ben stood only about ten yards away, his hand gripping the chain-link of the gate, watching.

The sounds of moist thrashing lessened.

JoJo watched Ben reach for the padlock. He swung the base around, aligning it with the shackle. And then he closed it.

It gave off the faintest click.

Over in the street, the Hatchling paused from his feasting. His head whipped around. He straightened up on to his legs over Dr Chatterjee's remains. A beard of scarlet froth dangled from his chin.

His large pupils pierced the night. Staring – it seemed – directly at Ben. But there was no way he could spot Ben. Not at this distance in the darkness.

There was a moment of perfect stillness, broken only by the crickets.

Ben's head bobbed a bit as he started breathing heavily. Then it seemed that something gave way inside him.

He turned and ran for the school's front door.

*That* the Hatchling saw.

The Hatchling sprang off Chatterjee. A few mighty leaps carried him across the parking lot to the fence. And then he vaulted clear over the gate, landing right in front of the bush in which JoJo was hiding.

His legs were close enough that she could have reached out of the hedge and poked his calf. The stink was overwhelming.

The front door of the school creaked open. JoJo could hear Ben plowing his way up the corridor inside, screaming at Mikey to split with him out the back.

JoJo expected the Hatchling to charge after him.

But instead it stayed there.

Perhaps it sensed her?

She mashed her hands even tighter over her mouth.

The Hatchling leaned forward and emitted a high-pitched whistle, steam misting all around his neck. The noise went on and on.

JoJo thought her eardrums might burst.

When at last the screech ended, even the crickets had been stunned into silence.

There was nothing except for the reek of the Hatchling and a ringing in JoJo's ears.

And then, in the distance, a faint ruckus.

A trash can knocked over. A car alarm sounded. The scrabble of claws on roof shingles.

They came pouring into sight from all directions. Up the streets, over bushes, streaming across rooftops.

Dozens and dozens of Hatchlings.

They bounded for the high school, not even slowing at the fence line. Instead they sprang over it like a plague of frogs.

The wall of the school vibrated behind JoJo. She heard smashing windows. Doors banging open.

And then the screams of the kids as the massacre began.

**ENTRY 42**     Patrick, Alex, and I had barely spoken for the entire drive back to the high school. We left the Mustang at the outskirts of town past the Piggly Wiggly. We entered the back fields through a gate over by the football stadium; Patrick had replaced the combination lock on it himself before we'd left. We edged around the outside of the stadium and slanted toward the school. The math-and-science wing lay ahead, a dark block in the night.

No Rebels were coming to save us. The helmet – the last lifeline we'd had – was buried beneath the dirt in Stone Spread. Nobody was left to help us.

'Look at the bright side,' Alex said. 'Now you don't have to blow yourselves up.'

Neither Patrick nor I laughed. It wasn't just that humanity's last chance at survival had been yanked away from us. It was that all hope had been destroyed, too.

Patrick and I had immunity from the spores, sure. That would let us scrape by for a few more months, maybe a few years if we were lucky. But at some point a Hatchling would catch up to us, sink his claws into our flesh, and then we'd be meat the same as everyone else. And in the meantime we had nothing to look forward to except watching all our friends grow older, each day bringing them closer to an eighteenth birthday that would snatch the life away from them. As for Alex – what would the world be like when we lost her?

My head was down, so I didn't even notice that Alex and Patrick had stopped walking until Alex called out to me.

'Chance? *Chance?*'

Something sounded very wrong with her voice.

I halted and looked up.

We were close enough now to see the school.

Every window in the math-and-science wing was shattered. The rear classroom doors flapped in the breeze.

My breath left me until there was nothing but a dull ache in my chest. The damage was immeasurable. I don't know how I knew that everyone was gone, but the building emanated lifelessness.

We moved closer. I neared a shattered window in Chatterjee's classroom. A dab of orange mucus clung to the tip of a shard.

I peered inside through the classroom doorway into the hall beyond.

There were parts on the floor. Of what I wasn't sure.

Shotgun barrel snugged to his cheek, Patrick drifted inside. Alex and I followed.

The hall looked like something from a horror movie. Streaks on the walls – some vibrant red, some deep crimson.

A discarded baseball cap. A partially filled pant leg. In a puddle of blood, a snapped-off claw lay shimmering, a dagger of amber.

We moved on numb legs down the corridor toward the gym. The double doors were laid wide, a scarlet handprint spotting one in the dead center. My chest heaved. Oxygen was hard to find.

As we drew close to the doorway, the inside of the gym crept slowly into view. Half of the beds were knocked over. Mattresses flung aside. Sheets puddled on the slick floor-boards. The freestanding whiteboard we used to keep track of everyone was split in half, the columns of names smudged. A doll missing an arm. A shattered flashlight. Someone's asthma inhaler. A few feathers from torn pillows still circled the air lazily – it hadn't ended that long ago.

Alex made a noise deep in her throat, backing away from the door. We flanked her in the hallway, Alex still facing the gym, Patrick and I aiming the other direction. Patrick kept the shotgun butt pressed to his shoulder, but the baling hooks swung limply at my sides. I couldn't seem to muster the strength to lift my arms.

We heard a creak above us.

We halted.

Tilted our heads up.

A panel in the drop ceiling slid back.

Bunny's head fell through the gap, plopping down on to the floor in front of my boots.

Another creak, accompanied by some rustling. Then JoJo stuck her head through the space in the ceiling.

When I let out my breath, it made a choking noise.

I held up my arms.

She slid out and fell into them.

She clamped on to me so tightly that my ribs hurt. I held her, her hair sticky against my cheek.

'Junebug,' I said. 'Did anyone else make it?'

She pointed at the ceiling.

A pair of skinny legs shot over the edge, dangling down. And then Rocky scooted into sight, swinging from his hands. He dropped on to the floor, landing on one leg, favoring a badly swollen ankle.

Eve crawled into sight next.

I had my hands full with JoJo so Patrick helped her down. Her sweater was torn right in half in the back, a cut bleeding through the fabric. Grease smudged her face. She came over to me and JoJo and put her arms around us both.

We stayed like that for a moment, breathing.

Rocky said, 'Ben and Mikey got away, I think.'

'Anyone else?' Alex asked.

Rocky shook his head.

'Small and sneaky beats big and strong,' JoJo said. 'I was in the hedge out front.'

'I was at the supply store,' Eve said. 'Rocky was keeping me company. When they . . . invaded, I yanked him with me back into the closet and slammed the door. A bunch of stuff fell on us. That's probably what saved our lives when they checked.' Her next breath came as a shudder. 'The noises . . .'

I thought she was going to say more, but she didn't. Her eyes had a faraway look that I hardly recognized.

My back was starting to ache, so I set JoJo down. We stood there in a ring, unsure of where to go or what to do next. I saw us all there in the hall as if I were outside myself.

A ragged little circle of six.

The last children of Creek's Cause.

**ENTRY 43**     We sat spread out across the bleachers because we didn't know where else to go. The sight before us was horrid. Every time you looked, you saw something new. A trail of dark splotches dribbling off into one corner. A wide smudge across the free-throw line where someone had been dragged. Maria Mendez's beanie cap along with a hank of her shiny black hair.

Alex had fetched a bag of ice from the cafeteria for Rocky, and he pressed it to his foot, which he kept elevated on the bench beside him. The swelling was colorful and bad — the bulge above the ankle was as big as a softball.

After a time Eve got up and walked over to the storage room. She dug a mop and bucket from the mess. Somehow the rolling bucket had stayed upright.

She wheeled it over to the edge of the basketball court. Slapped the wet mop on to the floorboards. Started scrubbing. We watched her. After a while it was clear that she was just smearing blood around.

It was no use.

But she kept on, her motions growing more and more furious.

I got off the bleachers and walked over to her. I touched her arm, and she swung away from me angrily and kept scrubbing.

Her breaths came fast and hard. She slopped the mop around so fiercely that it was like she was trying to dig through the floorboards.

I stepped around in front of her. I took her arm more gently. This time she let me. I pried the mop handle from her grip.

She sat on the floor and wept.

I sat with her and took her in my arms, and she sobbed like I'd never heard a person sob. An awful, torn-open, animal wail. She wasn't even worrying about staying quiet.

She couldn't.

Six beds.

We'd cleared space on the center circle of the basketball court. Our beds radiated out from the middle like the petals of a flower.

A breeze poured through the shattered casement windows. We lay there, staring up at the sports banners fluttering overhead.

I held my baling hooks crossed over my chest.

Alex twirled her hockey stick.

Patrick kept his shotgun alongside him – so still you might've thought he was inside a coffin waiting to be lowered into the ground.

Eve's breathing still hitched in her chest at intervals, the aftermath of her crying jag.

JoJo hugged Bunny.

Rocky kept the bag of ice wrapped around his ankle. He plucked out a strand of his hair and then another.

We listened to the deep, endless black of night.

**ENTRY 44**    For a solid week, we drifted.

It's amazing how pointless everything is without a clear goal. You'd think that would be self-explanatory, but still, it was surprising how mired we were in our own weariness.

As conflicted as Patrick and I were about being human bombs, at least that had lent some purpose to our existence.

Now we were just holed up, waiting to die.

We avoided one another. I suppose we were each mourning in our own way. And there was so much to mourn. Dr Chatterjee. The Mendez twins. Even the way of life we'd resurrected here for a brief stretch of time.

You'd be surprised how many things you can find in the wreckage of a massacre that bring you up short. One afternoon I came upon Eve in the hall holding a partially used pillar candle and sobbing. I didn't know what it meant to her, and I didn't want to intrude on her private grief to ask. Instead I silently retreated around the corner. Later that day I found one of Dr Chatterjee's shirts beneath an upturned mattress. It was still folded neatly. I lowered the mattress back over it. It was too hard to look at.

On the seventh day, Alex finally summoned the focus to unearth the television from where it had fallen in the groove behind the lowest bench of the bleachers. A hairline crack split the screen diagonally, but by some miracle the set still powered on when she plugged it into the battery. She kneeled there before it, checking deserted channels, praying to a long-dead God.

Rocky iced his ankle twice a day. The swelling was coming down, but it'd be another week yet before he could walk on it without pain. Though we were cautious, creeping around the halls like mice, we barely stood watch. There wasn't much point. The Hatchlings had already berserked their way through the school, and if they decided to come back for seconds, there wasn't a whole lot we could do about it anyway.

No one talked about the countdown to Alex's death. But as the days clicked toward the one-week mark, there was no denying that it was the only thing we were thinking about. And hovering above that deadline, even greater than all the anguish and rage, was the knowledge that we were too stuck in our hopelessness to even spend her last days well.

As morning broke on Seven Days Left, we rolled listlessly out of bed. Alex laced her fingers together and cracked them over her head as she stretch-yawned. Her socks thumped down on the sticky floorboards.

I watched her trudge over to the TV for her morning dose of static.

Click.

*Kkkrrrr.*

Click.

*Kkkrrrr.*

Click.

For an instant a wobbly image caught on the screen.

I shot off my bed so fast I nearly slipped and went down. I ran over to Alex and stared at the TV.

The snow wavered and then cleared.

A hefty bearded man wearing a white lab coat stood in a room, the walls behind him dressed with plastic sheets. A shoved-to-the-side desk bore a symbol on the front.

'— transmission for . . . survivors to . . . possible solution for the situat —'

And it was gone.

The others were behind us now, tense with anticipation.

We clustered around the screen as Alex fiddled desperately with the rabbit ears.

'What was that?' Patrick asked.

She fussed with the antennae some more, then finally gave up, letting her hands slap to her sides with frustration. 'I don't know.'

'Great,' Rocky said, limping off a few steps. 'We finally see an adult — someone with a fix for the whole stupid deal — and now we don't know where to find him.'

'The desk,' I said, 'didn't it have some kind of logo on it?'

'I didn't see,' Alex said. 'It was gone before I could see.'

A voice floated over from behind us. 'I did.'

We turned to look. Eve shouldered between JoJo and Rocky, crouching by the screen. 'It said "SPU" in blue and gold.'

A stir rippled through me. Excitement and — for the first time in ages — hope. 'Stark Peak University,' I said.

'They have a news station?' Rocky asked.

'It wasn't a news station,' Eve said.

'How do you know?' JoJo asked.

'Because there was a department sign on the wall beneath the plastic sheets,' Eve said. 'You didn't see it?'

'What did it say?' I asked, my voice humming with eagerness.

Eve said, 'Department of Virology and Immunology.'

We jumped up and down and threw high fives.

'That means a cure!' JoJo said. 'We could get immunity like you guys. Anecdotes!'

'I think you mean *antidotes*,' Rocky said.

'Whatever.'

I turned to Patrick. 'We've got a week to get Alex there. Once she's safe —'

'We come back, grab everyone else.' Patrick was talking fast, as excited as I'd seen him. 'Rocky's ankle should be healed up by then. We can either bring the fix to him or him to the fix.'

I turned to everyone else. 'We'll get everyone taken care of.'

That's when I noticed that Eve wasn't celebrating along with the rest of us. She was standing to the side, her arms crossed as if she were hugging herself. Her face was pale, except for her cheeks, which were flushed.

'I'm so happy for you guys.' She mustered a smile that died on her face.

I looked at her, not understanding.

'It's my birthday today, Chance.'

The gym, filled with the noise of our celebration just seconds before, fell silent.

I looked over at the cracked, forgotten whiteboard, the names and birthdays smudged from the Hatchling attack.

It all made sense now. I remembered what Eve had said when I'd kissed her on the bleachers: *I wish I wasn't older than you.* I thought about seeing her crying in the hall the other day over that half-used candle and it hit me like a strike to the heart: It was the candle from the birthday cupcake she'd made for Leonora on her last day.

Patrick and Alex lowered their faces, but not before I saw in their eyes a match for what I was feeling. Thundering grief, yes. But also remorse. We'd been so busy looking out for ourselves this past month that none of us had been looking out for Eve. So many times we'd counted down the days to Alex's birthday, and never once had we considered Eve's.

And all the while Eve had been there for us. Watching our backs. Guarding the supplies. Protecting JoJo and Rocky.

Making cupcakes for other kids so they wouldn't feel so alone as they headed toward the brink.

'I'm sorry I won't make it to Stark Peak,' Eve said.

JoJo burst into tears and ran off behind the bleachers to hide.

For a time the silence was broken only by JoJo's sniffles carrying over to us.

'If I'd checked the TV earlier,' Alex said. 'If we'd gotten reception a few days ago. If –'

'Sometimes things happen for a reason,' Eve said.

How could she say that? She was talking about her *life*. This was Eve. My friend. After everything we'd been through, what 'reason' could justify this? My body filled with bitterness. It felt like I was *marinating* in it. I wanted to yell and cry and break things.

Eve started after JoJo.

'I'll get her,' I said.

'It's okay,' she said. 'I should talk to her.'

I followed Eve and finally caught up to her over by the bleachers. I took her by the arms and said, 'I'm sorry, Eve. If I could do anything . . .'

'You can,' she said.

'What?'

'I care about you, Chance. A lot.'

'I care about you, too.'

'I know you do. But not like I care about you.'

'Eve –'

'We don't have to pretend anymore, Chance. That's the one good thing. There's no time to lie. I know how you feel about Alex. She's lucky to have someone like you feel that way about her.'

My face was hot. I felt a tear sliding down my cheek. No matter how hard I tried, I couldn't stop it.

I said, 'I don't want you to die, Eve.' With the words came even more tears, rolling down my face, dripping off my chin. My throat locked up; I wasn't crying except from my eyes.

She hugged me, and I hugged her back. I couldn't believe she wouldn't be here tomorrow.

'When the time comes,' she said, 'I want you to do it. Do you think you can do that for me?'

I nodded. Got control of myself.

I said, 'I do.'


Eve sat in a chair before the paint sink while Alex brushed her hair. We'd gathered in the art room around noon. Eve knew she'd been born in the afternoon, but she didn't know the exact time, so we had to prepare early.

Patrick looked out the window, his jaw clenching now

and then. JoJo sat at Eve's feet and held her hands. Rocky kept limping off to fetch stuff for Eve that she didn't even ask for – a glass of water, stale cookies, a half-empty box of tissues.

And I sat watching Alex brush Eve's hair. Ben's stun gun rested on the desk in front of me. Eve had waded into the mess of the supply station, venturing one last time into her domain, and come out with Ben's prized possession.

Alex finished with Eve's hair, and Eve looked at herself in the mirror and smiled. 'I look nice,' she said.

We all agreed.

It felt like some perverse wedding preparation.

Eve stood up and smoothed her shirt. 'Merry Christmas,' she said.

It was. And we'd completely forgotten.

The rest of us had lost track of what dates meant. All we knew these days were countdowns. I hoped I'd be strong enough when the time came to give Eve the only gift she'd asked for.

'People say being born on Christmas sucks because you don't get as much stuff,' Eve said. 'But I always loved it. Everywhere you look, people are celebrating. And even though it's not about you, it's like you're part of everything and everything's part of you.' She looked at us. 'I hope you get to Stark Peak. I hope you guys have a lot to celebrate soon.'

The others went over and took turns hugging her. I couldn't watch, but I heard JoJo start to cry. I was gathering everything I had for what was to come.

Gathering the strength I *hadn't* had for Leonora.

As Alex shuffled out with JoJo and Rocky, Patrick

paused by my desk. 'Want me to wait in the hall in case you need me?'

I looked up at him.

'No,' I said. 'I got this.'

He left.

I took a deep breath. And then another.

Then I walked over to Eve.

The sun through the window caught her eyes perfectly, making the yellow flecks sparkle. She saw how I was looking at her and smiled shyly.

There was that dimple in her right cheek.

Her dark hair looked lush and pretty. She always managed to keep her bangs perfectly straight. I took her hands.

We might've been heading out on a date.

I kissed her.

Her mouth was soft. She closed her eyes. A moment later I did, too. I put everything I felt for her into the kiss, and when we parted, we both took a moment, our foreheads touching, our breath mingling.

Her eyes darted to the canvas tarp on the floor. 'Maybe I should, you know . . .'

She walked over and sat on it nervously, her legs folded to one side. I brought the stun gun with me and sat next to her.

I lowered her gently on to her back.

I lay beside her.

I kissed her.

I stroked her hair.

'Be gentle with me,' she said.

'I will.'

'And when it happens, don't wait. Everything's gonna be different. I don't want to feel any pain.'

'You won't feel any pain. I promise.'

We stared into each other's eyes.

Our noses, close enough to touch.

I didn't love her like I loved Alex, but I loved her just the same.

I don't know how long we lay together, but the light shifted in the room and soon enough a chill laced the air.

I knew it would happen an instant before it did.

She shuddered.

Her pupils dilated, expanding out until they filled the space between her eyelids.

I reached for the stun gun. I didn't want to wait for those beautiful eyes to turn to ash and disintegrate.

I placed the tip of the steel rod against her temple.

My hand was steady. Not from courage. From love.

I leaned forward and touched my lips to hers.

The compressed air hissed, and the rod smacked forward, the stun gun jerking in my hand.

She didn't feel any pain.

Just like I'd promised.

**ENTRY 45**     I found the others in Mr Tomasi's room. Patrick and Alex had set up the classroom as cozy as they could for Rocky and JoJo. A bunch of clean mattresses laid side to side. A shaggy rug from the principal's office. The bookcase stocked with supplies and food that wouldn't go bad. Above the bookcase one of the ceiling tiles was pushed back; in case of trouble, JoJo and Rocky could use the shelves like ladder rungs and disappear into the drop ceiling as before.

They'd said that they couldn't sleep in the gym without us, and what with all the carnage aftermath we couldn't blame them.

Rocky lay on a raft of repurposed couch cushions. His ankle, resting up on a chair, was surrounded with ice packs. Over the past few days, the bruise had faded from purple to a jaundiced yellow.

'Stay off that leg and heal up,' Patrick said. 'We need you good to go when we come back for you.'

'We hate staying here,' JoJo said. 'Everyone died here.'

'It's safer than out there,' Alex said. She nodded at Rocky. 'Especially on that ankle. This is still the best location. It's already been mapped by Hosts and ransacked by Hatchlings, so they have no reason to come back. You've got shelter, bathrooms – plus plenty of food since now it's just the two of you.'

JoJo held up the stuffed-animal head by the ears. 'Two of us plus Bunny.'

'Right,' Alex said. 'I forgot about Bunny.'

'Know why I set you up in this room?' Patrick asked.

Rocky shook his head.

Patrick pointed at the window that faced out across the front of the school.

'Lookout post?' Rocky asked.

Patrick said, 'So you'll see us when we come back.'

He walked over to the wall, shrugged into his back-pack, and picked up his shotgun. Alex grabbed a pack of her own and shoved her hockey stick in so it was sticking up the way she kept it, like a samurai sword. I grabbed my baling hooks, slid the nylon loops over my wrists. Then I made sure the stun gun was seated firmly in my waistband.

Having the stun gun there made me feel a little bit like Ben. Considering the road ahead, that wasn't all bad.

JoJo looked over at me and then looked away.

'Eve's gone, right?' she asked.

I nodded.

'We'll be okay without her.' Her lower lip wobbled a bit. 'We'll be okay without you, too.'

'You won't have to be,' I said. 'We'll be together again, JoJo.'

'The university's in Stark Peak,' she said. 'That's where you said the Drones and Queens were headed. And the Hatchlings. All of them. It's Harvester *headquarters*.'

I looked at my brother. He was leaning back against the wall, shotgun resting over his shoulder. The brim of his Stetson dipped, giving me the faintest encouragement.

'Yeah,' I said. 'We're going into the dragons' den.'

'Why?' JoJo said. 'Why do you have to?'

'Because, JoJo,' I said. 'That's where the treasure is.'

**ENTRY 46**     Four grueling days later, I crept out of the cover of forest on to the granite ledge on the steep back cliffs of Ponderosa Pass. Patrick and Alex clambered up next to me, and we peered over the brink. All the hiding and crawling and hiking had left us filthy. Dirt crammed beneath our fingernails. Sweat stains on our shirts. Dead pine needles clinging to our tattered clothes.

And we'd only finished the easy part.

We lay on our bellies on the rock slab and gazed across the foothills to the highway bisecting the flats. The sky-line of Stark Peak rose jaggedly at the horizon – the end of the road in more ways than one.

The ground was littered with the debris of the great exodus. Abandoned vehicles. Brush and trash shoved to the sides of the highway like dirty snow. And the bodies of Hosts everywhere in various stages of decomposition.

I can't tell you how many dead Hosts we saw on our way here, puddling in the gutters, staining the forest floor, melting in drivers' seats. Their expiration dates had passed. They'd served their purpose.

Now it was down to the Drones and Hatchlings.

And us.

The vast scene below was so still that any movement seemed more pronounced. A broken gas-station sign hanging from a wire, twirling in the breeze. Vultures gliding through the air and feasting on carrion. A few roving bands of Drones picking through the wreckage, searching the trunks of empty cars. An injured Hatchling squirming on the shoulder of the road, left behind to die. His leg was bent the wrong way, a dagger of bone shoved out through his thigh. Even so, he was trying to claw his way to Stark Peak.

The challenge was daunting. Before we reached the city, we had to hike down off the pass, through the foothills, and across the flats past Lakewood and Springfield and a half dozen other small towns.

All without being seen.

'How the hell are we gonna do this?' Alex said.

I stared at the injured Hatchling, the bands of Drones, the gas-station sign twisting in the wind.

Then I pulled out Ben's stun gun and turned to her and Patrick.

Alex held up her hand. 'Lemme guess,' she said. 'You've got a plan.'

It took us the better part of four hours to climb off the mountains, traverse the foothills, and hike to the base of the pass. Two more hours to make our way unseen up the highway, moving from wrecked car to wrecked car, crawling through culverts, scurrying along drainage ditches at the edge of the road.

The Drones were sparse in number, moving in groups of three and four. At one point, while we hid behind a stretch of guardrail, we watched them pull a kid from an overturned van in the distance. Before we could react, they marched him off somewhere out of sight. We could hear him crying for help for a few moments after they'd passed from view.

We had to take a moment to pull ourselves together after that.

We came upon the gas station from the rear. The jangle of the door to the convenience mart almost scared me out of my boots. We safed the interior and then took turns in the bathroom.

The water worked. A year ago I never would've thought that one day I'd consider washing my face a luxury. I straightened up over the sink, let the cold drops run down the sides of my neck, cutting through the grime.

When I closed my eyes, I pictured all those Hosts we'd seen dotting roads and woods and highways. Every adult we'd ever known was gone. I shook off the thought and finished cleaning my face. A sign on the wall thanked me for not putting gum or paper products in the urinal. Another reminded me to wash my hands before handling food. How life used to be – when clogged plumbing and proper hygiene were primary concerns.

I came back out to find Alex chewing on a hot dog from the steel roller grill.

She shot me a look. 'What? I figure it's impossible for these things to rot. Plus, when's the last time you had a hot dog?'

I shrugged and joined her. It wasn't half bad.

Patrick drank yellow Gatorade and chewed a Slim Jim, his eyes on the dirty window. We waited.

An actual tumbleweed blew off the highway and through the pump stations. A neon-green Kawasaki Ninja motorcycle leaned against the air pump. Pieces of cracked black armor were scattered across the parking lot, as if a Drone had been accidentally run over. Something burned on the horizon, sending up a tendril of gray smoke.

Patrick grabbed a bag of sunflower seeds, and for a time the only noise punctuating the silence was him spitting out the shells. He'd built up a pretty good mound at his boots when he straightened up and flicked his chin at the window. 'There.'

Three Drones worked their way through the hulls of the burned vehicles at the side of the freeway.

Alex cleared her throat dramatically, pretended to fluff up her choppy hair, and glanced over at me. 'I'm ready for my close-up.'

Then she stepped out through the front door. This one also was keyed to a chime alert. The noise rolled across the pumps and the parking lot. Over on the freeway, the Drones' shiny helmets swung around.

Alex stopped by the pump. Pretended to spot them. Then ran back inside.

They followed.

Patrick hid in the snack aisle. I ducked behind the counter.

After a minute the Drones charged in.

Alex backed to the opposite wall, in clear sight.

The Drones swept into the mart, breezing right past me.

Alex threw an arm across her forehead. 'I'm just a helpless Unnamed Girl here for the taking.'

The Drones halted, seemingly confused.

I stepped behind them, stun gun raised. I placed it at the base of the nearest Drone's helmet and fired, steel rod smacking through the armor. Black smoke burst out, hot against my arm.

Before the remaining Drones could react, I spun to the next one and pierced his suit, too, firing the rod into the back of his shoulder. He shot forward across the floor and skidded into Alex's shins, knocking her over.

As I swung the gun toward the third Drone, he grabbed my wrist with an armored glove. The pressure was crushing. His other hand reached for my eyes, the fingers flexing. I had a premonition of him puncturing my eye sockets, gripping my head like a bowling ball.

Patrick seized him from behind, and the Drone's grasping hand swung wide. But his grip on my wrist didn't relent. I fought the gun toward his face mask, but he was much stronger than me. He kicked Patrick free and grabbed my wrist with his other hand, too, turning the stun gun around toward my own face. My arm trembled as I tried to move it away, but he overpowered me.

Patrick had flown into a rack of potato chips. He was trying to untangle himself, but the rack clanged around, stuck on his foot like a massive bear trap. Alex kicked her way out from beneath the now-empty suit of armor that had knocked her over.

For the moment I was on my own.

And a moment was about all I had.

I shoved the Drone with my other hand. No good. He continued to force the stun gun around until it was aimed between my eyes. The tip of the steel rod brushed my forehead. I fought it a few inches away, but the Drone bore down again. He was going to force me to shoot myself in the head.

I did the only thing I could.

I released the stun gun.

It tumbled between us, his helmet dipping to watch it fall. I caught it with my other hand. Jammed it against his stomach.

And fired.

The face mask swung up to look at me an instant before he geysered through the hole. He slid back on his boots a few feet but somehow managed to plug the hole with his finger and keep his balance at the same time.

I lunged forward with the stun gun and punched another hole in his thigh. He clamped over it with his other hand.

He looked at me helplessly, essence misting through his fingers like a slow-leaking balloon.

He was out of hands.

I raised the gun again. But I didn't need to use it.

He sank to one knee.

Stared up at me

And then his hands went limp at his sides, the last of the smoke sighing through the holes. His helmet bowed.

He stayed that way, kneeling like a disgraced samurai.

Patrick finally stepped free, showering bags of Cool Ranch everywhere.

Alex got up and set one foot on the black armor before her like a big-game hunter. She stared down at the suit appraisingly.

'It'll do,' she said.

**ENTRY 47**     JoJo hopped the Head of Bunny across the mattress fort and on to Rocky's arm. He was stretching his ankle this way and that. Over the past few days, it had improved a lot; he'd even practiced jogging in the halls. Bunny drew no reaction, so JoJo had her jump up and down on Rocky's head.

'Stop it,' he finally said.

'Why?'

'Because it's annoying.'

'Why?'

'Because who wants their head jumped on?'

Bunny's head jumped off Rocky's head and on to his shoulder. Then she hopped up and down there.

Rocky said, 'You are *so* irritating. Have Bunny stop jumping on me *completely*, okay?'

JoJo removed Bunny's head from her brother. Then she held Bunny's ears and swayed her an inch in front of Rocky's eyes.

Rocky was about to get mad when they heard voices outside. Rocky grabbed JoJo, and they flattened on to the mattresses. The voices grew louder.

Rocky and JoJo crept across Mr Tomasi's classroom to the windows and peered out.

Two high-school-age kids scurried through the gate on to the front lawn, shooting glances over their shoulders.

One of them wore a T-shirt that said STARK PEAK MON-ARCHS TRACK & FIELD, which sported the cartoon image of an old king with a scepter and crown. The king wore sandals with wings on them. The other kid was small and scrawny with thoughtful eyes. Shoes flopped on his feet. They looked four sizes too big.

The kids crept closer to the building, stopping by the classroom next door. JoJo and Rocky had to crane their necks to keep them in sight. A whispered conversation drifted up through the open window.

'– think it's safe?'

'I don't know. It *is* gated.'

Then came a familiar voice that sent ice up JoJo's spine: 'What are you guys doing here?'

Ben Braaten stepped into view. He headed toward the Stark Peak kids, walking right past the window where JoJo and Rocky perched. Mikey followed him, an even bigger presence. Their shadows flickered across JoJo's face.

'Look,' one of the others said. 'We're not picking any fights.'

'That's wise,' Ben said. 'What's your name?'

'I'm Nick and this is –'

'You're from Stark Peak High?' Mikey said. 'Monarchs suck.'

The old rivalry.

'Why are you in our town?' Ben asked.

'We just want to be anywhere but Stark Peak,' Nick said. 'The Invaders took it over.'

'Why'd you come here?'

'There's these kids who saved us from the Eyeless when

we were trapped up at the Lawrenceville Cannery. I'd met them before. They're from here. I came to find them.'

'Who?'

'The younger one's named Chance. The older one's Patrick.'

'They saved you?' Mikey said.

'Yeah. They have, like, superpowers or something.'

JoJo could only see Ben from behind, but still she sensed him bristle.

'Superpowers?' Ben said.

'Yeah. The Invaders knew Chance by name. And Patrick, too.'

'The Harvesters. Know Chance and Patrick. By name.'

'Yeah. They, like, analyzed Chance's body, and it showed some reading. They were searching for it. Chance and his brother have something the Invaders are scared of. Like a threat to them. They said Chance had to be "voided." But then he escaped. And he saved us.'

Mikey smacked Ben's arm. 'I *told* you. I told you there was something weird going on with that helmet and everything.'

Nick said, 'I thought it might be safer here with them.'

'This is *my* turf, not theirs,' Ben said. 'And I want you off it.'

'C'mon, man. We've been hiking for days.'

Ben stepped up on him. 'Let me make this clear. You're small and you're weak, and I don't want you around. You're not welcome here.'

'Look, it's daylight. Can we at least hole up until night-fall, when it's safer?'

Ben said, 'Start walking.'

Nick took a step back and looked at his friend. 'C'mon,' he said. 'Let's split.'

They jogged off through the gate and across the street, bent over in some sort of combat run. Ben and Mikey watched them go. A few feet behind Ben's head, JoJo and Rocky watched them go, too. Finally the Stark Peak boys vanished around the side of the Swishers' old house.

'Now,' Ben said, 'let's get my gun back.'

He started toward the school's front doors.

Mikey hesitated. 'I don't want to go back in there.'

'Don't be such a wuss,' Ben said. 'It's safe by now.'

'I don't know. We been out here awhile. What if one of them heard us?'

'No one heard us,' Ben said. 'Now, come on. We've got some searching to do.'

JoJo pulled away from the window and shivered. Next to her, Rocky let out a shaky breath.

They watched Ben and Mikey make their way into the school.

**ENTRY 48**     Getting into a Drone suit was harder than I thought. First I had to pry free the helmet, which took a crowbar from the gas station's garage and a lot of exertion. Once it popped off, more problems presented themselves. How could I get into the suit itself when it was all a single airtight piece? I couldn't exactly climb through the neckhole.

Alex and Patrick watched me work my way around the suit, searching for zippers, catches, hidden buttons – anything. But no, it was perfectly smooth.

I finally decided to put on the helmet.

It lit up at once, and I saw that I could control it like the Rebel helmet by issuing commands. Once I'd gotten the hang of it, I said, 'How do I get into the suit?'

Nothing.

'Get the space suit on me.'

Still it lay there, inert.

I said, 'Open armor.'

A seam opened down the midline of the armor. We watched in amazement as it peeled open from the neck to the chest to the stomach, as if being sliced with an invisible laser.

I sat on the floor and wiggled my way into the suit.

Then I said, 'Armor close.'

It zippered shut around me, conforming to my body. It

was incredibly comfortable – tough and flexible at the same time. It felt like a second skin, the technology knitting around my shape, seeming to anticipate my movements as I stood up.

I stared through the face mask at Patrick and Alex.

'Whoa,' Alex said. 'This is so weird. I totally want to kill you right now.'

The air tasted like metal and oil. I found myself getting light-headed.

Then I remembered: It was airtight. Aside from the tiny hole I'd made with the stun gun.

I took off the helmet and aerated it with the stun gun, punching two holes beneath the chin where they'd be hidden but close to my mouth.

When I put the helmet back on, the air tasted a bit fresher.

Patrick and Alex set about armoring themselves next. They'd never worn a helmet before, and they staggered around more than I did, finding their balance. They kept knocking into the shelves.

'You need to practice walking outside,' I said. 'More room.'

I walked to the door, reached for the handle, and tore it clean off.

'Oops.'

I dropped the handle on the floor and flexed my glove. It would take some work to acclimate myself to the strength contained in the armor.

We stepped out through the doors. Though I found the suit freakishly fluid, there was a half-second delay between my wanting to reach for something and my arm actually doing it.

Patrick practiced running around the pumps, his legs pistoning powerfully. Alex did deep knee bends and then jumped a few times, testing the suit's weight.

We were so occupied with our new armor that we didn't notice the two giant cattle trucks.

Not until they'd pulled into the gas station.

We turned as they eased up to the pumps. Three Drones filed out of each cab. They took a few steps in our direction. Halted in a line.

I could see our reflections in their face masks. I glanced nervously over at Patrick and Alex. The hole in the thigh of my brother's armor seemed obvious. The one in his stomach looked like a friggin' belly button. They were too obvious. There was no way the Drones wouldn't notice.

Bracing myself to fight, I looked at the Drones. Their unreadable face masks pointed at us.

My breath echoed around in my suit like crazy.

They stared at us.

We stared back.

Two of the Drones reached for gas nozzles and started filling up the trucks' tanks.

The others walked around to the livestock holds. They were packed with kids. A few bulging eyes peered through the slats. A little kid's fingers wiggled out the side near the bottom. Someone was shrieking, 'Can't breathe! Can't breathe!'

The gas pumps clicked off, and the Drones filed back into the cabs. They looked out the windows, nodded at us again.

We nodded back.

They pulled out, driving for Stark Peak.

The cries of children lingered in their wake.

I thought about those small fingers I'd seen poking out of the hold. No bigger than JoJo's. Something fired to life inside my chest. Anger. At Ben Braaten. At the pieces of our friends littering the halls of Creek's Cause High. At saying good-bye to Eve. At the Hosts and the Drones and the Hatchlings. At a new world where little kids were packed into the backs of cattle trucks.

I was staring at the Ninja motorcycle leaning against the air pump.

Fire spread inside me, my temper igniting. Maybe I could have stopped it, but I didn't want to. Yielding to the rage felt so much sweeter. I was already walking, my step charged.

'Chance,' Patrick said. *'No.'*

Rocketing out of the gas station on the neon-green Kawasaki, I thought, *Too late.*

I blasted toward the cattle trucks. As I zoomed up on them, it seemed like they were flying backward at me. I'd done plenty of off-road dirt-bike riding on the mounds behind Britney Durant's house, but those beat-up little motorcycles were nothing compared to this. This was flying a rocket.

I steadied the motorcycle and steered close to the first cattle car. I reached out an armored hand, grabbed hold of the rear gate, and clenched.

My hand literally crumpled into the metal.

I tore the rear gate open.

As it swung wide, my front wheel wobbled. I grabbed the grips with both hands, the bike cutting sharply, almost hurling me off. I righted myself just in time.

Kids were shouting and clamoring in the back. Two of the bigger kids released the ramp, which slid down and started sparking along the asphalt. The cattle truck veered and slowed some. But not much.

As I zipped ahead, one of the Drones reached out of the passenger seat and tried to knock me off the bike. I grabbed his arm and gave a little tug.

He hit the highway, black smoke bursting from his joints. The armor rattled off in various directions.

I revved ahead to the second cattle car. It was already slowing down.

I had no baling hooks, no gun, no real plan. But I had one advantage over the Drones – I wouldn't disintegrate if my armor got punctured.

I went to free the back gate, but the driver yanked the truck to the side, almost hitting me. I slowed down, cut across the back, and rode up along the passenger side. The Drone was just opening the door, his boot inching out toward the runner.

I made a fist with the armored glove and swung it into the door as hard as I could without toppling the bike.

The door slammed shut where his ankle would be. A blast of black smoke shot through the fractured suit down at the asphalt zipping by beneath us. The Drone blasted across the bench seat, flying over the Drone next to him and smashing into the driver. Both of them hammered through the driver's door, taking it right off the hinges.

The remaining Drone sat there in the middle, bolt upright and apparently stunned, as the truck barreled forward. Then he seemed to come to his senses. He slid across to take the wheel.

I eased over, figuring he was going to swerve into me.

The other truck was right there in the next lane, catching me by surprise.

I jerked the handlebars back, barely dodging the grille as it swept past.

I was in the tight space between both trucks.

There was nowhere to go.

I hit the brakes, hoping to let them fly ahead of me, but both of the drivers steered sharply in at me. There wouldn't be time.

I watched the walls close in.

There was no doubt about it. I was gonna get pancaked.

The sides of the trucks hit the outsides of the Ninja's grips, pinning the motorcycle in place.

I let go of the handlebars and hopped up on to the seat. The ground flew by below. One slip and I'd be spread across the highway. I tried to grab the trucks' slats, but there were no handholds. Through the metal bars, kids' faces appeared, cheering me on.

I reached for the top of the slats, but they were too high.

The handlebars bent and gave way. The bike started to crumple beneath me, dragged forward. The sides of the trucks crushed in on my shoulders. I bladed my body, riding the disintegrating bike like a skateboard.

The Drones kept steering into each other, smashing me between the walls.

I had one foot on the seat. One of the bike's wheels broke free and whipped away as if sucked into a black hole.

The trucks were side to side, zooming forward, closing even more.

The slats clinked against my helmet on either side, crushing in on it.

Blue electricity fizzled across my face mask.

I felt the helmet bulge around my head.

It was going to pop. And then my head would, too.

I knew that the Drone helmet was strong. I didn't want to bet my brain on *how* strong.

What was left of the Ninja dragged forward beneath me, a sled forging through a fountain of sparks. I was on the tiptoes of one foot, trying to keep some weight off my helmet, which was still held in a vise grip between the sides of the two trucks.

I was pretty much flying along the freeway suspended by my head.

The helmet cracked under the pressure, a fissure opening up around my neck. I could feel air rushing through the seam.

The helmet bulged even more, distorting my view through the face mask.

This was it.

I heard a *boom*.

My head blowing up?

Another *boom*.

The trucks didn't veer apart, but they started to decelerate. The asphalt treadmill beneath me slowed, slowed, and finally stopped.

The motorcycle gave a metal groan and collapsed.

For an instant I swung from my head.

'Hello?' I said, my voice strained and wheezy. 'Anyone wanna help me out?'

The weight of my body tugged my head from the

helmet with an audible pop, and I collapsed on top of the jagged, smoking Kawasaki.

I reached up and worked the helmet loose. Then, turning my body sideways, I squeezed my way up the narrow gap between the trucks. At last I squirmed out the front.

Through the cracked windshields, I saw black smoke and pieces of armor. A Drone stood on top of one of the cabs, shotgun in his hands, pointed down.

Patrick.

He had fired through the roof of the cab.

Then he'd jumped across to the neighboring cab and done the same.

A commandeered Ford F-150 pickup coasted into view from around the side of the wrecked vehicles, another Drone at the wheel. Alex yanked off the helmet and shook out her spiky hair. She must've driven up alongside the first cattle truck so Patrick could jump up on to it. She had one elbow out the rolled-down window and looked like something from a beer commercial.

She smiled that wide smile. 'Whoa there, Little Rain. Next time wait for the cavalry.'

I grinned.

Already the kids were streaming out of the cattle holds, running around us, whooping and clapping.

We threw high fives, bumped knuckles, and wished one another well. They took off quickly, heading every which way.

Every which way – except toward Stark Peak.

We were the only ones stupid enough for that.

**ENTRY 49**   JoJo and Rocky crouched in the cramped crawl space by the heating vent, their faces striped with slits of light from the vent's grille. They peered out on to the gym floor, watching Ben and Mikey dig through the wreckage of the supply station.

Leaving Mr Tomasi's room had been easy enough, scaling the bookcase and vanishing into the drop ceiling. But crawling down the English and history hall had been tricky, since they had to balance their hands and knees on the metal grid that supported the panels. One wrong move and they'd go crashing through the ceiling. Moving above the cafeteria was easy, since there was an attic-like space reinforced with wood. When they'd crept down the intersecting hall leading to the gym, they'd heard Ben and Mikey walking beneath them. Through the pencil-hole perforations in the acoustic tiles, they'd watched the boys making their way cautiously along the corridor below them.

Shadowing the older boys from a few feet above them had been slow, scary going.

Now JoJo and Rocky pressed their faces close to the heating vent, staring through the slivers between the thin slats. They were straddling a row of ceiling panels, their knees riding the metal grid on either side. A few feet to their left, an external vent looked out across the school's front lawn. A lazy breeze drifted through, stirring dust around them.

Mikey emerged from the supply station first with a fistful of energy bars. He righted an overturned bed, sat on it, and started cramming them into his mouth, one after another. Ben kept digging for a few more minutes and then finally waded out.

He said, 'When I find who took my gun, I'm gonna take it from him and shove it up his –'

'Who do you think took it?' Mikey said.

He glared at him. 'Who do you think?'

He walked over and snatched one of the energy bars from the mattress. He gnawed off a big bite and gazed across the gym.

His eyes snagged on something at the bleachers. His spine straightened.

'What's he looking at?' Rocky whispered.

JoJo pressed her finger across her lips. Even way up here, she was too scared to make the *shhh* sound.

Ben walked over to the bleachers. They were strewn with ripped clothes and sleeping bags and pillow feathers. On the bottom bench, the TV lay on its side, facing outward, static snowing the cracked screen.

Ben put a boot up on the bench next to the TV and hunched over to tie his laces.

JoJo pressed Bunny's head against her mouth. Her calves were starting to cramp.

An image wavered on the screen, catching Ben's attention. He rested a forearm across his knee and stared down.

Again the image undulated in the fuzz, a figure lost in a snowstorm. Ben righted the TV, turned up the volume to a white-noise roar, and fiddled with the rabbit ears.

Up in the crawl space, JoJo prayed the picture wouldn't clarify.

It didn't, but a snatch of a sentence emerged through the static: '– haven here on the northeast edge of Stark Peak –'

And then it went to full black-and-white specks.

Ben tugged at the antennae but couldn't retrieve the reception.

'Holy hell,' Mikey said. 'Someone else is alive out there.' He stood up, wrappers falling from his lap.

'Those losers,' Ben said. 'They went to Stark Peak.'

Too late JoJo sensed a vibration in the hall below. She stared down through the perforated tiles as movement swept by directly below her.

Shiny black.

Salamander orange.

The familiar stench rose through the holes in the panels.

Rocky's upper lip glistened with sweat. 'Oh,' he whispered. 'Oh, no.'

They felt the tremor of the gym's double doors flinging open.

Ben and Mikey turned to face what was coming. Mikey dropped the bar he was eating. Ben stepped away, his legs banging into a bed. He stumbled back, sat down abruptly on the thin mattress, and then stood up again.

JoJo and Rocky watched the forms ease into view below them.

Three Drones. Two Hatchlings.

They fanned out around Ben and Mikey.

Ben held up his hand. 'Listen –'

The Hatchlings pounced on Mikey and tore him in half at the stomach. He didn't even have time to scream. Each Hatchling dragged its bloody chunk a few feet away and fell on it. Hunkered possessively over their meals, they glared at each other with their pupil-filled eyes even as they devoured their spoils. The terrible smacking noises made JoJo's insides lurch up. She wanted to scream and hide and throw up all at the same time.

Ben's knees buckled. He tilted forward on his feet as if he were going to fall flat on his face, but then he caught himself. The Hatchlings rose from their feast and shook like wet dogs, whipping the excess blood off their faces and necks. They snapped at each other and then focused on Ben, circling him like sharks.

He spun around to keep them in sight. 'Wait . . . okay? Wait . . . *listen*. Just . . . listen. Take me to your leader. I have something he'll want to know.'

The Hatchlings rotated faster around him. Ben whirled on his heels.

The Hatchlings coiled. And then they lunged.

*'Chance and Patrick Rain!'* Ben screamed.

One of the Drones held up a hand.

The Hatchlings froze, their dripping fangs inches from Ben's face.

Ben's eyes were closed, his arms up, caging his head. 'I know where they are. Or at least where they're headed. And I'm willing to trade. The information you want for my life. Okay?'

He opened his eyes.

The Hatchlings cocked their heads, their jaws gnashing as if of their own accord. They did not back off.

Ben closed his eyes again. *'Okay?'*

The Drone flattened his hand, a command for the Hatchlings: *Stand down.*

The Hatchlings backed away until they were stooped over their respective meals. They tore back into the pieces of Mikey.

One of the Drones marched out of the gym.

Up in the crawl space, JoJo swallowed hard. Then she crept over Rocky, who was still frozen with terror, and made her way through the crawl space to the exterior vent.

After a minute she watched the Drone emerge. He stepped out on to the front lawn. He tilted his helmet back to the heavens, a blue glow illuminating his face mask.

Sending a signal.

A chill tightened JoJo's skin when she realized what that meant.

More Harvesters were on the way.

**ENTRY 50**   We drove into Stark Peak as if it were an ordinary day trip.

Except for the alien space suits we were wearing, of course.

Patrick was at the wheel of the big pickup. As we neared the city, other vehicles started to appear. At first we couldn't help glancing out at all the other Drones zipping past. They drove mostly big rigs – tanker trucks, livestock cars, moving vans – but there were plenty in normal cars as well. Many of the vehicles transported Hatchlings and children. The Drones drove without regard for lanes or signs, but somehow the confusion of angles all worked out. It reminded me of watching schools of fish on television, how they always seemed to know when to turn this way or that without ever bumping into one another.

Alex and I kept staring out the windows in disbelief until some of the Drones started staring back.

'Stop looking,' Patrick said, his voice tinny through the helmet.

We wound into thickening traffic until we were surrounded by enemies, too far in to back out. We were masquerading as Harvesters inside the beehive itself.

If they ever found out we were here, there'd be nowhere to run.

For a time we joined the flow of cars on the freeway. If

I ignored the thudding of my heart amplified inside the echo chamber of the suit, it almost felt safe.

Buildings started to spring up along the sides of the road. A cattle pen was packed with children, the kids mixed right in with cows and pigs. All those small bodies pressed between the livestock. They looked gaunt and miserable, sunk to the ankles in manure. Drones prodded them toward feeding troughs.

A line of Hatchlings stretched out of the slaughterhouse on the far side. They looked uncharacteristically calm, even patient.

It dawned on me what they were waiting for, the realization a wrecking ball to my chest. 'They're waiting in line,' I said. 'Like at a restaurant.'

Mercifully, the feeding zone passed from view.

The skyline loomed ever larger. The domino-tile slabs of apartment buildings at the edge of town. The formidable tower of Stark Peak Bank & Trust. And rising above it all, the upthrust spire of City Hall.

We exited the freeway. At the stoplight Patrick released the wheel and flexed his fingers. I could see indentations on the metal of the steering wheel where he'd gripped too tight with his armored hands.

Around us Drones paraded the streets in clusters and columns, bent to some greater purpose.

Patrick signaled to turn right, but Alex reached over and clicked it off.

'Aliens don't signal,' she said.

Patrick waited for an opening and turned.

We goggled at the city. It had been transformed into an alien landscape. Hatchlings strolling the sidewalks and tearing through cabinets in the shops. Drones training in Newbury Park, enacting series of movements that looked like tai chi. The giant bank building had been split open as if by an explosion, the exposed interior lined with transparent organic screens showing feeds from all around the world. Floor after floor of Drones were plugged into the screens by umbilical-cord-like wires attached to the sides of their helmets. Were they monitoring the footage? Patrick slowed as we coasted past the sight, and I spotted a Queen on each floor. I imagined hives like this dotting every city in the world.

On the sidewalks Hatchlings bickered and brawled. One skirmish turned violent, four Hatchlings going after a smaller one. They each seized a limb with fangs and nails, and an instant later he was quartered.

We rolled up on the giant courtyard before City Hall. A wave of Hatchlings swept by us on the broad steps, shoving and hissing. One slashed another, gouging his cheek, and then a fight broke out. More Hatchlings piled on, turning the riot into a mini-stampede. Several Hatchlings got trampled, leaving orange smears on the pavement. The others smashed through the window of a movie theater and tumbled out of sight.

Patrick kept driving. Just a few more blocks and we'd be through the heart of downtown, making our way to the cliffs that rimmed the northeast section of the city. Stark Peak University was perched on those cliffs.

As was – we hoped – our salvation.

As we coasted up to the next intersection, Alex gasped.

A female Hatchling stepped off the sidewalk on to the crosswalk. As she passed in front of us, we watched her with shock.

She was pregnant.

It was hard to tell at first, given that the females were rotund to begin with. But as she crossed before our windshield, we saw that the swelling around her midsection was pronounced enough to stretch the skin so tight it was translucent – just as with the Husks. Through the orange flesh, tiny forms were visible, swimming around like baby sharks.

'Now they've really got no use for us anymore,' Alex said.

Even after the Hatchling passed by, we sat there, stunned.

All at once we were banged forward in our seats. A truck, ramming us from behind.

Patrick accelerated off the line. A few more turns as we drifted through the outskirts of the city. Even here we marveled at all the industry. Buildings hollowed out, the interiors plastered with virtual screens. Hatchlings crouching on bus shelters, roofs, parked cars. In a few places, Drones were digging up the streets, churning through the concrete with bulldozers and excavators. They pulverized buildings, remaking the landscape into enormous molehills. The population thinned out here in the construction zones. The few Hatchlings and Drones seemed too preoccupied with their tasks to focus on us.

Patrick steered around fallen high-rises, mounds of glass and concrete, broken fire hydrants spouting water. Most of the streets threading to the northeast part of the city were blocked. We couldn't take the normal route around the cliffs to come at the university from the rear. And we couldn't risk reversing our way through the city center again.

Our only shot was to run the intact streets to the base of the cliffs and figure it out from there.

At last we reached the outskirts of the city. The freeway on-ramp had collapsed into a spill of rubble. There'd be no moving forward. Not in the truck at least. Patrick parked in an alley splitting a housing project, and we climbed out and crept to the end.

Across the freeway was the bottom terminal for an aerial tram that forged up the steep hills to the cliffs beyond. Thick steel cables connected the intermediate supporting towers. Cut into the cliff face in the distance were steep switchbacks.

Way up at the top, we could see a few flat buildings – the fringe of campus.

They looked peaceful. Undisturbed.

I stared longingly at the tram. If we rode it up, we'd alert the entire city. I looked back at the switchbacks and sighed. 'Gonna be a long hike.'

Patrick and Alex were looking at me but not replying.

And then I realized why.

In the reflection of their helmets, I saw the enormous Hatchling emerging from the alley wall to loom behind me.

I wheeled around, nearly losing my balance. Which, I'm sure, seemed most un-Drone-like. For a moment I'd forgotten that I was disguised by the armor.

The Hatchling leaned over me. I had to crane my neck to stare up at him.

His nostril holes quivered. Could he *smell* me?

I told myself not to move. Not that I could've done much anyway. When we'd hopped out to sneak a peek at the freeway, we'd stupidly left our weapons in the truck.

He leaned closer, closer, the horrid orange face bulging at me in the face mask's fish-eye view. His mouth spread. The fangs were smaller than I would have thought, two jagged rows of triangles.

I steeled myself. The smallest flinch would give me away.

His face knocked my mask. All I saw was a smear of orange dotted with two nostril holes. The stench was overpowering. I could practically feel it taking up residence in my lungs. I held my breath.

I waited to feel a flurry of claws disemboweling me.

But instead he pulled back, leaving a dribble of orange mucus across my face mask.

The giant Hatchling swung next to Alex. He leaned over her, plastering his face to her mask as well.

She stood motionless.

He snuffled in an inhale and stepped back, seemingly appeased. He stepped to Patrick, his clawed feet tapping the pavement.

Same thing. Lean in, big sniff.

He started to back up. Then halted, his head cocking in that awful fashion. He lifted his hand, raising a single long finger. We stared at the point of the claw.

Slowly, he lowered his arm and slid the finger into the belly-button hole on Patrick's suit.

Alex and I moved to tackle him.

But it was too late.

A quick jerk of his arm and he would impale Patrick.

We watched the ropy muscles of the Hatchling's back tighten as he drove his finger through Patrick.

I cried out, the noise reverberating around my helmet.

But no – the Hatchling hadn't shoved his hand into Patrick.

Patrick had shoved his hand into *him*.

More precisely, my brother had punched an armor-reinforced fist straight through the Hatchling's chest.

For a moment they were frozen there, the Hatchling staring down at Patrick's arm, sunk midway to the elbow through his rib cage.

Then Patrick ripped his fist out.

It was gripping the Hatchling's heart.

An organic confusion of torn pipes and ventricles dripping orange sludge.

Patrick dropped the heart at the Hatchling's feet.

Then he palmed the Hatchling's face and shoved him to the side.

The Hatchling tilted over like a plank of wood.

Patrick wiped his gloved hand on his suit, his voice issuing from behind that blank face mask.

'Let's go,' he said. 'We got work to do.'

**ENTRY 51**     JoJo dozed off in the golden dusk light, curled in the crawl space against the outside vent. A shuddering in the bones of the building woke her.

No – not in the building.

In the *world*.

The vibration turned to a rumble, so intense it seemed the building would tear itself apart. She looked over at Rocky, who clung to the metal grid as best he could, his body hovering above the ceiling panels. His wild eyes stared out from beneath the jumble of his curly black bangs.

The noise grew to a roar, and then JoJo watched with amazement as a massive meteor rocketed into sight, crashing into the parking lot and plowing through the cars and asphalt. It mowed through the fence and came to a smoking halt in the middle of the front lawn of Creek's Cause High.

Chunks of turf spattered against the side of the building. Some even landed on the rooftops of the houses across the street.

The meteor rotated open, cracked vertically from the middle. The cockpit housed three seats.

A feminine form in shiny black armor uncurled from the podlike wrap that passed for a pilot seat. She kept uncurling until she stood, tall and forbidding in the day's dying light. One arm, elongated like an octopus tentacle, tapered to a sharp point.

A Queen.

JoJo felt a gasp scrape its way out of her throat.

The Queen started for the school's entrance. Two Drones unloaded from the neighboring seats and marched behind her.

JoJo scrambled through the crawl space and took up a position next to her brother, peering through the vent into the gym. Ben was weak on his feet, swaying slightly as if drunk. The Drones hadn't let him sit this whole time.

The Hatchlings had long finished their meal. Only dark stains were left where Mikey's remains had been. They paced at a distance, eyeing Ben hungrily.

The doors boomed open one floor beneath JoJo and Rocky.

The Queen drifted into the gym and right up to Ben. Her Drones fanned out beside her.

Ben drew in a breath and raised a trembling hand. 'There's . . . I have information you, um . . . If you'll spare my –'

The Queen's face mask flickered with glowing blue amplitude bars. 'Where are Chance and Patrick Rain?'

'A TV . . . transmission . . . Alex, she used to check . . .'

The Queen leaned in. Despite her menace, her movements were elegant, the seamless black suit bending gracefully around her. 'Where?'

'Stark Peak,' Ben said. 'There's . . . uh, some kind of haven or something somewhere on the edge of the city. I don't know any more than that. I swear I don't.'

The Queen seemed to scan his face. 'I believe you.' Her mask danced again with the blue light. 'Thank you.'

She drew back her squirming stinger of an arm and plunged it through Ben's midsection.

Rocky gave a tiny yelp, and JoJo grabbed his hand.

The Queen lifted Ben up. His glazed eyes stared down at his impaled stomach. His legs churned, feet kicking listlessly.

The Queen said, 'We will tear the outskirts of the city apart.'

Then she flung him to the floor in front of the Hatchlings as if slinging a steak to a pack of dogs.

The Hatchlings fell on him.

He did not last long.

Next to JoJo, Rocky was hyperventilating. She looped an arm around his neck, pulled his head close, and whispered in his ear, 'Ben didn't say that they were at the *northeastern* edge of the city. And he doesn't know they went to the university. Which means we still have a shot.'

Rocky's lips were parted, his head nodding with each breath. 'Shot . . . at what?'

'At warning them. We have to go.'

'Go where?'

JoJo cast a look down at the Queen, who continued to give orders to her Drones.

'Follow me,' JoJo whispered.

She straddle-scampered back through the crawl space atop the hall, away from the gym. Bunny's head thumped along beside her, clenched in her fist. Then JoJo slid back a ceiling panel, stuck her head through, and scanned both directions.

Clear.

She swung down and dropped through. Then she peered up at Rocky.

'What are you, crazy?' he whispered. 'Where are you going?'

'Come on already. Don't land on your bad ankle.'

She heard footsteps moving across the gym toward the doors to the hall. She stared at the closed doors, panic building.

Her next whisper was strained through clenched teeth. '*Now*, Rocky.'

He slid out, landing evenly. She grabbed his hand. They ran for the front exit and skidded through just as they heard the gym door clang open behind them.

JoJo dragged her big brother toward the meteor.

Rocky halted as they approached it. 'No,' he said. 'No *way*.'

They turned back to the school. Shadows became visible behind the inset windows of the front doors. No more time.

JoJo dove into the meteor cockpit. Rocky jumped after her.

They scrambled on to the row of podlike seating structures. Behind was a tiny cargo space.

She could hear boots moving across the lawn, closing in.

She and Rocky slid over the headrests, piling on top of each other in the cargo space. They shoved themselves as low as they could. A few bulky bags filled with hard equipment dug into their backs.

Three shadows fell across the meteor opening. JoJo's face filled the tiny gap between two of the chairs, a band of light falling across her eyes.

The Queen and the Drones ducked to enter. They turned to sit.

That's when JoJo realized she didn't have Bunny's head.

Her eyes strained to find it.

On the curved base of the pilot's seat pod.

Right beneath the Queen's lowering rear end.

At the last second, JoJo snaked her hand through the gap, grabbed Bunny's ears, and snatched the stuffed animal into the cargo space with her.

It was so close that her knuckles brushed the smooth armor at the back of the Queen's thigh.

The seats rocked slightly as the Queen and Drones adjusted their positions.

A grinding sound as the meteor zippered itself closed.

A vibration rattled JoJo's teeth in her skull. The roar grew to an earsplitting decibel level, and then the meteor rose up slowly, slowly. When it rocketed off toward Stark Peak, it left JoJo's stomach behind.

Her mouth, like Rocky's, was open.

She would have been screaming if she could've caught her breath.

**ENTRY 52**    By the time I hiked off the last switchback in the cliff face and tumbled on to level ground, my calves ached, my thighs screamed, and the sun was nothing but a seam of fuchsia at the horizon. Alex and Patrick were up top already beside the stalled aerial tram perched at the cliff's edge. They sat side by side next to their packs, enjoying the sunset. Patrick was wearing his black cowboy hat again.

It looked like I'd interrupted them on a picnic.

After cresting the first hill past the freeway, we'd shed our armor. It was too heavy for the terrain. We'd followed the path of the aerial tramway overhead, hiking beneath the steel cables to the base of the cliff. We didn't come across a single Drone or Hatchling the entire way. The Harvesters seemed to be concentrated in the city, remaking it to their liking.

More and more the university seemed like a haven.

At the top of the cliff, Patrick and Alex gave me a moment to recover, and then we readied our weapons and walked toward the grouping of buildings. The closest, a three-story rise that housed the departments of history and literature, was empty. We stepped inside, the click of the glass door sending an echo through the abandoned halls and up the stairwells. We walked through the lobby, across the atrium, and out the other side.

The chemistry building was deserted. As were physics

and biology. From a central quad, we peered down at the law and business schools below. Dark windows. No signs of movement.

A ghost campus.

We were losing light fast, and the winding paths were confusing. After a few more detours, we found ourselves back at the central quad. A big fountain sat stagnant. Dead leaves clustered around picnic tables. A mountain bike lay on its side in the middle of a wide lawn, the front wheel spinning lazily in the breeze.

'This place is confusing,' Alex said. 'We keep walking in circles.'

'Maybe we're too young to be at college,' I said, and she laughed.

'I don't see any Department of Virology,' Patrick said. 'What if we came all the way here for nothing?'

I turned in a circle, my eyes settling on a sign at the edge of the quad. It said STARK PEAK MEDICAL SCHOOL and had an arrow pointing to the far edge of the cliffs, around the bend where we'd climbed up. I walked over to the sign and peered up the dirt path.

The sunset backlit the big white building of the medical school. Next to it was a low-lying concrete structure, almost a bunker, with slits for windows.

Lining the edge of the roof like gutters were what appeared to be pipes. They pumped mist into the air all around the building. The surrounding parking lot had no cars, just a row of golf carts near the door. Odd.

I signaled to Patrick and Alex, and we crept closer. We hid behind a groundskeeper shack and peered out at the building.

Sure enough, a metal plaque bolted to the concrete read DEPARTMENT OF VIROLOGY AND IMMUNOLOGY. The pipes pushed out slow, steady bursts of mist.

'What *is* that stuff?' Alex asked.

The mist reached us now, flecking our cheeks.

I stepped out from around the groundskeeper shack. Opened my mouth.

Smiled.

'Salt water,' I said.

My pulse quickened with excitement. We ran across the parking lot to the door of the bunker.

It was locked.

But beside it was a keypad with an inset security camera. My trembling thumb jabbed at the red button.

Nothing happened.

I jabbed at it again.

A moment later the front door clicked open.

It slowly swung wide.

As we stepped inside into a glass-walled box of a room, air blasted down at us, making our hair flutter. The door sealed behind us, trapping us in. In the ceiling, the noise of hidden fans revved to life. We spun around, staring up at various vents. A UV light came on, glaring through the Lucite walls, bleaching everything to A-bomb white. The air tingled around us.

After a while the lights dimmed. The fans quietened. A second door clicked open ahead of us. We squinted at it, trying to blink our eyesight back to life.

Patrick stepped through the doorway first.

A man's form emerged slowly from the glare. A heavy guy with a bushy beard – the guy from the TV transmission.

Several other scientists were arrayed in the background, wearing scrubs or sweats and white coats. The room looked like some kind of control center, with monitors and servers and consoles. A few slender windows provided scant light. Pipes twisted from giant tanks of water and disappeared into the concrete walls. I guessed they fed the outdoor misters.

The door whistled shut behind us.

The man with the beard spread his arms. 'Welcome! I'm Dr Brewer.'

Patrick said, 'Are you in charge?'

'No.' A skinny woman with horn-rimmed glasses stepped out from behind him. 'I am.'

Alex smacked Patrick on the arm with the back of her hand. 'Sexist!'

Patrick shrugged. 'She was hidden.'

The scientists eyed us with delight, whispering in wonderment, as if they were laying eyes on some never-before-discovered Amazonian tribe.

I caught only snatches of what they were saying.

'– can't believe anyone actually made it –'

'– older one looks eighteen already –'

'– reach of the television signal –'

'Uh,' I said, 'we're *right here*.'

'I'm sorry,' the skinny woman said. 'Our social skills have atrophied. I'm Dr Messing. But please call me Laura.' She offered a slender hand.

We stared at it.

The bearded man said, 'I think it's safe for you to lower your weapons now.'

We hadn't even noticed that we were in fighting posture. Alex relaxed first, her hockey stick clanking to the floor.

Patrick let the shotgun swing down by his side. I released the baling hooks so they dangled from their nylon loops.

Alex shook Laura's hand.

'You're safe now,' Laura said.

One of the scientists in the back started crying but stopped when everyone looked at him.

Laura gestured to a steel staircase at the rear of the lab. We stepped through another sealed Lucite door to see that it twisted down to a huge underground facility.

'I'm sure your journey's been trying,' she said. 'What do you say we get you cleaned up?'

**ENTRY 53**     The meteor smashed down in the city center, churning up the sidewalk in front of City Hall like butter. The cockpit split open, and the Queen and her Drones exited, storming toward the high-rise of the bank building.

As soon as they cleared from sight, JoJo and Rocky poked their heads up from the cargo hold and peered out.

Drones and Hatchlings everywhere.

'Great plan, JoJo,' Rocky said. 'I don't know why I listened to an eight-year-old. I'm *two years older*, which means . . .'

He kept on, but JoJo wasn't paying attention anymore.

She watched the Queen disappear into the bank. The outer wall of the building had been removed, so you could see right inside, like a cross-section diagram in science class. Drones were hooked up to virtual monitors on all the floors.

The Queen strode regally across the lobby and plugged herself into a massive screen.

A moment later the movement in the city stopped. The Drones halted all at once – on the sidewalks, in their vehicles, in the surrounding buildings. The Hatchlings, cuing to them, halted as well.

A paralyzed moment.

And then, at the same time, every last one of them started moving again, heading for the city outskirts.

They'd received the Queen's order and were bolting to the fringes of the city in search of Chance and Patrick. The numbers were awe-inspiring.

But JoJo and Rocky had one thing going for them. They knew not only which part of the city outskirts to search – they knew that their friends were at Stark Peak University.

Rocky hadn't even noticed that the city had cleared out. His face was covered in a panic sheen of sweat, and he was still looking at JoJo, rattling nervously, '. . . survive all this time to become Hatchling snacks because my dumb younger sister wouldn't –'

JoJo reached over, gripped the back of his neck, and turned his head.

Empty streets. Empty buildings. A newspaper blew through the desolate City Hall courtyard.

Rocky finally shut his trap.

JoJo squirmed out of the cargo space, climbing from the meteor. She took in the deserted city.

Rocky clawed his way out. 'What just happened?'

Already JoJo was walking over to an abandoned Smart Car. 'This one looks about our size.'

Rocky trudged behind, still gazing at the quiet city all around. 'Wait. *What?* I've never driven.'

JoJo yanked open the door, eyed the dangling keys. 'How hard could it be?'

Rocky white-knuckled the steering wheel as they careened through a trash can, banged off a streetlight, and sailed up an alley, clattering against its brick walls. JoJo was on the floor of the Smart Car, working the pedals with her hands, one foot waving up and bonking him on the cheek. They'd been lucky enough to get through the city center without seeing a single Harvester, but if they Wile E. Coyote-ed themselves into a wall now, that wouldn't count for much.

'Gas!' Rocky cried. 'Gas!'

They flew out of the alley, accelerating toward the edge of an overpass. Rocky's eyes bulged as he looked ahead to where the ground fell away past a flimsy guardrail, a four-story drop to the crumbled freeway.

'*Brakes!*' Rocky screamed, and the brake discs screeched. The giant drop zoomed up on them, filling the windshield.

The car slowed, slowed, knocking into the guardrail and sending the metal strip plummeting down into the wreckage. Rocky braced himself for the fall, but the car miraculously halted right at the brink.

Rocky opened one eye. Then the other.

The front tires lost their purchase and bumped over the lip, the car collapsing another two feet on to the chassis. Rocky shrieked, and JoJo's legs flailed. She kicked him in the jaw.

'Don't move,' Rocky said. 'Just . . . *don't move.*'

They stayed that way, perfectly still, the drop teetering before them. JoJo's sneaker smooshed Rocky's nose to one side.

Moving excruciatingly slowly, he reached for the door handle. Clicked it open. Pushed the door wide.

'Ready?' he said.

JoJo's voice came back muffled against the floor mat. 'What? *No*, I'm not ready. I can't even see what's –'

'One . . . two . . . *three*!'

Rocky seized JoJo's ankle and rolled out the open door,

dragging his sister with him. She was still half in the Smart Car when it tilted forward over the edge. She covered her head, swinging upside down as the car fell away, slipping off her curled body like a shucked shell. It plummeted down and smashed into the wrecked freeway below.

Rocky hauled her up by her ankle, and they lay at the brink of the overpass, panting. A moment later they heard movement below. They flattened against the ground.

Clattering. Footsteps. Heavy breathing rode the wind up to them.

At last JoJo risked a peek over the edge.

A band of Hatchlings surrounded the Smart Car, sticking their heads through the shattered back windows. One shoved his face against the cracked windshield. They sniffed and clawed their way around the crumpled metal.

JoJo drew back and lay down out of sight, her cheek pressed to the asphalt.

She and her brother stared at each other, their noses inches apart. Her breath ruffled his curls.

After a while they heard the Hatchlings move on up the freeway. They waited until there wasn't the faintest sound below. Then they hauled themselves to their feet.

Across the freeway the cables of a gondola traced a bumpy course over several hills and up a cliff face, showing them the route they'd need to follow.

JoJo pointed a half mile to their side where a concrete staircase zigzagged down from the back of some housing projects.

'We can get down there,' she said.

**ENTRY 54**     The jets pelted me, intense enough that I thought they might leave bruises. I rinsed away the antibacterial soap, turned the lever, and took a moment to make sure my skin was still intact. As I toweled off, I realized why the water pressure was so insane – it was a decontamination shower.

They'd laid out cargo scrubs for me in various sizes. I dressed in a pair that fit, pulled on my boots, and emerged from the bathroom. One of the scientists – a lanky guy who didn't talk much – waited for me outside. Moving through the contained facility was a pain, because every room was airlocked – the door behind you had to shut before the one ahead of you opened. The guy guided us through, tapping a digital key card to various panels. I felt like a rat in a trick maze.

Alex and Patrick were waiting with all the scientists in a big central lab that had cloudy glass walls on all sides. Because they could fit some of the scientists' clothes, they had better wardrobe options. Patrick wore jeans, a white T-shirt, and, of course, his Stetson. Alex was in workout gear – yoga pants, a T-shirt whose sides she'd torn down under the arms like one of her hockey practice shirts, and some kind of jog-bra thing.

Distracting.

They were in mid-conversation, and I gleaned they'd already told the scientists some of our story.

Though Laura was the boss, Dr Brewer was pretty animated. She watched him with amusement as he waved his hands around.

'You have to understand,' he was saying. 'As a Biosafety Level 4 lab, we work with some crazy sh – some crazy stuff in here. You see all these vents?' He stood, gesturing with excitement. 'They're HEPA filters to kill any atomized biohazard before it's released to the outside world. And the blowers over the doorways? They ensure negative pressure – a constant inward flow designed to keep any airborne pathogens from leaking.'

He sat down at one of the specimen tables. 'So when we got word of what was happening out there ...' He leaned forward, stabbing a chubby finger into the top of the lab bench. 'We reversed the system. Airflow, filters, blowers, vents – all of it. Instead of keeping air from leaking *out*, we keep it from leaking *in*.'

The chair cocked back so far under his weight that it looked like it might give way. He crossed his arms and nodded proudly. Blocky red lettering across his stretched-out T-shirt proclaimed, TRUST ME, I'M A SCIENTIST!

I was struggling to adjust to being in a room with adults. Aside from Dr Chatterjee, we hadn't interacted with grown-ups for months, and it felt weird now.

'But how did you get word of the infection before it was too late?' Alex asked.

'It took a while for the spore concentration to reach us up here,' Laura said. 'And Zach – Dr Brewer – turned the front office into a comms station. We watched the infection spread on TV, studied the pathogen-dispersal patterns, and figured out in a hurry that we were in trouble. I made the call to lock down the facility. We're equipped for such contingencies in the event that an internal leak forces us to quarantine scientists in here. We have food stores, bathrooms, even an exercise room.'

She toyed with a locket around her neck, noticed she was doing it, and quickly lowered her hand. I wondered whose pictures the locket held. Her children? Husband? She wasn't wearing a ring. One thing seemed certain: Whoever her loved ones were out there, they were already dead.

She cleared her throat. 'Zach got a broadcast signal up pretty quickly. We've been sending out occasional alerts directing survivors here.'

'How many have come?' Alex asked.

Laura pursed out her lips. Rolled them over her teeth. Bit down. 'Just you.'

'But we *have* caught a few staticky incoming signals,' Zach said. 'More survivors out there. San Francisco. London. Hong Kong. All kids, of course.'

I felt an uptick in my heartbeat, a flare of hope. Survivors. More kids on various continents. Did I dare to dream about a change in fortune? A rebellion? The young shall inherit the Earth?

Not yet I didn't. I beat down the thoughts. Focused on what was before us.

'You're lucky the Drones haven't tuned in,' I said. 'And followed the signal here.'

Zach said, 'I don't think they know to scan for our wavelengths.'

'So you're a virologist?' Alex asked.

'Nah.' Zach shook his head, his long, wavy hair bouncing. 'That's Dr Messing.' He beamed at her. 'Chief of Viral Special Pathogens Branch. Ain't that right, boss?'

Laura gave an awkward thumbs-up. Her wrists were so thin that the cuffs of her white coat gaped around them like the sleeves of a wizard's robe. She had a few light freckles on her nose. She was probably one of those adults who looked way younger than she was.

'I worked at the Institute of Parasitology,' Zach said. 'So technically I'm a parasitologist. But that's a mouthful, isn't it?'

'What do you prefer to be called?' Alex asked.

He grinned. 'Awesome.'

'How do you know so much about what's going on out there from up here?' Patrick said.

'Are you kidding me? We've got the best view imaginable! Right down into Stark Peak.'

Laura said, 'We have airtight suits that allow us to leave the compound. We've run several missions to the observatory over in the astrology building.'

'We've been watching the Second Gens,' Zach said. A glance at Alex. 'You call 'em Hatchlings, yeah?'

She nodded.

'They seem to have a susceptibility to –'

Patrick, Alex, and I all spoke at the same time: '*Salt.*'

He stared at us in surprise. Then nodded. 'Right on.'

One of the male scientists piped up from the end of the table. 'We retrofitted the outdoor misters from the university cafeteria – you know, the ones they use for air-conditioning? They're a defense contingency.'

'We were just testing the lines when you guys showed up.' Zach turned to Laura. 'We got a blockage on the east wall, by the way. I'll fix it after dinner.' Swiveling back to us, barely taking a breath. 'If those Hatchers get near, we'll turn 'em into orange goo.'

Alex smiled. 'Hatch*lings*.'

'Them, too.' Zach sprang up and walked over to the nearest glass wall. It was opaque, a smoky gray. 'Speaking of that, check out what we have inside Hot Suite C.'

When he tapped the glass with his fingertips, it turned from smoky to clear.

I barely had time to marvel at the effect when the sight beyond took away my breath.

In the hot suite lay a dead Hatchling on a gurney, much of his flesh eaten away.

Alex, Patrick, and I stared through the giant pane into the cell-like room. It was shocking to see a Hatchling like that. I knew it was dead, but I couldn't quell the drumbeat of fear starting up in my chest.

'When we recalled the gondola, this guy was in it,' Zach said. 'A nasty little jack-in-the-box surprise. He'd trapped himself in there, you see.'

'How'd you kill him?' Patrick asked.

'A chiller-unit vapor-compression pipe to the head. As you do.' Zach flexed his biceps like a strongman. 'He started to heal the wound with alien kung fu magic so I had to take the head clear off. I gotta say, it was pretty badass.'

Laura grinned and rolled her eyes. 'The act of heroism might have been accompanied by some girlish shrieking.'

'There exists no evidence of girlish shrieking,' Zach said. 'But there *is* evidence of said badass kill.' He gave a game-show assistant's wave through the glass. 'We dragged his body back here where we could experiment on it.'

One of the other scientists cleared her throat. 'It took a lot of trial and error before we got to a saline solution. Ate through their flesh like acid.'

'Yeah,' Patrick said impatiently. 'We know. You said you have some cure or something? Immunity from the spores?'

Laura shook her head. 'I'm afraid we don't have anything like that.'

Alex stood up so fast the lab stool toppled behind her. 'But the transmission. It said you had a solution.'

The scientists stared at her, caught off guard by the sudden show of emotion.

'Alex turns eighteen the day after tomorrow,' I said. 'We only have two days.'

Laura nodded solemnly. 'Well. She'll be safe in here at least.'

'Safe?' Patrick said. 'For how long?'

'For as long as *we* are, I suppose. If we take one sip of outside air, we die.' Laura looked at Patrick. 'Now, you mentioned you're eighteen already. So why aren't you –'

'We'll get to that in a minute,' Patrick said. 'We went through hell and high water to get here. If you don't have immunity, then what solution *do* you have?'

Laura deflated. Even Zach's energy sapped. Reading their expressions, I felt a familiar chasm open up in my gut.

'It's a solution we *had*, I'm afraid,' Zach said. 'Past tense.'

Hopelessness swept through me. Alex righted her chair and sat down, her shoulders sagging. To have come this far to find nothing seemed unimaginable.

Patrick took off his cowboy hat. Ran a hand through his hair. Seated the Stetson back on his head. 'Explain,' he said.

'Well, the plan we *did* have,' Laura said, 'came from reverse engineering. We took the spores from air samples we'd collected and made our own version. We used their weaponized pathogens, stripped them down, and retrofitted them for our own purposes.'

'Kind of like viral vectors,' I said.

All the scientists looked at me funny.

'No, Chance,' Laura said. '*Exactly* like a viral vector. That's what we made. We used a lentivirus because —'

'It's a nice roomy virus,' I said. 'Like smallpox.'

'How is he this smart?' Zach asked. He looked at me. 'How are you this smart?'

'I'm not,' I said. 'I've just had this conversation before. Go on.'

Laura took off her horn-rimmed glasses and folded them in a slender fist. 'So just as the spores acted on adult humans, our viral vector would act on the Hatchlings, wiping them out.'

'How does it kill them?' I asked.

'Given Second Gen's susceptibility to salt,' Zach said, 'it'd be great if we could dump all the Hatchlings in the ocean, right? But most of our population centers are nowhere near the ocean. So the question we asked ourselves was, what commodity exists wherever people are threatened?'

Alex leaned forward and shoved her fists into her cheeks, clearly in no mood for an academic exercise. 'I give up.'

'The average human body is point-four percent salt.' Zach's bright little eyes glittered with excitement. 'Roughly

341

equivalent to the salt levels in the ocean. So I'll ask you again: What commodity exists wherever people are threatened?'

It dawned on me. *'People,'* I said.

Zach's fingers hovered over the table between us. 'You, Chance, like me, have two hundred grams of sodium chloride running through your veins. That's forty teaspoons of common table salt. And so we created an airborne pathogen that weaponized that salt. We'd inject it into an infected human –'

'A Host,' Alex said.

'A *Host*, and then that Host would disintegrate, turn into a saline aerosol the way the first wave of adult humans did when they released the spores. The infection would spread from Host to Host until the air was full of seawater mist.'

'Wiping out the Hatchlings,' I said.

*'Exactly,'* Zach said. 'We'd use the invaders' own slaves to destroy them!'

The idea excited me so much that I'd forgotten what he'd said about its not being viable anymore. But now I came crashing back to reality. And it hit me why it couldn't work, not anymore.

'They're all dead,' I said. 'The Hosts. So they can't spread anything.'

'As far as we can see,' Laura said, 'over the past few weeks the entire population of Hosts has dropped dead.' Again she fingered the locket around her neck. 'It took us weeks and weeks of around-the-clock work to come up with the solution. A few days too late.'

She walked over to the south-facing wall and placed her palm against it. The smoky glass turned clear. The adjoining room looked to be some kind of high-containment storage facility with gauges and dials, swirling freezer mist, and a dozen or so metal canisters. An embedded window in each canister showed a suspended syringe loaded with a cloudy white fluid.

Laura stared wistfully at her creation. 'A gorgeously engineered weaponized pathogen, and we have no means to disperse it.'

I felt it first along my spine, like an electrical charge. It prickled my skin, lifted the thin hair on my arms. I looked over at Patrick and found him staring back at me, already on the same page.

'What if I told you Patrick and I had the perfect dispersal weapons?' I said.

Zach tugged at his beard. Laura blinked at us rapidly. 'What?' she asked.

'Us.'

**ENTRY 55**     The cafeteria, cramped and dim, felt like a cave. We'd eaten military MREs – mushy beef Stroganoff, squeezy cheese on crackers, and apple jelly from tubes. Zach had fired up a trio of Bunsen burners, and we clustered around them now, roasting marshmallows on sterilized test-tube cleaners. I gripped the bristle end, letting the marshmallow impaled on the handle catch fire. I like mine *charred*.

It was early-morning late. I'd already explained the basics of my and Patrick's crazy genetic freakishness to the scientists, who'd listened with a mix of skepticism and wonder. Zach and Laura had peppered us with questions all the way through.

*Yes*, our DNA is designed to replicate a viral vector on a massive scale and release it.

*Yes*, the virus we release is engineered to reproduce inside the Hatchlings, triggering them to pass it from one to the next until there's a sufficient concentration to reach around the globe.

*Yes*, a secondary benefit of this dispersal is that it will wipe the Harvester pollen from the air, making the planet safe for humans.

And, of course:

*No*, we can't guarantee that your viral vector will work precisely the same way.

'But this is seriously advanced biotechnology,' I said. 'Think about it. The Rebels set up the dispersal mechanism in our DNA *years* before even knowing what specific viral vector they'd have to inject into us. I'm guessing it's a pretty plug-and-play setup.'

Laura said, 'We can't stake two children's lives on "plug-and-play."'

Alex sat on a bench with her hands wedged under her thighs, palms down. Her shoulders were drawn up by her ears. She did not look happy.

'What better options are there?' I asked.

'Better than having two of you *explode* yourselves?' Zach said. 'I can think of several.'

'Like what?' Patrick said.

Zach's mouth bunched, making his beard ripple. But he didn't have a reply.

I started tentatively, 'Look, I'm not saying we *will* do it, but if we *did* do it, what would be the most effective way?'

Zach leaned forward and blew out his flaming marshmallow. 'Well, you'd want to get to a high altitude in the middle of a dense population. You'd need the initial effect to be immediate – infecting a bunch of others quickly is the best way to ensure the virus'll spread throughout the city. Once the entire city is infected, our algorithms show that the air concentration will be sufficient to carry to neighboring cities. And from there we hit wind streams, and off we g –'

'Zach?' Laura said. '*Not* helpful.'

'Oh. Right.' He chomped down on the marshmallow, then turned bright red and let it fall from his mouth on to the floor. 'Sorry. *Hot*.'

'Perhaps we should table this discussion,' Laura said.

Alex blew out a shaky breath.

For a while we chewed and stared at the neat blue flames. Except for Zach. He was regarding us.

'I always wanted to have kids,' he said. 'Especially if they turned out as cool as you guys.'

Laura looked at him, and her eyes were puffy and sad. 'Maybe someday you still will.'

He made a little noise in his throat and spiked another marshmallow on the makeshift skewer.

Alex finally lifted her head. 'Why do you think this happened?'

'As in a cosmic why?' Zach said. 'I doubt that any of us can offer a better answer than you guys could.'

Laura said, 'We do know that the fossil record shows five major extinction events where at least half of the planet's species died off.'

'That *is* what we're staring in the face,' the scientist next to her said. 'Extinction.'

Patrick said, 'Unless we can stop it.'

'The worst part has been watching what it does to us,' Alex said. 'How it takes over our bodies.'

Zach made another of his little thoughtful noises.

'What?' Alex said.

'You assume you're in charge of your body now?' he asked.

'Of course I am,' Alex said.

'Can you make it stop growing? Sprouting hair? Growing fingernails? Can people with Type 1 diabetes decide to make insulin?'

'At least our brains are still our own,' Alex said. 'Our thoughts.'

'Are they?' Zach smiled. His tone wasn't malicious in the least. You could see he loved this kind of stuff. 'Can delusional schizophrenics control what's coming into their heads?'

'But they're sick,' I said.

'More readily definable as such. But I'm not.' He shot a smile at Laura. 'Not diagnosable at least. But when I get anxious, I perseverate – obsess on stuff, I mean. When I get scared, I can't just force myself to think happy thoughts. Some of that is learned, sure, but some of it is genetic. Hardwired into my brain. We're not as in control as we'd like to think.'

'You know what Alex means,' Patrick said. 'The way spores take over people. It's not natural.'

'Ah.' Zach raised a finger. 'And here we arrive at naturalistic fallacy. Just because something is natural doesn't mean it's good, right? Cancer is natural. Earthquakes are natural. Animals eating their young is natural. Antibiotics are not.'

'That's assuming that there's even a distinction between natural and unnatural,' Laura said. 'If humans are natural and Earth's resources are natural, then how could we make something unnatural? Why is, say, nuclear waste any different from a beaver dam or bird droppings?'

'Fair enough.' Zach stood up and walked over to a row of big lockers against the wall. 'But my point is, the Harvesters aren't doing anything to us that doesn't happen all the time in nature.'

'What are you *talking* about?' Alex said. She was getting flushed, ovals of pink coming up under her cheeks. Her spiky hair shot out in all directions, and she looked tough enough that I wouldn't have wanted to take her on right now.

'Brine shrimp,' Zach said. 'Also known as sea monkeys. They're transparent. Until they get infected by tapeworms. The tapeworms make them turn a vibrant red and gather in clusters in the water. Why? So they'll be spotted and eaten by flamingos. You see – this species of tapeworm can only reproduce inside flamingos. So they reprogram the brine shrimp to suit their own purposes just as the Harvesters reprogrammed human adults by turning them into Hosts.'

'And,' Laura said, 'just as we were hoping to *re*-reprogram them with our viral vector.'

Standing by his locker, Zach started to don a puffy white suit. 'The examples are countless. There's a tiny worm that invades crickets, grows to adult size, and turns the crickets suicidal. The crickets seek out the nearest body of water and drown themselves. Then the grown worm wiggles out. Why? Because the worms have to be in water to mate.'

Zach pulled on a giant boot. He was on a roll now, and it was clear that when he got on a roll, no one could stop him. 'The emerald cockroach wasp stabs a cockroach with a stinger sense organ.' He looked over at us. 'Just like the Harvester Queens have. Except the wasps use theirs to feel inside the cockroaches' brains. They inject venom into specific brain areas that take away the cockroaches' motivation to move of their own accord. Then the wasp walks the cockroach to its lair by one of its own antenna like a dog on a leash. It lays eggs inside the cockroach, and when the offspring hatch, they devour the cockroach. They even eat the organs in a specific order that guarantees the roach will stay alive until the larva can become a pupa and spin a cocoon inside the roach.'

Alex made a gagging gesture with a finger.

Zach was now ensconced in his airtight suit up to his neck. He held a helmet under one arm. He looked like a mix between Neil Armstrong and the Pillsbury Doughboy. 'Which raises another interesting question. We love to talk about free will. But is there any such thing? Is the infected cockroach still a cockroach? When does it stop being a roach? When does it become part of the wasp?'

'Like the Hosts,' I said. 'They became part of the Harvesters.'

'They did. We're looking at good old-fashioned parasitical warfare.' He tugged on his helmet and secured the latches. It was completely clear, giving him 360-degree sight lines. He spoke into a wire microphone that floated before his chin, his voice coming through clearly. 'Which is why we need to ready our defenses to kick some Hatchling ass.'

He started to shuffle out. 'I gotta fix that blockage in the saline-mist line on the east wall. Be back in fifteen.'

'That's fine, Zach,' Laura said with a grin. 'It'll give the rest of us a chance to speak.'

He flashed a thumbs-up and waddled out.

Laura turned to us. 'He's excitable,' she said.

'That's okay,' Alex said. 'We like it. Everything's felt dead for so long, it's nice to see someone with a spark of life in him.'

Laura fiddled with her locket. 'He does have that.'

One of her colleagues called her over, and they began discussing supply inventory. That gave me, Patrick, and Alex a moment to huddle in relative privacy.

'We have to talk them into letting us use their viral vector,' I said.

'Or steal it,' Patrick said.

'Either way we've gotta get our hands on one of those syringes and get down to the city center.' I stared at my brother. 'I'll inject myself. You go back for JoJo and Rocky.'

'We both take it,' Patrick said. 'You remember the odds for success. We both have to do it, and then Alex goes back for them.'

'Do I get a vote?' Alex asked.

'No,' Patrick said at the same time I said, 'Yes.'

She looked from my face to his. 'You Rains are *beyond* impossible.'

A loud chime sounded – some kind of alert – and then Zach's voice came in over the loudspeaker unit. 'Uh, guys? I think we got a problem here.'

**ENTRY 56**     Laura bolted through the doorway of the cafeteria into the hall, the scientists surging after her. We grabbed our weapons and backpacks and followed them as best we could. Running through the corridors was infuriating because of their segmented nature, each sliding door needing to seal behind us before the one ahead opened.

At last we made it through and up to the comms center. Laura brought up Zach's image on one of the giant wall monitors. He was standing by the keypad at the front door, peering into the security camera. His bearded face loomed large on the screen, cast green by the camera's night vision.

'Hello? Are you there, Laura?'

She clicked a button. 'I'm here. What's wrong? You scared us.'

Zach said, 'I have a . . . well, see for yourself.'

He stepped away from the camera, visible in the dawn light. His finger and thumb squeezed a fold in his suit at his thigh. Laura leaned over the console, bringing her face close to the monitor.

Then she jerked in a breath.

When she bowed her head, I saw past her to what she was looking at.

A tear in the fabric of Zach's suit. He was pinching it closed with his gloved hand. A few loose threads waggled in the air. He stared down at them.

'Shit,' he said.

'Maybe the spores didn't get through,' Laura said. 'Maybe that's why you haven't been infected yet. Maybe –'

'No,' he said. 'I already feel funny.' He pressed his other hand to the helmet over his forehead. 'The leak in the suit – it's tiny. And I sealed it off pretty quick. I think the spores haven't built up a high enough concentration in my body yet. But I can feel them in there, working. It's . . . interesting.'

His chest heaved a few times.

My mouth was dry. I hadn't known Dr Brewer long, but I liked him a lot already. The other scientists were staring through the Lucite entry room at the door beyond. He was right there on the other side.

Zach looked back at us and managed to produce a smile. 'When an ant dies, the others take its body and dump it far, far away from the colony to protect the surviving members.' His breathing grew more labored. 'In case it was infected.'

'No,' Laura said. 'No, no, no. Zach, listen to me. You don't *know* you're infected. The spore concentration could have thinned in the air.' Her hands flew across the keyboards. She brought up a screen on another monitor showing various readings of air particulates.

'Laura, it's okay. Let's make this easy now.'

She stared at the readings on the screen, and her shoulders curled, as if she were folding in on herself. None of the rest of us could move.

'Hello?' Zach tapped the camera screen with his finger. 'Is anyone there?'

Laura still couldn't respond, so I stepped forward.

'Yes?' I said.

'Chance?' Zach said. 'Kids?'

Patrick and Alex came forward next to me.

'The future rests in your hands.' Zach's beard shifted, and again he showed a hint of that goofy smile. 'I guess it's always rested in the hands of kids. But you know what I mean.'

'We'll do our best, sir,' Patrick said.

Zach stared into the lens. 'Laura?'

She finally looked up. 'I'm here,' she said.

Zach pulled back his shoulders, straightening his spine. 'It was a pleasure working with you, Dr Messing.'

Laura's voice was raspy. 'It was a pleasure working with you, Dr Brewer.'

Zach gave a nod. 'Good luck, doctors.'

Still pinching shut the tear in his suit, he walked over to the nearest golf cart at the edge of the parking lot and climbed on. Then he drove off.

Laura clicked the mouse, and another surveillance angle came up. We watched the golf cart motor across the parking lot. It bumped up on to a grassy slope and headed for the edge of the cliff by where the aerial tram was perched. Halfway across the lawn, Zach shuddered.

A storm of particles released inside his suit, swirling in the glass helmet, turning it into a snow globe. Then he slumped over the wheel.

The golf cart rolled forward off the cliff.

There was no crash, no noise, no nothing.

Laura took a step back from the console and sat down on the floor. Her hands lay loose in her lap.

No one knew what to say.

The scientist standing next to me sobbed a few times

and then silenced. Another wandered off and sat on a chair in the corner. Alex chewed her lip. Patrick took his hat off and held it against his chest. He studied the frayed stitching along the band.

Slowly, the scientists started to head back to the lab below.

I was the only one who noticed it.

A dot of movement on the monitor.

No – make that two.

Entering the field of the wide-angle security lens, two forms rushed along the edge of the cliff. One of them carried something swinging at its side.

They passed the spot where Zach had tumbled over the brink and veered toward the building.

Toward us.

As they came closer, I blinked a few times, unsure if I could trust my eyes.

Rocky and JoJo.

'Uh, guys?' I said.

No one turned around.

*'Guys!'*

At that, several heads snapped to attention. I pointed at the monitor.

Alex said, 'You have *got* to be kidding me.'

Rocky and JoJo were gesticulating at each other and pointing up various paths. They were arguing. Which seemed about right. JoJo swung Bunny's head by the ears and whapped her brother on the crown.

They finally agreed on which way to go and ran right past our building, vanishing off the edge of the screen. A moment later they came back and stopped in the parking lot, looking around. Looking everywhere, it seemed, but at our building.

Now they sprinted off in opposite directions, neither one correct.

Alex slapped her forehead with the palm of her hand.

Patrick said, 'Let's go get 'em.'

He started for the door when JoJo reappeared on the monitor. She pointed at our building and started jumping up and down and shouting. Rocky emerged from one of the trails, and they ran for us.

Now they appeared on the other screen, the one linked to the surveillance cam by the door. JoJo leaned in so close we could see up her nose. Her breath fogged the glass. I could see her hand bobbing as she punched buttons indiscriminately.

All this time Laura hadn't stirred from her position on the floor. I stepped past her and clicked the button. 'JoJo?'

'Chance? Chance! You gotta get out of here. There's no time. They're coming.'

'Wait. *Who?*'

She and Rocky jockeyed for position, and I caught a glimpse between their shoulders.

A Hatchling stood behind them at the edge of the cliff.

We watched with horror.

Another flew up over the brink, landing beside it. And then another.

They'd scaled the cliff face with their claws.

A few more came over the edge, and then we stopped counting.

A wave of orange poured over the lip, sweeping toward us.

**ENTRY 57**   I couldn't figure out how to buzz the door open for JoJo and Rocky. They were screaming into the camera now, their faces mashed together as if they were trying to crawl through the lens.

I hauled Laura to her feet. 'Open the door!' I shouted.

She blinked twice and then snapped back to life.

With trembling hands she keyed in a code, and the door clicked open. JoJo and Rocky leapt through into the decontamination room. As Rocky swung the door closed behind them, one of the Hatchlings hammered into it, knocking them both on to the floor. The door whammed shut and autolocked. Already the fans and UV lights were going, sterilizing the air around Rocky and JoJo in the Lucite-walled room.

There came a dull thud and then another, the percussion quickening as more and more Hatchlings hurled themselves against the concrete walls. A clawed hand struck the slit window, leaving an orange dab. The windows were narrow, but still wide enough that a Hatchling could wriggle through. It was only a matter of time.

'The saltwater misters!' one of the scientists cried.

Laura initiated the system, saline solution humming through the pipes. A moment later we heard screeching from outside. The other scientist called up various feeds on the monitors. The sight was horrendous – Hatchlings melting along the sides of the building or staggering away, clawing at themselves. More and more swept in toward us, trampling the wounded.

'There are too many,' Laura said. 'We'll never hold them off.'

The decontamination process finally finished with Rocky and JoJo, the glass door clicking open. JoJo spilled into my arms, terrified.

'Ben told them where you were,' she said.

'Wait a minute,' I said. 'Ben's alive?'

'He *was*,' Rocky said. 'But after he told them where you guys were, they didn't need him anymore. The Queen, she . . . she fed him to the Hatchlings.'

JoJo's voice, hushed with horror: 'It was awful.'

Alex lowered her head, closed her eyes for a second. We didn't know what to say or feel. Ben had shown his true colors again and again, but even he didn't deserve that fate.

JoJo said, 'We raced here to warn you.'

'Thank God you did,' Laura told her. 'We'd have been down below. They would have caught us off guard. It would've been a bloodbath.'

'It still might be,' another scientist said, pointing to the monitors.

The mound of carrion at the base of the walls was growing, flesh layering on top of flesh. Each new wave of Hatchlings used the mounting pile as a foothold to jump higher toward the windows.

A melting face rose into view, smacking the pane, all black eyes and flaring nostril holes. The glass spider-webbed. Another vaulted into brief view, soaring above the glass. We waited to see him drop.

But he didn't.

The monitor showed that he'd flung himself on to the mister line itself. His body stuck on the pipe, liquefying. His bubbling flesh plugged the spray openings, providing a clear lane through the mist for the others.

'Fall back,' Patrick said.

Laura staggered toward the stairs and elbowed a big red punch button on the wall. The Lucite door behind us slid open. She gestured at the spiral staircase beyond. 'Go, go, go!'

The scientists shoved us forward, so we stumbled on to the landing. Then they piled through after us. One of the scientists banged into a rolling chair and fell over. He looked up at us.

The rest of us were already through the glass door on the landing above the twisting steel stairs.

Another Hatchling hit the cracked window. The fissures spread to the edges of the pane. A chip of glass spit out and tapped the floor.

Looking across the threshold at the comms center, Laura lifted her hand to the red button on our side of the doorway. Her palm hovered an inch away.

'Please,' the scientist said. 'Please wait.' He used a chair to pull himself up, but it rolled out from under him and he toppled over.

Another Hatchling struck the window, the glass cascading away.

Laura jammed the heel of her hand into the button, and the glass door whipped shut.

The scientist on the floor shuddered. His eyes went to ash and disintegrated. He rose. We stared through the tunnels of his head. Through them we could see the shattered window.

Hatchlings jammed the narrow gap, bent arms and legs and snapping faces. The neighboring window gave way next, clogged by Hatchlings clawing to get through.

The first batch of Hatchlings fell.

Directly into the saline tanks.

They screeched and thrashed, and the water turned a boggy orange.

Then the others tumbled through. They spilled over the consoles, on to the floor.

That got us moving.

We flew down the stairs, our feet hammering the steel steps. At the bottom another containment door. Alex hit the button, and we stumbled through, banging into one another, nearly tripping.

We ran through the airlock toward the heart of the warren. My only thought was to head for the relative safety of the main research area and living quarters. Alex waited to close the door behind us.

We managed a brief sprint before hitting the next wall. Another button, another wait, another brief sprint. We made balky, painstaking progress.

As the next wall sealed before us, we looked back down the corridor through the four Lucite doors we'd put between us and the horde.

The Hatchlings were piling against the door at the base of the stairs. It looked like a wall of orange. Only a few twitching limbs and blinking eyes were distinct.

The door gave way.

A female Hatchling, large and rotund, bounded out

ahead of the others. She gathered speed as she approached the next door and leapt at it, curling up. She shattered through with battering-ram force.

She fell to the floor, stuck through with shards, a quivering mass. The others charged over her, pounding her into the tiles.

We moved frantically down the next segment of corridor, this one leading into the main research area. Laura ran ahead, reaching the next threshold. She fished a digital key card from her pocket and held it over the inset panel, ready to open the next door the instant Patrick got the one behind us shut. The halting movement was torture. Each delay felt like an eternity. The airtight chunks of hall smelled of sweat and fear.

Hatchlings were making up ground, sprinting and crashing through door after door like rampaging hurdlers.

Now they were in the airlock chamber right behind us. The door between us and them slid shut in seeming slow motion. Patrick kept jacking the red button as though that could make the barrier move any quicker.

The throng closed in on us, shoving their putrid scent before them. At last the door sealed right between us.

It was clear there wouldn't be enough time for us to get to the next section.

As the lead male hurtled at the glass, Patrick stepped back and squared to fight. Behind us Alex snatched the key card from Laura, tapped it to the panel, and then shoved Laura through into the next airlock chamber. Alex slammed the key card to the panel again to close the door between her and Laura. As it rolled shut, Alex Frisbeed the card down the hall past Laura so it would be locked in there with her.

Laura fell over, nearly losing her horn-rimmed glasses. Then she rose and ran for us. The closing door sealed and she pounded her fists against it.

An instant later the male's torso punched a hole right through the door by me and Patrick. The Hatchling hung there a moment, jagged glass teeth sunk into his gut, his juices leaking down the pane beneath him.

Contaminated air breezed through. All around us the scientists shuddered and transformed into Hosts. JoJo screamed, the noise so high-pitched it sounded like a whistle.

Other Hatchlings smashed their way through.

As I turned to face off with the scientists, Patrick fired a few shells from the Winchester, a rock-salt fusillade tearing through the lead ranks. The Hatchlings screeched and writhed, their bodies gumming up the gap.

I spun through the scientists, swinging the baling hooks, tearing out throats and impaling heads. Murdering these people who had been so good to us. Moments ago they'd been our friends.

Next to me Alex made fast work of the others with her hockey stick. Laura watched from the other side, one hand pressed to the Lucite, sobbing.

Alex jabbed a finger at Laura, indicating the next chamber and the waiting key card. *Go.*

Laura turned and ran.

Rocky and JoJo were backed into a corner, a scientist Host lunging at them. His hands were inches away when I caught him through the temple with the tip of my baling hook, slamming him into the wall. He fell down in a broken-doll sprawl.

JoJo hopped up, snatched the key card from the dead Host's belt, and tapped it to the panel. It did nothing. Laura wasn't yet through the next door. JoJo waved the key card again and again over the panel. At last Laura tumbled through ahead, the door zippering shut, allowing ours to glide open.

Patrick held the rear, walking backward and firing shot after shot. Barely holding off the horde. We'd left plenty of bodies as obstacles. Some of the Hatchlings seemed confused by the recently turned Hosts, snatching at them with their jaws and then turning on one another.

We'd bought a little time.

We ran through, sealed the door behind us. UV lights beamed down, sterilizing the air and making us sweat. We caught up to Laura after the next door. We'd wound up in the nexus near the main lab, the corridor splitting off in two directions.

The Hatchlings had finished their brawling over the Hosts. A multitude of heads lifted, staring through the two barriers at us.

The effect was unsettling.

Laura was breathing hard, her face red and swollen. Though she was no longer crying, she was still catching her breath. '. . . rear stairwell . . . this way . . . another tank filling the rear misters . . .'

At the end of the corridor was a large steel door with a heavy cylindrical handle.

'We're there,' Alex said, charging down the hall. Patrick, Rocky, and JoJo followed.

I hesitated. Then I grabbed Laura's key card and ran the *other* way.

The halls were parallel, so Patrick could see me through the glass walls. For an instant we were running side by side. He looked pissed.

'What are you doing?' he yelled.

There was no time to answer. I peeled away, watching my brother fade from sight. Behind me the sound of shattering glass, scrabbling nails, and grunts carried up the corridor.

I ran across the lab and slapped the smoky glass with my palm. The high-containment storage facility on the far side came clear. I tapped Laura's key card to the panel, and the door slid open.

I stepped into the swirling mist. The window behind me morphed from transparent back to its smoky glaze. The metal canisters were cold to the touch. My fingers almost froze to the latches as I unclipped them. I grabbed two syringes, shoving them into one of the cargo pockets of my scrub trousers.

I started for the rear door.

The smoky pane exploded in at me.

A huge female barreled into the canisters, knocking them all over the place. I raised my baling hook, but she backhanded me as she rose. I'd been kicked by horses before and I can tell you: She hit me much, much harder. I slid across the tiles and knocked my head into the wall, my cheek burning, yellow spots dotting my vision.

A large clawed foot set down inches from my nose. The floor shook as her other leg stomped down. She was straddling me.

I managed to turn my aching head to look up as she leaned over me.

**ENTRY 58**     Claws and jagged little fangs.

That's all I saw.

They zoomed in at me.

My baling hooks were twisted behind me, held to my wrists only by the nylon loops. There'd be no time to grab for the handles. My hand groped the floor around me.

It seized on a spinning canister. The latch had been knocked open. I shot my hand inside. My fingers closed around the syringe filled with cloudy white fluid.

I could feel the Hatchling's breath now. A drop of saliva fell, striking my neck and sizzling.

Grabbing the syringe, I jammed it through the top of the Hatchling's foot and depressed the plunger.

The effect of the viral vector was instantaneous.

She reared back, her mouth gaping. She didn't even have time to screech before she disintegrated, her jaws opening ever wider as her skin and muscle melted from her head on down, a sheet of orange slop puddling to the floor. I rolled free before the spill hit me.

More Hatchlings poured into the main lab; I could see them through the shattered window. I ran to the rear door, used Laura's key card to get through. As the Hatchlings barreled at me, I closed the door. One hand curled around the edge at the last second but lost its purchase as the glass whipped shut.

The hall behind me ended with another steel door. I ran to it, my breath and footsteps echoing like crazy. I could hear the Hatchlings approaching, but I didn't look back.

I reached the steel cylindrical handle and yanked to turn it. It didn't give. I put more strength into it, and at last it spun. I whipped it around and around, banging it with my palm, ignoring the sound and the stench, closer every second.

As last the lugs released, and I ripped the door open. It wasn't until I slipped through and turned to tug it shut behind me that I dared to lift my eyes.

Hatchlings filled the corridor – not just wall to wall but leapfrogging over one another, crowding the space from floor to ceiling in their eagerness to get at me. One was near enough to reach through the gap and swipe at my face, his claw opening a thin seam on my cheek. Roaring, I slammed the door against the weight of them. As it banged shut, it lopped off the Hatchling's finger. The crooked digit lay at my feet, twitching.

I gulped in a breath and stepped back.

Something rustled behind me.

I yelled and spun around, but it was Patrick.

The others were there, too. We were in a tiny metal room protected by steel doors on either side. A rear staircase rose to a third door that led outside. Apart from a small tank of saline solution feeding the mister pipes through the walls, the room was bare.

I was panting. 'I got two syringes.'

'You're an idiot,' Alex said. 'A *brave* idiot.'

Hatchlings pounded at the steel doors.

Laura fumbled her glasses into place. 'You have to go,' she said.

'The spores,' Alex said. 'If we open that door, you'll die.'

A dent appeared in the metal, but it looked like it would hold.

Laura raised her slender arms to gesture to the four walls. 'This is the last safe place on Earth for me,' she said. 'I'm dead already.' She pointed up the brief run of stairs. 'Open it,' she said. 'Go.'

None of us moved.

'I won't have you die for nothing,' Laura said.

More banging. Another dent. Now the drywall at the edge of the frame started to crumble. Rocky yelped, and JoJo pressed Bunny's head over her eyes.

Laura climbed the steps. Put her hand on the doorknob. She smiled back at us. ' "The future rests in your hands," ' she said.

Then she opened the door.

Fresh air rushed in. She stiffened on her heels. Shuddered. Behind her horn-rimmed glasses, her eyes turned to tunnels. Then she tumbled down the stairs.

Her head smacked against the floor, and she was still. Her glasses spun away. Her necklace was pulled to one side, her locket cracked open.

It held a tiny photograph.

Of Zach.

That tiny locket tore a hole right through my chest. But I had no time to dwell on it. Alex and Patrick were already at the top of the stairs, peering through the outside door.

'Get up here,' my brother said.

I jogged up and peeked through.

The parking lot was overrun with Hatchlings. I looked past the groundskeeper shack and on to the quad, but that, too, was covered with bodies swarming toward the building. More and more clawed up the cliff edge, pouring over the stalled gondola.

We had nowhere to go.

I scrunched my eyes shut. Opened them.

'Guys?' I said. 'I have a plan.'

In tight formation we burst from the doorway, Patrick and I holding the tank of saline solution on either end, with Rocky and JoJo flanking us. Alex took the lead with the shotgun. The tank – no bigger than a giant picnic cooler – was heavier than you could believe. It was slippery, hard to grip. The water slopped up our arms as we ran. My baling hooks twisted from their loops, clattering against the side of the tank. We ran-hobbled toward the groundskeeper shack twenty or so yards away.

The element of surprise let us get about halfway there before the Hatchlings took note. A single head swiveled to note us, and the rest followed in a wave, like cornstalks rippled by the wind. Hatchlings charged us from all sides.

Alex fired, pivoted, fired, pivoted, sending out wide sprays in every direction. Ducking beneath the raised shotgun, Patrick and I did our best to keep making progress. When Alex twisted to get off another shot, a surge of Hatchlings threatened our exposed flank. Rocky swiped at them with Alex's hockey stick, but it had little effect. JoJo dipped her hands in the tank and flung salt water at them. Scalded, they stumbled back, knocking into the others behind them.

Still holding one side of the tank, Patrick smashed into the shack, knocking the rickety door off its top hinge. We tumbled inside, losing our grip on the tank. Somehow it kept from shattering when it landed. Salt water sloshed over the sides, but most of it held.

Alex filled the doorway, facing out, firing, jacking the shotgun, and firing again.

'I don't mean to sound pushy, Chance,' she called over her shoulder. 'But if you could do whatever you're doing in fast-friggin'-forward, that'd be swell.'

As Rocky redipped our weapons in the salt water, I tore through the cabinets. Watering cans, hoes, shovels. For a terrified moment, I thought I'd misstepped – that there wouldn't be one here.

But there it was, collecting cobwebs in the corner.

A weed sprayer.

I thumped the plastic four-gallon sprayer on the floor and spun off the cap.

Alex held down the doorway, keeping Hatchlings – barely – at bay. They thumped the walls. Wood splintered. Shadows flickered between planks. The shack wouldn't last long.

JoJo grabbed a watering can, dipped it in the salt water, and flung it out from between Alex's legs. The Hatchlings leapt away, their bodies sizzling as the saline ate through their flesh. The others kept a few feet back from the wet grass, afraid to step forward.

Patrick and I picked up the saline tank and tipped it. The first pour knocked over the empty weed sprayer. Rocky set it upright and held it, and we managed to direct the stream from one corner of the tank through the small opening.

In the back a few planks splintered inward behind the

wall-mounted shelves. Sinewy arms twisted into sight, knocking stuff over, clawing the air. Just out of reach.

At last the sprayer tank reached full and started overflowing.

I screwed the cap on. Ripping off my backpack, I tossed it to Rocky, who put it on. Then I picked up the weed sprayer by its straps and slung it over my shoulders. I wielded the fiberglass wand and pulled the trigger.

A spray shot out.

Perfect.

'Ready?' Alex shouted.

JoJo handed her watering can to Rocky and filled another with what was left in the tank.

'Ready,' I said.

From there it went like clockwork. Alex turned and tossed Patrick his shotgun. Rocky tossed Alex her stick.

Patrick stepped through the doorway and fired twice. Rocky and JoJo darted out beside him and flung salt water from the watering cans in wide, arcing sprays.

As Rocky and JoJo parted, I shot between them, filling the air around us with saline mist.

The Hatchlings screeched and bucked, in total disarray. You'd have thought I was wielding a flamethrower.

We forged forward into the sea of Hatchlings. They folded into place behind us. I waved the wand in a 360, keeping a constant sphere of mist around us.

We made slow but steady progress toward the edge of the cliff. I'd thought I'd be able to ration the saline solution, but the Hatchlings were too dense. I had to keep the trigger depressed. The tank was already half empty.

We made it to the cliff, several Hatchlings waving their

hands frantically against the mist before tumbling off the brink. As they plummeted, they took out several Hatchlings scaling the walls. At last we reached the edge. I sent a cloud of salt mist down over the cliff face to protect our rear guard. More Hatchlings peeled off and fell away. Now we only had to fight facing in one direction. We moved sideways along the brink, the ground crumbling behind our heels. When I glanced back, the drop seemed bottomless. The tank on my back – now three-fourths empty.

We made for the aerial tram.

Fighting our way along the cliff, our backs to thin air. The sprayer started to sputter, running out of juice.

At last we banged into the tram. It floated a few feet off the ground, ready to descend.

I wafted the last of the mist through the cabin. Two Hatchlings pawed at their melting faces and pitched through the doors on the far side.

As Patrick, Alex, Rocky, and JoJo piled in, I turned to face the driving throng and pulled the trigger. Nothing happened.

I ripped the weed sprayer off my back and threw it at them. It bonked off a Hatchling's head. He was undeterred.

From behind, Patrick and Alex each grabbed one of my shoulders and meat-hooked me into the cabin. Rocky slammed the door shut after me.

I pounced up on to the operator's seat. The bubble front window showed nothing but open skies and Stark Peak way down below.

Home-free sailing.

I yanked the lever to release the brake.

Nothing happened.

**ENTRY 59**     In disbelief, I pulled the lever again. And then again.

Hatchlings piled on to the cabin from all sides, a round-about view of waiting death. The floating tram swayed from side to side. Gentle at first. And then not.

I started punching other buttons at random, but nothing happened. 'You have *got* to be kidding me,' I said.

'It might have been wise to ascertain that the lift was working *before* we blaze-of-gloried ourselves out here,' Alex said.

Patrick rested the shotgun barrel across my shoulder. I looked over at it. He covered my ear with one hand and pulled the trigger with the other.

At close range? The whole ear-covering thing? *Not* that helpful.

The front bubble window shattered out, a confetti throw of shards into the abyss. Patrick stepped past me and up on to the control panel so his torso and head were sticking out into the open air. He faced back over the top of the tram.

'I see the brake,' he said.

He aimed above the cabin with his shotgun. 'It'll either knock off the brake or hit the cable and send us plummeting to our deaths.'

'*Patrick,*' I said.

The shotgun wobbled. He could only hold it with one hand; he needed the other to grip the frame of the blown-out window. He looked down at me. I could barely see his eyes beneath the cowboy hat, and they looked amused.

'What the hell,' he said.

And then he fired.

We torpedoed off the edge of the cliff, and for a moment I thought we were gonna just keep falling.

But no, the tram was still clinging to the steel cables overhead. A slew of Hatchlings tumbled over the cliff in our wake, several more sliding off the roof.

Patrick fell back inside, falling across the open cabin and hammering against the rear window.

Rocking violently from side to side, the cabin whipped down toward the first supporting tower. As we reached it, the tram pitched to the side. JoJo and Rocky screamed. We were gonna smash right into the tower.

We clipped the edge of the massive metal post. One wall of the cabin was sheared off, door and all. Rocky and JoJo got knocked over the back bench, plastered to the rear window with Patrick. As we seesawed to the other side, Alex slid out backward on her belly toward the opening. Her fingernails dug for purchase on the cabin floor, but there was none to be found.

I fell out of the operator's chair, tangling in a seat belt. As I slipped through, it lassoed my head and one arm, holding me in place.

I reached out and grabbed for Alex's hand. It slipped from my grasp. My fingers caught hers, hooking them with my knuckles, but the centrifugal force was too great, pulling her away.

Alex slid back, her legs falling through the opening. Her hand shot out and grabbed my leg. Her arm flexed, her hand gathering a fistful of fabric above my knee. For an instant we held that awkward equilibrium. Movement flickered above. A Hatchling stuck his head over the edge of the roof, leaning down past the sheared-off opening to swipe at Alex. All the while we hurtled toward the next tower.

Behind Alex the mountainside flew by in a blur. My stomach muscles strained as I reached for her. The Hatchling lowered himself, clinging to the roof, the tips of his nails scraping Alex's back. She hung on to my leg, her teeth gritted. I could hear my cargo scrubs tearing. I prayed they'd hold.

They tore.

More precisely, the cargo pocket ripped open.

Sending both viral-vector syringes rattling across the floor of the cabin.

Helpless, I watched them go. One glided straight off the sill, sailing into the void.

The other banged against the side of a bench, spun lazily for a moment on the floor, and then flew out after it. I watched our last hope zip across the threshold, free in the air.

Alex shot her other hand out behind her and grabbed it. Her body stretched as far as humanly possible, her legs dangling in space, one hand gripping the syringe, the other holding on to the torn flap of my cargo pocket.

The Hatchling finally reached her. With a lunge, he closed his claws around her forearm just above her fist clenching the syringe.

Alex screamed.

But she didn't let go.

The Hatchling shook her arm, the acid sending up curls of smoke. I smelled burning flesh.

Still Alex held on to the syringe.

And to my leg.

My fingers were inches away from her hand as it gripped my torn cargo pocket.

The fabric gave way.

Alex went weightless. Her hand flailed up.

With a final effort, I surged forward and grabbed for her wrist.

Caught it.

As I raked her back inside the cabin, she twisted around and kicked the Hatchling in the side of the head so hard that his skull caved in at the temple. He released her forearm, plummeting off the roof.

As he fell, the other tram zipped past, being hauled upslope as a counterweight. It plowed into the Hatchling, sending him flying, a jumble of broken limbs.

The cabin was still swinging like mad. I ripped Alex in to me and gripped her as tight as I could. She hugged me back. That felt so good I didn't even notice that my shoulder had been dislocated. When I shifted, it popped into place again with an audible click.

Alex fumbled the syringe at me, and I shoved it into the cargo pocket on my other thigh. Her skin bore the acid mark of the Hatchling's three-fingered grip, puffy and swollen.

In the rear, Patrick held on to JoJo and Rocky, bracing against the benches with his legs. The cabin hammered through the next supporting tower, the steel rise sailing past, missing us by inches.

We were really flying now.

Two-thirds down the hill and picking up steam. The city loomed larger and larger. We were bouncing violently, the whole view gone jerky. If we didn't slow the tram, we were going to fly right off the steel cables.

Alex and I managed to claw our way to the operator seat.

The ground whipped by below. Pitted rocks thrust up from the brush like molars.

We scoured the controls for anything resembling a backup brake. No luck.

I climbed up on to the control panel and pulled myself through the shattered front window, driving the baling hooks into the roof so I could hold on.

Alex grabbed my leg. 'What are you doing?'

I screamed back into the wind, 'Maybe I can activate a brake up there by hand!'

She just pointed ahead.

The bottom terminal was coming up fast.

I kicked myself up on to the roof, using the baling hooks like ice picks, my body swinging around crazily. I dragged myself toward the mount where the wheel set rolled along the steel tracks. I spotted a red emergency-brake lever to one side, intact but pitted with pellets from Patrick's shotgun.

The cabin blasted through another supporting tower, bucking high and then dipping so low that treetops whacked the bottom of the cabin.

It bounced me right off the roof of the tram.

I floated peacefully, the world rotating around me. The cabin sailed by beneath me, out of reach.

I was going to fall hundreds of feet and break apart on the rocks below, and there was nothing anyone could do about it.

As I spun upside down, one of the steel cables flashed by in my peripheral vision. I twisted and flung out a baling hook.

And snared the cable.

My falling weight ripped the handle from my fist.

But the nylon loop held, biting into the flesh of my wrist. I kicked and writhed, sliding down the steel cable as if it were a zip line.

I risked a look ahead of me.

Four faces filled the cabin's back window, staring at me helplessly. Beyond them the bottom terminal. If they hit it at this speed, there'd be nothing left but blood splotches.

I yanked myself up, swinging my other baling hook on to the cable.

I was picking up steam now, zip-lining along, closing the gap between me and the tram. When I tucked my legs up into my stomach, balling up my body, I went even faster.

I approached the cabin as the cabin approached the bottom station.

There'd be almost no time.

My eyes were watering like crazy, but I blinked away the tears, squinting into the chill wind.

I closed in on the tram.

Hoisted my body up just before I hit the rear window.

I slid across the top of the cabin.

Knocked the brake as I glided past.

The wheels screamed their complaint. The current tore away wisps of gray smoke.

The tram slowed drastically, which only made me feel like I was speeding up. I zipped right across the roof.

Just before I flew off the other side, Alex popped up from the broken front window. She was right in front of me, braced like a baseball catcher.

I hammered into her.

She made a sound: *Oomph*.

She clutched me in a sweaty embrace. We fell on to the control panel and pinballed to the floor. I landed right on top of her. We were nose to nose.

Above us the wheels squealed. In the back, Rocky and JoJo burrowed into Patrick.

Through the shattered bubble window, we watched the bottom terminal loom. Larger.

Larger yet.

'Did you slow us enough?' Alex asked me.

I stared down into her green, green eyes. 'Let's hope,' I said.

We held each other, braced for impact.

The impact didn't disappoint.

At first it was a catastrophic confusion. Rent metal. My teeth vibrating in my skull. A science-fiction warble of the steel cable snapping. The air filled with glass. We banged to earth so hard it felt like the floor swung up to hammer us.

Freed from the cables, the cabin skated across the lobby of the terminal like a hockey puck. Fancy light fixtures whipped by overhead.

A great shattering announced that we'd penetrated the

row of lobby windows facing the street. Sparks showered up as we hit the asphalt. Rocketing toward the intersection, we ran over a female Hatchling. Then two males.

We ping-ponged off a parked truck, careened through the intersection, passing a busload of Drones who stared out the windows at us as we flew past. Spinning slowly, we coasted up on to the sidewalk and came to rest, rocking gently on a bed of shrubs in front of the courthouse.

We coughed and hacked and groaned. The air was filled with dust and smoke.

'Is everyone alive?' Patrick shouted.

'Mostly,' I said.

We pulled ourselves from the wreckage. The city center still looked relatively empty, the search parties presumably still out at the periphery. But there were scattered Hatchlings and Drones. And they were already running for us.

We bolted up the steps into the courthouse. Through the lobby, a courtroom, a judge's chambers, and out a window into an alley.

Footsteps behind us.

Through another window into a department store, sprinting up the aisles, knocking over mannequins, getting tangled in clothes.

The footsteps still coming. More of them now.

Out a side door, across a street, up another alley, hiding behind a giant black Humvee.

We panted and panted, peering beneath the high chassis at the department store across from us.

'. . . can't run . . . anymore . . .' Rocky said.

After everything we'd gone through, I, too, felt at the

end of my endurance. My legs throbbed. My lungs burned. My shoulder ached.

Across the way our pursuers came into view in the windows of the department store, heading to the sliding front doors. Coming right in our direction.

Rocky stifled a sob.

A creaking sound came from behind us.

We whirled around in terror.

But it was just JoJo, holding open the giant wooden door of an old church right behind us. We'd been so focused on hiding that we hadn't even noticed it.

She smiled, keeping Bunny's head tucked under her arm.

Alex headed inside. 'Sanctuary,' she said.

**ENTRY 60**     We huddled in the bell tower like low-rent Hunchbacks of Notre-Dame. We'd scampered up the creaky wooden ladders, losing ourselves in the network of walkways and scaffolding that threaded around the old apse. From here we could keep an eye on the city below.

Patrols of Harvesters tore through the streets and alleys. We'd closed and barred the weighty oak doors of the church beneath us. The stone façade was impenetrable. More important, the Drones and Hatchlings centered their search a few blocks away from the department store, figuring we'd had time to get in a bit more distance from where they'd last seen us.

The setting sun sent an orange glow across the tower, reflecting off the giant bronze bell overhead and casting us in a twilight hue. We leaned against the brick walls. It had been hours since our escape and it still felt like we were catching our breath.

I rubbed the aching tendons around my shoulder. It didn't help. My cheek stung from where the Hatchling had sliced it with his nail. Alex tended to the cracked swelling on her forearm. Rocky and JoJo were off to the side, tucked into the corner of the belfry. Rocky had curled up like a puppy and fallen asleep. JoJo was sitting cross-legged, hopping Bunny up and down in her lap. The

Head of Bunny had never looked worse. Tattered, dotted with acid burns from Hatchling spatter, a missing half-marble eye. But JoJo loved her just the same.

Patrick sat with his elbows resting on his knees, his black Stetson slanted. He looked well rested and calm. I had no idea how that was possible, but that was Patrick for you.

On the stone floor between me, Patrick, and Alex sat the single syringe. Miraculously, it had remained unbroken in my cargo pocket.

One viral vector.

And – in me and my brother – two dispersal bombs.

The math sucked.

The three of us did our best not to look at the syringe, but it was screaming for our attention there between us. It felt like some macabre game of spin the bottle. Which – if you really thought about it – was kinda appropriate.

Alex looked away, and I followed her gaze. To the west across Stark Peak, the City Hall spire rose, the highest point in the skyline. It used to represent such hope for me. I remember marveling at it on our third-grade field trip. They'd even let us on to the roof for an up-close look. We'd stood at the base, leaned back on our heels, and stared at it thrusting into the sky. It was the first time I'd ever encountered vertigo from looking *up*. But especially for us kids from a farm-and-ranch town, it seemed to hold all the promise of what mankind had to offer.

And now, there on that spire, we would make our last stand for mankind.

How had Zach put it? *A high altitude in the middle of a dense population.*

Yup, City Hall spire seemed just about right.

*If* we could get there.

*If* the scientists' viral vector worked with whatever dispersal mechanism had been implanted in my and Patrick's DNA.

*If* the engineered, weaponized pathogen worked against the Harvesters.

I pushed my doubts away. We had one play to make, and we would have to make it. There's no point second-guessing your final option.

'We're down to our last day,' I said.

Alex stayed still, but her eyes shifted over to me. 'Before I die. Or before one of you does.'

'What does *that* mean?' JoJo asked.

'New Year's baby,' Alex said. 'I was born just after dawn. Tomorrow's December thirty-first. The last day where I still get to be me.'

'I know that,' JoJo said. 'But Patrick and Chance are gonna save you, right?'

I said, 'That's right, Junebug.'

'So what does she mean that one of *you* might die?'

No one answered.

'The streets are too busy to make a move,' Patrick said to me. 'We gotta wait for it to die down a little.'

JoJo said, 'Why can't you just do whatever you're doing here?'

'We need to get as high up as possible,' Patrick said. 'For wind currents and all that.'

'What *are* you gonna do?' JoJo asked, fear taking over her voice.

Patrick met my eyes. 'We're not sure yet.'

'Yeah,' I said. 'We are.' I leaned forward, took the syringe, and put it back in my pocket.

'No,' Patrick said. 'No way.'

'You guys can be together,' I said. 'It's always been you two.'

A tear rolled down Alex's cheek. 'No,' she said. 'It's always been us *three*.'

'We don't have that choice,' I said. 'Not anymore. One of us has to, or everything's over.'

JoJo was crying now. 'I'm scared,' she said. 'Why won't you tell me what's happening?'

Patrick's gaze didn't waver from me. 'I won't let you,' he said.

I looked at him. 'Big brother, you don't have a choice.'

Patrick got up and walked out of the belfry.

JoJo started to sob.

I looked at Alex and nodded for her to leave me and JoJo alone.

Alex got up, picked up Rocky, and carried him out.

I opened my arms, and JoJo crawled into my lap.

I did my best to explain to her what was going to happen tomorrow. My best wasn't very good. She beat at my chest with her little fists and then collapsed into me and cried so long I thought she'd never stop. The sun went down, and I rocked her in the darkness until at last she quietened. Her breaths were still jerky.

'Will you come down from here with me?' I asked.

'What for?'

'To finish our story.'

'No,' she said. 'No, I won't.'

She got up and ran from the belfry.

I sat for a while, tasting the night air.

Tomorrow at this time, I'd be dead.

I gave myself a couple extra minutes to study the moon. How beautiful it was, blood-orange and ripe.

A harvest moon.

I found Patrick and Alex down in the vast chamber of the church, talking quietly. As I approached, Alex held out her hand.

I took it. Then Patrick took her hand and mine, the three of us standing in a circle, dwarfed by the huge golden altarpiece. Before us was a simple wooden table covered with a white linen cloth. It was so peaceful here.

I glanced over to where Rocky and JoJo were conked out in the pews. Sleeping peacefully.

I said, 'You guys have to take care of them.'

Alex nodded. 'We can't as well as you. But we'll do our best.' She wiped her cheeks, not letting go of my hand. I felt wetness on my knuckles.

'When we go tomorrow, we'll set them up here in the bell tower,' I said. 'They'll have a good view of the city, so they'll know when it's safe to come down.'

'Chance,' Patrick said. 'We got it.'

We stood at the altar, the three of us. No one knew what to say.

Alex finally broke the silence. 'Since my mom left, it's just been us. You guys got me through. You're the best family I ever could have asked for. All that matters . . .' She swallowed, hard. 'All that matters is us.' She looked up. 'Big Rain? Little Rain? I love you guys. I know you know it. But I wanted to say it.' She stared over at the massive altarpiece. 'I wanted to say it here.'

I was too choked up to reply. I couldn't see Patrick clearly beneath his hat, but – as crazy as this sounds – I think he might've been choked up, too.

Alex let go of our hands. Then she hugged me. I figured that was my cue to leave them there alone. I wandered off to one of the pews in the back and fell asleep beneath the celestial vaulted ceiling.

I woke up with her body pressed against mine. Before I could say anything, she kissed me.

Kissed me deep.

She pulled back, and my spinning mind took a moment to fasten on to reality.

Stark Peak.

End of days.

In a church.

My last night.

Alex.

I sat up. We faced each other on the pew there in the rear of the church. I looked around for my brother, but he was nowhere to be seen.

Alex took my chin. Turned my face back to hers.

And then I kissed her. I couldn't help it. Her mouth, her lips, her eyes – I wanted to lose myself in her. For a time I did.

We pulled apart, breathing hard, our foreheads touching. Her eyes glinted in the darkness.

'You're both in my heart,' she said. 'But you . . .'

'What?' I said.

'You *are* my heart, Chance. I can't imagine living without you.'

My own heart was doing things inside my chest it had never done before.

I said, 'I'm glad I won't have to live without you.'

We kissed again, hard, her arms wrapped around my neck, mine around her waist.

And then we parted.

I felt like I was being ripped in half. From her eyes I could tell she felt the same.

She walked off quietly toward the nave, her footsteps pattering softly on the old stone tiles.

I took a deep breath and turned back toward the altar.

Patrick was standing there in the aisle, no more than ten feet away. Staring right at me.

Before I could say anything, he walked away.


I lay there staring at the ceiling, guilt and fear crushing in on me. I had the sensation of being trapped in a rowboat in the immense, roiling ocean. So tiny. Everything else so huge. Doom tapping its foot, biding its time.

A hand shook my boot. I sat up.

JoJo stood at the end of the pew.

'You okay, Junebug?'

'I'm bigger than I thought I was.'

'Yeah,' I said. 'Me, too.'

She gazed at me with her giant eyes. Bit her lip. Held it between her teeth until it stilled. 'I'm ready to finish our story now,' she said.

I got up and took her hand. As always, I was struck by how small it felt in mine.

I grabbed my backpack, and together we climbed up into the scaffolding. I pulled out my notebook and my last two pens. We sat together, side by side, our legs dangling off the suspended planks.

There couldn't have been a prettier place. It was like we were floating in the dome with its beautiful murals. All the great stories laid out in paint and stained glass. Adam and Eve in the garden. Cain sneaking up on Abel. Christ's eyes turned to heaven, the crown of thorns trickling blood down his temples.

I wrote entry after entry, JoJo and I talking quietly, catching up on everything that had happened since we'd been apart.

When we'd written our way through to our arrival at the church, JoJo leaned into my side. 'Where should we end it?' she asked. 'With us sitting here on the scaffolding?'

'No.'

I handed her the pen. She took it. Her eyes glittered with tears.

'You'll take over,' I said. 'Write down everything that happens. You're the keeper of the human record now.'

She blinked and tears fell. 'But I want you instead.'

I rested a hand on her dirty hair. 'You'll keep me alive this way.'

**ENTRY 61**     This will be my last entry. I won't have time to write, you know, before. JoJo's got it from here. So this is our good-bye. I hope everything goes well. I hope you can live safe and free.

Thanks for sticking with me.

**ENTRY 62**    Circumstances have conspired to allow me to pick up the pen and notebook again. Things didn't go as planned.

In fact, what happened was devastating.

But since you've been here for most of the ride, I figure I should take you through the bloody end.

**ENTRY 63**     All the next day, we crouched in the bell tower waiting for the streets around us to clear. But — if anything — the Harvesters' search in this area of the city had intensified. It seemed only a matter of time before they'd bring a battering ram and knock down the church doors.

More essentially, our time was running out. We watched with mounting impatience as morning turned to day, day to evening.

As the sun started to trace its descent, every minute grew more agonizing.

Alex would die at first light of day.

I chewed my thumbnail to the quick. Alex paced in tight circles. Patrick kept watch by the jagged parapet, silent and steady, barely moving.

He hadn't said anything about seeing me and Alex last night.

I hadn't either.

And Alex and I didn't mention it to each other either.

The good thing about knowing you're close to dying is you don't have to waste your time poking at painful spots. You can just let everything be what it is.

I knew Patrick would forgive me. I knew he still loved me. I knew he was way more upset about losing me than he was about me and Alex kissing.

So it was behind us already. There was only one thing in front of us.

That spire taunting us from the western horizon.

The sun inched lower and lower. Hatchlings and Drones crowded the blocks below.

As the horizon extinguished the last rays of the last day, our frustration reached a near-panic pitch. The movement below showed no signs of diminishing.

Midnight.

Two a.m.

Four.

There was no more time to wait. Alex circled past us again, heading for the far side of the bell tower, giving me and Patrick a moment of privacy.

He pulled away from the parapet. 'We go now,' he said to me. 'We've no longer got a choice.'

I turned to get Alex, but Patrick grasped my forearm, gentle yet firm. I looked back at him.

'The best part . . .' Patrick's voice went hoarse. He steeled himself and started over. 'The best part was having a brother like you.'

I wanted to say something, but my words were blocked by the lump in my throat. He must've read the emotion in my eyes, because he gave my cheek a gentle tap with his palm.

Then he turned away quickly and headed for the stairs.

The Humvee flew away from the curb, plastering a band of Hatchlings across the grille and windshield. The tires spun over their corpses, caught, and hurled us forward.

By the time we reached the first intersection, it seemed

the entire city knew about us. Every Hatchling and Drone in sight came at us.

We blasted up the dark streets, Patrick steering skillfully. And then there was a loud booming sound, and the city grid lit up.

Every streetlight, every fluorescent in every building, even the glaring arena lights at Stark Peak Stadium. Up ahead the City Hall spire glowed yellow and orange, still decorated for last year's fall feast.

We let it guide us in.

We whistled between vehicles, smashing into Hatchlings. We clipped Drones, sending them spinning off in mist-blasting trajectories. It was mayhem.

As we breached the city center, cored-out buildings rose all around us, each illuminated with hundreds of virtual screens showing live feeds from everywhere on the globe. Our world in the clutches of Harvesters. On every high-rise floor, floating as far as the eye could see, Drones and Queens were hooked into the network they'd created.

'How's our rear flank look?' Patrick shouted.

I twisted in the backseat to look behind me.

The sight literally took my breath away.

The streets, the city, the mountains beyond were alive with so much movement I couldn't see the ground. Hatchlings swirled in at us from every direction, a flood pulled toward a drain.

I tried to swallow. Couldn't.

'Um,' I said. 'Not so great.'

As I turned to face forward, I saw the same view to our left.

And our right.

And ahead.

We were the eye of a living hurricane.

It looked like a war zone, but not a modern one. More like one of those battlefields you see in period movies when Roman infantries blanket the earth and you can't believe you're seeing that many bodies bent to a single cause.

The cause for every Harvester in Stark Peak was to kill us.

This was it. Our last run.

We skipped up the curb, the front tires popping, and skated down the wide steps into the giant courtyard before City Hall. All the while Hatchlings hammered off our hood. Our windshield cracked. The roof dented in so hard that the metal kissed the top of my head.

We plowed through endless bodies. They racked up against our bumper. The stripped wheels gouged concrete.

'We're not gonna make it!' Alex shouted. 'There's no room for us to get out and run!'

'Then we won't,' Patrick said.

He stomped on the gas pedal, blasting through the Hatchlings, aiming straight for City Hall's doors.

'You might want to fasten your seat belts,' Patrick said.

Alex and I clicked ourselves in.

The Hummer hammered up the front steps of City Hall and barreled at the big double doors. The crash slammed us forward in our seats.

The SUV stayed there, rammed into the mouth of the shattered doorway.

Bruised and bleeding, we popped off our seat belts.

Patrick kicked out the cracked windshield. We slid across the hood, slick with Hatchling guts, which burned where it touched our skin. Scraping it off, we fell into the empty lobby.

The unvented air stank of dead fish. Massive aquarium tanks lined the walls all around us, mineral deposits whitening the glass like mold. Already Hatchlings were crawling through the Hummer after us. Others smashed through the floor-to-ceiling window panels flanking the front doors, streaming in two bodies wide.

Patrick *shuck-shucked* the Winchester and blew out one of the tanks. Rank green water swept across the marble tile, eating into the Hatchlings' feet.

He shot the next tank. And the next.

Salt water flooded the lobby, melting the Hatchlings. They screamed as if caught in lava.

We waded through toward the fancy marble stairs. Bloated fish bobbed across the tide. Already the water was draining from the lobby, pouring out the front door and the shattered window panels. The Hatchlings didn't slow. They hurled themselves on to the wet tiles, jellying against the marble. Others trampled over the disintegrating flesh only to bubble into the mass.

They were willing to sacrifice themselves. And they had countless numbers.

We'd bought some time. But not a lot.

The horde was making progress as we scampered up the wide stairs. From that long-ago field trip, I remembered the route we needed to take. Alex and Patrick followed me to a rear stairwell, and we bolted up three more sets of stairs and spilled on to the roof.

There the spire was, lit up like a mirage, convenient metal rungs running up one side as on a telephone pole.

There was only one problem.

The base was encased by a big protective metal cage.

We pulled up short, our chests heaving.

It must have been a safety precaution added in the years since I'd been up here, designed to prevent unauthorized access.

Like, say, the unauthorized access needed to save the lives of everyone on the friggin' planet.

Patrick ran up to the big metal gate and tugged at it. Locked. I tried to wiggle between the bars. No luck. Alex started to scale the bars, but about ten feet up they ended in an encircling overhang, the bottom studded with razor wire.

We regrouped outside the barred gate. Clipped to one of the rungs, out of reach just above the cage, a climbing safety belt swayed in the wind, mocking us.

From our perch we could see much of the city. Every square inch, it seemed, was covered with Hatchlings. One rotund female for every twenty sinewy males. They bounded toward us, individual forms lost to the scope of movement.

The city lights cast our shadows across the rooftop, distorted and severe.

Patrick and I watched the incoming avalanche with stunned disbelief.

Alex was cursing skillfully, a torrent of frustration. And then she stopped.

Patrick looked over at her. 'Run out of words?'

''Cuz I got a few more,' I said.

'The janitor's closet,' she said. 'Second floor by the stairwell. Remember?'

Patrick and I shook our heads.

Already she was running back for the stairs, gripping her hockey stick tight. We followed her, leaping down four steps at a time.

The clamor rose up from below. Fighting every instinct in our bodies, we ran toward it.

We reached the second floor. Sprinted to the janitor's closet.

At the end of the hall, the vanguard of Hatchlings spilled into view off the top of the wide marble steps. Their feet and ankles were scalded with salt water and couldn't hold their weight. They collapsed, and others clawed over them.

Alex pawed at the door to the janitor's closet. It was locked.

Patrick shot the knob off with his Winchester.

Alex sprang inside.

A few of the Hatchlings broke free of the morass and started for us. Patrick tore a hole through them with rock salt. I readied my baling hooks for the next charge, sweat tickling the sides of my neck.

Alex stumbled out again, gripping a massive key ring. 'Got it!'

We jumped back into the stairwell. Ran up and up.

On to the roof, locking the door behind us.

Over to the gate.

As Patrick and I watched the roof-access hut behind us nervously, Alex tried key after key. At last there was a click.

We turned. Alex stood triumphantly by the open gate, wearing her unimprovable smile. We all gulped in a breath.

Around us we could hear the entire city crashing toward us, a galaxy folding in on itself. Light from the high-rises shimmered over us. Movement from around the world scrolled across the virtual monitors.

For a single instant, we were the center of the universe.

A body thudded against the door behind us, yanking us back to reality. And then another hammered the wood, breaking the spell entirely.

Patrick breezed past me, brushing against my side.

Lifted the keys from Alex's hand.

Stepped through the gate.

And shut it with a clang.

From inside the metal cage, he looked back at us. And then he threw the key ring through the bars and off the top of the roof.

I stared after it, incredulous.

I grabbed for my cargo pocket.

Empty.

I looked back up as Patrick tucked the syringe into his boot. He'd lifted it from me.

My chest lurched with emotion. My throat clutched. We were only a few feet away.

The brim of Patrick's hat gave the faintest dip. 'You got it from here, little brother.'

Seven words, a continent of meaning.

I grabbed his shirt through the bars. 'No – goddamn it!' I was sobbing. 'My most important job is to protect my brother.'

He looked at Alex. 'Not anymore,' he said.

My fist was still twisted in his shirt. He held my hand until I relaxed it. The sound of Hatchlings banging on the door behind me faded away. Everything faded away but me and my brother.

He gave my hand a squeeze and let go.

He looked over at Alex. 'I promised I'd keep you safe, Alexandra.'

He pulled her to the bars and kissed her.

When he let go of her, she literally reeled. I caught her, bracing her with an arm across her lower back. She was crying, too.

My brother turned and started scaling the metal rungs.

At the same time, the access door burst.

My sorrow turned to rage.

I charged the Hatchlings as they spilled on to the roof. I swiped and gashed them with my baling hooks, Alex at my side with her hockey stick. She was screaming, veins standing up in her neck.

Acid flecks splattered over us, but we didn't care. The Hatchlings fell away. We kicked and hacked them back through the access door. Alex toppled a huge air-conditioner unit down the mouth of the stairs. It wedged up against a clot of fallen bodies, blocking the narrow passageway.

For now.

We turned back to Patrick.

He was two-thirds up the spire. He was wearing the climbing safety belt, though he hadn't used it.

Not until now.

Breathless, Alex and I watched him clip it to the rung. He let his weight sag back.

He pulled the syringe from his boot. Looked down. The brim of his hat dipped as he gave us a final nod.

Fighting away tears, I nodded back.

And then he slammed the needle into his thigh.

He leaned away from the spire, the cowboy hat falling from his head. The wind riffled his hair.

He didn't explode.

He turned to mist from the top down, like an image pixelating, a mosaic drifting away bit by bit, a dandelion with millions of seeds. He floated apart until his body was no more.

If it weren't so gut-wrenching, it might've been beautiful.

Patrick, turned to glorious rain.

**ENTRY 64**     The Hatchlings hurled the air-conditioner unit from the access hatch and blasted on to the roof as if sprayed from a fire nozzle.

Alex and I turned to face them.

But as the breeze swirled down at us, they puddled instantly where they stood. As they fell away, only one remained standing.

The sole female in the group.

She stiffened. And then walked to the edge of the building. She lay down on her back. As Alex and I watched with amazement, her stomach pulsed and then burst open, releasing a stream of orange mist.

Alex and I looked out across the city.

Dozens of females scaled to various high points – billboards, rooftops, streetlights – and burst open.

A New Year's fireworks display.

The orange mist spread across the blocks, a growing cloud, eating through the male Hatchlings below. The streets filled with the sounds of screeches, the anguish of the dying.

As we watched with astonishment, the mist coated the armor of the Drones and Queens. The acid seemed to gnaw through the suits, because they burst from their armor, one after another, bleeding out into the air.

I heard an echo of the Rebel's words when I'd asked

about the Drones and Queens: *They've been accounted for as well.*

No matter how much we'd hypothesized that the dispersal mechanism built into my and Patrick's cells was plug-and-play, there'd been no way to know for certain that the weaponized pathogen would act the same as the Rebel's serum.

Not until now.

All over the city peaks, female Hatchlings continued to burst. The wind whipped the orange mist toward Ponderosa Pass, Creek's Cause, and beyond. I don't know how long Alex and I stood there watching the concentration of mist thicken and sweep away to cities and states unseen. It was near impossible to tear our eyes from the sight before us. After a time we noticed something on the virtual monitors in the hollowed-out bank building.

Hatchlings were disintegrating by the Gateway Arch in St Louis. Females climbed to high points across the city and exploded, laying waste to Drones, Queens, and male Hatchlings.

Like the great Dusting, but in reverse.

I recalled another piece of the Rebel's speech about the serum: *It is engineered to spread at a massively accelerated rate.*

Once the trend spread to Chicago and caught the lip of the East Coast, Alex and I shuffled toward the access roof. We had to wade through bodies of Hatchlings all the way down through City Hall. The building was lined with decomposing flesh, the stench nearly unbearable.

At last we stepped out into the vast courtyard.

All around us a landscape of destruction.

But then we heard a cry of joy.

JoJo and Rocky sprinting up the main thoroughfare, flapping their arms and hollering at us.

I lifted a hand in greeting. Alex and I hadn't spoken, not since Patrick's death. There was too much grief and wonder.

We watched the kids approach, whooping and screaming. JoJo waved Bunny's head by the ears. At last she slammed into me.

We stood there for a moment, the four of us in the wide expanse of the courtyard. Orange mist spun all around us, like we were inside a snow globe.

'Patrick,' JoJo said, looking around frantically. 'Where's Patrick?'

My chest felt bricked in, my lungs tight. 'He's gone,' I said, and saying it made it real and permanent.

JoJo squeezed me harder, and I felt those bricks falling away, all the emotion opening up. It was hard to breathe, but I managed.

Rocky's forehead was shiny with sweat. 'How?' he asked.

'Saving us,' Alex said. 'Saving everyone.'

The mist settled over the surrounding high-rises, texturing the asphalt and abandoned cars, and I thought about how it wasn't just mist. It was Patrick. He was the air, and he was life, and he was the reason it would be safe here for the next twenty-four thousand years.

In that safety was freedom. And yet with freedom came a new kind of fear. All my life I'd always thought it was what I wanted. Freedom. But I realized now it was a kind of void, too. There were no Harvesters to fight against. No parents to look after us. No aunts and uncles.

No big brother.

It was down to just me to shape myself and the world however I wanted. I could strive. I could fail. And at the end of the day, who I would become – what my world would become – would rest on my shoulders.

Next to me Alex held her hand to her mouth, and I could tell that the same kinds of thoughts were flooding through her. No matter what we faced, at least I had her at my side. And she'd have me at hers.

Far in the distance, I thought I heard the confused cries of kids locked away in holding pens somewhere. Then the wind shifted, and there was a sound unlike any I'd heard in over two months' time.

Quiet.

I thought of those incoming signals Zach had told us about. Survivors out there for us to find.

Something tumbled toward us from above, riding the wind. A black cowboy hat.

Patrick's.

I watched the hat twirl in the air. It landed at my feet. I crouched. Picked it up. Stared at it, feeling a lifetime of emotion gather at the back of my throat.

I put it on.

Taking Alex's hand, I turned to face the faintest gleam of light to the west.

The first rising sun of the New Year.

'Come on,' I said. 'We got work to do.'

It ended in sacrifice. I suppose we always knew it would. That we couldn't possibly make it through unscathed. But I never dreamed it would turn out the way it did. The way the world went upside down and our lives with it. Now that it's over, I hope you take something away from what happened to us. Two brothers and a girl from Creek's Cause - who would've ever thought we'd make a difference?

The world changed.

We changed it back.

# Acknowledgments

I'd like to thank:

— Melissa Frain, Kathleen Doherty, Linda Quinton, Amy Stapp, and Alexis Saarela of Tor Teen, for giving me a YA home

— Lisa Erbach Vance of the Aaron M. Priest Literary Agency, Stephen F. Breimer, Marc H. Glick, and my team at CAA

— Maureen Sugden, Philip Eisner, Missy Hurwitz, Dana Kaye, expert readers

— Librarians, who fired my imagination from the start

— Booksellers, for decades of support

— My wife. My daughters. My Rhodesian ridgebacks, Simba and Cairo

# *He just wanted a decent book to read ...*

Not too much to ask, is it? It was in 1935 when Allen Lane, Managing Director of Bodley Head Publishers, stood on a platform at Exeter railway station looking for something good to read on his journey back to London. His choice was limited to popular magazines and poor-quality paperbacks – the same choice faced every day by the vast majority of readers, few of whom could afford hardbacks. Lane's disappointment and subsequent anger at the range of books generally available led him to found a company – and change the world.

*'We believed in the existence in this country of a vast reading public for intelligent books at a low price, and staked everything on it'*
**Sir Allen Lane, 1902–1970, founder of Penguin Books**

The quality paperback had arrived – and not just in bookshops. Lane was adamant that his Penguins should appear in chain stores and tobacconists, and should cost no more than a packet of cigarettes.

Reading habits (and cigarette prices) have changed since 1935, but Penguin still believes in publishing the best books for everybody to enjoy. We still believe that good design costs no more than bad design, and we still believe that quality books published passionately and responsibly make the world a better place.

So wherever you see the little bird – whether it's on a piece of prize-winning literary fiction or a celebrity autobiography, political tour de force or historical masterpiece, a serial-killer thriller, reference book, world classic or a piece of pure escapism – you can bet that it represents the very best that the genre has to offer.

**Whatever you like to read – trust Penguin.**